I Believe You

Jeanne Grunert

Bricks & Brambles Press
Prospect, Virginia, USA

Book Layout ©2013 BookDesignTemplates.com

Ordering Information:
Quantity sales. Special discounts are available on quantity purchases by corporations, associations, and others. For details, contact Bricks & Brambles Press: www.bricksandbrambles.com

I Believe You/ Jeanne Grunert -- 1st ed.
ISBN 978-1522915102

For my husband, John.

David Majek yawned, lacing his fingers together and raising his hands over his head, stretching to the ceiling. He dropped his hands with a thud onto the desk in front of him on top of the piles of papers he'd brought home from work. Multiple spreadsheets were open on the desktop monitor, but nothing there made sense, either. Whether it was because he was tired or there really were discrepancies in the Triad Fund he couldn't tell. He rubbed his tired eyes, glanced at the cold mug of coffee to his right, and yawned again.

I should call it a night, he thought, shuffling the papers around once more. But he also knew that once he sank into bed, he wouldn't sleep. Cathy's side would remain cold and empty. The hours would tick by until dawn, when he'd rise early once again to more coffee and endless work. Anything to keep his mind off of Cathy's absence.

"Um, Dad?"

His teenage son Josh stood in the doorway. David leaned back in the creaking office chair. "Hi, Josh. You're up late. Everything okay?"

"Um, Dad?" Josh shuffled his bare feet on the hallway carpet. "There's a guy outside."

"Outside where, Josh?"

"On the corner."

"So?" David waited.

Josh wandered over to the couch before finally circling back to his father's desk near the door. "Well, he's like, watching the house or something."

"What?" David pushed back his chair. He narrowly missed tipping over the congealing coffee. "What is he doing?"

"He's standing on the corner. I think he's taking pictures with his cell phone."

"How did you notice him?" David rose from his chair and strode past his son to the living room. A warm pool of light from the accent lamp on the hall table provided the only illumination in the room, but he could make his way past the sofas and coffee table, up the little step past Cathy's baby grand piano to the front windows. Josh turned on the lamp on the end table next to one of the sofas and followed his father to the front windows.

David pushed aside the heavy burgundy velvet and rayon drapes covering the window and peered through the mullioned panes. It was a cool, misty April night. An offshore breeze blew salt-scented mists through the oaks and sycamores lining Edgewater Drive. He pressed his palm against the cold glass and wiped at the mist until he realized it was outside, not condensation on the glass. Joshua joined him on his right hand side, pointing down the slight hill to the base of Edgewater Drive where it curved away from Walnut Street.

"He's there. Under the streetlight." Josh pointed.

"When did you see him?"

"Eddie saw him about an hour ago. He just came and got me now because the guy didn't move."

Each corner of Hunter's Run, the Long Island housing development where the Majeks lived, had old-fashioned street lamps that reminded David of the lamp that greeted the children into Narnia. David strained to see through the swirling mists. Rainwater shimmered on pavement and fresh green leaves.

David peered into the shifting mists. For a second he thought he saw a form near the lamp. A tall man wearing some sort of hat, it looked like to him.

"Oh, yeah, Eddie said the guy was at his school today, too."

"What?"

"He said that he and Chris saw the guy at school today. They ran to tell a teacher, but by the time the teacher got there, the man was gone."

"Can you get Eddie for me, please?" David asked. Josh pounded upstairs to find his little brother.

David leaned back against the barrister bookcase containing Cathy's music. He hadn't the heart to get rid of them, and dusting wasn't even on his radar. To give away her music was unthinkable, the final act acknowledging she was gone, not coming home. Sometimes late at night when he couldn't sleep, he wandered down to the living room and sat at the piano bench, resting his cheek against the music stand. Her fingerprints were still there, ghostly imprints of a full life cut short, a life filled with laughing and playing music, preparing for her next class at the university, practicing to play piano at church on Sunday. He wondered what his sister Eva had thought when he'd asked her not to dust the piano, but she had just nodded mutely and gone on to clean the rest of the house, instructing her workers to do the same.

Now he leaned against the bookcase, wedging his tall, lean frame between the upright case and the cool plaster wall, peering out from behind the curtains like a burglar in his own home. The strange man hadn't moved. He still leaned against the lamp post, collar turned against the cold and damp, fedora pulled low over his forehead. The family room clock chimed 11:30.

He studied the man. Strongly built, with broad shoulders, unless the coat had padded shoulders. What was he doing there? As David watched, the stranger reached with his left hand into the flap of his coat pocket, pulling forth a small object. Maybe a pack of cigarettes? David shook away the image of a 1940s gangster film, when he realized it was a smartphone. The man raised the phone, and clicked. It took David a second to realize the man was photographing his house.

"That's it," David muttered under his breath. Confront the asshole or call the police? He reached for his cell phone and was just about to dial when footsteps thudded back down the stairs.

Eddie followed his older brother. His tawny hair was long and tousled, his bangs falling over his dark-circled brown eyes. He needed a haircut, but Cathy had always arranged such things. Alex had been here around Christmas to take his brother into town for a haircut; David supposed he would have to take his son from now on. He shook his head and raised his hands to sign to his son.

Have you seen him before? David's hands moved fluently in American Sign Language.

Eddie peered out the window, then nodded, glancing back to his brother, then to his father. He patted his hands together in the sign for "At school."

Josh nodded. "I told you," he said quickly to his father, his words tumbling out. "Ed says it's the same guy..."

David held up his hand to pause his middle son, then turned back to Eddie. *What did he do?*

Eddie shrugged, made Os with his hands, then raised opened hands with fingers spread and palms out. *Nothing*, the gesture said. He brought V fingers to his eyes. *Watching*. Then signed, *Waiting*.

The man outside had stepped closer to the Majek's home. Just a few feet away from the lamp post, but enough to disturb David.

Suddenly, a black sedan screeched to a halt by the curb. The man raced to the passenger door, threw it open, and slid into the front seat. David glimpsed the Cadillac logo and a New York license plate; the last letter a Y, but he couldn't get anything more than that. With a puff of exhaust fumes the car vanished into the misty night.

"Well," David said, tapping his phone. "I'm still calling the police."

"You think it has anything to do with...Mom?"

"Mom was killed by a hit and run driver," David said quietly, "I don't think so, but he may be casing the neighborhood."

"Casing it? Like in the movies?"

"Yeah, something like that." David waited until the phone clicked through to the 5th Precinct. He quickly relayed details to the dispatcher, who promised to send a car around to take his statement. Josh and Eddie waited until he was done. David continued. "He may be trying to see who's home, who's coming and going, things like that, so he can rob the neighborhood."

"Wow."

David signed to Eddie, *Time for bed*. Eddie lifted his chin. David knew he wanted to wait up for the police. *I'll get you if I need you*, he signed. *Go*.

"C'mon, Ed." Josh took his little brother by the hand and pulled him back towards the stairs, where the two thudded back up their rooms.

David leaned against the cool panes of the front window, watching Edgewater Drive. Mist swirled against the newly blossoming maple trees. Light from the lamp post shimmered in rain-slicked golden smudges on the black pavement. Lights flashed; a police car turned the corner and cruised slowly up to the Majek's Tudor. David stepped away from the windows and back to the front door to let the police in to take his statement.

Cathy, he thought for the thousandth time that day, *I wish you were here.*

Did the strange man watching the house have anything to do with her death? Probably not, but as he opened the front door onto the cool, misty April night, and the scent of the wet asphalt and moist earth reached him, he shivered.

2

The next morning dawned bright and clear. By the third shriek of the snooze alarm, David stumbled into the shower, bleary-eyed and thick-headed. He shuffled into the kitchen by 6 a.m. to get everyone out of the house on time.

David poured six cups of water into the coffee pot and added a hefty helping of French Roast. While the coffee perked, he turned on the small flat screen television mounted on the wall to the left of the stove with the sound muted so he could listen for the boys upstairs. He clicked to CNBC. Rapidly flickering green and red symbols reported on overnight trading in Hong Kong and Eastern Europe. Upstairs Joshua's bedroom door slammed followed by the sound of the shower running.

David poured a glass of orange juice for himself and one for Eddie. He shook one of Eddie's pediatrician-prescribed vitamins into his hand and set it with the juice on the placemat next to his cereal bowl, spoon, and box of Captain Crunch.

He glanced at his watch and hurried to the bottom of the stairs, shouting, "Joshua! Get Edward down here now! He'll be late for the bus."

"Why do I have to do everything around here?" Josh grumbled as his feet pounded to Eddie's door. David heard the thump of Eddie tumbling to the floor, doors slamming, Josh laughing, something hard - a basketball? - hitting the back of the closing bedroom door. David shook his head and walked back to the kitchen, still studying the television.

Joshua breezed into the kitchen, his dark hair sill wet and slicked back over his forehead like a seal. "You didn't dump your brother on the floor again, did you?" David asked

"How else do you get a deaf kid up?" Josh opened the cupboards, peering into the depths as if different breakfast options would magically appear. He finally chose a box of toaster pastries and popped two into the toaster. He pushed the box back into the cupboard without securing the flap, grabbed a clean glass from another cupboard, and poured himself a large glass of milk.

"Did the police say anything last night?" Josh asked.

David poured himself a cup of scalding coffee. He shook his head. "No, they just took my statement and left. It's just good to have a record of what happened. You know...in case something else happens."

Josh nodded. The bathroom door upstairs slammed. The hot water heater in the basement kicked on with a bewildered squeal and the pipes thrummed.

"Sounds like Ed's in the shower," David said.

Josh walked back over to the fridge. "You got someone to watch him after school today?" He poured a second enormous glass of milk, gulped it down, and belched loudly. "I've got Driver's Ed today until almost four, but I can be home after that if you need me."

"I appreciate it, but Aunt Eva is coming by today with one of her cleaning crews. She said she would wait here until I came home from work." His younger sister, Eva, owned a White Glove Maid Service franchise. Her crew kept the house livable until he could either find a full-time live-in housekeeper or a way to juggle parenting, housework and career at the same time.

Hiring a full-time housekeeper was the best option, but finding one who spoke American Sign Language and didn't mind babysitting a deaf child after school had been nearly impossible. He had placed ads, called agencies, but to no avail. The few candidates who made it through the screening process didn't strike him as trustworthy.

"Get your laundry together and get it in the basket," David warned his son, thinking of what Eva had asked of him. "The ladies on the crew will wash anything, but only if they know it needs to be washed."

"Do we have to sort it by color, like Mom used to make us do?"

David smiled, remembering the time when Cathy, fed up with the way the boys simply stuffed their dirty clothes under the bed, had pulled out every dusty sock, every crusty pair of jeans, and thrown them all in a jumble into the washing machine. The boys had worn pink underwear for weeks thanks to a burgundy sweatshirt left in the mix. They never forgot to separate their wash after that incident.

"Just put dark stuff in one pile and light stuff in another in the bathroom. The maids will figure it out."

Josh grabbed his toaster pastry in midair as it popped up out of the toaster slot, flipped it back and forth between his fingers as it burned the tips. "Yowaza! That's hot. Okay." He leaned against the counter, chomping his piping hot pastry.

The Majek Investments logo, a lion with his head thrown back in a roar, flashed across the TV screen. David grabbed the remote and clicked the sound on.

"....an analyst from Majek Investments, Jack Noble, will be with us at noon for the Lunch Hour Report to discuss oil futures and the ramifications of the North Atlantic pipeline on stocks..."

David swore under his breath and jammed the mute button. Josh stopped chewing, holding the toaster pastry in midair. "You didn't know?"

"No, I didn't know. Crap!"

"Maybe he tried to call you."

"He wouldn't. Your uncle should have."

"Maybe he doesn't want to disturb you."

David ripped his cell phone from its clip on his belt. He called up his missed call log, and scrolled through the list. "Damn it! How did I miss this?"

"Maybe you were preoccupied."

David glanced at the display. His brother's call had come through at the same time he'd been talking to the police dispatcher. It must have gone to voicemail.

"You just missed a call. It could happen to anyone," Josh shrugged

"Grandpa put me in charge of the company." David poured a cup of scalding black coffee. "The only way that Jack could be on television is if Constantine told him to go ahead. And Constantine is not supposed to be making these decisions. If I didn't answer the e-mail message, he should have called me. He knows he can call me anytime, day or not, with company matters."

Josh chewed his pastry methodically, swallowing it with big gulps of milk. He wiped his mouth on his sleeve. "Maybe you should talk to Uncle Constantine about it."

"You sound like your mother."

"Well, she was right a lot of time. You get mad at him, but you never talk to him."

"I do talk to him."

"Yelling isn't talking, Dad."

"I don't yell."

"You're not as bad as Grandpa, but close."

David picked up his coffee cup and sucked in scalding sips until he felt calm again. "If your grandpa sees this report before I make it into the office to straighten this out, I'm screwed."

"No, you'll just get yelled at. You're still majority shareholder in Majek Investments, right?"

David eyed his middle son over the rim of his coffee cup. How did the child turn into a wise young man? Joshua, 16 going on 66. He had Cathy's wisdom and patience and David's dark Eastern European looks. Josh saw him staring, crossed his eyes and stuck out his tongue. David laughed.

Eddie sailed into the kitchen, burgundy polyester uniform blazer slightly askew over the tails of his Oxford shirt. His gold and burgundy striped class tie was unknotted, his khaki pants wrinkled. His navy blue backpack bulged with books and his tablet. He thumped it on the floor by the back door, waved to his father, and plunked himself down at the kitchen table, pouring a heaping bowl of Captain Crunch. David opened the refrigerator and handed him the milk, which Eddie liberally poured over the sugary breakfast cereal. He prepared to dig into the cereal, but David waggled his hand and caught his eye. He made a quick motion of plucking an imaginary pill with his fingers and popping it into his mouth, and then pointed to the vitamin and juice. Eddie shrugged; palms open wide, as if wondering what his father wanted.

David shook his head, mimed taking the vitamin again. Eddie sighed and plucked the vitamin without more fuss, drinking down the juice. David nodded. Eddie dug his spoon into the sugar squares floating in his bowl.

David's cell phone chimed. He touched the screen to switch back to telephone mode. "Yes?"

"Dad?"

"Alex!"

Joshua grinned and shouted across the kitchen, "Hey, Dr. Bro!" Eddie saw the change in his brother's expression, glanced from Josh to David, and then looked back at Josh. He shrugged palms up. Josh tapped his fingers on his wrist. Eddie smiled broadly, happily, at the mention of his eldest brother's name.

"It's so good to hear from you," David said, "but isn't it a bit early for a college student?"

"Not for a medical student. I haven't gone to sleep yet. I was up all night studying for my pharmacology final today."

"You'll do well, I'm sure."

"I guess so." Alex cleared his throat. "Uh, Dad?"

"Yes?"

"I got a letter from the bursar's office in my mailbox yesterday. I think you might get a copy of it tomorrow."

"The bursar's office? What did they want?"

"The check you sent in to pay for my tuition for the summer session bounced."

"What?" David strode from the kitchen to the family room without pause. "That's impossible. I have $100,000 in that account."

"I thought it must be a mistake," Alex said.

"Let me check," David murmured. He pulled open the top right desk drawer, rummaging around amidst papers, pens and the calculator until he found the box containing the check book. Even though he kept his accounts on the computer, he found it easier to keep a paper ledger to see his finances at a glance. He flipped it open. "Yes, there should be just about $100,000 in the account."

"Maybe you wrote a check to the investment house from that account?"

"No, I use this account only for your tuition and household expenses. I wouldn't make that mistake."

"Well, I just wanted you to know. If it isn't a problem, could you just make sure that the tuition is paid, please?"

"Sure, Alex."

"You sounded a little angry when you answered the phone, Dad. Everything okay?"

David looked out the windows in the family room to the gardens behind the house. The pink dogwood in the corner of the yard was just showing a hint of color, and the daffodils Cathy had planted underneath its spreading branches were turning jaunty faces to the sun. "We had a little oddity here last night, and then this morning, I turned on the television set to see someone I didn't authorize about to appear on television. Nothing I can't handle, but I'm dreading your grandfather's reaction when he finds out."

"How's he going to find out? Just don't tell him."

David laughed.

"Oh yeah," Alex said. "It's Grandpa. I forgot."

"Right. I thought it was Grandpa calling me when you rang."

"Well, I'm sure it will sort itself out."

"You sound like your brother."

"We had a good teacher. Mom."

There was a pause. Alex finally said, "You mentioned an oddity? At the house? Something wrong?"

"Nothing wrong. Just some man standing on the corner snapping pictures. At eleven at night."

"What? Did you call the police?"

"Yes, so it's all taken care of."

"Maybe it's related to what happened to Mom."

"Alex," David sighed. "I doubt it has anything to do with Mom's case."

"It was a hit and run. They never caught the guy. Maybe it's related."

"You and your brothers have quite the imagination."

From the kitchen, Joshua called, "Dad? Eddie's bus is here."

"I heard," Alex said. "I've got to go too, Dad. Thanks for looking into the case of the missing payment for me."

"Love you, Alex."

"Love you too, Dad."

David switched off the cell phone and slipped it back into its holster. He trotted to the kitchen just in time to see Eddie shrugging into his coat in the doorway from the kitchen to the mudroom. David held up his hand like a traffic cop – stop – then mimed knotting a tie and tucking in a shirt. With a martyred sigh, Eddie complied, tucking in his Oxford shirt, fussily knotting his tie while outside, the bus driver honked his horn.

David thrust his backpack at him, handed him a $5 bill for lunch, and kissed Eddie on top of the head. He raised his hand, pinky finger and index finger pointed skyward, middle two fingers folded down, thumb out in the ILY gesture. I love you. Eddie flashed ILY back, and headed out the back door. David stepped through the mudroom door to the back porch, watching as his youngest raced down the driveway, crooked tie flapping, jacket loose and unbuttoned. The driver flashed his lights once, signaling that Eddie had boarded, and pulled away from the curb. As he was about to step back into the mudroom, a black Jeep pulled up to the curb, idling.

"Josh! Your ride is here!"

Josh had his backpack in hand. "You need lunch money?" David called, but Josh shook his head.

"I'm good, Dad. Later."

David returned to the kitchen, locking the back door behind him. Instead of cleaning up the mess of breakfast dishes, he returned to the family room. He switched on the computer and pulled the rolling office chair back, settling into the worn seat. He accessed the Internet and typed in his bank's URL. A few clicks and passwords later, he accessed his accounts.

"Oh no!" he whispered under his breath.

Someone had accessed his account nine days ago and withdrawn most of the money. He stared at the lines of type, scanning for any other suspicious activity. He saw his checks written each month to his credit card companies, checks to pay the tuition for Harvard and St. Mary's School for the Deaf. He saw checks to the oil company, the electric company, the gas company. Everything appeared normal until nine days ago when someone had completed an electronic withdrawal that had wiped out almost every last cent in the account.

They had my user name and my password.

No one had his user name and password...except Cathy.

And Cathy was dead.

He cradled his head in his hands. *Could this day get any worse? What the hell was happening?*

Breathe, he told himself, *just breathe*. He reached for his cell phone, to call work and let them know he would be a few minutes late. With a deep breath, he dialed the office and left a quick message for Joan, his administrative assistant, letting her know he had a small problem at home and would be about an hour later than usual. Next, he dialed the bank to report the theft. The theft reported, his information taken, he next called the detective handling Cathy's case. Halloran wasn't in, so he left a message there, giving the man his cell phone number. Then, with a knot of lead in the pit of his stomach, he shut down the computer and walked slowly, heavily back upstairs to finish dressing for work.

This day, David thought, *cannot possibly get any worse.*

3

"Good morning, David." Joan smiled as David strode into the executive suite of Majek Investments. A central waiting room dominated by a mahogany desk greeted anyone privileged enough to access the inner sanctum. Two doors, one on the left and one on the right, led to the Majek brother's offices. Five years ago, David had the office on the left, his father the one on the right. Today, Constantine's name adorned the left-hand office, while his name shone subtly on the brass plaque on the door of his father's former office.

"Good morning to you, Joan." He rested his briefcase on the floor and accepted the pile of mail Joan handed to him. She waited quietly while he scanned the envelopes, handing back to her all but six business letters. She fed the advertisements into the gaping maw of the shredder tucked next to the old-fashioned typewriter return on her L-shaped desk, then waited for instructions for the rest.

"Make sure the prospectuses go to the appropriate broker or investment advisor. See that Henderson gets the invoices; I don't recognize the top one, have him look into it. There's a charity ball invitation too, near the top, which Cathy and I attended last year. You can see if my brother wants to go."

"He's got a girlfriend?"

David shrugged. "So he claims." He picked up his briefcase. "Any calls?"

"None so far." Her phone shrilled. She raised her index finger for him to wait, and he did so with a smile. "You just jinxed yourself."

"It was inevitable."

"Majek Investments, Joan speaking. How may I help you?" She paused, grimacing at David over the half-moon rims of her reading glasses. She tapped an impeccably manicured red fingernail on the receiver, nodding at the unseen caller. "Yes, Mr. Majek. Mr. David is in now. I'll tell him you're coming up."

"Oh God," David groaned. "Not my father. Not today. Not now."

"Yes, and I'm afraid he's already on the elevator."

"Is Con in yet?"

"I haven't seen him. Shall I have him paged?"

"Yes, try the third floor, the foreign equities office."

Joan nodded and reached for the telephone. "If the detective working on my wife's case should call, or my bank, buzz me no matter who I'm with."

"Even if you're with Mr. Majek senior?"

"Even if I'm with the good Lord himself, Joan."

"One and the same around here," she murmured. He smiled at her fondly before stepping to his office door. He slipped his left thumb into the lock scanner. The top light on the three-light panel turned green and he keyed in this month's sequence of letters and numbers. The bottom two lights blinked red, yellow, and then green. The door lock disengaged with a shrill beep. He stepped into his office and flipped on the overhead lights.

He hadn't changed the decor since his father's retirement party five years ago. Tibor Majek, a legend on Wall Street, had finally decided to accept a reluctant retirement at the urging of his Board of Directors. David had been unanimously voted into the CEO's chair, while his brother had struggled for the two-thirds majority to gain the title of Executive Vice President. It was only at Tibor's urging that the two board members had changed their vote. David always wondered what they had said to Tibor in private about Constantine. His younger brother took foolish risks, it was true, but some of those risks paid off for their clients and, with the right coaching, he could parlay those risks into benefits for the firm.

Inside the warm office, golden sunlight spilled through two enormous windows overlooking the manicured grounds of the office park and the fountain at the entrance to Mitchell Field Gardens. The vertical blinds were open. David closed the one on the left slightly, turning the acrylic rod so that the light wouldn't create a glare on the three computer screens he had set up on his desk and the credenza behind him. He extracted a pile of papers he'd meant to review the night before and plunked them onto the ever-growing pile of work on his desk, then switched on the computers, keying in three separate passwords and user names which only Joan had access to.

He clicked on the flat screen television mounted over the meeting area at the far end of the room, noting with satisfaction that Joan had already fluffed the pillows on the striped couches and made sure his private coffee urn was perking. He poured himself another cup of black coffee and returned to his desk. He had just finished deleting sixty of the seven hundred or so emails in his inbox when his father burst into the room.

Tibor Majek entered rooms like a tornado ripping across the plains, thick white hair flung back over his head as if caught in a whirlwind. The ninety-year old Czech immigrant strode into the room, rubbing his hands together vigorously. Joan swiftly shut the door behind him. The older man's jet black eyes bored into his son while he drank in the office, nodding with satisfaction at the state of the empire.

"David, *můj syn*," Tibor's booming voice rattled the diplomas and awards hanging behind him. David smiled to himself as he shut off his email. He rose from his Aeron chair, and crossed in front of the desk to receive the bone-crushing bear hug from his father.

Tibor gripped David by the shoulders and took a step back, scanning David's visage. The two men could see eye to eye; they were evenly matched. "My son, how are you?"

"I'm fine, Papa," David said. "To what do I owe this pleasure?"

"I was afraid you were ill," Tibor said, striding to the windows and peering out from between the vertical slats at the office park beyond. "Give that I saw that Jack Noble, on the television this morning. Was that your idea or your idiot brother's idea?"

"Constantine made the decision late last night, when he was unable to reach me by telephone," David said smoothly. He walked back to his desk and settled into his chair, resting his hands under his chin while regarding his father pacing in front of the desk.

"Unable to reach you? I ask you again, were you ill? You are the CEO of Majek Investments. You must always be available."

"I was dealing with something."

"Dealing with something? What does this mean? One of the children was ill?"

"We had a strange man outside the house last night. Stalking it, so to speak. Taking pictures."

His father whirled around, nostrils flaring. "KGB?"

"No, Papa," David said patiently. "There's no KGB in the United States."

"The KGB are everywhere!"

"The Cold War is over, Papa. The good guys won. I don't know who this man was, but he was acting suspiciously, so I was on my phone with the police when Constantine called." A little white lie never hurt anyone, and it seemed to satisfy his father.

"How did you know he was there, this man?"

"The boys told me about it, and I looked out the window, and I saw him. He had a camera. He was taking pictures of my house. Then, this morning…well…."

"Well? Well what?"

David hesitated. He hadn't meant to tell his father about the theft from his account, but some instinct made him confide in him. "Someone hacked into my bank account and stole a considerable amount of money. But it's all right. The bank has their men looking into it."

Tibor leaned over the desk. His nostrils flared again. His dark eyes sparked with anger. "It is all right? They steal from you and this is all right? Why not just toss money from the rooftop of this building, this building that I bought, me, Tibor Majek, a man who worked his way up from office boy to head of the company, to CEO, to owner, in less than 20 years? Me, who grew up with a shack and a dirt floor, now a multi-millionaire...it is not all right that these animals should steal from a hardworking man!"

"Papa, what I meant to say was–"

"You young people! You do not know the value of money. If you had to work for it when you were young–"

"Papa, please calm down."

"I AM CALM."

"Pop."

"All right, all right!" Tibor sank onto the crimson and tan striped couch in the seating area of the suite, waving his hand towards David's desk. "Tell me again. This hacking. What it means?"

JEANNE GRUNERT

David leaned back in his chair, crossing his arms over his chest. "Someone accessed the bank account I use to pay our monthly bills. I keep separate accounts for investments and cash reserves." Tibor nodded. "The account I use to write checks against was accessed by someone with my password and user name."

"So not really hacking – they did not safe crack."

"No, they had the combination. But I didn't give it to them, that is for sure."

Tibor nodded. "Who has this, your user name and password? The boys? Your sister, Eva?"

"No. The only other person who had it was Cathy."

"Ah," Tibor said. He looked away from David. "I see you have had a bad morning indeed. It is hard, the memories. It is not so much about money, then, that bothers you. I understand now."

"Well, having $100,000 stolen right out of your account is bad, I'll grant you," David said. "But having Jack Noble on television today representing the firm actually worked out to my advantage. I doubt I could have concentrated enough to be coherent, let alone represent us well, in my current frame of mind."

Tibor nodded slowly. "Constantine should still ask. You are the boss now!" He thumbed his right fist on his knee for emphasis.

Joan paged him through the telephone intercom. David held up his left hand, palm out, to ask his father to pause while he picked up the receiver with his right. "Yes, Joan?"

"Your brother is here now. Shall I send him in?"

"Yes. Please."

Tibor lapsed into silence, resting his chin on his cupped hands, staring at Cathy's portrait in the center of the framed photos on the credenza.

"Constantine is here."

Tibor glanced away from the photos towards David. His eyes hardened. "Good. Have him come in here so I can give him a piece of my mind."

"I'll handle this, Papa."

"I am the founder of this firm. I put you in charge. You are in charge."

"I am," David said evenly. "And as I said, I will handle it."

"He is my son."

"As am I. But Constantine's behavior while in its employ is now my problem."

"Bah!" Tibor dismissed him with a flick of his wrist.

"I'm quite capable of handling Constantine."

"You always were."

"Indeed. Things are no different now than we were boys."

"They are very different," Tibor said. "You are men now. You have pride. You have ambition. He has pride. He has ambition. Someday, they will clash."

"Then why did you lobby so hard for him to be my Executive Vice President when the Board almost voted him down? You were against it originally, if I remember correctly. Why the change of heart?"

"Because he is a Majek!" Tibor thundered.

David just sighed.

There was a soft knock, and then his younger brother peered furtively around the doorframe. "David? Joan said you wanted to see me. Oh hello, Dad."

"Constantine," Tibor said. "Enter."

"Yes, Con, come in." David waited while Constantine decided between sitting near his father, who was glowering at him from his seat on the couch, or in the guest chair in front of David's desk. He finally decided upon the desk chair.

"You wanted to see me, David? I'm very busy this morning. The Asian markets are very volatile and–"

"Why did you assign Jack Noble to the CNBC spot without my permission?" David demanded. "You know I make all media appearances, and in the event I am unavailable, I assign someone else."

"You weren't available last night when I tried to reach you." Constantine licked his lips. A single bead of sweat appeared on his right temple. He ran a hand over his rumpled white shirt and blue striped tie.

Was he wearing that yesterday? David thought. *I could have sworn he was wearing that yesterday.* Tibor studied Constantine as well from his perch on the sofa.

"I called your cell phone, and when you didn't answer, I texted you."

"I saw only one text, and that just said to call you. It didn't give me any context."

"Well, I didn't want to bother you."

David leaned back and folded his arms across his chest. "I see."

"I mean, it was after eleven and all...and with the children, I didn't think you'd want me calling you at home..."

"In December, less than a month after Cathy died, you called me when that pipe burst in the office. Do you remember that?"

Constantine shifted in the visitor's chair. "Well, that was different–"

"True. You could have dealt with that yourself."

"No, I couldn't. How was I supposed to know what to do? We had water gushing everywhere, on the file cabinets, the computers..."

David uncrossed his arms and leaned forward. He held up his hand, palm out, rigid, to stop his brother from speaking. "I don't know, and I don't really care why you didn't call me this time,

Constantine. I'm telling you, I represent Majek Investments. When the media calls, I answer. When the shareholders call, I answer. Not you."

"Papa..." Constantine squirmed in his chair to face his father. "It's not fair! I'm your son, too."

"You are both my sons, it is true," Tibor said heavily, nodding towards David and Constantine. He braced his hands on the arm and seat of the couch and pushed himself upright. He seemed to fill the room, blazing with fierce pride. He jabbed an index finger in the air towards Constantine. "I have chosen David to move the company forward, and I have chosen well. Constantine, this is between you and your brother. I will leave you now. David, call me tonight." It was a command rather not a request. David nodded.

"Yes, Papa, I will."

Standing erect, his stride free of infirmities, his mane of snowy white hair thick, the legend of Wall Street stepped from the room. He slammed the door shut behind him. The pictures rattled again on the walls. "Goodbye, dearest Joan. Give my regards to your husband, yes?" His booming voice pierced even the thick wooden door. They waited. Joan buzzed the intercom twice. Tibor had left the executive suite.

Constantine slumped in the visitor's chair across from David's desk, chin on chest. "It wasn't fair how you took me on in front of Dad like that. You humiliated me on purpose just to keep your power."

"Fair or not, you acted rashly, and I was just in my actions." David s stood and paced towards the window.

"What the hell were you thinking, putting Jack Noble on the show to represent us? I've half a mind to call CNBC and tell them to cancel the spot, or phone it in from my office."

"I thought of that," Constantine shifted around to watch his brother. "It's too late. The segment is on at noon, but they're filming it now. They didn't want a phone-in segment. You would have had to leave at five this morning to get to Wall Street by seven to film the interview, David. That's why I asked Jack to go."

"I would have gone– "

"And who would have watched the boys?"

"You could have," David snapped. "You're always saying that to me now – 'Who will watch the boys?'" He mimicked Constantine's whiny tone, then drew in a deep breath. "You're using Cathy's death as an excuse to undermine my authority, and I won't have it, Constantine. I can't. Not with Papa forever questioning my decisions, and half the board of directors muttering all the time about 'That's not the way Tibor would have done things.' Enough is enough."

"You think you're so wonderful," Constantine grumbled. "The oldest. You always get it all."

"What was that? I didn't quite hear you."

"I said that I can make decisions, too. I'm part of the Majeks of Majek Investments, and I'm capable of making a sound business judgment."

"I know you are," David said. Weariness descended upon him, and he wanted suddenly to reassure his brother. "When Cathy died, you stepped into my shoes here quite well. You handled everything here in the office wonderfully during those weeks when I was coping with everything at home, and I do trust your judgment, Con. I do. But the media is something entirely different than deciding who handles which investment account and whether we open a new hedge fund. You do those things wrong, we lose a million dollars or we face fines and penalties. You handle the media wrong, we could lose the business."

"That's absurd."

"Is it? How many millions of potential investors watch CNBC every day? How many of our current clients would wonder if they've invested their millions well if we put a poor spokesman on for the company?"

"All right," Constantine rose to his feet. "You've made your point and I'm sorry. Okay. Are you happy now?"

"You're just lucky Papa wasn't the one who scolded you."

"You're a bastard," Constantine muttered as he stormed out of the room, slamming the door behind him.

No, not a bastard, David thought. *More Tibor's son than anything else, that's for sure.*

4

When David pulled his Yukon into the driveway, his sister Eva's White Glove Maid Service van was parked in the driveway behind her Toyota 4Runner. He pushed the automatic garage door opener and eased the Yukon into the garage next to Cathy's dusty Buick LaCrosse.

He grabbed his briefcase stuffed with twice the number of papers he'd brought home yesterday, secured the garage door with the keypad on the outside wall, and strode to the back door. It was propped open with a bucket. A blue-handled mop stood sentinel inside the bleach-scented water. From deep within the house, the blare of salsa music from the Spanish radio station muted the roar of a vacuum cleaner.

Eva appeared around the corner of the dining room, carrying a sleek chrome toolbox in her left hand filled with furniture polish, various rags, and a feather duster and a pack of Marlboros in her right. She wore the black slacks and black uniform polo shirt her staff sported, the breast pocket adorned with a white-gloved butler's hand swiping an imaginary finger over non-existent dust. She skidded to a halt, almost running smack into her oldest brother.

"Oh hey! I wasn't expecting you home on time." She glanced guiltily at the pack of cigarettes in her hand and stuffed them into the open top of the box.

David hugged her, leaning over so his chin rested on her nest of curls. He towered over the petite little Eva. Her hair smelled like lemon furniture polish, dryer sheets, and stale cigarette smoke. "Am I always late?"

"Usually." She stepped back and smiled at him. Her whole face lit up and her right cheek dimpled. "Lucy is vacuuming upstairs, and Carol is finishing in the downstairs powder room. I've got laundry running, and I thought I'd stay for dinner since I brought it myself. Is that okay?"

"You're cooking for me? More than okay. Wonderful!"

Eva led the way into the house, stepping through the mudroom and into the kitchen. From the laundry room just off the mudroom, the dryer hummed, with the washer's drum beating a counterpoint. The bleach-scented air told him that clean clothes would be his by nightfall. He knew he had to keep up with the laundry, but he always forgot, and then scrambled on Saturday to catch up. Cathy had pinned a note that said, "A laundry a day keeps the chaos away!" on the wall over the washing machine, and he often thought truer words were never spoken...as long as someone else did the sorting, washing, drying, ironing and folding.

"Eddie wanted to play some game with his friends from school involving armies blowing things up," Eva continued. "He asked me before he logged onto the Internet, so I said it was okay. I hope it was. He promised to start his schoolwork when he saved the world or defeated the opposite army or whatever the point was of the game. I couldn't keep up with his hands. He was a little excited about today's meet up."

"Yes, it's fine," David said. "Cathy used to let him play with his friends on the computer all the time. The kids are into some kind of war game. It's got a little history in it and less violence than most, so we said okay. The boys in his class agree on a time to get together and play like we used to do with our friends when we were kids, except they all meet online, while we met at the playground or the bus stop for a game of kickball. It's a different world."

"That it is." She hefted the box of cleaning supplies to her other hand. "Lucy's still upstairs, vacuuming, and I've got one more load of laundry in the dryer. I think Lucy's done with your bedroom, so go right on up."

"Thanks, Chief." He smiled at her. "You sure I can't hire you to be my full time housekeeper?"

"You can't afford me," she teased.

"You're worth your weight in gold, that's for sure."

"I'm skinny. And short. I won't let you get off that cheap. Double my weight in gold and throw in Con's weight, too."

"Ha. I'm serious, though, Eva. You know I don't trust just anyone in my home. Are you sure I can't persuade you to hire someone to manage your business and you can come work for me?"

Eva shook her head. "I prefer working for myself, but thanks anyway. You have Con to boss around all day."

"What's he been whining about now? How I'm treating him unfairly?"

"Not at all," Eva said serenely. "You can be a tad bit demanding. But you do need a housekeeper. Did Papa blow into the office like a hurricane?"

"You know that old saying, blows in like a lion and out like a lamb? Our dear papa blows in like a lion and trumpets out like an elephant. He's 90 years old and as crazy as he was when we were kids. I don't know how Mom stood it for so long."

Eva laughed. "May we all live long enough to be terrors to our children in our old age. So he made an appearance and blasted his way into the office? What else happened?"

"Let me get changed and I'll tell you all about it."

He took the stairs two at a time, loosening the Windsor knot at his throat and humming happily for the first time in a long time.

He passed Lucy in the upstairs hallways outside of Joshua's room, methodically vacuuming in neat vertical lines over the plush steel gray hall carpet. "Hello, Lucy!" he shouted over the vacuum. Startled, she jumped, realized it was David, and smiled, waving. She continued vacuuming, and David, humming happily at the thought of a clean house and ironed clothes, stepped into the master suite to change.

He emerged a few minutes later wearing a light blue polo shirt, khakis and loafers. Techno music pounded from behind Joshua's closed door; Eddie's door was closed. Eva had turned off the radio in the kitchen. At the bottom of the stairs, he glanced into the living room and family room to see if Eva and Lucy were there, but sounds from the kitchen told him the women were starting dinner preparations.

Lucy had set the table for dinner, laying four place settings. The oven was already preheating, and a roast wrapped in foil rested in a deep-sided pan, with a neat nest of round new potatoes surrounding it in a succulent brown glaze. Through the kitchen windows he saw Carol loading the floor buffer and vacuum cleaner into the rear of the van. Eva's cleaning kit was also on the driveway awaiting its place in the organized cleaning mobile.

He scanned the room for his sister, but she wasn't there. Lucy smiled and pointed towards the laundry room.

"Thanks, Lucy."

He found Eva ironing his business shirts. Eddie's white button-down uniform shirts had already been starched and ironed, and a row of crisp dress shirts hung on plastic hangers from the overhead rod. A metallic button clanked inside the dryer, as jeans tumbled about in the basket. His nose twitched at the scent of clean linen, bleach, and lavender fabric softener. Eva worked her magic with the iron, a ballet of creasing, folding and motion he could never fathom. She nodded crisply as she finished each shirt and snapped it out to let it settle on the hanger. She buttoned every button, and reached for another shirt.

"Hey," Eva smiled at him. "So how was your day after Hurricane Dad?"

"Lousy," he admitted. He hoisted himself onto the top of the closed lid of the washing machine, letting his long legs dangle over the front. As he sat and recounted the previous 24 hours to his sister, he felt a little better. Sharing his problems with her, like he used to do when they were kids, as well as the smells of roasting meat mingling with the clean scent of the fresh laundry had cheered his spirits immensely.

When he finished his tale, Eva spit on her index finger and lightly tapped the iron. Steam hissed. Unfazed, she grasped the handle and proceeded to iron another shirt. "How did that fellow, Jack, do on the television program?"

"All right. I saw the segment early in the morning; he recorded two, which they ran throughout the day. He wasn't great, but he didn't disgrace the firm. Honestly, so many other things happened that it was the last thing on my mind. I'm actually relieved I didn't have to be on camera today. I was so upset about my account being hacked, I'd almost forgotten it."

"What did the police say?" She finished the shirt, buttoned into a hanger and paused.

"About the man? They said he hadn't broken any laws, except maybe loitering, and as you can imagine, they've better things to do than chase down a man for loitering. As for my money, yes, the bank is looking into it, and their security and insurance people are also looking into it. It's strange, though, Eva. Whoever took the money had my user name and my password. The only person in the world who knew that, aside from me, was Cathy, and believe me, they weren't things anyone could just guess."

Eva stood on her tiptoes and checked on the line of shirts hanging from the clothing rod suspended from the laundry room ceiling, reaching up to pluck a bit of microscopic lint off of the nearest one. It swung gently on the hanger, casting spectral shadows from the harsh glare of the ceiling light. "Hackers are getting more sophisticated every day."

"I think this was more than the average hacker, Eva."

"But who could it be?" Eva stared at him. "Not one of the boys, surely?"

He shrugged. "I don't know. Not yet. The bank said they will refund my money; I think their insurance covers it. I closed out the old account, opened a new one. This account only I know of, and I'm not telling the boys."

"You just told me about it," she pointed out.

"Why would you need money?" he teased. "You have this glamorous maid service to run."

"Shut up," she said mildly to her oldest brother. "I'm the Northeast's most successful White Glove Maid Service franchise, did you know that?"

"Congratulations."

"I've got twelve vans running six days a week," Eva said proudly. "Each van employing a two-person crew. I've created twenty-five jobs in total, including the woman running my office. It might just be a maid service, but I'm building an empire just like Papa did."

David nodded. "I know. And I am proud of you, little sister. But now, with all of these connections, all of these wonderful women working for you, why haven't you found me a full time housekeeper yet?"

Eva sighed and pushed a corkscrew curl away from her forehead where it had escaped from the barrette holding her wild hair away from her face while she worked. She grasped another clean shirt from the laundry basket. With a practiced flick of her wrists, she snapped it open over the ironing board. She raised the can of spray starch, and shot a thin jet at the collar. The hot, metallic scent of starched cotton filled the air as she methodically swept the iron over the cloth. She pressed the collar, the cuffs, and creased the sleeves. All the while David waited quietly from his perch on top of the washing machine.

"Did you call that service I recommended? I gave you the card."

"I'm leery of agencies, Eva. I don't trust their screening process. I don't want just anyone in my house."

"You're as stubborn as Papa," Eva said. She thumped the iron down, hard.

"I won't be like Papa. I promise. I know it was hard for you after Mom died."

"Why do you think I own a maid franchise?" Eva examined the shirt with a critical eye, a surgeon giving the patient a once-over before pronouncing it cured. Satisfied, she plucked the shirt off of the ironing board, draped it over a wire hanger and buttoned it to the collar. Before she pulled the next shirt off of the pile in the basket, she raised her eyes to meet his gaze. "I had the perfect training for it after being drafted as the Majek family maid at 14. Papa should have called an agency for a housekeeper, not used me as cheap labor. He could well afford it. So can you."

"He thought he was training you to be a fit wife."

"Bah." Eva spat, ostensibly at the iron to test its heat, but he knew better.

"I promise I'll call an agency."

"I'm going to hold you to that promise. Your housekeeper doesn't need to be perfect. She just needs to get you through the basics of the day so you can focus on business and loving your sons, especially Eddie. He needs you the most now."

Eva examined the water reservoir on the iron. Assured there was enough in the steam tank, she plucked the next shirt from the pile. It was one of Eddie's school shirts she had missed. She grasped it by the shoulder seams and snapped it over the ironing board. Something white, the size of a walnut, shot from the breast pocket. It sailed over the ironing board, and rolled between the washer and dryer.

David hopped down and peered into the dark, cobwebby space between the two machines.

"I'm sorry," Eva fussed. "I usually check the pockets better before I put the shirts in the laundry. I hope it wasn't anything important."

David grimaced and thrust his hand in the dark crack, feeling the gritty linoleum floor with his fingertips until he touched a small, smooth, cool object. He prodded until it rolled into the light, revealing a balled up piece of paper. He picked it up and straightened. He carefully pulled apart the corners of the paper crisped by the dryer. The ink was smeared from the washing machine, but he could make out the crest of St. Mary's School for the Deaf at the top of the page. It was a letter, but half of the words were illegible; creased and worn from their tumble through the washer and dryer.

"What is it?"

"I can't make it out." David squinted at the faded page. "But if I had to guess, I'd say Eddie had a note to bring home, and he stuffed it in his pocket instead of giving it to me. I'll go upstairs and find out what it's all about. How long until dinner?"

Eva glanced at her watch. "About half an hour." She reached for the iron. "Oh, before I forget – this time around, I left the music area of the living room as you asked. Lucy didn't dust there. I'd really like to clean the piano and dust the music books next time I'm here." She didn't meet his gaze as she turned the steam up on the iron. In a smooth practiced motion, she snapped a shirt open and flattened it across the ironing board. "It just seems so sad to see it dusty." She glided the iron back and forth over the cuffs and collar.

"It feels worse to me to disturb it. The last thing she did that day was play that piano. She had her church music books out on the stand...." David hesitated. He forced himself to swallow against the lump in his throat. "That night, after I returned from the hospital, and after I'd told the boys, I just lost it. I tumbled all the sheet music she had up on the rack into the bench and slammed the bench shut. She was choosing the hymns for Sunday's Mass when something interrupted her and called her out of the house that day."

"The police still don't know why she went to that shopping center?"

"No." David fisted his left hand and softly punched it into the palm of his right, repeating the gesture rhythmically as he paced in front of the washer and dryer. "She wasn't purchasing anything at the store –didn't have any shopping bags. She left the house in a hurry. I know because she always put her music away when she was finished practicing. I could see from her notes that she'd gotten about halfway through Sunday's music when something interrupted her. If the police could only find her cell phone!"

"And that was the only thing missing?"

"The only thing." David nodded. "Her purse had spilled out onto the parking lot after the car hit her, and her wallet, her keys, her makeup case had all tumbled out. When the police gathered up the evidence later, I noticed her cell phone was missing. She wouldn't leave the house without it."

"The police haven't looked into it?"

He shrugged. "They don't think it's connected to the hit and run. They say a passerby probably snatched it and ran off with it. They keep saying her death was an accident."

"But you don't think so." Eva placed the iron upright on the ironing board, switched it off, and jerked the plug from the wall socket.

"No."

"You're sure she didn't run out for something?"

"No, no, and no. Something urgent drew her from home that day and brought her to that parking lot."

"You realize you might never know what."

"I'll take that risk. In the meantime, let's go upstairs. I need to talk to Eddie."

He found Eddie diligently at work at his laptop, looking up fish in the Yellow River of China. David flicked the overhead light to let Ed know he was standing in the doorway. Eddie glanced away from the screen, nodded, and beckoned him into his kingdom. The dark blue walls were hung with framed posters of African animals – lions, elephants, tigers. On top of the bookcase, the filter on his turtle terrarium blew bubbles into the water. To the right of the bookcase, a twenty-gallon tropical fish aquarium on a stand shimmered with colorful mollies, guppies, and swordfish. His bed was made but rumpled, with the dark blue quilt hastily pulled up to the pillow. The shades were open. Only one dresser drawer wasn't closed all the way, a sweater sleeve snagged in the aperture.

Eddie finished writing something on the pad at his right side, then turned his full attention to his father. David pulled the crumpled ball of paper from his pocket and put it on the desk.

Eddie stared at the ball of paper. A pink flush suffused his cheeks and he squirmed in his seat. He looked up at his father and shrugged weakly.

David spread his hands and shrugged back. He pointed to the paper.

Eddie bit his lip. He folded his arms across his chest.

David felt his temper rising. He thumped the desk with his fist, hard. That got Eddie's attention.

David pointed again to the paper.

Eddie's cheeks turned crimson. He slapped the keyboard on his laptop back into life, then stabbed the keys with his fingers, opening an internet browser. David leaned across the back of the chair to see the screen. The crest of St. Mary's School for the Deaf appeared in the center, followed by a login and password. Eddie typed in his mother's name, then a password.

"How the hell do you know Cathy's password for school?" he demanded, then he realized Eddie was facing away from him. He moved to Eddie's left so that his son could see his hands, and he signed, *How you know Mom's password*? having to spell out the last work because he didn't know the sign. Eddie's right hand scooped in front of his face like he was grasping a fistful of air.

You guessed it? Some guess, David thought. He watched in fascination as Eddie clicked through various screens to access what appeared to be a bulletin board for teachers to communicate with parents. *I can't believe I didn't know this existed*, David thought with a rising sense of unease. Cathy must have checked on the kids, in this way. What had he missed?

He saw a series of messages, about one a month, addressed to him and Cathy. The messages began in January, approximately six weeks after Cathy died. They were all from a Mrs. Caruthers. Eddie clicked on the last one. David quickly scanned the message.

"Edward," he said aloud, "I can't believe you didn't show me this."

Eddie had apparently failed to complete his year-long assignment. David remembered at the start of the school year that Cathy had been annoyed that the sixth grade teacher had given all the students a year-long assignment. They had the choice of building a website or blog, or writing a hundred-page report on the subject of their choice.

Eddie explained that they worked on it a little at a time, each week handing in an assignment, so that they would complete it by the end of the year. David recalled some kitchen table discussions last September, but he couldn't remember what Eddie's project was about.

Just something else Cathy had been handling on her end of things, while he was off running the family business. But this family was his business. In fact, it should have been his only business.

Eddie looked up at his father questioningly. David nodded. He pointed to the work project on the screen, and Eddie nodded. His fingers flashed over the keyboard until a new window opened. He typed in the URL "Cooking withEddie.com."

A website opened on screen.

It was a blog, actually. David saw a banner with pots, pans, spoons and a chef hat at the top emblazoned with "Cooking with Eddie." At the top of the sidebar on the right hand side of the blog, it read: "Hi! My name is Eddie and I am a 6th grade student at St. Mary's School for the Deaf. My teacher has assigned us a year-long project and I am going to make a cooking show online to teach you Czech cooking, and I will write about Czech culture. My dad's family is from the Czech Republic and they are very proud of their heritage.

My mom will help me with my assignment. She will narrate the videos while I sign them so that everyone can understand my cooking show. I hope you like it."

He watched in astonishment as a video appeared on screen. A lump formed in his throat when Cathy stood at the kitchen island next to Eddie. He tapped the screen next to the sound icon, and Eddie quickly unmuted it.

"....and my name is Cathy, and this is my son, Eddie, and we are going to show you today how to make a simple beet salad with onions...."

Eddie signed the recipe, smiling happily at his mother on camera. He paused to chop, slice and dice the beets and pour them into a bowl. But it was Cathy that David couldn't keep his eyes off of. Cathy, with her beautiful sweep of red-gold hair, her laughing eyes, the red apron he had given her last Christmas. She loved to cook, and he loved to indulge her hobby. He could not believe that these videos would live on for as long as the web lived on, showing his lovely wife and his son cooking happily in the kitchen.

Eddie paused the video. He looked at his father. Slowly, he unfolded his arms and began to sign. David could barely keep up with the torrent of communications that flowed from his son.

...and I have 10 more to make or I'm going to fail, I'm going to fail sixth grade!

Okay, slow down, David signed back, holding up his hand.

Eddie complied. B*ut then Mom died...no one to help me.*

David sighed heavily. His closed left "A" hand resting on his right palm moved from his chest to Eddie. Eddie repeated the gesture, moving the hands from David to himself as if he couldn't believe what he was seeing.

Yes, Eddie, I'll help you. He formed a fist, palm up, and circled it. *Saturday.*

Eddie glanced back at the computer screen, and David saw him looking at the frozen video at Cathy's face, turned in profile. Eddie's eye swam with tears.

David knelt down by the desk and put a hand on Eddie's knee. Then he raised both hands to his face, fingers spread, drawing gentle tears from his eyes. He pointed to Eddie, and wrapped his arms around himself in a hugging gesture. Eddie shook his head vigorously. *No.*

David raised his hands hesitantly, and then made Eddie's special sign for Cathy – tapping his heart, three times.

Eddie dropped his head to the desk and cried.

David enfolded him in his arms. He dropped his face into Eddie's toffee-colored hair, and his own tears mingled with his son's. Eddie's breath hitched as he sobbed, wiping his nose on his sleeve. David wiped his own tears from his cheeks, hoping Eddie hadn't seen him, but his son had. He took a shuddering breath and looked in wonderment at his father. Then he raised his hands to his own tear-streaked face, fingers spread, drawing them down, and then pointed to his father.

Eddie tapped his heart again.

David nodded. He tapped his own heart, three times. Then he drew his hands up and together, then apart in a rending motion. *My heart is broken, too*, his gesture said.

Eddie threw his arms around his father, pressing his cheek to David's chest. David glanced down at the wad of paper on the desk. It could wait.

He drew Eddie into his arms again and rocked him gently, stroking his hair until his tears subsided.

5

"David! Josh! Dinner is ready. Get Eddie too, please." Eva slid the roast pork from the oven as David entered the kitchen.

"Dinner smells delicious!"

She loosened the foil on the roast and nodded. "Can you get Eddie, please?"

"He'll be here in a bit. I told him it was time for dinner."

Josh walked into the kitchen rubbing his stomach. "What can I do to help?"

"Can you grab the potatoes, please?"

Josh spooned the roasted potatoes into a serving bowl. Eva sliced the pork, while David slid a bowl of green beans into the microwave. Eddie trotted into the kitchen and gave his father a watery smile before sliding into his accustomed place at the far end of the table.

It was wonderful to have a homemade family meal again. The boys dug into Eva's perfectly crisp-tender pork loin and new potatoes. Eddie even ate his portion of green beans without making too many faces. Amidst the happy banter, David could almost imagine Cathy was just out for the evening with her friends, or perhaps teaching an evening class at the university.

The boys cleared the table. Eddie rinsed the plates and put them in the dishwasher. Josh began scrubbing the roasting pan.

"Thanks again, Eva. This was wonderful," David said from his accustomed place on the far side of the round kitchen table.

She leaned back with a sigh of contentment. "For all my bitching, I do love to cook a big family meal."

"You're welcome anytime..." David smiled

"You're really pushing it, aren't you?"

"I wouldn't have gotten where I am today if I didn't push people."

Eddie stood at the sink with his back to them, so Eva leaned forward and whispered, "Did you find out what the wad of paper was all about?"

"He needs to complete a school assignment," David said. "He started a blog with Cathy, but after she died, he didn't keep it up. The teacher sent home a warning note."

"I'm surprised she didn't call," Eva said.

"Maybe she did," David replied calmly. He glanced at his middle son diligently scrubbing the roasting pan. "Joshua? Anything to add?"

"What's this? What did I do now?" Josh didn't turn around. He used the spray nozzle to rinse soap from the pan, then set it in the drain board. He grasped the vegetable bowl and started rinsing it without looking toward his father.

"Sure you don't want to tell me anything?" David asked.

"About what?"

"About phone calls from Eddie's school."

Josh rinsed the bowl for so long David thought he'd rinse the floral pattern right off the china. Finally, he shut the water off, grabbed the dish towel, and turned to face his aunt and father. He dried his hands. Eddie poured detergent into the dishwasher, his back still to the others in the room.

"How did you know?" Josh gulped.

Eva sat back, and crossed her arms over her chest. "Gotcha."

"Joshua..." David rumbled.

"Well, it was only a few times," Josh protested. He twisted the dish towel in his hands. Eddie shut the dishwasher door. He pressed the start button, then glanced at everyone. David waved him away. Eddie left the kitchen.

"Isn't he in trouble, too?"

"You're older. You should know better." David folded his arms over his chest and appraised his son. "Okay, out with it. How many times did Mrs. Caruthers call? And what did she want?"

"She only called three times," Josh protested. "Well, okay, four, but the other time was the day Mom died, and I assumed you'd talked to her when you called the school to let them know Ed would be out for the rest of that week."

"And you pretended to be me?"

"Um, yeah."

Eva laughed. David glared at his sister. "Don't laugh," he admonished. "You'll only encourage him."

"Oh, come on, David." A smirk played across her lips. "Don't be such a stick in the mud. How many times did you cover for me and Con?"

"Wait, what? Dad, you pulled this off too?"

"He used to pretend to be Grandpa when I cut school," Eva said. "Didn't you, David?"

"Well, just a few times..."

"I didn't go to gym class once my entire freshman year in high school. Not once!" Eva scraped back her chair. She walked to the kitchen island and reached for a package of Marlboros in the outer pocket of her purse. She tapped out a cigarette and grabbed a red plastic lighter. "Your father does a fantastic impression of Grandpa." She left the kitchen and exited through the mudroom. The screen door was open, and the rich smell of tobacco wafted into the kitchen as Eva enjoyed a cigarette.

"Mrs. Caruthers called four times?" David prompted his son. "And the first time was the day Mom died?"

"Yeah," Josh said. "She called around four-thirty. I got home from school at four and Mom wasn't home. It was weird, Dad. She...she left her music open all over the piano, and it looked like she'd just run out for something quick. Ed wasn't home. The phone rang, and I picked it up, and Mrs. Caruthers asked for Mom. I was just joking around and I said I was you. We do sound a lot alike, don't we?"

"Since your voice changed, yes, we do," David replied. "What did she want?"

"Ed didn't go to his last class that day," Josh said. "Wait - you didn't know?"

"No, I didn't. Why didn't you tell me?"

Josh shrugged. He placed the towel back on the oven handle. He turned back to the sink and started wiping the chrome faucets with the dish sponge. "I don't know. It's just...well, that day sucked, that's all. A little while later the police called, and they said Mom had the accident. I tried to call Uncle Constantine to find out what to do, and he wasn't available, and so I had to call Uncle Blake. And then Ed came pounding into the house and he was crying. I couldn't get it out of him why he was crying. I was trying to tell him something happened to Mom. He just ran upstairs to his room and wouldn't come out until I got hold of Aunt Eva and she came over...and you weren't there. We had to wait until you flew home overnight. So it was all just a big mess, and I'd forgotten about that day."

David mulled over what Joshua said. Finally, he asked, "When were the other times the school called?"

"Well, after that time, she thought whenever I answered the phone that I was you. She called in February about some kind of project Ed has due for school. I told him to get on the stick and get with it, and he just sort of shrugged and went back to reading about birds in the Amazonian jungle or whatever other book he's got going. Then Mrs. Caruthers called again in March, and in April. Honest, Dad, I was going to tell you. It just never seemed like the right time."

"Well, it's the right time now," David snapped. "Now Eddie's got three weeks to do ten of these blog posts or videos or whatever he's got to do, and now I've got to help him with it."

"I'm sorry."

"Next time, don't cover for your brother."

Eva returned to the kitchen. "What did I miss?"

David eyed Josh instead of looking at his sister. "I'm just finding out now that my son is cleverer than I was at covering for his sibling."

Josh shuffled uncomfortably under his father's gaze. "Aw, gee, Dad."

"I really ought to punish you."

"What about Ed?"

"Oh, I'll get to him soon enough. No video games for the rest of the week."

"The week! Dad!"

"Unplug the Xbox One from your room and leave it in my bedroom closet," David commanded. "Now."

Josh stomped from the room muttering under his breath. A few minutes later, they heard a door slam upstairs, a clatter, and then Josh shouted down, "Done. Are you happy?"

"Ecstatic," David murmured.

Eva laughed.

Eva stayed for coffee and a quick game of Sorry with Eddie, after which she had to go. She shrugged into her coat and gave the boys hugs and kisses. David walked her to the 4-Runner.

"Will you be over for dinner on Sunday with Dad?" David asked. "Con said he could make it, but that mysterious girlfriend of his can't. Have you met her yet?"

"No, but they seem to go out an awful lot," Eva said. She played with her car keys as they paused.

"They like to go to that club in Huntington Harbor," David said. "Ocean Blue, I think it's called."

"I'll never understand Con's fascination with bars and clubs. I hate them."

"Me too," David said. "But how else are you going to find a husband these days?"

"I'll clean the home of a rich bachelor and he'll be so enamored with his shiny white toilet that he'll sweep me off my feet." Eva stood on tiptoe and kissed David on the cheek.

"As Papa would say, 'You're not getting younger, Eva!'"

She shut the car door and rolled down the driver's side window. "I promise I won't die an old maid."

"Not when you cook like that, you won't," David replied. "

"Bye David. I love you. Call me anytime."

"How about coming back tomorrow? We're partial to Italian food!"

She laughed as she drove away. He could see the red glow cigarette as she stopped at the corner. Shaking his head, he made his way back into the house.

David strode to the family room, where he attacked the stack of reports he'd brought home from the office. Most concerned the Triad Fund, a series of three hedge funds the firm had opened last fall.

David managed the Blue Chip Fund, which invested heavily in Fortune 500 companies. His fund yielded modest returns and seemed to attract safety-conscious investors content with moderate growth. Constantine, on the other hand, had launched an aggressive investment fund that brought fund members into tech IPOS early enough for them to capitalize on the initial buzz. He was eager to read the latest balance sheets from his brother's funds, especially since Con's fund earned a huge return last fall, considerably over the market average. The third fund in the Triad was Betty Goldfarb's Social Conscience Fund, or as he and Con joked, the Crunchy Granola Fund. It had only recently launched, and he needed to review the current status. Betty's fund invested in renewable energy, third world development projects and similar companies, and it attracted aging hippies and Baby Boomers who wanted dividends without the blood of corporate America on their hands.

Josh and Eddie tumbled into the family room just as he'd begun reading the first report. "Dad, can we watch T.V.?"

"All right," David said absently. "Can you watch with just the closed captioning?"

"Yeah, I guess so," Josh said. He signed to his brother and the two began arguing over what to watch. They finally agreed on a program that seemed to involve flesh-eating vampire zombies. Soon, David was lost in his reports, and the boys were cheering on the zombies.

Around ten., he chased Eddie upstairs to bed and reminded Josh to finish his homework. He was so engrossed in the report that he forgot to check in on Eddie, but by the time he lifted his head and glanced at the clock, it was eleven. Eddie was probably already asleep.

He turned his attention back to assets and liabilities, investments and returns, and another hour passed. His brother's recommendations were included on hastily scrawled notes stuck to various pages inside the bound reports. Joan had also read them, adding a few arrow stickers to sections she knew he'd want to study. He found himself shaking his head, removing Con's stickers, balling them up and tossing them into an ever-growing pile on his desk. Joan's comments held deeper insights than his supposed vice-president did; it was as if Con had used up a stack of sticky notes just to make it look like he had read the reports.

"Tell me something I don't know," David muttered after reading yet another inane comment about social media and the most recent IPOs. Did Con honestly think these comments were helpful? Of what value was any of this?

He finally slammed the sixth report shut and leaned back, pressing the pads of his index fingers into his eyelids, rubbing his tired eyes until he saw colored dots darting this way and that. It reminded him of their childhood, when he had sat down each night at the wobbly Formica kitchen table in their little house in Bellerose, Queens, diligently going over his math homework while Con snuck glimpses at a comic book he'd tucked between the pages of his social studies textbook. Mama was at the stove, stirring red cabbage in a gigantic pot, while Eva sat on the floor in front of the stove playing with her Raggedy Anne doll she loved so much.

"You gotta do your work," David muttered to his brother, glancing up at him over the edge of his raised algebra book. "If you don't read the book, you won't be able to answer Sister Benedict's questions tomorrow and she'll stick you in the corner again."

"No, she won't. I have a system," Con said confidently, smiling and nodding.

"A system?"

"Yeah, a system. The answers are always in the first sentence of each paragraph anyway, or the last one. The middle is just a whole lot of junk. I read the first and last on the bus tomorrow and I'll know enough so she won't knock my block off. You just waste your time with that crap."

"It's not crap," David said. "You'll see. Someday, you'll see. When I'm smart and running a company, and you're driving a bus or something, you'll see."

He woke from his doze with a jolt. His eyes snapped open and he glanced back at the report on his desk. How was Con earning 16% returns on his fund with social media and internet IPOs when he seemed to barely put the time into the analysis needed for success? David shuffled through the papers again, reading his brother's scant comments. I'm doing everything right, he thought, and my fund earns just about market or a little less. Con does everything the quick way and gets triple my return. How?

He pushed his chair away from the desk and stuffed the reports back into his briefcase. I'll get Joan to read this too, he thought as he switched off the desk lamp. Maybe she can give me a second opinion. Joan had been his father's administrative assistant for a decade before Tibor had announced his retirement. Since assuming control of the firm, David had recognized a steady, quiet brilliance in the executive assistant. It was clear to him she could handle bigger and better things.

David glanced at his watch. Just about midnight. He dropped his briefcase onto the couch and mused on this as he left the family room, passing by the little table to the left of the family room that housed their collection of family photos and the small lamp they kept switched on to illuminate the pathway from the family room to the stairs and the kitchen.

He started toward the stairs when something compelled him to walk towards the piano which stood sentinel in the darkened alcove of the living room. A draft of cool evening air gently touched his cheek. Where had it come from? All the windows were closed, weren't they?

He shifted the heavy red drapes to check the windows; they were closed and locked. He peered down Edgewater Drive. Next door, the Miller's Rottweiler barked as he trotted along the chain link fence encircling their property. Curious to see what had set the dog off into such a frenzy, David peered towards the street lamp on the corner of Edgewater and Walnut.

His heart fell. The watcher had returned. The man in the trench coat cupped his hands around a small cell phone and snapped a photo of the Majek's Tudor. The Rottweiler whined, snarled, and barked. The man stuffed the cell phone into his pocket and regarded the Majek residence with cool detachment. David could see a glint of eyes, a hint of white skin under the brim of a hat. The sight stirred indignation at the invasion to his privacy.

I've had just about enough of this, David fumed, dropping the curtain back over the window.

He slammed open the front door and sprinted down the block. The Rottweiler howled and stood on his back paws, looping his massive shoulders over the chain link fence. David sped by. The fellow in the trench coat bolted towards Walnut Street. David lengthened his stride, his feet pounding the pavement, arms pumping in the chase.

"Stop! Damn it, Stop!" David shouted. The man didn't glance back, but doubled his pace.

David closed the distance. His chest grew tight, his breath hot and forced in the back of his throat. His legs ached but he refused to stop. Lights clicked on at the Miller's house. On the corner, light spilled from Mrs. Jansen's front door as she opened it to peer at the commotion. Gasping for breath, David stopped at the street lamp in front of the Jansens. He leaned heavily against the lamppost, resting his forehead on the cool metal.

Mrs. Jansen opened her front door. Her gnarled hands tightened the belt of her pink velour robe. White hair stood in a halo of pillow puffiness about her head. "Mr. Majek, is that you? What is it? What's the matter?"

"Man! On your lawn!" he wheezed. He put a hand to his chest. A burning pain shot from his chest, blooming like fireworks into his arm. He forced himself to breathe deeply, but the pain continued.

"Oh dear," Mrs. Jansen murmured. She wrung her hands together and backed into her doorway. "Oh dear, I must call the police."

The pain subsided. David could breathe more easily now. He wiped the sweat from his face with the back of his hand and peered around, cursing himself for being so out of shape that he'd let the man get away. Something fluttered on the damp lawn to the right of the street lamp. He dropped to his knees and fumbled in the grass. His fingers closed on a small scrap of paper, which he plucked from the dewy grass and thrust into his pocket just as a police siren whooped from around the corner.

He clutched the lamp post, using it to heave himself upright. His chest still felt tight, and his heart hammered too quickly for his liking. If I die, he thought suddenly, what will happen to Alex and Josh? What about Eddie? Who would raise Eddie?

Mrs. Jansen suddenly stood beside him, tugging his arm, speaking urgently.

"Mr. Majek? Are you all right? Mr. Majek?"

"I'm – I'm fine." The dizziness swept past, clearing his mind. Now he breathed in and out without difficulty. Just a stitch in my side, he tried to convince himself, just out of shape. I just need to start going to the gym....

A black and white pulled up the curb, lights flashing. Two officers exited the vehicle and came over to them.

Mrs. Jansen was speaking to a police officer. "...and I looked out of my window and there was a man standing there. What time was it? Goodness, about midnight. I got my baseball bat out, you know, in case he tried to break in but then Mr. Majek came running from his house, shouting. So you see, I knew he saw the man too."

"Mr. Majek?" The officer who addressed him was tall and rangy, with a boxer's shoulders and a disarming smattering of freckles across the bridge of his nose. His partner was a medium built African American man who walked the perimeter of the lawn, shining his flashlight in swift arcs over the grass. David felt the crumpled paper in his pocket, and slipped it into the palm of his hand.

"Yes?"

"We had a report of a similar event earlier in the week at this address. Was it you who called it in?"

"Yes, I telephoned the precinct about it the next day," David said. His fingers tightened around the paper. It was a well-worn business card. He glanced down. He turned the card over in his fingers. Something was written on the back. His eyes widened. He fumbled with the card, trying not to let the officer see his expression.

"Something wrong?" The officer frowned.

"I – I found this on the ground." He was sweating again. How did liars manage to keep lying without getting caught? Everything in him wanted to run, get away as quickly as possible. Instead, he forced himself to take a deep breath. He handed the officer the well-thumbed business card. "Yes, I phoned in a similar complaint last week. My sons alerted me that someone was on the street corner. We noted he had a camera and was photographing the house. Then he disappeared. At that time, we didn't see which way he went. Tonight, I saw him again and gave chase. He fled around the corner, towards Walnut Street."

The officer took the paper from him. "This business card says Majek Investments," he said. "Did you by any chance drop it?"

"I have my own personalized cards. This is one of the blank ones we keep in the reception area. It just has the general office information on it."

"The address on the back, written in pencil," the office said, turning the card over. He looked up. "This is your address?"

"It is."

"Do you recognize the handwriting?"

"No. But – well, you're right. Maybe I did drop it."

"You said you didn't a moment before."

"Maybe I did. I don't know. May I have it back?"

The officer hesitated, glanced at it, then nodded, handing it back to David. "Are you sure you dropped this?"

"Yes. I must have had it in my pocket. It's mine."

"I see." The officer stared at him until David had to look away. "Can you describe the man?"

"I couldn't see much," David said. "He wore the same costume as the other night. An oversized trench coat, khaki, belted, with old-fashioned shoulder pads that made him look big. He's not that tall – he just looks tall, I suppose. Maybe around six-two? Medium build."

"Black? White?"

"White. He's Caucasian."

The officer jotted notes on his pad. David shifted from his left to his right foot like Eddie when he had to go to the bathroom. He needed to get away, now, and look at the business card again.

"Nothing here," the second officer said, reporting back to the man taking David's report. Mrs. Jansen offered her story, and Mrs. Miller wandered by with the beast of a Rottweiler on a hefty chain leash. David gave the dog and his owner both a wide berth, circling around the back of the police car to where the second offer was radioing in a report.

When the policeman clicked the receiver back into the console, David asked, "Can I go now? My children are home alone, and I don't want to be gone too long."

"Did Officer Nylan get your statement and your address?"

"Yes, he did."

"Fine. We'll be in touch if we find out anything."

"Thank you."

David walked slowly up the hill back to his house, grimacing when the knifelike pain sliced his chest again. He paused, forcing himself to breathe deeply. Stress, he told himself, and lack of sleep, and...

What will happen to my kids if something happens to me now?

A gentle spring breeze stirred his dark hair. A shower of tiny, sweetly scented green florets tumbled to the pavement from a maple tree. David had a sudden vision of Cathy the year he had met her, twirling around on a darkened Bellerose street under the arching maples on a May evening like this, laughing, her skirt flying out in all directions, her red-gold hair tumbling in thick waves down her back. She had been so joyful, so full of life, everything in her spirit turned upward to the sun and forward to the future. A lump rose in his throat, and a single maple blossom floated down as he stepped onto the path towards his open front door. Angrily, he kicked it aside, and slammed his way back into the house to dial the number on the piece of paper.

He had lied. He well recognized the handwriting.

It was his father's handwriting on the back of the card.

6

Joshua waited for David on the front stoop. His son scratched his belly under a thin gray t-shirt. He shuffled his bare feet. He peered down the street towards the flashing lights. Other neighbors switched on their porch lights, lights clicking on in living rooms and kitchens all up and down Edgewater Drive. *The Miller's Rottweiler is going to bark himself hoarse,* David thought as he stumbled up the steps to the Tudor's arched front door.

"What's going on, Dad?" Josh's eyes widened. "Geez, Dad, you'd make a vampire look healthy. You okay?"

"Fine," David insisted. "The Watcher was back." David shivered. I've given the lurker a name, a title, even. It made it seem all the more real – and all the more frightening.

"No way!" Josh hesitated a moment before stepping back into the house after his father. David shut the front door and slid the deadbolt into place. "Whoa. Cops. And Mrs. Jensen in all her old lady glory."

"He was standing on her lawn."

"Did she have the Louisville slugger with her? One time when we were walking past her house and Mom stopped to talk to her, she said she kept a baseball bat under her bed."

"Joshua..."

"Okay, sorry. But whoa, the scary dude is back? Should I wake Ed?"

"No. Let him sleep. Just go back to bed. The police will handle it from here." David slumped onto the couch. He put his head in his hands.

"But – Hey Dad, you really don't look good."

"Would you get me a glass of water, please?"

Josh returned in seconds and handed his father a glass of ice water. David sipped, feeling the burning subside in his chest. He nodded his thanks and held the glass between his palms, letting the icy smoothness cut through the fog that threatened to descend again. *The card*, he thought numbly. *Papa? What are you doing, Papa?*

A cool whispering breeze touched his cheek and vanished.

"Dad?"

"I'm fine, Joshua. Thank you for the water." He rose and strode back to the front door, locking it and sliding the deadbolt in place. "Can you turn off the lamp on the side table?"

"Sure." Josh flipped on the overhead light by the stairs and David made his way slowly up, pausing for his son to join him.

"Dad, you sure you're okay?"

"I'm fine. Really."

They walked together up the stairs, two men of almost equal height, David feeling his steps drag behind his young son's. He thought again of how quickly time fled, of moments that seemed like just yesterday when the boys had been infants and he and Cathy had taken turns rocking them when they were fussy. Now it was as if the roles were reversed, and Joshua was trying to parent him. He saw his son sneak a concerned glance at him from under lowered lids, and then they parted with a murmured "Good night" at Joshua's bedroom door.

David entered the master suite. He turned on the night table lamp, kicked his loafers off, and sank onto the counterpane. He slid the business card from his pocket and studied it carefully, turning it over and over again in his hands. He hadn't made a mistake. It was his father's deep, curling old-school penmanship on the back. He'd written David's address in pencil, the thick letters slightly smudged from the damp grass.

What the hell was going on?

He would have sworn he wouldn't be able to sleep a wink, but he fell into a deep, dreamless sleep, fully clothed on the top of his bed with the bedside light on until the alarm shrilled at five. A sprinkle of salt on his cheek from a dried tear the next morning was the only sign he had slid momentarily into weakness.

By the time he finished his shower the next morning, David made up his mind on the course of action he would take. Decisiveness was a key quality he prized in his employees, and he felt better as soon as he had made up his mind about his next steps. A battle plan formed in his mind.

After showering and shaving, he made sure the boys were awake and ready for school. Josh and Eddie ate breakfast quickly and accepted ten dollar bills from him for their lunch money.

As Eddie hurried out of the house to catch the bus, David caught him. He ruffled Eddie's hair and kissed him gently on the top of his head. Ed squirmed in his father's unexpected caress. The school bus groaned to a rumbling halt at the curb. Ed thrust his V for victory sign in the air and shot out from his father's arms into the raucous signs of his friends on the bus who pummeled him with happy insults as he bounded aboard, two steps at a time.

Joshua had already left for school with his friends. This morning David tidied the kitchen, stacked the dishwasher so quickly he chipped a cereal bowl, and knotted his tie while peering into the mirrored shine of the steel polished refrigerator. He gulped a third cup of black coffee, hurried out and locked the back door behind himself. The Yukon's engine revved as he backed out of the driveway. Half an hour later, he eased into his reserved spot in front of the office building in Mitchell Field and took the elevator to the second floor executive suite.

Serene, unruffled, as if she left and returned to Majek Investments only after changing her clothes and freshening her lipstick, Joan accepted the stack of reports from David without demur. But she did hesitate and raise a neatly shaped brow when he made his request.

"Please read the oil future reports and give me your recommendations."

"Me, David? I'm not a broker. I'm not an advisor. I'm—"

"—a trusted member of my senior staff," David said firmly. He handed the final report to her from his bulging briefcase and snapped it shut. "Your notes were thorough and showed insight and forethought. I would like your recommendations on my desk this evening, if it's not inconvenient."

It was the first time he had ever seen her flustered. "I – yes, of course." The surprise vanished, replaced by her usual quiet grace. She did, however, look twice at the reports, and he thought he saw her index finger twitch, as if aching to pick up the blue ballpoint pen on her desk and begin jotting notes.

"Yes, and print a copy. Leave it in the folder of papers I'm to take home."

"Yes sir."

"Do I have any pressing engagements this afternoon?"

She scanned his calendar on the computer. "You have a meeting with Allen Hendrickson at two., a conference call with the Los Angeles branch at three, and a regularly scheduled sales team meeting at four."

"Reschedule Hendrickson for this morning, postpone Los Angeles until later this week, and give my regrets to the sales team. I'll most likely be out this afternoon."

"Yes, sir."

"Thanks, Joan."

Once inside his office, he tried to telephone his father, but there was no answer. His father didn't believe in answering machines or cell phones, so he gave up after ten rings, figuring his father was out for his walk or just ignoring the phone as he sometimes did. He'd call again later. The business card was tucked into his breast pocket. He wasn't going to let it out of his sight until he saw his father again.

David quickly checked the 600 emails waiting for him, trashing more than half and answering a few urgent notices. The private coffee urn on the credenza beckoned, and he poured another cup of coffee, then returned to his desk and opened the top drawer of his desk where he kept a stack of business cards wrapped in a green rubber band. He flipped through them until he found the three he wanted, and then he slid the rest back into the drawer.

His first call was to his doctor's office in Glen Cove. The receptionist put him on hold for several minutes, and Jim himself answered. They were old friends from their New York University days.

"Well, I wasn't expecting the great doctor himself to pick up."

Jim got right to the point. "My nurse said you had chest pains last night and shortness of breath. Did you go to the emergency room?"

"No, and I'm not going now, if that's what you want me to do."

"It's not what I want you to do. It's what I insist that you do. David, with your family history – "

"Just my mother, Jim. My father is healthy, hearty and hale at age ninety, and likely to outlive us all."

"Still, David, I don't like those symptoms. Did anything precipitate them?"

"Let's just say I went for an impromptu jog."

"Exertion can trigger a coronary event. I'd like you to go to the nearest emergency room –"

"I can't, and I won't, so please don't ask me again. I can, however, stop by your office this afternoon if that's convenient?"

"It seems it will have to be. But promise me one thing?"

"Yes?"

"If you have any symptoms again today – shortness of breath, chest pain, pain in your arm, indigestion, sweating – you will go directly to the nearest emergency room."

"I will not set foot in a hospital."

"David, you might have to. Promise me."

"You're worse than my sister."

Jim chuckled. "Can you make it here by one-thirty?"

"Yes."

"Fine, I'll tell my receptionist to pencil you in. Be there and be on time, please."

"Yes, sir."

"Oh, shut up with that." Jim paused. "David?"

"What?"

"If you get any chest pains again – shortness of breath, nausea, anything remotely resembling what you experienced last night – I want that wonderful admin of yours to call 911 immediately. Don't mess with this."

"I'm never going to set foot again in a hospital. I barely made it in when Cathy had the children, and only under threat of death or divorce if I wasn't there when she gave birth."

"This isn't something you can play around with, David."

"No."

"We can discuss it at one-thirty."

"At one-thirty, then."

That task accomplished, he tried his father again, and when his second attempt was unsuccessful, he made another phone call, listening to the recorded message, pressing one, pressing three, and waiting until finally the line rang into his brother-in-law's law office. Cathy's father had been a Nassau County family court judge, and her only sibling was a well-regarded attorney in Mineola. Blake picked up the phone on the second ring, barking, "Blake Tarleton," into the receiver.

"You're worse than me on the telephone. Hello, Blake."

"David!" He heard Blake's chair creak, and pictured him sitting back in the heavily varnished wooden swivel chair that had been Judge Tartleton's seat of power for over 40 years. "I'm glad you called, bro. How are you doing?"

"I'm holding on. Did I catch you at a bad time?"

"Never a bad time for family. What can I do for you?"

"Blake, when Cathy and I made out our wills a few years ago after Eddie was born, did we designate guardians for the kids?"

"I'm not sure," Blake said. "Can you hold on a minute while I check? It's in the files here but in another room. I won't be but a minute."

"Certainly."

He waited in the blessed silence of the law office's phone system; they eschewed messages on hold, of which David was profoundly grateful. Joan knocked quickly while he was on hold, and he called her in. She entered, sliding a note onto his desk. Con wanted to see him. He nodded and said, "I'm on hold. Tell Con I'll buzz him when I'm off the phone. I won't be long." She nodded and left quietly, shutting the door softly behind her.

A minute later, Blake returned to the line. "David? I have your file here. No, actually, you didn't specify guardians. I have a note that says that Cathy was supposed to call me to let me know who would accept guardianship, but she never did. I guess it slipped her mind."

"I suppose so. What must I do to assign guardians?"

"First, they must be over age twenty-one. I would suggest someone with the means and the ability to care for all of your children in one household, and someone prudent enough to oversee their finances since you will leave them considerable assets."

"Indeed. Blake, is this something I can call you about when I've made my decision?"

"Yes. When you have someone in mind, speak to them privately about it, and if they agree to the guardianship, I will update the paperwork."

"Fine. Thank you. I'll call you back later this week."

"Okay." Blake hesitated. "How are you doing, though? I mean, with everything? Is there any further word on the hit and run?"

"No. I wish there was."

"When did you last speak to the detective on the case?"

"About two weeks ago," David said. "I don't think they're working on it very hard, frankly. It seems like it's already low priority."

"Let me call again," Blake said. "I can shake something up. I'll use my mean courtroom voice."

David laughed. "Let me know if you get results."

They caught up quickly, Blake asked about the boys, asking after his father, brother and sister. Soon the conversation had run its course, and David, promising once again to call back later in the week with the final choice of guardian, hung up the phone feeling better than he had in days.

He rang Joan and let her know he was available, and soon Constantine entered the room. "Mind if I have some coffee?"

"No, have as much as you want. I'll get more for myself, too."

David motioned to the seating area so that they could sit more comfortably, and Con sank onto the striped couch, stretching out his long legs. David noticed that Con's gray suit trousers were slightly wrinkled, as if he hadn't had them cleaned or he had slept in them again. It rang a bell with him, and he searched his memory, realizing that Con had also looked a little disheveled a few days ago. He scanned his brother's face and noticed a fine mist of dark stubble on his chin. Con saw his scrutiny.

"What? Did I spill coffee on my shirt or something?"

"No, no, nothing like that. You just look a little – different."

Con stirred his coffee slowly so that the three sugars he'd added would dissolve. "If you must know, I didn't go home last night."

"Oh."

His brother smiled. "Lisa."

"Oh, that." David swallowed a smile. "Good. Great. Are you happy?"

"Happy? She's fantastic." Con's smiled vanished. His eyes darted nervously to the carpet and back to his brother's face. "I was wondering..."

"Yes?"

"I was wondering, David, if I could ask for a raise."

David almost choked on the mouthful of bitter coffee he was about to swallow. "Excuse me," he said, coughing. "I thought you just asked me for a raise."

"I did."

"You received a raise last year, did you not?"

"I did. But it wasn't enough."

"If memory serves me, it was 5 percent."

"But you promised me a bonus."

"A performance bonus, which you did not earn last year, although I must admit you're on track to earn one this year. The Triad Fund seems to be doing extremely well." David leaned forward from his seat on the opposite sofa, softening his tone. "Con, I'm sorry. But if I give you a raise and you haven't achieved the goals set for you, all of the vice presidents and executive directors are going to be in my office demanding raises. It won't do for me to show favoritism to anyone. You understand, don't you?"

"I guess." Con looked away.

David decided to address the issue of the reports now, too. "I could really use your assistance now, Con," he said. "Those oil futures report you reviewed last week. Can you please work with Joan to build a comprehensive set of recommendations?"

"Joan? But she's our secretary."

"She's got potential," David insisted. "I think her skills are underused. I've asked her to take a look at the reports, too."

"Oh, all right," Con said. "But I'm working on the Asian Tiger Fund now."

"I know, and I know that is important to you. But will you do this for me?"

"Of course. You know I will. You just have to ask me anything and I'll do it for you, David." Con looked down into his lap. "But...David, I kind of need the money now."

"For what?"

"I... oh, never mind."

"No, Con, tell me. Even if I can't grant you a raise, there's nothing that says brothers can't lend brothers money, is there?"

Just then, the intercom buzzed. "David?"

"Yes, Joan."

"Neil is on the line for you."

David leaped to his feet and crossed to his desk. He motioned for Con to wait, but Con put his coffee cup back onto the service tray by the urn and waved his brother aside. "No, don't worry about me, David," he said. "I just thought asking for a raise was worth a shot. You're right. I was wrong."

"Con, if you're in some kind of financial difficulty, I can lend you money. I don't have a problem with that."

Con shook his head, smiling wanly. "No, it's okay. I'll find a way."

"Are you sure I can't lend you the money, Con? I really mean it. I may come off a hard ass now and then, but you're my brother, and brothers support each other, right?"

"Right," Con said, walking to the office door. "But no, David. I'm fine now. Everything will be okay."

The phone buzzed again. Joan's voice floated over the speaker. "David, your morning conference call with the investors is on line one."

"Con—"

"Take your call," he said again. "No worries, David. Everything is fine."

A chill descended on him as he watched Con disappear around the doorframe. Why did his words strike him so oddly? The phone line buzzed again, commanding his attention. He pressed the button and turned his mind back to the business of the day.

"No, Jim. I won't," David said.

The nurse slid the needle out of David's arm. "Bend your elbow," she barked, pressing a cotton ball firmly on the site where she'd taken the blood samples.

Jim, known to most of his patients as Dr. Bjork, sat on a stool on the opposite side of the examination room studying David thoughtfully. When his nurse left, carrying the tray with neatly marked vials of blood, Jim waited until the door closed behind her and the two old friends were left alone in the exam room. David leaned back in the uncomfortable chrome and plastic chair and said, "Screw you and your tests. I'm not doing it."

"You're being an ass, David. You know that?"

"So I've been told."

"How would you like it if I told you how to do your job?"

"You wouldn't dare. I've doubled your investment in six years. I know what I'm doing."

"And I've kept more men like you out of an early grave than you can count," Jim snorted. "When did this phobia of yours start, anyway? I don't remember you being this silly about hospitals when we were in college."

"That's because I never got sick." Jim slid off the stool and David held out his arm for the bandage, which his old college buddy slapped onto his arm. "Ow. Nice bedside manner."

"Man up," Jim said mildly. "You're lucky I didn't slap you with a Sponge Bob bandage. That would go over well at your next board meeting." He leaned against the examination table. "You're forty-eight years old and you ran down the block and had chest pains and dizziness. You have a significant family history of early coronary disease – your mother died from a heart attack when she was your age, didn't she?"

"She did." David picked up his shirt from the hook on the wall behind the chair and slid it on over his undershirt, buttoning it with his right hand so swiftly his fingers moved in a blur.

"And you've experienced a significant emotional trauma this year. Don't you think you owe it to your kids to get this checked out?" Jim folded his arms across his chest and leaned back in his chair.

"I am getting it checked out. I allowed you to do an EKG here, didn't I?" David didn't look at his old friend. He searched for his tie and found it hanging on the same hook where his shirt had been.

"After so much whining I almost went out and bought you a lollipop, yeah."

"Well. So what did it tell you?"

"That you need a stress test with an echocardiogram."

"Why can't you do this test here, like the EKG?"

"An echocardiogram is a sonogram of the heart - a picture. I need a special machine for that. I don't have it here."

"Well, then. They won't get done. I won't go to a hospital."

"If you have a massive coronary on my watch, you will go to a hospital whether you like it or not." Jim stared at him until David looked away. David knew his old friend wasn't joking anymore; he was deadly serious.

"Are you saying I'm at risk for a heart attack?" He tried to keep the tremor out of his voice.

"I'm saying there is something showing on your EKG, and I need you to go for more tests."

"Can the tests be done in an office somewhere?"

Jim shook his head and muttered as he pulled his tablet from the pocket of his lab coat and touched the stylus to the screen. "If I find a laboratory for these tests that's in an office, a standalone office, not at a hospital, will you go?"

"How long will they take?"

Jim hesitated. "Block off the entire morning. The stress test itself takes about an hour, but I want them to take some pictures of your heart afterwards, so that will add another hour." He added quickly, "You'll have to fast the night before, too. No caffeine, no food or drink except water for 12 hours before the test."

"Pictures don't sound too bad," David said grudgingly. He stood to knot his tie in the little mirror hanging next to the hook in the doctor's office.

"David, I don't think you're taking this seriously enough," Jim said quietly. He clicked a few more buttons on his tablet, and then slipped it back into his pocket. "I've asked Marge at the front desk to get you in for the test on Monday. You'll have to fast the night before, so nothing to eat from dinner until after the test."

"All right."

"You're not taking any medications now, are you? I know I prescribed sleeping pills for you after Cathy died. Are you taking them?"

"No."

"Are you sleeping?"

"Sometimes."

"David...."

"Look, don't nag me, Jim. I wasn't even going to come in today if it hadn't taken me so much by surprise, those chest pains. I thought they were just from exertion – it's been longer than I thought since I've done any running."

"If you get a clean bill of health after the tests, you should take it up again."

"I haven't gained an ounce since college and you know it."

"I'm not saying you've gained weight. In fact, you've lost almost ten pounds since Cathy died, and on your frame that's a lot. You're starting to look gaunt, David. You could actually stand to gain a little back. No, I'm talking about for your health. Your heart is a muscle, and it benefits from exercise the same as your arms or your legs. And it's a good stress reliever, which I think you need, frankly. Managing money for the world's richest people can't be the easiest job, not with your father breathing down your neck all the time. No offense."

David smiled. "None taken. You've actually met him and survived to tell the tale."

Jim laughed. "Oh, yeah. He's an incredible man, and I know you love him a lot, but being in the family business can't be easy."

"No, it's not." David smiled ruefully. "It's rather like trying to juggle porcupines."

"And then there's Cathy. You're still grieving. So many questions unanswered about her death. There's a reason we speak of the heart as the center of emotions. Grief takes time to heal, too."

"And you can see a broken heart on an x-ray or whatever you're going to do?"

Jim sighed. "Your blood pressure is 150/98, and I can see from the cords on the side of your neck that you're a bundle of stress. I know what your job is like. You're managing a 100-person office and a satellite office on the west coast. You're juggling your elderly father – who on a good day isn't an easy man to handle – and you're trying to be both father and mother to your kids, including a handicapped child." David opened his mouth to protest. Jim held up his hand. "No, don't tell me he's fine. No matter what a great kid Eddie is, and I have no reason to think he's not a great kid, it's still got to be a little more challenging than raising your typical kid, which is challenging enough. Now we throw a gallon of gasoline onto your stress fire and give you a theft of almost $100K from your bank account and someone stalking you. Gee, David, did I leave anything out?"

"Well, when you put it like that..." David slumped back onto the hard plastic chair. He put his head in his hands. "Jim, how the hell did I end up here?"

"In my office? You drove on the Long Island Expressway."

"Very funny. You know what I mean." He looked up at his old college buddy. "We were in college, chasing girls and beers, sometimes in that order, sometimes not. And then I met Cathy. And I fell head over heels in love. And I thought I had it made – perfect wife, perfect life. Now I'm widowed, I'm running my dad's company, and I don't know which was to turn."

"You want my advice?"

"No, I just want to chit chat."

"Ha. Listen, David – my advice? Take a month off." David snorted. "Seriously, you need a vacation. Take a month off. Your family still owns that beach house in Cutchogue, right? Pack up the kids, pack up the house, stare at Peconic Bay for a month from a deck chair and get your life and health back in order. You've got too much stress right now."

"I'll take it under advisement." Suddenly, he was very, very tired.

He had one final stop to make before heading home to rustle up supper for the boys. Jim's office in the North Shore Towers was just one exit away from his old Bellerose neighborhood, and since his father wasn't answering his telephone today, he decided to swing by for an impromptu visit. More like a confrontation, David thought as he waited at a traffic light. He glanced to his right at the cluster of four stores with a pang of nostalgia. Kids clustered outside the candy store, bikes leaning against the metal lamppost. Trashcan overflowed by the corner. The kids uncovered Marino's Italian ices and dug into them with the little wooden paddle-shaped spoons. Schott's Candy Store was still there, and on the right, the German deli. But the hair salon had been replaced by a liquor store, and the end shop was vacant yet again. The light turned green, and the car behind him honked. He moved forward.

A few blocks later, he turned right, then right again three blocks into the close-knit Queens community. The houses were set a driveway apart from one another, stacked like the tiny houses on a Monopoly board on top of sixty by ninety lots. *Paradise to the immigrants like my parents*, David thought as he eased the Yukon into his father's narrow driveway. Next door, a Vietnamese lady watered her yard with a garden hose while a chubby toddler played with a dandelion. David smiled at her, but she scowled and looked away.

His father's grass was neatly trimmed, and the stone lions on the front stoop of the Cape had been recently whitewashed. He gave the one on the right a fond pat on the head as he knocked on the front door; he had spent many happy afternoons with his brother Con playing games on those lions, imagining riding them, racing them like the chariots in Ben-Hur. *How does time fly so quickly?* David wondered, fingering the card in his pocket. *How do we move from playing at imaginary chariot races to this?*

There was no answer at the front door, so David walked around to the rear. His father stepped from the garden to see who was parked in his driveway. Tibor wore a white sleeveless undershirt over ripped old trousers and heavy brown leather boots from his days serving his mandatory two years in the Soviet army. His hands were crusted with soil, and sweat dripped from his brow. He wiped it off with a white handkerchief and beamed when he saw David.

"David! An unexpected pleasure!"

"Hello, Papa."

Tibor threw his arms around David in a sweaty bear hug. "What? Why so stiff? You are angry, *můj syn*. Come and have a glass of tea, and we will talk about your troubles, yes?"

"Yes, we will."

Tibor had been spading the earth around the rose bush in the center of the elaborate parterre garden. The parterre, or kitchen garden, had been his mother's pride and joy, and David was relieved to see it still as he remembered it. The small yard, flanked with wooden stockade fencing in the back and chain link fences to the right and left, was divided into small symmetrical planting beds edged with scalloped brick. In the far back corners stood dwarf apple and pear trees, and in a circle in the center of the garden, his mother's American Beauty rose bush. His father had somehow managed to find a bucket of rather ripe horse manure, and he had been spading it into the earth, turning the rich brown soil over so that he could mingle the fresh manure near the roots.

"You shouldn't do such heavy work anymore, Papa," David said. He noted the lettuce bed planted in neat, diagonal stripes of color: lime green, red tipped, oak leaf and other varieties of lettuce. Radishes waved their rough leaves from the border. Young tomatoes were waiting their turn in the garden, still housed in their garden center pots near the garage.

"It's my pleasure, my exercise," Tibor said. He walked to a round white lattice table where a sweating Tupperware pitcher and a sleeve of plastic cups waited. "Here, take tea."

David slid onto the metal bench that fit neatly around the table, and his father sat down opposite him. He poured two glasses of the strong, icy tea. He handed a glass to his father, then reached into his pocket and pulled out the business card. He slid it across the table. "Papa, what do you know of this?"

"Eh?" Tibor squinted in the bright sunlight at the card. He picked it up, studying it. David watched his father's reaction. For a moment, Tibor said nothing. Then he shoved the card back across the table. "It's a card. Why?"

"It's not the card I'm asking about, and you know it."

"What do I know? I know nothing." Tibor wouldn't look at him. He gazed across the garden to the rose bush. "I have to get back to my gardening. Your mother's rose, it is looking sad these days." The lush green shrub rustled in the light breeze.

"Papa," David asked quietly, "Why?"

"Why what? You make no sense!"

Tibor tried to leave the table, but David's shot out his hand and grabbed his father by the wrist. "Papa, I want answers. Twice now a man has been watching my house. Photographing it. He went to school to see my son. The police find nothing. I find this, this card, with your handwriting on the back of it. You gave this man my address. I want to know why, Papa."

"I don't know what you are talking about."

"Oh, I think you do," David said. He released his father's wrist. He forced himself to take a sip of the unsweetened iced tea. "You're having me watched and my family watched, too. I want to know why. Why, Papa?"

Tibor sank onto the metal bench opposite David. For a moment, he was silent, turning the sweating red Solo cup in his soil-crusted hands. A bee buzzed lazily over the table, then bumbled on. The Vietnamese lady next door clattered about her trash cans as she shut off the hose. She shouted to her child, then banged the screen door shut.

"It is not what you think."

"You lied to me. When you came to my office, I told you about the man. I told you how frightening it was and how Eddie had seen him at his school, and you pretended not to know anything. KGB my ass. You hired this man. Now I want some answers."

"Sometimes it is best not to ask the questions. Then you do not get answers you do not like."

David shoved his bench back and rose to his feet. He towered over the table, his shadow looming on the concrete pad behind him. "I'm done talking," he said.

Tibor looked up at him.

"If you don't answer me, Papa, I have nothing to say to you. Clearly, you find it necessary to keep tabs on me at work, to drop in unexpectedly. Joan said last month she caught you peeking into the files – no, don't look so shocked. Yes, she told me, but you wouldn't find anything there. Everything is on the computer now, and you don't have the password.

"It's not enough you spy on my work, that you check on my every move. It's not enough you undermine my decisions, that you create havoc wherever you go. No, that's not enough. Why all of this? And all you can say is that I won't like the answer."

Tibor finally spoke. He said hoarsely, "You won't."

"Let me be the judge of that. I ask you one final time, Papa. Why are you having me followed?"

Tibor closed his eyes as if praying. Finally, he looked up. David stood with feet apart, fists clenched. He met his father's eyes.

"All right," Tibor sighed. "I will tell you. God help me, I will tell you."

"I'm listening."

"I thought you killed Cathy, and I wanted to protect my grandsons."

8

David sank back onto the bench. Around them sounds of the afternoon continued as if his world had not just cracked in two. Sparrows chirped happily from the trees, and game show music blared from the neighbor's television set. Children blocks away at the elementary school roared approval of someone's home run in the ball field; the sound carried from the same school that he, Constantine and Eva had attended all those years ago. His chest felt tight and heavy. He found he was holding his breath and drew in more air as a drowning man gasps; then with a whoosh, he exhaled.

"You thought I killed Cathy? Good God, Papa. Why in heaven's name did you think that? I was in Los Angeles the day she died!"

David rose to his feet and strode away from his father. He stopped near the garden hose curled like a plastic green snake in the new spring grass.

"The day before she died, she called me," Tibor said hoarsely. "She says she is worried that you might have done something foolish.

She asked me questions about some papers she found on your desk. You left them behind when you left on your last business trip."

"When I was opening the Los Angeles office? She called me too. She didn't mention anything about them other than the fact that I'd left them on the desk in the family room, and she asked if they were important. I said yes, they were, but they were needed at the office in New York. I told her to call the office and they'd send a messenger for them."

"Did the office pick them up?"

"I don't know." David suddenly realized he hadn't seen them since. "I spoke with her once more that evening, and the next day...well, the next day was the day she died. I assume someone picked them up."

"What were they, David? She was asking me questions about the Triad Fund, but that is not something I know about."

"The Triad Fund is the hedge fund Constantine and I established. It's actually three funds. I manage the first, Con the second, and Betty Goldfarb, the third. The first fund, the one I manage, invests in blue chip stocks. Con's fund invests in new technology. Betty's fund is a socially conscious fund investing in renewable energy. She's having trouble getting that one to generate good returns, but the investors like it because they feel their money is doing some good. Mine is returning only about average, but Con's is doing extraordinarily well."

Next door, the Vietnamese lady sounded as if she had given her toddler every saucepan and lid to bang together. Tibor waited a moment until the clamor subsided before he continued. "Now you see, though, why I hire this man to watch you. The day after Cathy calls to ask me about these papers, she is killed. Did someone pick up the papers?"

"I assume so. Why in the world do you think she didn't - and that she was killed over these papers? It makes no sense, Papa. I think you're imaging things."

"I look at you, my son, and I think, 'What if my David is in trouble?' What if he did do something funny with the hedge fund?'"

"Papa, I still can't believe you thought this of me. I've never given you cause to doubt my honesty. Never."

"Pah," Tibor waved him away. "Anyone can fall. Look at that man that was just in the news." He spit a wad of phlegm at the name onto the concrete pad of the patio. Tibor had known the latest villain in the media's investment scandal circus casually through the same social circles, but he had never liked the man, and the feeling was mutual. "He did not need all that money, but he was tempted, and look where it got him? Prison. A son, dead by suicide. A company, ruined. Anyone can be tempted, David."

"I did nothing wrong, Papa. Nothing. I swear to you. But did Cathy really think...?" He felt tears prick his eyes. He blinked them away.

"Ah, David. Cathy loved you. She loved you so much. But she knew how hard you try to fill my shoes. To become bigger and better than the old man is impossible, and she knows this."

"Papa," David said, folding his arms across his chest. "That's nonsense. I'm my own man. I don't want to be you."

"The summer before she died, Cathy was worried about you," Tibor admonished. "When we went as a family to the beach house in Cutchogue, you did not come. You stayed behind, commuting to us on the weekend as if we were the job and the job was your family. You had many business trips. You missed Eddie's fifth grade play. You did not see Joshua's baseball team win the trophy. Cathy thought...Cathy worried.

"Oh, don't look like that. She never thought you had another woman! Cathy worried that you loved your profit and loss statements more than time with your family."

David reached for more tea, then realized the pitcher was almost empty. He thumped his cup back on the table.

"So when she found something among my papers, she assumed the worst? That I would be capable of breaking the trust of my clients, of my father, of putting all of our lives in jeopardy?"

"Greater men than you have been tempted, David."

"Why didn't she come to me?"

"Perhaps she was going to. Perhaps that is why she was killed."

David folded his arms around himself. He wanted to rush from his parent's house back to the office and demand to see the Triad Fund documents, to call an immediate, emergency meeting of his senior staff. But if his father was right, and someone had killed Cathy over an issue in the paperwork...if her death wasn't an accident...he could be putting himself in deadly peril if he made a move too soon. He must be cautious. He finally spoke.

"Let me set the record straight, Papa. I did not embezzle funds. I did not play games with our clients' fortunes. All I did was make the worst decision of my life that summer by spending so much time on work that I missed my last weeks with my wife, and with our family as a whole.... a time we can never get back. That is the worst thing I have ever done in my life, Papa, and believe me, it is far worse than embezzlement. It leaves a bitter legacy."

"Then fix it." Tibor stood up and faced his son. "You are still doing this running, David. Yes, yes, I know. I am a meddlesome old man. But the man I hired, he keeps tabs on you. He says you work too hard. Eddie is not supervised after school every day. You never did call an agency, did you? Eva cannot be a wife to you. She is a good woman, my daughter, but she has her own life to lead. Now I ask you,

David. While we look into this mess, while we find answers to the papers Cathy saw, will you sweeten the bitterness of your life?"

"My life is not bitter."

"It is not sweet."

"My sweetness is buried with my wife."

"David, she may be dead, but you are alive." Tibor gestured towards the rose bush. "Do you know when your mother planted that?"

"It's always been there."

"She planted that rose the day we moved here," Tibor said. "She built the garden around it. She wanted sweetness at the heart of everything she did. Your Cathy was like that, too."

"I've got to go, Papa."

"Majek Investments will still stand if you leave for a while. Your brother can take on more responsibilities. Neil Taylor is a good CFO...he can do more. Betty Goldfarb is a good compliance officer...she can do more.

"But you, David Majek, you are a father first. Your children need you now. Will you be there?"

David strode to garden entrance. He paused and said, "I'll look into these papers, Papa. Tell your man not to spy on us anymore."

"David, be careful! These papers could be dangerous. Cathy may have been killed for them."

"I will be careful, but I think you're blowing this all out of proportion," David responded. "Perhaps there was something among the paperwork I brought home that was troubling. But Cathy didn't know anything about finance, Papa. She didn't understand a hedge fund from a mutual fund, and she couldn't even balance the damned checkbook. I handled all the money, Cathy handled our lives, and she did it beautifully. I'm awful at it. I don't remember my kids' teachers, I can't remember to pick up fish food or turtle food, and I let the laundry pile up. But I do know my job, and I know my place, and my place is at the helm of Majek Investments. My clients and employees expect no less of me than they did of you. So stay out of this. Don't make this into something more than it is. I'll find those papers, I'll look at them, and when I do, you'll see it was nothing, nothing at all."

"I hope so," Tibor said sadly. "I hope so."

"See you Sunday." David turned on his heel and strode to the Yukon.

Tibor called after him, "So I am still expected for dinner? You are not disowning your old Papa?"

David shouted rudely in Czech.

"Don't talk to me like that!" Tibor roared, shaking his fist. "I am still your father. You do not tell me to be quiet!"

But David couldn't hear him anymore over the roar of the Yukon's engine and the chatter on the radio. He turned 1010 WINS up as loud as it would go, letting the sound of the traffic report drown out his thumping heart.

Could there be truth to what his father had said? He hadn't so much as glanced at the December hedge fund reports. Cathy's death had knocked him senseless, had turned his world upside down. He remembered flying back to New York in a black haze, huddled in the back of the plane with his eyes closed so that the stewardess would leave him alone. He remembered the car service driving him straight to the morgue, where he identified her body in the green-tiled room that smelled of bleach. He remembered the questions, the police, the children crying...Cathy's brother, Blake, sobbing.... Eva staying with the kids, making sure they were fed, making sure he ate and slept and stayed alive to pick out funeral clothes and flowers....

He almost missed his turn off onto the Long Island Expressway as the memories of last November flooded his mind. *Papers*, he thought to himself as he steered among the tractor trailer trucks, cabs and vehicles on the congested expressway, *what papers did I bring home in November?*

November, David thought as he drove, *was almost end of the year.* There were monthly statements to review for each fund; a balance sheet, cash flows, and other paperwork. He couldn't remember.

But he also didn't remember seeing the folders on his desk after Cathy died. She must have called the office as he'd requested and had someone pick them up. It was the only logical explanation.

As traffic slowed to a trickle thanks to rush hour volume, he plugged his cell phone into the car's system and dialed the office. Joan picked up on the first ring.

"Joan?"

"Yes, David? How did your appointment go?"

"All right. The usual. Listen, I have a question to ask. It may seem odd. I need your discretion."

"Need you ask? What's the question?"

"Back in November, when I was in Los Angeles opening the new branch office, just before my wife died, did she call you for anything?"

"Cathy, call me? No, she didn't call me. Oh, wait. I was out sick that week, remember? Terrible stomach flu. We had a temp in that week."

"Oh, right. I'd forgotten."

"Is there anything I can do for you?"

"No, no. I'll have to look into this myself," David said. "It's just about some paperwork that might have been misplaced. I thought that Cathy had them, but now it turns out she didn't. It's not urgent. It can wait until the morning."

"Very well. You had about a dozen telephone calls while you were out, and I cleaned out your email and forwarded you only the urgent ones. Everything else is fairly quiet today."

"Is Constantine there?"

"Yes, he's actually right in front of me now. Want to talk to him?"

"Yes, put me through, please."

David slid the Yukon into the right line, which seemed to be crawling a little faster than the middle lane. He had only three more exits before he could leave the dreadful Expressway traffic. Constantine's voice filled the car's speakerphones.

"David? How was your appointment?"

"It was okay. You know Jim. You go in for a tune-up, he adds on a tire rotation, safety check and a valve job."

Con laughed. "I know. That's why I avoid doctors, too."

"I stopped by to see Dad on the way home."

"Oh? Everything okay there?"

"Yeah, he was outside gardening. Are you coming to dinner on Sunday? Two o'clock. Like in the old days. Eva's cooking, so you don't have to worry about my food killing you."

"Good. You can cook bacon and eggs and that's about it."

"Con... back in November...the day Cathy died...did she call you for any reason?"

A pause. "Call me? No, not that I can remember. Why?"

"Nothing. Seems like some papers are missing. I brought them home from work, and Cathy asked me about them that day. I was just thinking about it today and realized I never followed up on that."

"David, it's been five months, almost six. If nobody asked about them, they're probably right where they should be. Did you ask Joan?"

"I asked Joan. She was out with the flu that week."

"Oh yeah. That's right. Well, do you want me to look for these papers?"

"No, no, not now. I'll take care of it another time." David navigated around a minivan loaded with what looked like an entire hockey team. "How did the meeting go today with the website committee?"

"New rules coming out of the Fed about disclosure again. Betty's on it. We'll probably need to update the various disclosure documents we send out to new clients, though."

"I see. Well, let marketing work with legal on that."

"Already taken care of."

"Thanks, Con. You're always on the ball with this stuff. Takes a big load off of my mind."

They spoke briefly of other matters, David getting an efficient recap from his brother on the day's events and decisions. As he finally coasted to the stop sign at the end of the exit ramp and to the last stage of his journey home David had to admit his brother could indeed handle things smoothly during his absence. Maybe his father was right. Maybe he should take some time off this summer. *Soon*, he thought as he turned onto Northern Boulevard. *I can take a break soon.*

He glanced at the dashboard clock. It was almost four-thirty. The boys would be home − and hungry. Normally, he didn't get home until well after six, but tonight he'd surprise them with an early dinner. He coasted off Northern Boulevard and onto Glen Cove Road. The CVS where Cathy had been killed was in the first shopping center on his right, the drug store surrounded by a dentist's office, the pet store that Eddie loved, and a dry cleaner. It was a little strip mall set just beyond a busy intersection, and less than a mile from the Majek's house.

At the corner of the intersection, the Rose Diner held court in all her sleek chrome and neon splendor. The diner had been built in the 1950s when fewer people drove, and the parking lot was woefully inadequate for the steady stream of customers seeking their amazing twenty-five cent milkshakes, the price kept the same since 1955. They even had a bicycle rack outside for the many cyclists who passed on Northern Boulevard on the weekends and stopped for a snack; local kids regularly rode to the diner, too.

It really was possible that Cathy had been meeting someone there and had simply left her car in the strip mall parking lot for convenience sake. Despite the many signs proclaiming "Customer Parking Only: All Others Will Be Towed" many locals parked in the strip mall lot to dash into the Rose for a shake and fries to go.

David decided he'd treat the boys to the Rose's to-go menu. Eddie in particular loved their milkshakes. He pulled his car into the CVS lot, trying not to look at the fourth aisle, third spot. That's where the Brookville Police had told him Cathy's car had been. She had been killed a few steps away. Although the Rose was always packed with people, the strip mall had been quiet at two o'clock on a Tuesday afternoon, and only the elderly owner of the dry cleaning establishment had seen the accident. He'd reported a man behind the wheel of a black SUV, but given that it was Long Island, and every other household owned a black SUV, without a license plate number, a make or model of the vehicle, the police had nothing to go on.

No wonder Papa thought it might be me, David thought uneasily as he locked the Yukon and strode across the asphalt towards the Rose Diner. *He only knows a few people with black SUVs.*

But somewhere out there was a black SUV that had killed Cathy. *And behind the wheel,* he thought as he reached for the door handle of the diner, *was the man who should pay for Cathy's death. But how to find him? How?*

9

"Oh hey! Rose Diner shakes!" Josh grabbed the nearest to-go bag and dug into it to view his treasures. David snatched it away from him.

"That one's your brother's. I got you the chocolate cherry shake. It's in that bag." He pointed to the one next to the opened bag.

"Awesome! Let me get Ed!"

Josh ran upstairs to tell his brother about their favorite meal while David placed the bags by his sons' spots at the kitchen table. Should he bother with plates? Plates meant washing dishes, which meant another fight between Josh and Eddie about whose turn it was to stack the dishwasher. How did Cathy handle all of this so easily? Maybe the kids fought around here and she just kept it from me. *If so, I should call the Vatican about her sainthood, because they're driving me nuts...and I'm not even around them all day.*

With a shrug, he decided real silverware and plates would be optional tonight. David left the kitchen and was halfway upstairs when he met Josh coming down.

"Ed doesn't want dinner," Josh announced.

"What? But it's his favorite!"

"He says he doesn't want it."

"Is he sick?"

"I don't know." Josh shrugged. "Hey, I'll eat his burger if he's not hungry."

"Wait until I talk to him," David snapped and veered to the left at the top of the stairs towards Eddie's room.

Eddie sat at his desk, chin cupped in his hands, watching the computer screen. He was in a chat room of some sort. David glanced at the screen to see that Eddie was chatting with someone who called himself Lucky 7. It looked at first glance like typical boy stuff - games, pets, school.

Eddie glanced at his father. David touched his head and stomach with slightly bent middle fingers asking Eddie if he was sick. *No.*

David brought his right hand to his stomach, then up a bit and pointed to Eddie. *Aren't you hungry?*

Eddie sighed and shook his head. He glanced at his laptop screen and shut the lid.

Please come downstairs, David signed. He patted an imaginary seat behind him. *At least sit with us.*

Glumly, Eddie nodded. David chopped his hands together, the left digging into the web of his right. *Is anything annoying or bothering you?*

Eddie just shrugged. *Don't bother with me*, he gestured, and although he didn't return the sign, he simply slipped off his desk chair and padded past his father in his stocking feet. David sighed in exasperation and glanced back at the laptop. He reached out and raised the lid a little to peek at the message. It wouldn't hurt, he thought. Not this once.

Lucky 7 had typed: They won't believe you

Eddie (Turtleman) typed: I know

Lucky 7: So what u gonna do?

Turtleman: I won't say anything

The conversation ended there. Puzzled, and a little concerned, David walked slowly from his son's bedroom to the master suite. He wondered as he changed into sweats and a t-shirt what was going on with Eddie. Turn down Rose Diner shakes? A Rose Diner chocolate shake was Eddie's favorite food in the whole world. And what was this stuff about not believing him? Who wouldn't believe Eddie, and about what?

But by the time he got downstairs, Eddie seemed to have forgotten his disinterest in food. David walked into the kitchen to see Josh and Eddie engaged in a duel using French fries as swords, laughing and giggling over their food. Josh slurped happily at his chocolate cherry shake, and Eddie smiled at his father, giving him a thumbs-up as he sipped his own milkshake. David smiled back and reached for a plate for his meal. *I'll put my own plate away tonight*, he thought, glad for a peaceful evening for a change.

Although David slipped into bed exhausted, his insomnia kicked in full blast as soon as he switched off his bedside lamp and pulled the duvet up to his chin. It was as if switching off the bedside lamp set off all the rapid-fire thoughts in his brain. Memories, forgotten words, tasks from his day crowded his consciousness, making sleep impossible.

A chilly spring breeze stirred the curtains in the master bedroom window, and moonlight spilled in cascades and ripples onto the dark blue carpet. The mirror over Cathy's dresser seemed to whisper with ghostly forms as the curtains stirred. Alex had told him that the secret to naturally overcoming his insomnia was not to fight it. He tucked his arms behind his head, closed his eyes, and simply observed the thoughts parading through his mind.

What if his father was right and Cathy's death wasn't an accident? What if she had been murdered? And what if the key that unlocked the murder was found among the missing papers?

He wracked his brain thinking of the missing paperwork, but for the life of him, he couldn't remember the folders Cathy had mentioned. It was likely he hadn't even looked at them while he was rushing around the house the Sunday before his flight to Los Angeles. Flying made him so anxious he broke out into sweats and chills and this trip had been especially pressured. He was opening Majek Investment's first branch office, making history for the family and the firm. A press conference was scheduled for that Tuesday morning, and the major financial channels would be covering the opening. As he slipped into a doze, memories drifted to the surface.

"My son, pride is too easy a word for how I feel today," Tibor had said that Sunday afternoon. They'd scheduled a big family dinner to celebrate the office opening even though Thanksgiving was just days away.

Since Thanksgiving was so close, Cathy had made pumpkin risotto, homemade bread and oven-roasted autumn vegetables. Tibor, who swore he would never eat a vegetarian meal a day in his life, raved about the dishes and asked for seconds. David, Eva, Constantine and Tibor gathered around the mahogany dining table while Cathy hastened into the kitchen for the coffee and dessert. The November day was overcast and blustery. A crackling fire bathed the living room in a warm golden glow, touching Eddie's cheeks with crimson as he lay on his stomach coloring by the fireplace. Josh sat on the couch, ostensibly with the family but texting his friends. Alex was still away at school, although he would be coming home for Thanksgiving. A typical autumn night, one that David thought would be repeated for many years to come.

"It's nothing you wouldn't have done, Papa," David had said. Cathy poured coffee and passed a bottle of brandy along with a bowl of whipped cream to Constantine so that they could each fix their own Irish coffees. Crispy sugar cookies complemented the rich coffee, a deceptively simple dessert that melted in David's mouth and made his stomach rumble just thinking about it months later.

"Aw, don't be modest, David," Con said, heaping sweetened whipped cream into his coffee. "You know you want to brag about your latest coup. C'mon, just for once, brag a little."

Cathy laughed and punched Con lightly in the shoulder as she passed behind his place at the table. "You make it sound like David's modesty is false modesty, Con. Lay off."

Eva laced her coffee liberally with brandy but passed on the cream. She passed both to her father who looked suspiciously at them. "What is this?"

"It's for your coffee. Makes it sweet."

"And happy," Con added, raising his cup with a smile. Tibor scowled and passed both the brandy and whipped cream back to Cathy, who had slid back into her place at the dining room table nearest the kitchen. She added a touch of both to her coffee.

David took his coffee black while Con went on. "Well, David, this really is a time for celebration. New hedge funds opening this year, new office opening. Before you know it, you'll build Papa's empire up beyond what George Soros and all those other hedge fund managers have done."

"I couldn't have done it without Papa," David said, raising his white cup to his father.

"Here, here!" Cathy cried, raising her coffee cup and clinking it with David's. "To Papa!"

"To Majek Investments! Long may the family reign!" Tibor shouted as they clinked coffee cups together.

David felt himself drifting off to sleep, but something in the scene nagged at his memory. It was a look Con had given to his father...as he slipped deeper into sleep, he thought that Con looked hungry. *How can he look hungry when we just ate that huge meal?* was his last thought before sliding into the pool of dreamless slumber.

The next day, David woke both boys early. Josh and Eddie pounded downstairs in time to gulp down cereal and milk and squabble about whose turn it was to stack the dishwasher. Squabbles between the boys involved many rude gestures, pushing and shoving.

"Will you two knock it off? I'm in no mood for this!" David shouted. He grabbed Joshua and pushed him into the mudroom, pointing to his backpack. "Time for school."

"It's his turn to stack the dishwasher."

"Yes, it is. I'll deal with him. Go." From his wallet, David plucked two ten-dollar bills and handed one to Josh, who stuffed the bill into his front jeans pocket and bolted out the back door, running to his friend's jeep idling by the curb.

Eddie sullenly kicked the doors of the cabinet under the sink, shuffling his feet on the area rug and whacking the door like it was a soccer ball. David tapped him on the shoulder and flattened his hands, signing *Knock it off.*

Eddie pointed to the sink full of dishes and jerked his thumb towards the mudroom. His intention was clear. It was Joshua's turn.

Can you do me a favor and just do it? David replied.

The television flashed market symbols for London, Paris, and the rest of the European Union. David grabbed the remote from the counter and clicked the sound on.

"...markets opened wild this morning in the European Union after Karl Schmidt, the European Union President, announced he would not allow a bail out of Greece or Poland after the tumbling currency rocked markets...."

Eddie had stopped rinsing dishes and stacking the dishwasher. He hadn't realized his father wasn't looking at him but over his shoulder at the television set. David wrenched his gaze from the television back to his youngest son. He caught only the end of the Eddie's sign *...not eating.*

Who?

Teeny.

David wondered who the heck Teeny was. His gaze flicked back to the television set, but Eddie reached out and tapped him in the chest to get his attention.

My turtle is sick.

That explained it. Teeny and Tiny were Eddie's turtles. *What do you want me to do?* David signed. He didn't mean to be abrupt, but he must have frowned, because Eddie stuck his lower lip out clenched his jaw as he responded.

Find a vet.

A turtle vet?

Yes.

Eddie, I don't know if there is such a thing!

I love Teeny. Don't let him die!

David sighed and reached out to touch Eddie on the shoulder by way of apology, but his son jerked away. The school bus squealed to a stop in front of the house. The driver honked and flashed the lights once. Eddie grabbed his backpack from the floor of the mudroom and raced for the back door. David hurried after him, handing him the second $10 bill for lunch and expenses. Eddie stuffed it into his uniform blazer pocket. He whirled around and rapidly signed; *Vet for turtle. Okay, Dad?*

David threw his hands up in the air. *Fine, fine! Yes! Turtle vet!*

Satisfied, Eddie ran to the school bus. The driver honked and flashed the lights twice to let him know his son was safely aboard, and the bus groaned away from the curb belching diesel fumes.

David clicked off the remote and unplugged the coffee pot, frowning at the television set. Dumping the rest of the coffee into the sink, he stacked the rest of the dishes quickly, not bothering to rinse them. Screw that. It's not like one time is going to clog the damned thing anyway. He hurried upstairs to knot his tie and don his suit jacket. More was on his mind than a sick red-eared slider turtle. By the time he locked the house up and turned the Yukon off of Edgewater Drive, he had forgotten about Eddie's turtle.

The Majek Investment Building bustled with activity at eight on that Friday morning. Many Asian and European traders and advisors arrived on the third floor at four in the morning to work with their counterparts overseas and complete the day's transactions before France's CAC, London's FTSE and the Hong Kong markets closed. News today from the European Union wasn't good, and after unlocking his office and turning on his computers, he headed upstairs to check in with the managers of each division. Constantine was already in the glass-walled conference room on the third floor on a conference call with several of the Asian managers. David nodded at his brother through the glass and continued on. Con would be tied up for another half hour at least. He had plenty of time for his plan.

Each of the three floors of the Majek building was constructed along the same basic floor plan. Windows surrounded the outer walls of the square-shaped building, and private offices for the senior staff lined each of the walls. In the corners of the second and third floors were conference rooms and restrooms. On the western wall of each floor was a larger space, with the first floor dominated by the employee cafeteria, the second had the executive suite stacked above, and the third, the Records Room. It was here that David was bound on this morning, a man on a mission.

Because of the confidential nature of the paperwork handled by the company, most of the investment applications, human resources paperwork and other sensitive documents were locked in the Records Room once they were processed. Row upon row of putty-colored file cabinets locked into a coldly lit room held the personal records of their clients for the past three years. Older files were moved annually to Granite Mountain Storage, a West Virginia company that maintained their paper-based records. Records were also inputted into their secure online system, but many financial papers required signatures, and these were kept in old-fashioned hard copies on the third floor. It was here, David thought, that some of the answers he was seeking may lie.

Over and over again, the nagging question of the paperwork he'd brought home on that fateful day last November returned to haunt him. If he had only paid more attention to it, or if he had only listened to Cathy...but he had been so preoccupied with the opening of the new office. There was a press conference at nine, clients to greet, employees to meet...it had all seemed so important that morning, but by the afternoon, when he was rushing to catch an emergency flight back to New York, none of that mattered anymore.

Today he was on a mission. He tapped the keypad on the door of the records room, entering his employee ID number, social security number, and personal access code. The door light flashed red, then green, and the lock clicked open. Cool ink and paper-scented air rushed out as he slipped inside. David strode among the banks of files, checking the dates on the cabinets. He scanned the fronts of the cabinets where typed cards announced the contents, the dates, and the alphabetical lists of its contents, but he couldn't find the Triad funds, and he had no idea where to start. Joan usually entered the Records Room whenever he needed files pulled.

"Where the hell is that file?" he muttered between clenched teeth. He should have sent Joan to look for it.

"Can I help you, Mr. Majek?"

David recognized Lin Liu, a new junior investment clerk who had started with the firm only a few months ago. She was standing on the other side of the bank of files when he walked in and had popped around the corner of the cabinets when she heard him muttering.

"I'm sorry if I startled you, Lin. Yes, maybe you can. Can you show me where the files are for last year? It seems as if they've reorganized the room since my time here as an intern."

"One row over." She pointed behind her. "Starts with the Adelphi Fund nearest the door, ends with Zephyr against the back wall. They're marked with the year and the fund; from there, you've got to find the actual files you need. It's a little confusing if you aren't used to it. Can I help you find anything?"

He smiled at her. "No, thanks, I've got it."

"Okay. Well, let me know if I can help you."

Impatiently, he crossed to the aisle of file cabinets Lin had pointed. Why won't she leave? He wanted the room to himself. At this point, he trusted no one with the files.

After a few more minutes of rustling papers and closing cabinets, Lin finished her task. Her footfalls tapped briskly in icepick thin heels to the door. She drew the handle down, opened the door and a rush of sound washed in, a babble of voices, tapping keyboards, shouts and laughter. She disappeared back into the open desk area beyond. The door closed behind her leaving David with only the whisper of the air conditioner and the hum of the fluorescent light banks overhead.

He bent his tall frame to peer at the faces of the cabinets searching for the Triad fund. Third cabinet from the back wall he struck gold. With a click, the latch opened and he was able to thumb through rows of neatly labeled files. He wasn't sure which applications he had taken home accidentally that night, so he grabbed all of the folders for Triad I, II and III, and pulled them from the hanging files. There were about thirty files in all. Behind the rows of cabinets were three small desks like the study carrels from a college library. Pulling out a scarred and battered chair, he sank into the hard seat and spread the files onto the desk.

Abbingdon, Abel, Bianchini...with each name, he opened the file and scanned the paperwork. Each application was two pages long, listing the applicant's name, address, date of birth, social security number, reference numbers, banking information and investment information, plus the designated heirs if the investors should die before closing their accounts. He nodded with satisfaction as he scanned each set of paperwork. It all looked complete down to the bank's purple embossed stamp at the bottom of each form. Like many major investment firms, Majek Investments did not receive funds on its own. They subcontracted this service to a clearing house with direct ties to worldwide financial institutions. Majek used Grazziola, a fund management firm in Manhattan. Each set of papers was stamped with the Grazziola seal, and in the event an investor sent in an actual paper check, a copy of the cleared check was stapled to the forms.

David flipped through each file, feeling his frustration mount. He couldn't see anything wrong with the paperwork. It all looked so mundane, so normal. He'd seen paperwork like this a thousand times in his career. Moistening his thumb, he flipped faster through each folder. Finally, he reached the end of the stack, no further along in his quest than he had been at the beginning.

He gathered up the folders and carried them back to the open file cabinet. As he stuffed each set of ten into a hanging folder, he realized he had only eight left at the end. He should have thirty in total, if memory served him correctly. That's how many investors they'd welcomed into the Triad Funds and none were allowed to exit until the first year was up. Counting a second time, he came up with twenty-eight folders. A third count yielded the same answer. He replaced the last eight, closed the file cabinet and turned, leaning against it deep in thought.

There were two files missing. He wasn't sure where they should have been in the stack - near the beginning, the middle, the end or somewhere in between. But instead of thirty files, he had twenty-eight.

Could they be the two files Cathy said were at their house? But where were they now? They weren't at their home. By now, he would have found them. Eva would have found them while cleaning. Even the boys, although they had their own laptops in their rooms, sometimes logged onto the family room computer if they were too lazy to return to their rooms. Someone would have noticed two business folders on the desk, but he knew the top of his desk was clear except for the tray where he kept the bills to be paid, the tray where he kept things to be filed, and the datebook where he and Cathy had recorded family obligations, dental visits, school functions and the like. They just weren't there.

If I find the folders, David thought with growing certainty, I'll find the papers, and they'll lead me to the reason Cathy went out that day, and that will lead me to the reason she's dead.

The door to the Records Room clicked open, the sound from the other side filtering into the file room as the door opened, then falling abruptly as it closed. David stood up straight and walked towards the entrance. As he rounded the corner of the file cabinet bank, he was astonished to see Constantine looking furtively around the Records Room.

"I thought you were in here!" Con said a little too heartily. He glanced at the row David had just exited. "Is there something I can help you with?"

"Funny, that's what Lin Liu said a few minutes ago," David said.

"Lin? Oh, the new junior investment advisor. Yes, I saw her in the hallway just now and she mentioned you were in here. I was curious, I confess. What's up?"

"Weren't you just in a meeting?"

"I stepped out to use the men's room. What, are you checking up on me now?"

"No, no." David gave a little self-deprecating laugh. He walked to the door, brushing past Con. Con followed him out into the noisy open area where rows of cubicles housed the Asian and European traders, their assistants, and others handling the overseas markets. David strode towards the elevator, Con close at his heels.

"So what were you looking for?"

"A folder," David said, "for the Triad Fund."

"Oh. Anything wrong?"

David stopped abruptly. "No. Why should something be wrong?"

"I don't know. You sound tense, that's all." Con began walking down the line of desk towards the conference room. "Hey, if you need anything, let me know."

David glanced at his brother and continued walking towards the elevator. Lin Liu also stood waiting for the elevator. She smiled at

David, who responded with a frosty smile of his own. "No, nothing. I found out exactly what I needed."

Con had already stepped back into the meeting room. David could no longer see his retreating form, but as the elevator doors slipped open, he motioned for Lin to enter before him. He stepped in and the doors slid shut. "Lin, you didn't by chance tell Constantine where I was, did you?"

"Why yes, I did," she said with surprise. "But he came bolting out of the conference room and said you were looking for him. I hope I didn't do anything wrong."

The elevator stopped on the second floor. David stepped out. "No, nothing wrong. Thank you."

Why had Con left the conference room? Was he really just curious about what David was up to, or was there a deeper reason?

10

David finished discussing various strategies with his senior management team by ten o'clock. Now he was ready to tackle the growing mountain of paperwork in his office. As he entered the executive suite, he suddenly remembered Eddie's turtle. Joan held the telephone to her ear nodding and murmuring polite pleasantries to whoever was on the other end.

"What is your name again, sir?" His assistant tapped a manicured fingernail on the edge of her desk. "I see. Please hold." She pushed the red hold button. "I have a Mr. Scalia on the telephone. He says it's important that he meets with you today."

"I don't know a Mr. Scalia. Where is he from?" Salesmen often pretended to be friends or business acquaintances in order to meet with him. Often they sent Joan flowers, candy, and gifts, but instead of accepting them, she enjoyed directing delivery drivers to the local nursing home to share her bounty.

"He claims your father called him last evening and suggested he contact you directly. Said you would know what it's about. He's from a firm called Scorpion Investigations."

The Watcher! David nodded. So his father finally accepted that he wasn't to blame for Cathy's death. David had to smile; he had intended to call his father for the investigator's information today. The old lion had already pre-empted his first move. "I'll see him."

Joan pressed the blinking telephone line button and returned to the call. "Mr. Scalia? We are located in the Mitchell Field Office complex. There's a sign for the Majek Investment Building. What time suits you?"

David raised his hand. She put the caller on hold and waited for instructions. "See if you can get my father into that meeting too. If not, I'll still meet with this Scalia alone, but please call my father and see if he can join us."

"Should Constantine be in this meeting, too?"

David hesitated. "No. Just my father and me."

"Very well." Joan returned to the call, and David strode into his office.

Muting the television, he rolled back the Aeron chair and adjusted the monitors on his three computer screens. A few minutes later, Joan rapped on the door and entered. He looked up from the email he was typing while numbers flashed and scrolled across the second and third screens.

"You have a one-thirty appointment and your father can make it. He seemed delighted by the invitation. Anything you need for the meeting?"

"We'll be ordering lunch." Eddie's worried face flashed before his mind's eye. "I have a favor to ask."

"Shoot."

"It's kind of a big favor."

"Oh dear. No, I can't marry you."

"Who do you think you are, Miss Moneypenny?"

She laughed. "Yes, Mr. Bond. Go ahead."

"I need you to find a turtle doctor."

"A what?"

"A turtle doctor, a veterinarian who specializes in turtles. Eddie's pet is sick." David raked a hand through his dark hair. "I know, I know...it's just a stupid pet store turtle. But not to Eddie. Cathy bought him those two creatures for his last birthday, and he's very attached to them. You know how he is with animals."

"You need a herpetologist."

David blinked. "A what?"

"Herpetologist. Biologist who specializes reptiles."

"Sounds like a doctor specializing in other kinds of diseases."

"You're awful." She laughed, shaking her head. "How can you not know these things?"

"My mind is packed with dollars and cents, not words."

"And your clients thank God for that." She bustled over to the coffee urn, checked it was full, and readied the set of china mugs for guests. As she counted the sugar and creamer packets, she said, "What about the university where Cathy taught?"

"C.W. Post?" He paused, hands hovering over the keyboard. "Why didn't I think of that? They have a wonderful life sciences department. And it's less than fifteen minutes from my house. Joan, you're a genius and a lifesaver."

"Yes, I am. I'll call to see if anyone is available to look at a turtle. Does tomorrow suit you?"

"Tomorrow suits me just fine." David sighed in relief. "And Eddie will be very grateful. He's so attached to those turtles." He peered at his email. "How do you spell recompense?"

"I thought Constantine was bad, but you've got to be the world's worst speller." Joan returned to his side and read the email over his shoulder. "You need to change that from it's to its. And change the c to an s in recompense. There is spell check on emails, you know."

"I know, but I have you."

"Send the copy to me first, and I'll polish it and send it out. If it's going to the vice president group at Chase Bank, you want it to make an impact. The right impact," she added.

"Right, Chief." He paused. "Hey Joan?"

"Yes?"

"Do we have a master list of just the names of the investors in the Triad Fund? Not the applications – I want the names, in alphabetical order, of all 30 investors."

"I can print it out for you," Joan replied.

"Can you do it so that no one knows I'm looking at it?"

"Yes." She hesitated. "Is something wrong?"

"No. Not that I know of. I just went to look for something upstairs and two folders were missing. I can't figure out which ones."

"That's odd. I'll get that printout for you."

"Thanks."

The telephone on her desk rang. Joan strode to the reception area to answer it from her phone, and David returned to his work. Hours passed swiftly. Joan had left his office door open, so when Constantine entered the executive suite, David heard his brother plainly.

"Hi Joan. Any messages?"

"Six, including one from Lisa. She sounds nice. When are you bringing her here to meet me?"

"I get to meet her first!" David called from his desk.

Constantine popped into his brother's office. "Morning. Saw you upstairs on three – is everything all right?"

"Everything's fine. I was just checking on the Asian and European groups, but you'd already handled the Asian team. Well done. How are the funds doing?"

"Asian Tiger is taking a beating, but Triad is holding up." Con leaned against the doorframe of David's office, nodding confidently. "The Triad Fund seems sound today. Most of your funds in Triad I are invested in U.S.-based companies, so unless the markets take a nosedive from the uncertainty overseas, you should be fine. Betty's social conscience fund is putting along. That one doesn't seem to do anything, frankly."

"I know." David pushed back his chair. "I'm thinking of pulling the plug on it, but I wanted to give it at least a year, if not two. She's been after me for years to add socially conscience funds to our offerings, and I think she's right about it; it appeals to a certain customer group. Once we get them signed up with Triad III, then they sign up for other money management services, and we get their business."

"True," Con said.

"How's your Triad fund doing? Triad II, Tech?" David folded his arms across his chest and waited.

"It's doing great!" Con gestured at the coffee urn. "Can I grab some coffee from you instead of running down to the employee cafeteria?"

"Sure, help yourself." Con poured a large mug of coffee and liberally laced it with sugar and creamer. David watched his brother stir his coffee, clanking the spoon against the ceramic mug. "Con, about that raise..."

"Oh David, don't mention it again." Con waved his wet spoon in the air. A few droplets of coffee sailed to the credenza, and he wiped them off with the palm of his hand, then swiped his hands on his suit pants. *Just like when we were kids*, David thought as Con ambled back to his desk. Con sank into the visitor's chair uninvited. "I mean, I would love some more money...I've got some unexpected expenses..."

"From what?" Just then, Joan leaned into the doorway of his office, rapping softly on the door.

"This and that," Con said, then looking down into the creamy depths of his coffee. He took a sip, grimaced at the heat, and sipped again despite his scalded lips.

"David, I have an appointment for you at 11 a.m. at C.W. Post University," Joan said. "A herpetologist named Dr. Donahue in Life Sciences Building 316 will see the patients. Bring them both, he said, and he'd be delighted to meet with you and take a look at Eddie's turtles. He knew Cathy, and he wanted to express his condolences."

David nodded. "Thanks, Joan." He clicked his cell phone from the holster on his belt and tapped the stylus on the screen, opening his text message service. "Hang on, Con," David said. "I've got to text Eddie and let him know I found a turtle doctor."

"Turtle doctors?" Con snorted. "Now I've heard everything. It's a stupid pet store turtle."

"Yeah, but it's Eddie's stupid pet store turtle." David pressed the send button, slid the stylus back into the cell phone's groove and clicked the device back into his belt holster.

"If it dies, can't you just replace it?"

"Don't you remember the fiasco with Eva's goldfish?"

"The one she won at the church carnival? Oh God. I'd forgotten about that."

David had been around Joshua's age that summer, just turning seventeen. The Majeks had gone to the St. Gregory Festival in June, and Eva had won a little orange comet goldfish in a toss-the ping pong ball into the fishbowl contest. Delighted with her new pet, she'd carried it home in a plastic bag, and even bought it a bowl, gravel, food and a plant with her allowance money. She took good care of the little fish, and when she left for Girl Scout Camp after the Fourth of July, she'd asked David to look after Goldy.

"You have to use these special drops in his water to get the chlorine out," Eva said. "If you don't, he'll die from poisoning."

"Okay, okay," David had said, while rushing out the door with his father. That summer he had worked part-time at Majek Investments as an intern and he didn't want to let his father down. "I'll change the water. I promise."

But he'd forgotten. Eva had called from camp to remind him. "Don't forget to change his water and feed him."

It was a hot July morning when Con burst into David's room. "Goldy's dead!" he shouted.

"He can't be dead." David tumbled out of bed, pushing a shock of hair out of his eyes.

"I'm telling you, he's floating belly up."

And so he was. David and Con stood mutely by Eva's dresser, staring at the white belly of the goldfish floating near the top of his little bowl. His fins looked slimy, the water cloudy. David gulped. When was the last time he'd bothered to change the water? Eva had been gone for three weeks. He'd done it the first week, but not the second or third, and the fish's wastes had built up in the small bowl until it suffocated.

"Eva's going to kill me."

"I know!" Con snapped his fingers. "You got money?"

"I have money. Dad's paying me just like a real employee." It was a point of pride with him that he'd cashed his first paycheck last week with the roaring lion and Majek Investments logo on it. He sorted the mail and filed paperwork, but he was a bona fide employee of Majek Investments.

"Let's go to the pet store and buy another."

"We can't do that! She'll know!"

"It's a stupid fish," Con scoffed. He poked the bowl with derision, and the dead fish floated forlornly amidst a sticky-looking cloud. "There must be hundreds like it. She'll never know."

They hopped onto their bicycles and pedaled two miles to the local pet store. David let Con choose the fish. They pedaled back to the house, buried the old goldfish under their mother's rose bush, and cleaned the bowl until it shone. David even remembered the water-conditioning drops. The new fish seemed happy in the bowl, and David diligently cared for it until Eva returned from camp the following week. He'd forgotten all about the dead fish until he heard Eva's wail. "That's not Goldy! What happened to Goldy?"

Con plunked his coffee mug onto the edge of David's desk. "Okay, so maybe you can't sneak in a new turtle if Eddie's turtle dies. What's wrong with it, anyway?"

"I don't know. He said something about it not eating. Something else about a soft shell. Do turtles get soft shells?"

"I only know about soft-shelled crabs, and they're delicious."

"Yeah, me too. I don't know anything about turtles."

"Well, I guess you'll learn tomorrow."

"Guess so. Hey, watch your coffee mug – you're leaving a ring."

Con scooped up his mug and wiped the desk with the palm of his hand. "Sorry about that. Happy now?"

"Ecstatic." David grinned at his younger brother, but his grin faded. "Con, are you sure I can't lend you some money? I felt bad about turning you down for a raise the other day, but you understood, right?"

"Oh David, you know I did." Con scooted back in his chair and stood, gulping the rest of his coffee. "Don't worry about it. I'll make do with what I have."

"I just don't understand what expenses you have now." David gazed steadily at his brother, who flinched and looked away. "I mean, you're single, your condo is paid for...right?"

"Right."

"So what's going on?"

"Nothing." Con squirmed under his brother's piercing gaze. "I just ran into a spot of trouble. Some...bad investments."

"Ah." David nodded. "I see. And you didn't want to tell me because it's an investment, right?"

"Right," Con rushed into the opening in the conversation. "I mean, how would it look if the senior vice president of Majek Investments, son of the great Tibor Majek, made crappy investment decisions in his personal life?"

"We all make mistakes. Even Dad lost money sometimes, Con. No one has to know about that, right?" David asked. "So if you still need cash, let me know. I can lend you some to cover your losses, just to get you by. I'm sure Dad can lend you some, too."

"He lent Eva money; did you know that?"

"No," David said with genuine surprise. "I didn't. How come?"

"She needed a loan to expand her business, and Dad offered her the loan without interest. He said banks would charge her too much."

"How do you know all of this?"

Con shrugged as he walked towards the office door. "It slipped out when Eva was talking to me the other day. She had a spot of financial trouble when she expanded, and Dad covered for her. Hey, are we still on for dinner at your house on Sunday?"

"Yes, come by around two."

"Is Eva cooking?"

"What, my cooking isn't good enough for you?"

"Your cooking turns my stomach." Con smiled at David.

"Why don't you bring your new girlfriend to dinner on Sunday?"

"To a family dinner? I'm not sure she'd feel comfortable with that yet. We've just started seeing each other and family dinners are sort of...well, you know. Family."

"That's okay. I promise Dad won't bite."

Con laughed. "We're all a little overwhelming, I think. I'll wait and introduce her gradually to everyone. Maybe over the summer. If Dad's okay with it, I'll bring her with me for a weekend at the beach house in Cutchogue or something."

"Well, be sure to introduce us. We're all dying to meet this mystery woman you're spending so much time with."

"I promise to introduce her. Soon. See you later."

David watched as Con crossed the reception area. His office door clicked open and snapped shut. David returned to his desk, pushed aside the papers and frowned over the response from Chase Bank that flashed across the screen. Joan must have already sent the email.

The rest of the morning passed rapidly, with meetings, phone calls, papers to sign, and emails to answer. He was just settling back at his desk after a meeting with his IT staff when Joan buzzed him. "David? Mr. Scalia is here."

"Show him in."

David stood as the door opened and Joan ushered the private investigator into the room. Victor Scalia was rail thin and nearly six feet tall, with receding black hair and a neatly trimmed goatee. He wore a charcoal gray suit and yellow and gray checked tie. Extending a confident hand, he said, "Scalia. Victor Scalia of Scorpion Investigations."

"David Majek."

David appraised the man as they shook hands. His father tended to hire wisely, if sometimes hastily, and David found himself approving of this man who had caused so much trouble for his family over the past several days. He frowned. Scalia's build wasn't right for the Watcher – too tall, too thin. Was there someone else?

"Please, sit," David gestured towards the seating area at the far end of his office. "My secretary will order lunch for us. We're just waiting for my father to arrive."

"Thank you." Scalia went right to the point. "I want to apologize for the other night. Your father asked us to be discreet, and normally I'd handle the case myself. But we had several men out sick, and I had new employee following you this week. He wasn't particularly good at his job and I've let him go."

David was surprised by the forthright apology and revelation. Scalia took a seat facing the windows, and David perched on the edge of the opposite sofa. From the reception area, he heard his father's rumbling voice, Joan's soft reply. A harsh tap on the door and his office door flung open, bouncing with a thud off the drywall behind it before it slammed shut. Tibor strode into the room, his white hair wild from the walk from the parking lot up to the office. He wore a threadbare business suit, a yellowed, white collared shirt, and a bow tie. David shook his head ruefully at his father's outfit and stood for Tibor's bone crunching embrace.

"Papa."

"*Můj syn*," Tibor said. "My son, how are you?"

"I am fine, Papa. I believe you know Mr. Scalia."

The men shook hands. Joan entered after knocking, bearing menus from the deli that catered the Mitchell Field Office Park. "I'll order sandwiches and drinks. They should be here in about ten or fifteen minutes."

David didn't even look at the menu. "My usual."

"Ham on rye and an iced tea, please," Scalia said.

"Roast beef," Tibor barked. Joan nodded briskly, still holding the unused menus, and shut the office door behind her.

"Now," David said without preamble, returning to the sofa. "My father told me last night that he hired your firm to follow me."

Victor looked at Tibor, who nodded. "It is true," Tibor said. "I am sorry, Victor, but your man dropped the address card I gave him. I had to tell David. That is why I called you last night and suggested you call David directly. He also has need of your services."

"As I told David, I fired the man," Victor said. "It was sloppy work and on behalf of my firm, I apologize."

"Yes," Tibor said. "Good. Well, tell David everything. From the beginning."

David listened while Victor shared the tale, recapping what Tibor had told him yesterday and adding more details. He leaned back against the sofa, folding his arms over his chest.

"Your father called me a few months ago, asking me to look into the matter of Catherine Majek's death," Victor said. He raised his eyes to David. "Your wife?"

"Yes, my wife."

"From my research, she was a fine woman. Well regarded and even loved by everyone who knew her. I'm truly sorry I never met her."

David was surprised by the sincerity in the man's voice. He was beginning to like Scalia despite his feelings about his family's privacy being invaded. He nodded. "Go on."

"I'm a former New York City detective. And I still have contacts with the Nassau and Suffolk County police. Your wife's case, I'm afraid, is already in the cold case file. They've chalked it up to an accident, and they had so few leads to go by, they've already moved it to the back burner. Too few police officers, too many budget cuts."

"Catherine's death was murder," Tibor barked. "Murder by automobile."

"A hit and run is classified as an accident; vehicular homicide, Mr. Majek," Victor said. He reached into the breast pocket of his suit jacket and removed a small notebook with a black leather cover, flipping it open to reveal his notes. "It's usually charged as manslaughter.

"I checked with the police, and the only lead they have is from a witness from the dry cleaners, and another at the Rose Diner who saw a black SUV speeding away after striking your wife. So we know the car that hit her is a black SUV. No make, model or year noted by either witness.

"Your father asked me to look into your past, your background, and to watch your comings and goings," Victor continued. "Followed by your sister, Eva and your brother, Constantine. Your father suspected foul play and spoke of some paperwork your wife was worried about. Can you tell me about that?"

David stood and paced the area in front of his desk, thinking aloud. "It was last November," he began. "I brought home some papers for the Triad Fund. It's a new hedge fund we opened last year."

"What exactly is a hedge fund?" Victor asked.

"It's an invitation-only fund, a collection of investments hand-picked by an expert. The Triad Fund is our first foray into the world of hedge funds. It was my idea, actually, to start one, and my father and Constantine were enthusiastic about the idea. Changes in regulations made it easier to start one, so we launched Triad last year.

"Three of us – myself, my brother Constantine, and Betty Goldfarb, one of our most trusted investment advisors, picked stocks and other investments around a theme. We have managers oversee the daily fund operations and receive a percent of the profits, but our names are on the funds, and we established them. Triad I is my fund. I chose American companies who manufacture a variety of goods within the United States. They're midsized firms looking to grow larger, and I visited each one over the past two years to ensure they were worthy of investment. I wanted a fund that investors could feel proud of, one that produces superior returns."

"And does it?" Victor jotted notes.

"Does it what?"

"Produce superior returns?"

"So far, it produces solid returns, but the fund is new; we really don't know the success or failure of these ventures before some time has passed."

"I see," Victor nodded. "Please continue."

"My brother manages Triad II. It's a basket of up-and-coming technology stocks – Facebook and Twitter's IPOs were in there, among other things. The hot, trendy stuff. He loves technology and likes to get in on the ground floor if he can. His fund is returning an astonishing three times over average."

Victor looked at Tibor. "That sounds like a lot. Is that unusual?"

"Very unusual," Tibor rumbled. "Especially for Constantine."

"Papa," David protested, pausing in his restless pacing. "That's not fair. He's a good hedge fund manager, although he does take more risks than I'd like."

"Perhaps yes, perhaps no. He can work miracles and he can fail miserably. He is not like you, my son. You are steady and strong. He blows like the wind..." Tibor waved his hand wildly. "...where it will, unpredictable."

"And the third fund?" Victor asked.

"Triad III is a social conscience fund," David replied. He moved to the windows, pushing aside the Venetian blind to gaze out at the parking lot, the grassy swards between towering office buildings. "We've wanted to offer one for a long time. They don't make a great return, but they do attract a certain clientele."

"What kind of clientele?"

"Baby boomers, mostly, who want to put their money in companies that aren't raping the environment or pillaging third world countries."

"Good luck with that," Victor commented.

David laughed. "Precisely. No matter how hard you try, no one's hands are clean these days. You understand it well, Mr. Scalia."

Victor nodded. "So how is that fund doing?"

"As well as can be expected, although I'm not thrilled with its performance. Again, too soon to say for sure."

Scalia considered his notes, then sat back and tapped his pencil against his knee. "I've heard about hedge funds, but I've never actually met anyone who invested in one. I'm a retired cop, and a business owner, so as you can imagine, I tend to play my investments safe – mutual funds, bonds, a bank account."

David nodded.

"So how does someone invest in a hedge fund? Walk me through the process. Could I get into one?"

"Probably not." David turned away from the windows and sank back onto the sofa next to his father facing Victor. "Unless you have at least three million dollars to invest."

"Three what?"

"The initial investment is three million dollars," David replied. "Minimum. Most people invest much more. I don't think we have anyone in the fund now who invested less than $5 million."

"That is actually quite low," Tibor said. "Most begin at $10 million."

Victor swallowed. "How does someone invest in the fund? I mean, do they just call up and say, 'I want in?'"

"Typically, the hedge fund managers – Jack Noble, who works with my brother Constantine, Bart Solomon who oversees my Triad fund, and Betty's assistant, Jenna Warren – reach out to some of our wealthier clientele through personal telephone calls, luncheons, that sort of thing. In 2013, the SEC lifted the ban on hedge fund advertising, but we choose not to advertise our funds."

"We don't need to," Tibor sniffed.

"No, we really don't," David agreed. "Once someone contacts us about the fund, we send them a document called an operating agreement. This spells out how the fund works. Sending an operating agreement is required by law, by the way. Majek Investments works a typical twenty-five over five."

"What does that mean?"

"The first five percent of the returns belong to the investors, but after that, the fund manager receives twenty-five percent of the gains and the investors split the remaining seventy-five percent. In our company, I receive half of the fees and my fund managers receive half. We do it that way because myself, Con and Betty are very active in managing our funds. Normally a CEO wouldn't do this kind of work, but I enjoy it. It's intense at times, but I like to stay in practice."

"Managing funds requires practice?"

David thought of all the years he had spent behind a desk, first as an intern, then as a personal wealth manager and investment advisor, and finally as his father's right hand man. "Would a gold medal Olympic athlete stop working out just because the Olympics are over and he's begun training others? Yes, managing funds takes practice." Tibor nodded agreement at the analogy.

"What's this like in terms of dollars and cents?"

"Well, here's an example. Let's say I have ten investors for a hedge fund. Each investor contributes ten million." Victor paused, as if waiting for the punch line of a joke, but David was absolutely serious. He continued. "That's a total of a hundred million."

"Does the money go directly to Majek Investments?"

"No, we use a specialized firm, called a fund administrator, to receive and manage cash flows. It's considered standard operating procedure for an investment firm to partner with an accounting firm or a bank to handle large sums like that. We use Grazziola in New York City; they're a well-established firm."

Victor nodded. "Okay. So people fill out paperwork and mail in checks to this company."

"Yes, or wire transfers, which are more common these days. Most money changes hands via computer nowadays. The paperwork is then sent on to us; they deposit the funds into an account, which we then use to buy and sell stocks, bonds, land, whatever we're investing in. Returns are sent back into Grazziola as well. Most of the actual money is handled by Grazziola, until we need a transfer into an investment vehicle. Then one of the six I mentioned earlier – myself, Con, Betty, Jack, Bart or Jenna – can activate a transfer or fund distribution, if appropriate. I must co-sign everyone else's transfers, and either my father or Con must co-sign mine. Two signatures are always required on transfers over ten million; below that figure, I am the only one with sole signatory power. Everyone else must have a co-signer to ensure the transfer is valid."

"Go on."

"Well, in my example, I now have $100 million to invest in the fund. Let's assume I've set the fund up to invest in stocks. The fund goes up in value as the returns are recorded – let's assume a forty-percent return."

"Is that good?"

"Yes, it's a healthy return for a hedge fund. I like round numbers for examples. My fund is now worth $140 million. The first five percent of that forty million in returns goes back to the investors. Anything over that gets split twenty-five percent to me, and seventy-five percent to the investors. The capital gain on that forty million is reduced by two million, or the five-percent hurdle rate. It's called a hurdle rate because you have to 'jump' over it to earn your money."

"I'm getting lost in these numbers," Victor confessed. "What's the bottom line?"

"The bottom line is that if my fund made forty percent, I'd have very happy investors and I'd be able to buy a second mansion somewhere. In my imaginary scenario, I'll take home about four million and Bart, the day-to-day manager, gets about the same."

"In one year? Does that really happen?"

"Last year, my best fund managers made over a million dollars each in commission, Mr. Scalia," David said quietly. "My salary as CEO is modest, but my take-home pay, if you figure in performance bonuses and commissions from when I was a fund manager, typically amounts to a million dollars per year or more. Usually more."

"You also have considerable private investments?"

"Yes. My home in Brookville is paid for; we have no mortgage. Aside from my son's Harvard medical school tuition, which is a hefty bill indeed, and Edward's private school tuition, we live rather simply. No flashy cars, no lavish vacations."

Scalia nodded and jotted another note. "Tell me more about Cathy. How was your wife involved with these funds, David? From my research, I understand she was a professor at C.W. Post University. How much does a professor make these days? Did she invest along with you, or did she keep her money separate?"

"Cathy didn't work for the money. Cathy loved performing and sharing music, and she loved teaching. When you come right down to it, she never really had to work. Her family was well off, and when her father, Judge John Tarleton, died a few years ago, he left a trust fund split between Cathy and her brother. I can't touch it."

"Who inherited it when she died? Her brother?" Scalia tensed and leaned forward.

David shook his head. "When she died, her half of the trust went to her heirs: our children. They can access the funds when they each turn twenty-five. A trust is a separate financial entity; I have no claim on it, not even as her spouse. The trust is handled by the law firm of Loeser and Klein in Manhattan." Victor noted the names. "When the children come of age, they will have to appeal directly to

Loeser and Klein to withdraw funds or receive a monthly stipend. It will be a nice stipend to supplement whatever they make in life. As you can see, Mr. Scalia..." David turned his gaze to his father and pursed his lips. "I had nothing to gain by my wife's death, and frankly, everything to lose."

"David..." Tibor pleaded, spreading his hands wide.

David turned his attention back to Victor. "If Cathy and I had ever divorced – and we weren't even remotely thinking of it, we were very happy together – she took that trust fund with her. Cathy didn't lack for anything she wanted, but she was an unusual woman. She wanted little in life except the freedom to be a wife, mother, musician and teacher. She didn't care for fancy things. For her birthday last year, I bought her a tree. Does that tell you what you need to know about my wife?" Victor squirmed slightly while David continued. "I tell you, Mr. Scalia, if Cathy was killed – and I'm still not convinced it was intentional – it had nothing to do with her personal life."

"And everything to do with those papers," Tibor said.

"Did Cathy deal with any of your personal investments here or at home?" Victor asked.

"No, I handled all of our family's investments," David said. "My wife wasn't very good with money. In fact, I handled all of our family's financial affairs. Cathy got involved in my work by accident. I was traveling to the West Coast last November. We had just opened an investment office in Los Angeles, since we now have a considerable number of clients in the L.A. area and it is easier to serve them when the office is local. Many like to meet their investment advisors in person, especially when we're handling millions of dollars of their money."

Victor scribbled more notes. "And what happened?"

"I'd brought papers home from the office, as I normally do. I thought I'd taken all of them with me on my trip, but I was in a hurry to pack my briefcase, and I must have left some on my desk. I have a small home office in the family room. Cathy found some papers on the desk. She called me in Los Angeles to ask if I needed them sent by messenger overnight, but they needed to go back to this office."

"What were they?"

"Applications for the Triad Fund," David said. "We don't accept just anyone into the hedge fund, Mr. Scalia. When Joan's out of the office, things get mixed up, and the temp who had organized my paperwork to take home didn't do a very good job. Those papers should never have gone home with me in the first place. Normally, applications must be kept locked up at the office. They contain personal information including social security numbers and such that you don't want to carry around with you. If they get lost, it can be a nightmare." He hesitated, considering the missing two folders. Tibor saw his hesitation and raised an eyebrow at him, but David shook his head. He wasn't ready yet to speak of those two folders. His mind flashed to Constantine, pouncing on him by the elevator, a glittering smile on his brother's lips. No, he was not ready yet....

"So," Victor said slowly, flipping through the pages of his notebook and reading through his hastily scrawled notes. "These papers that Cathy had at home shouldn't have left your office. A temp mixed them in with files you needed to take to Los Angeles but you left them on your desk at home. Cathy called you to tell you she'd found them. What did you do?"

"Cathy called to say she'd found the pile of paperwork. She asked me what I wanted her to do with it – she thought it might be important. I said she should call the office and have them picked up."

Joan knocked and entered at David's response, followed by a delivery man bearing bags of sandwiches, drinks and chips. They spread the lunch out on the coffee table and opened up sandwiches and bottles of iced tea, taking a break from the conversation to dig into their lunches. Joan and the delivery man left.

"So Cathy called you," Victor said around bites of ham and cheese. "And she said you left papers behind. Was she worried about them?"

"She didn't sound particularly worried to me," David replied around a bite of his BLT. "She just said I'd left paperwork at home, and did I need it? I told her to call Joan and have someone from work come by and pick it up."

"But Joan wasn't in that day."

David sipped his iced tea. "Correct. Joan was out with the flu. I assume Cathy spoke with the temp, or with my brother."

"And your father."

"Yes," Tibor frowned. He chewed his roast beef sandwich methodically and swallowed before responding. "She was upset, worried. She asked questions about the fund. Then she said she would call the office. That was the last time I spoke with her."

"What time did you speak with her, Tibor?"

"Around two-thirty, I think."

"And she was killed at approximately three-fifteen?"

"Yes." Tibor said. David nodded.

"And neither of you have any idea what brought her out of the house in such a hurry? David, your report to the police said that she left in a hurry. How did you know she left in a hurry?"

"Her music books were open on the piano," David said. "And Eddie was due home from school at any minute. She played piano for our church, and she was working out the music for Sunday's service. She never left the house when Eddie was expected home – she always met the school bus."

"Did the police look at the cell phone and house phone records?"

"They were supposed to, but they never did." Despite his steady control, a hint of bitterness entered David's voice. "It seemed as if Cathy's case wasn't very important to them."

"They did not care," Tibor said. He balled up the white waxed paper from his sandwich into a tight knot between his palms, thrusting it into the white bag on the coffee table. "Can you make them care, Mr. Scalia? I will pay you well if you can solve this. Someone murdered my Caterina, my daughter, the mother of my grandchildren."

"Tibor, you don't know it was murder," Victor cautioned. "I agree, it might be tried as manslaughter for a hit and run, but you shouldn't throw around the term murder like that."

"What else do you call it?" David asked.

Victor shook his head. "Now," he said, "your father tells me you have other matters going on. What is this about money missing from your account?"

David glared at his father, who shrugged and looked away. "He says tell him everything, I tell him everything. If it solves the case, tell him."

David hastily explained about the missing money. Finally, after Victor had taken copious notes and all but filled his little black notebook, David asked, "So what did you find out from all the cloak and dagger stuff? You checked on Eddie, you watched my house. Learn anything?"

"Not much," Victor admitted. "But we started with you and your family, and had just moved on to tailing your sister. We haven't gotten to your brother yet. Do you still want me to proceed, Tibor?"

Tibor stared at David. "Should I, David?"

David looked down at the scuffed toes of his black Oxford shoes. A hundred thoughts crowded his mind at once. He thought of Con's request for a raise. He heard Cathy's bright laughter, and saw the swirl of her red-gold hair. He saw Eddie's hands fluttering in sign for a sick turtle, and he thought of Eva's dead goldfish and the lengths they had gone to hide it. He thought of unusually high returns and short cuts on homework. He thought of Eva asking their father for a loan after expanding her business too quickly, yet bragging to him of how well she was doing. He swallowed.

"Yes," David said finally. "I hate this, but I think we need to know the truth. I have an idea. Con saw you come into the office; why don't I tell him you're a consultant I've hired to help out with some of the fund paperwork? That will give you access to almost everything here in the office, but especially to the Triad Fund files. You can look around and see if you can find the missing paperwork, or anything else suspicious. You can bring in anyone else you think necessary to the job, too – perhaps someone more versed in white collar crime or financial crime. I don't know what to look for, but my dad seems to think it all hinges around those papers Cathy found. Damn it, but I wish I'd paid more attention to them. Maybe...maybe..."

"My son," Tibor said gruffly, pressing his hand over David's hand. "Do not blame yourself."

"No, David," Victor said quietly. He rose from the sofa, and David and Tibor stood, too. He held out his hand and they shook hands all around. "You can't blame yourself. That's an excellent idea, and I'd like to proceed with your plan, if that's all right with you. And I'd like to speak with your sister."

"She doesn't have anything to do with Majek Investments," David said, walking Victor to his office door while his father settled again on the sofa.

"No, but by all accounts, she was very close friends with your wife. Perhaps she may have additional insights."

"How much do you charge, Victor? Is it by the day or are you on retainer?"

Victor brushed his question aside while Tibor barked from the sofa, "I am paying him. Do not worry about this. If he finds Cathy's murderer, it is worth any amount of money."

"All right," David said. As he opened his office door, he wasn't surprised to see Con leaning on Joan's desk, chatting. Joan pursed her lips in annoyance, but smiled with relief when she saw David and Victor exiting the office.

"Con," David said brightly, as Victor stepped forward and held out his hand. "I'd like to introduce you to a consultant Dad suggested. Victor Scalia, my brother, Constantine Majek."

The men shook hands. "Consultant?" Con asked. "For what project?"

"Triad Fund," Victor said smoothly. Con cast a startled look towards David.

"Why? The fund's doing well."

"We need help with the documentation and the marketing materials because of the disclosure changes," David responded. "Victor is an investment communications specialist. I know you've got your hands full with the Asian and European markets, and Dad suggested that Victor's team could step in to help write the fund updates and prepare mailings to the clients. I thought it was an excellent suggestion, so Dad and I interviewed Victor and just hired him for a few weeks to work on the project. How many weeks do you think you will need, Victor?"

"Oh, probably until the end of the quarter," Victor smiled. Lines crinkled around his dark blue eyes.

"Excellent. Joan, please find Victor an empty cubicle to work from on this floor. I'd like him as close to the executive suite as possible."

"I'll call Katie in Human Resources to arrange it," Joan said.

David walked Victor to the elevator while Con ambled into David's office to say hello to his father. "What do you think?" David asked, nodding towards his brother.

"I think," Victor said quietly, his shrewd gaze following Con's retreating back. "There's more going on here than you think."

David walked Victor to the elevator. The two men exchanged business cards and shook hands. When the elevator had whisked his guest back to the ground floor, David returned to the executive suite. Con eyed him speculatively as he sauntered back to his office, but David merely closed the door firmly behind himself to have privacy with his father.

"Well? Did I do the right thing by hiring him?" Tibor demanded as soon as the door closed.

"I'm not sure," David said slowly. "I liked him, but I'm still unconvinced he can solve the mystery of Cathy's death. The police..."

"Bah, the police." Tibor waved his hand as if brushing away a fly. "They do nothing."

"What I'm saying, Papa, is if the police couldn't find clues, perhaps there are no clues to be found. Maybe it really was just an accident, and a panicked driver ran off. Or maybe he really didn't know he hit someone. Some crimes never get solved."

"You act as if you don't want to know."

David hesitated. "Maybe I don't want to know."

11

Tibor's nostrils flared. "I did not raise a coward."

"I'm not saying I won't pursue this, Papa. I'm simply saying that sometimes the truth is hard to bear."

David's cell phone rang. He clicked it from his belt and answered. "Yes?"

"Dad?"

"Alex!" For the first time all day, a genuine smile creased his face, his cares and worries forgotten at the sound of his son's voice.

Tibor, hearing his eldest grandson's name, perked up immediately, shouting, "Tell him I say hello!"

David cupped his left hand over his ear, holding the phone to his right, trying to block his father's shouts. "Alex, how are you? Is everything all right?"

"Everything is fine. Is that Grandpa I hear? Tell him I say hi."

"He says hi!" David called to his father before turning his attention back to the phone. "Did the payment make it to the bursar's office all right? I did a wire transfer from another account. The bank is still investigating the theft."

"Yes, I logged in yesterday and it said my account was paid, so I'm all set for summer school. Thanks, Dad. I have another favor to ask, though. Actually two favors."

"Ask away. Anything."

"Can I come home this weekend and stay for about two weeks? They're painting my apartment and I'm between sessions now...summer session doesn't start until after Memorial Day. I was wondering if I could come home and stay in my old room. I can watch Ed after school, maybe help around the house.... you know."

"Alex, you're the answer to your father's prayers," David said.

"Whoa, don't get so dramatic with me, Dad!"

"No, really. Aunt Eva was nagging – er, reminding – me the other day to call the housekeeping agency." He gazed at his desk, where the business card Eva had given to him lay in a jumble in the top desk drawer along with the neat stack of cards he deemed important. "I could really use a hand now."

"You sound kind of stressed out."

"I am."

"Josh texted me...he said you went to the doctor yesterday. He was worried about you. We know how you hate going to the doctor, so he figured it must be serious. Is everything okay?"

"I'm fine. I have to go for some kind of test on Monday."

Tibor's eyes narrowed. "What? What is this test?"

David hushed his father. "I'll tell you in a minute, Papa."

"What test, Dad? If you went willingly to a doctor, even to Uncle Jim, it's bad."

"Just some sort of scan, that's all."

"You're talking to a doctor," Alex said tersely. "What scan?"

"Something called an echocardiogram."

"With a stress test?" Alex asked sharply. For a second, he sounded like Tibor. David winced.

"Yes, that's it. Don't get excited. It's just Jim being overly cautious."

"Dad...what aren't you telling me?"

"Nothing, nothing. What favor do you need, Alex?"

Alex muttered something under his breath and sighed. "You know, you can tell me these things.... Anyway, I'm hoping to come home this weekend. I can get the eight o'clock train out of Boston's South Street Station tomorrow morning into Penn, and then take the Long Island Rail Road from Penn to Locust Valley. I should be there around two, maybe a little after depending on the trains. Can you pick me up?"

"Can I pick you up?" David laughed. "Nothing can stop me. Eddie and I have an appointment tomorrow morning, but we should be free by then and I'm sure he'll want to come with me to pick you up."

"Terrific! Then I'll see you tomorrow. And then I want you to tell me everything - absolutely everything. Tell Grandpa I love him and will see him on Sunday."

David clicked off the call and slipped his cell phone back into his belt holster. He smiled broadly and his father waited expectantly. "Alex is coming home," he said.

Tibor's weathered face cracked into an answering smile.

"He'll be here tomorrow."

"For the weekend?"

"Until Memorial Day. End of May."

"Good! It is good!"

"Yes," David smiled. "It is very good."

David awoke on Saturday morning to the scent of strong coffee. It was already past nine, and sunlight streamed through the open window, spilling in bright golden pools on the dark blue rug in the master bedroom. After showering and shaving, he dressed in casual jeans and a polo shirt and strode downstairs.

Josh sat watching the television in the kitchen and eating a small mountain of Captain Crunch. "Morning, Dad."

"Hi, Josh." He peered at dark, viscous-looking fluid in the coffee pot. "You made coffee, I see."

"Eddie and I made it together. He rode his bike over to Chris' house to pick up some kind of gizmo to carry the turtles to the vet today."

David grasped his white Portuguese ceramic coffee mug from the cabinet and reached for the coffee pot. He peered into the oily depths and hesitated, holding the carafe in mid-air as the contents squirmed rather than swished. He put the cup and carafe back onto the counter and considered his breakfast options instead. Briefly, he craved some of the sweet cereal his son ate, then decided to be good. He opted for a piece of toast. While he waited for his toast, he asked, "When did Eddie leave?"

"About half an hour ago. He should be back soon."

The back door flew open and, as if on cue, Eddie bounded in. His t-shirt was wrinkled, his jeans grease stained near the right cuff where he'd probably gotten the fabric caught in his bike chain again. He carried a clear plastic terrarium with a green perforated plastic handle and lid.

David signed quickly. *Ready by 10:30. Change your clothes.*

Yes! Eddie signed with a grin and sprinted upstairs.

"That kid loves those turtles more than a reptile has a right to be loved," Josh mused.

"I had no idea reptiles could elicit such feelings." David's toast popped up and he buttered it. Finally gathering his courage to try the coffee, he poured a mug of the thick black liquid. He peered into the inky depths of his mug. "Um, Josh... how much coffee did you guys use?"

"One to one ratio, just like you said to do."

"One what to one what, Josh?"

"One cup of coffee to one cup of water."

"Josh? For future reference, it's one tablespoon of coffee to one cup of water."

"Oh. Well, Eddie thought you liked it strong. He wanted to do something nice to thank you for taking his turtle to the biologist guy."

If I leave my spoon in it, will it dissolve metal? David wondered. The boys had made several cups of the noxious brew. Debating his options, he raised the mug to his mouth and took a tentative sip. The thick, oily brew was so strong he gagged.

Josh paused in mid chew. "Is it okay?" he asked around a mouthful of Captain Crunch.

Sputtering, David managed to nod. He turned the hot water tap on full blast, poured out half the cup, then diluted the coffee with hot water. Shutting off the taps, he turned to Josh, who continued to stare at his father. "It's a little...strong."

"As strong as Grandpa's espresso?"

"A little stronger."

"Oh wow. That bad?"

"Rocket fuel." David winced. He picked up the mug and tipped it to his middle son. "*Naz drovie!*"

It wasn't as dreadful diluted with hot water...or else his high tolerance for caffeine had made even the highest octane coffee in creation bearable. While Josh ate, eyes glued to the Three Stooges movie playing on the television set in the corner, David quietly poured the rest of the pot into the sink. He emptied the filter basket, replaced the filter, and spooned out enough granules for a reasonable three cups. Refilling the coffee maker with water, he started the brew again. With a last glance at the diluted mix in his cup, he poured that down the sink, too.

Munching his toast, he asked "Josh, can you do me a favor while I'm out with Eddie?"

Josh was carrying his empty bowl, spoon, the milk and the cereal box, balancing the bowl and spoon on his forearm. "Yeah, sure, Dad. What do you need?"

"Can you tidy up your bathroom, please, and put out towels for your brother?"

"Aw man, Dr. Bro gets the red carpet. He knows where the towels are."

"It's polite, Josh. And please put sheets on his bed and make sure his room is ready for him. Can you do that for me, please?" He wiped his mouth with the back of his hand, then realized he had just done something he was always nagging the kids not to do. Fortunately, Josh hadn't seen him.

Josh dumped the cereal box and spoon onto the counter with a clatter. "Yeah, sure, I guess so. When is his train coming in?"

"Around two or so, but given that he's changing trains twice, once at Penn and once at Jamaica, I'm betting he might be late."

"Okay. What are we having for dinner tonight, then?"

"Dinner..." David ran a hand through his hair. "I'd forgotten about dinner."

"How about steak? That's easy, and we can make it in the broiler. Steak, baked potatoes, peas or something."

"Okay." David grabbed a pad of paper and pencil from the kitchen drawer and jotted notes to himself. "I'd better do the grocery shopping. What else do we need?"

"Everything," Josh grinned. "It's us, remember?"

"Oh, I remember. Three boys. I can't keep any food in this house for more than an hour."

David quickly wrote down the usual staples – bread, milk, eggs. Josh finished loading the dishwasher and sauntered back upstairs. David peered into the cupboards and found them bare, as usual; except for a box of Ritz one of the kids had left open, a jar of peanut butter, and a few cans of tuna fish. I've got to get a housekeeper, he thought again. I can't even keep enough food in the house for the kids, let alone remember all this stuff. How did Cathy do it all? How did she keep us all clean, fed, clothed, our schedules straight and yet still manage to teach three classes a semester at the university – plus her private students? It was insane. David closed the cupboards and made a few final notes to himself when his cell phone rang.

"Yes?"

"Hey there!" Eva shouted over the whine of a vacuum cleaner. "I'm at work, but I wanted to check in with you to see how many we'll be for Sunday dinner tomorrow."

"Seven, unless Con brings his girlfriend."

"Seven? Then Dad was right. I called him earlier and he said that Alex was coming home. You must be looking forward to seeing him." Eva's muffled voice came over the cell phone as she turned to one of her workers, giving instructions about what to clean next. "Sorry."

"No problem. I guess…figure on eight and if we have leftovers, we have leftovers."

"Okay. Then I'll be over around two tomorrow to start cooking."

"Thanks, Eva." Before she could click off, he said quickly, "Eva?"

"Yeah?"

He swallowed. "You gave me a card for a housekeeping agency," he said. "And I left it at work. I was going to call them today. Do you remember their name? I can look them up online."

"Sure," Eva said. "Excelsior Housekeeping Service. Jen, the owner, is a friend of mine. I send her clients who need live-in or daily housekeepers, she sends me people who are really looking for weekly cleaning. We send each other business all the time."

"Excelsior," David nodded, writing down the name on the pad next to the grocery list. "Thanks."

"Are you going to call them?" Eva asked with surprise evident in her voice.

"I think I have to. The kids are down to a sleeve of stale Ritz crackers and a jar of peanut butter, and I think we'll be out of coffee by tomorrow."

"That's a national crisis."

"Damn straight."

"How can you be out of coffee? I left you a full container."

"Let's just say the boys tried to make me coffee today."

"Oh dear." Eva laughed. "Espresso?"

"More like crude oil, but it was the thought that counted. Anyway, I'll call your friend today and see about a housekeeper."

"You won't be disappointed," Eva promised. "And to tell you the truth, David, I'm relieved. We were all a little worried about you."

"We?"

"Me, Dad, Con," Eva said. "We know it's been rough since Cathy died. Even Papa noticed, and that's saying something."

"Yeah," David said just as Eddie trotted down to the kitchen bearing the terrarium. Inside, Teeny and Tiny huddled together on a large flat rock in the corner while water sloshed around the bottom. "I've got to go. Time to take the turtles to the vet."

"Turtles to the vet? Now I've heard everything."

"It's a long story."

"I can only imagine. Bye, David. See you tomorrow."

"Bye."

Eddie had changed into a clean polo shirt, probably one that his aunt had laundered for him, and a less wrinkled pair of jeans and navy Converse sneakers. He'd used water to slick back his wavy hair. How grown up my baby is beginning to look. He had shot up another inch over the past year, and his face was taking on angles and planes closer to Cathy's Scotch Irish ancestors than to his own Czech heritage. David nodded at the turtles and signed, *Ready?*

Eddie nodded.

I've got to make one phone call, David signed, pointing to the cell phone.

Eddie scooted onto a kitchen chair and waited patiently, swinging his legs and kicking at the rungs of the chair while David tapped access to the internet on his Smartphone. He quickly found the website for Excelsior Housekeeping Services in Mineola, and dialed the number. A perky young woman answered on the second ring.

"Excelsior Housekeeping Services! This is Jennifer speaking. How may I help you?"

"Jennifer? My name is David Majek, and my sister, Eva Majek, recommended your firm to me." David leaned his left hip against the counter and watching Eddie as he peered at his turtles, squinting his eyes to see through the cheap plastic sides of the container. "I'm looking for a housekeeper, five days a week."

"Mr. Majek, it's a pleasure to speak with you," Jennifer replied. "Eva's mentioned you often. Are you looking for a live-in housekeeper or a daily?"

"Daily, I think. I'd want someone to arrive around 9 in the morning and stay until six. Some nights they might need to stay a little later if I'm stuck at work or something. I'd pay overtime or however you work it if that's the case. Really, someone I can trust is more important to me than anything else."

"I see," Jennifer said. He heard tapping, as if she were typing notes. "And where do you live?"

"Brookville."

"Thank you," she affirmed. "What kind of housekeeping work do you need?"

"Oh, um, the usual, I suppose. Cleaning. Shopping. Preparing meals. Laundry. Watching my youngest son when he gets home from school."

"How old is your son?"

"Eleven. Eddie is eleven. But..." David hesitated. "My son is deaf and mute. He communicates very well through American Sign Language, and if you have anyone who speaks ASL that would be ideal. But if not, Eddie uses his tablet to write messages to adults who don't speak ASL. He's quite proficient at communicating."

"I see. Well, let me call around and see who I have available. Would you like to meet the candidates first or should I just have someone ready to start next week?"

"No, no," David said. "I want to interview the candidates please. I'm very particular about who I allow inside my home, especially when I'm not here."

"I understand completely," Jennifer said. "Please be assured that the housekeepers assigned by Excelsior are fully bonded, licensed and insured. They undergo rigorous screening before we allow anyone to work with our clients."

They quickly discussed prices, which David thought were reasonable given the hours, and Jennifer promised to call him back in the afternoon with potential interviewees. Eddie kicked harder at the rungs of his chair, drumming his fingers on the table, until David motioned for him to stop. Wait, wait, he signed with one hand rather than the normal two.

Eddie pointed to the turtles, then to the clock over the sink. *I know, I know*, David nodded. *Time to go. One more minute.*

"Very well then, Jennifer. I'll await your call. You can reach me on my cell phone."

She took down the number. "Thank you. I'll speak with you later."

He clicked off his call and nodded to Eddie, who leaped to his feet. David pointed to the backdoor, and Eddie hefted the container and started for the door. "Josh!" David called towards the dining room and the upstairs, raising his voice to a shout. "We're leaving now for C.W. Post. Back in about an hour."

"Okay!"

"Please answer the phone and take a message!" David yelled back. "Don't pretend to be me, okay?"

"Yeah, yeah."

"Joshua...."

"Okay, Dad. Hope the squirt's turtles are okay."

Eddie balanced the terrarium on his knees from his perch on the rear passenger seat of the Yukon. Their housing development was serene on this Saturday, a picture of an early spring morning. Mrs. Jenkins was outside watering her garden. Eddie beamed when he saw her, waving madly. She waved back, her wrinkled face creasing into smiles. A memory from when Eddie was small flashed through David's memory. Cathy used to visit Mrs. Jenkins, with Eddie in tow. He'd toddle back home gnawing at a homemade oatmeal cookie twice the size of his fist. He wished he wasn't driving so he could sign to Eddie and ask him if he still visited Mrs. Jenkins.

That memory awaked others. He'd forgotten a great many things about when the boys were young. Along with the memories, he felt a rush of sorrow tinged with anger at the busyness of his corporate CEO life. For a split second, he wished he wasn't Tibor Majek's son; that he wasn't expected to be a financial wizard, a corporate superhero, able to transform dollar bills into six figures in a single bound; that he wasn't the man everyone turned to for answers when things went wrong. The weight of his life pressed upon him, and he felt his chest tighten, squeezing. David gripped the steering wheel and set his jaw; this was not the time for sentimentality. He didn't have time anymore for regrets. His life was what it was, and he had accepted every milestone, every responsibility piled onto responsibility along the way. Now was not the time to daydream.

The traffic on Northern Boulevard was surprisingly light for a Saturday morning as he crested the hill near C.W. Post's campus. Cathy had taught as adjunct faculty in the music department for about five years, returning to classroom teaching after Eddie entered St. Mary's School for the Deaf. Before that, she'd played piano for church, for weddings and funerals and such just to keep in shape, as she laughingly called it. He almost made the left hand turn into the first gated entrance which led to the Humanities, Arts and Music buildings, but he stopped himself in time. At the second entrance, he waited by the traffic light, then turned left through the massive iron gates. C.W. Post had been the home of the cereal magnate, and the main buildings were from the days of Long Island's Gold Coast. A sandstone wall surrounded the stately oak and maples, the glistening swathes of velvet lawn, the waving pink tulips flanking the driveway. David coasted to the guard gate, explained his errand, and was waved towards the Life Sciences building. He gazed into the rearview mirror and saw Eddie eagerly examining the buildings, and the few students and faculty walking between buildings on this May morning.

The Life Sciences building was easy to find, a glass and steel three-story facility behind the Administration building. He parked in a Visitor's slot and Eddie scrambled out of the car, carefully balancing the terrarium. David pointed to the sign, and Eddie nodded, slipping his left hand into David's while carrying the terrarium in his right.

Once inside the building, David consulted the signboard and found Dr. Donahue listed on the third floor. Eddie led the way up the stairs, with David now carrying the terrarium in both hands like a sacred vessel. David walked slowly up the three flights of stairs while Eddie scampered ahead, pausing and beckoning his father, Faster, faster!

David smiled wanly and pressed a hand to his chest. He didn't want to admit that the squeezing felt worse, and now a burning sensation, like heartburn, churned in his throat. Ah, the coffee, he thought to himself, tasting the remnants of the boys' gift to him that morning. I am so glad I didn't drink more than a little bit. Wow, this hurts. He pressed a hand to his chest again, rubbing the area near his sternum. Pausing for breath on the second floor, the pain subsided. Eddie had already reached the top and waited, tapping his foot.

Finally, David and Eddie arrived at office 316. The door was open, and inside, laboratory tables topped with black granite and glistening steel sinks lined the room in orderly rows. A doorway in the back corner revealed an office overflowing with books, papers, and what appeared to be fish and reptile samples mounted and stuffed. But around the perimeter of the room were, dozens of fish tanks. Eddie placed the turtles onto one of the tables and raced to the first tank, pressing his palms to the glass. Filters gurgled and bubbled, and a school of large-mouthed fish surged within the depths. David flinched as dozens of razor sharp teeth suddenly gnashed towards Eddie's hands on the opposite side of the glass.

"Amazonian piranhas," a man called from the corner. Dr. Donahue strode towards David and held out a soft, doughy hand. "Brian Donahue."

"David Majek."

"Dr. Majek's husband?" Dr. Donahue asked in surprise.

"Why yes," David said, startled. "Have we met?"

"Briefly, two years ago," Dr. Donahue said. His blue eyes softened with compassion. "We met after the faculty recital, at the reception. I'm afraid I interrupted you; you were on your phone reading emails. Something at the office."

"It's always something at the office." He vaguely remembered the pudgy scientist in a sea of faces congratulating Cathy for a wonderful performance. The music faculty played a welcome recital at the start of every school year, and Cathy had played three Debussy pieces. A lump formed in his throat as he remembered how graceful, how beautiful she had appeared on stage, like a fairytale princess with her cascades of red gold hair, the dark sapphire blue formal gown and silver slippers on her feet. Cathy, swirling among the crowded reception, greeting her students and future students, introducing him to her colleagues. She had loved her work, David thought suddenly. I don't think she ever felt burdened, the way I do. She often felt overwhelmed by the amount of work on her schedule, especially when she had to play a concert, and she never felt she had enough practice time at the piano. But she had loved teaching, and the students loved her, and it showed that night, with more teenagers than he thought possible rushing to shake his hand and say how much they enjoyed his wife's classes.

"I was on a few faculty committees with her," Donahue said as he walked over to where Eddie had moved on to study a tank of turtles similar to his own pets. "I got to know her quite well. She was a bright light snuffed out too soon."

"Yes." David cleared his throat. "This is my son, Eddie. I think my secretary mentioned that he is a deaf mute..."

"She did, and I speak a little bit of ASL," Dr. Donahue said. He tapped Eddie on the shoulder and moved his hands clumsily to sign hello. Eddie's face broadened in a smile; anytime a grownup even tried ASL, he was pleased. He held out his hand formally to shake Dr. Donahue's hand, and the professor laughed.

"What manners!" Dr. Donahue pushed his tortoise shell rimmed spectacles back to the bridge of his nose. "Well, what do we have here...is this the patient?" He pointed to the terrarium.

Eddie nodded.

"*Trachemys scripta elegans*. The red-eared slider turtle. One of the most popular pets in America. Do you wash your hands after playing with them?" Dr. Donahue asked. David translated for Eddie, who shrugged, then nodded. "Make sure he washes his hands after touching them or cleaning the tank," Donahue mumbled to David as Eddie unlatched the top of the carrier so that the doctor could look at his pets. "They can carry salmonella."

David nodded.

Dr. Donahue turned on a bright light clamped to the side of the laboratory table and adjusted the steel gooseneck so the light shone fully on Teeny. He clucked his tongue, and gently touched the shell. After spending a few minutes examining Teeny, he moved on to Tiny, who seemed to pass his scrutiny. He returned to Teeny while Eddie peered anxiously at the doctor's face, searching for clues.

Well? Eddie questioned with hands.

"Can you translate?" Dr. Donahue asked David, who nodded.

"You can also type messages on the computer," David suggested. "Or give him things to read. He's an avid reader."

"I'll give him a copy of my book," Dr. Donahue promised. He turned on the water at the lab table and made a great show of washing his hands, even though he had no soap, wiping them dry on the edge of his lab coat. David rolled his eyes. Cathy would have had a fit. Dr. Donahue was worse than the boys.

"Eddie, Teeny has something called soft shell disease," Dr. Donahue said. He walked over to a bookshelf and pulled out a heavy volume, thumping it onto the granite tabletop. Eddie trotted over and stood on sneakered tiptoes to peer into the pages as Dr. Donahue flipped it open to the section he sought. The biologist pointed to a page and Eddie scanned it, biting his lip. When Eddie looked up, David continued to sign for him as Dr. Donahue spoke.

"Turtles in the wild eat many things – water plants, snails, insects. Teeny needs more calcium in his diet. He is not getting enough nutrition, so his body is taking calcium from his shell. If he doesn't get some help, he will die. Tiny looks better but he is showing signs of the disease, too. I'll give your father a list of things to buy, including new food, and things to do to help Teeny, but you must understand that some turtles do not make it when they get this sick. We will do everything we can to help Teeny, but I can't promise anything."

David finished translating and waited. Eddie frowned, dropped his eyes, and nodded. Then he looked back at his father and queried, *Can we get what he says?*

Yes, David nodded. He opened his hands wide. *All.*

Mollified, Eddie smiled at the doctor in thanks. Dr. Donahue said, "I'll write your list now. You can find everything at the supermarket or at a local pet store, but you've got to be consistent with this from now on."

He disappeared into his office while Eddie snapped the lid back onto the turtle carrier. When Dr. Donahue returned, he handed a sheet of paper to David, who scanned the contents.

"Romaine lettuce...okay.... cuttlebone? What's a cuttlebone?"

"It's something sold in pet stores for birds," Dr. Donahue said. "Normally it is mounted on the side of a bird's cage, but for the turtles, I want you to place it in a shallow dish of water. The cuttlebone will release calcium into the water, which the turtles will drink. It will help their shells heal."

"Okay."

The rest of the list seemed fine, so David slid it into his pocket. "How can I thank you?"

"Oh, it's my pleasure," Dr. Donahue said. He nodded towards Eddie, who had wandered back to examine the reptiles and fish in the tanks. "He seems like quite the conscientious young man."

"He loves animals and nature," David said. "He wants to be a scientist of some sort or a veterinarian when he grows up."

"Would he like a tour of the lab before you leave?"

"Would he?" David smiled. "I think it would be Christmas and Halloween rolled into one for him."

"Now that is special!" Dr. Donahue laughed. David tapped Eddie on the shoulder and signed the good news, and Eddie's eyes sparkled. His grin said it all.

Dr. Donahue led the way, pointing to each aquarium while David translated in ASL for his son. Most had signs explaining the rare and exotic species housed within. Eddie seemed especially taken with a large tank of fellow red-eared sliders.

"Do you see how active they are?" Dr. Donahue explained while David signed. The turtles swam, sunbathed under a heat lamp, and crawled about on the rocks. "Your turtles should look like this. You may need to adjust the heat lamp, like so." He showed Eddie the angle and height of the lamp, and Eddie nodded, carefully noting the positioning of the lamp.

They moved on to the snakes, which David did not care for all that much except for one ivory and orange diamond-patterned snake which the biologist identified as a corn snake. Dr. Donahue reached into the cage and pulled the reptile out, letting Eddie touch and hold the snake. Eddie held it out for David to pet, and David gingerly tapped the scales with his fingertips. The snake flicked his tongue and David jumped back. Eddie grinned and caressed the snake before handing it back to Dr. Donahue.

"The snake was just smelling you," Dr. Donahue reassured David.

"With his tongue?" David asked incredulously from his safe position several feet away.

"It's how snakes communicate." Dr. Donahue place the snake into its aquarium. "This is a corn snake, a very sweet, harmless snake. Don't worry. They don't bite people. They eat mice and insects."

"Okay." David eyed the reptile as Dr. Donahue clicked the lid of the aquarium into place.

They moved on to a roomful of mounted specimens, which David found much more to his liking and Eddie seemed less interested in, and then to Dr. Donahue's office.

"How much do I owe you?" David asked quietly as Dr. Donahue fussed about in the drawers of his desk for the book on turtles he had promised to give to Eddie.

"Nothing, nothing." Donahue waved him away. "I had to be at the lab this morning anyway to feed the specimens since my graduate student is away for the weekend. It was my pleasure to meet and encourage such an intelligent young man. I hope you do become a biologist or a veterinarian, Eddie; you will make a fine doctor." Eddie glowed from the compliment as David translated the scientist's words.

Dr. Donahue found the book and pulled it out of the desk. "The Big Book of Turtles," David read, and Eddie pointed to the byline. "Why doctor, you're an author!"

"I wrote this as a children's book," Dr. Donahue said modestly, handing the copy to Eddie. Eddie shook his head. "What, you don't want it?" He waited while Eddie grabbed a pen from the desk and pushed it into the biologist's hand.

"He wants you to sign it," David said.

"Well!" Dr. Donahue exclaimed. "You're making me into quite the celebrity."

He autographed the title page with a flourish, then shook Eddie's hand and gave him the book. Eddie hugged it to his chest like a treasure. "You've made his day," David said as they walked back to the doorway of the lab. Eddie threw his arms around Dr. Donahue and gave him a big hug, which made the pudgy scientist laugh.

"Oh, I enjoyed it," Dr. Donahue said. "Anything for Cathy Majek's family. She was really a treasure for the school and she is deeply missed by all. But most of all by you, I imagine."

"Indeed." A sudden thought came to David. "Didn't they plant a tree in her honor or something?"

"Yes, over by the music building," Dr. Donahue said. "She loved trees and gardens of all sorts, so her students thought planting a tree in her honor was apt. Didn't you get the letter inviting you to the ceremony?"

"I did, but I had to work," David lied. In truth, he couldn't bear to go. "Do you think we could see it?"

"Of course! It's easy to find. We're between spring and summer session now, but there should be a few students about if you get lost. Just follow the path between the buildings and past the hideous steel modern art caterpillar or whatever the thing is on the lawn. Eddie can leave his turtles in the car; it's warm enough and they'll be fine for a few minutes."

"Thank you." David shook his hand again, and he and Eddie moved off after waving farewell to the doctor.

When they got to the car, David put a hand on Eddie's shoulder and signed carefully. *They planted a tree for Mom*, he said. *Can we go look? Leave the turtles in the car.*

Okay, Ed nodded. He pointed back to the biology building and made his cheeks puff out so that he did a fair imitation of the doughy scientist. *He was nice.*

Yes, he was. David nodded. *Leave the book in the car too.*

They walked together down the cement paths, nodding to students as they walked by. Some smiled at Eddie, who of course had to walk along the edge like a tightrope, balancing on the bricks that lined the path. Kids never walk anywhere, David mused as he beckoned Eddie to follow him down the curving path. They trot, jaunt, skip or walk a tightrope; anything to make the walk an adventure.

Ahead of them was the monstrous steel caterpillar Dr. Donahue had mentioned, a hulking beast set on the lawn, clearly intended as artwork and instead coming across like a leftover prop from a science fiction movie. Eddie ran towards it as if to climb on it. David grabbed him by the shoulder and shook his head. No, not a playground. Eddie just shrugged and skipped ahead.

They reached the music building. Unlike the modern steel and glass Life Sciences building, the music department was housed in a Greek temple-style classical brick building with sweeping stairs and large, arched windows along one side, which David knew led to the auditorium. Across a grassy quadrant was the administration building, the theater and the Humanities building. In the center of the grass quadrangle was a newly planted pink dogwood tree, Cathy's favorite. David gestured for Eddie to move near, and the two stood side by side, reading the bronze plaque at its base.

Dr. Catherine Majek, Music Faculty

The dates of her birth and death were inscribed below, with the words, "Your music lives on."

David felt a lump in his throat. Eddie's hand crept into his own, and he gave his son a reassuring squeeze. A breeze ruffled their hair and sent a spray of pink petals spiraling to his feet.

From the open windows in the music building, he heard the deep throated chords of a Chopin polonaise tumble down to them. The F# minor, David thought uneasily. It was an ominous, darkly textured piece that had been Cathy's favorite and the one she had been rehearsing the week that she died.

As the music rumbled down to them, the throaty chords echoing across the quad, a dark shadow fell over Eddie. His son stood next to Cathy's tree, tracing the words on the bronze plaque with his index finger. David suppressed a shiver and gazed up at the sky. Not a cloud.

Where had the shadow come from?

He whirled around, looking for the source of darkness that seemed to envelop his youngest son as the dark trills and passages of Chopin cascaded down. No one was in sight. He peered to the right, to the left, but nothing blocked the bright light. The shadow pulsed, loomed, then vanished as quickly as it had come. The music ceased. All was golden again, warm spring, blue skies and twirling pink petals.

Eddie raised his eyebrows questioningly.

What was that? David signed. *The darkness. Did you see that?*

Unperturbed, Eddie shrugged. He tapped his heart three times. *Mom?*

Eddie nodded. He walked away slowly, hands stuffed in his pockets. David hurried after him and grasped him by the shoulder to halt his progress. Slowly, David shrugged, then tapped his heart three times again. *It was Mom?*

Eddie pulled his hands from his pockets and signed. *Haven't you seen her before?*

Seen her? Where? Mom is dead, Eddie.

Yes, but she watches over us, Eddie signed patiently, as if David were the child and Eddie, the parent. He pointed back to the tree, then tapped his heart.

Eddie, that's not possible.

I knew you wouldn't believe me.

Eddie, Mom is in heaven, with Jesus and the angels and the saints. I told you that. That is where good people go when they die.

Yes, Eddie nodded, *but she watches us too. She comes to me sometimes, like a shadow. Sometimes I see her out of the corner of my eye.*

David was speechless, his hands frozen by his sides.

She is afraid for us.

David paused trying to figure out why his son would say that. He signed, *Why, Eddie?*

Because of who killed her.

Who, Eddie? Does she say who?

Eddie turned and walked away. This time, David did not follow, but stood stock still. The breeze caressed his brow. He folded his arms over his chest and shivered. Across the quad, a shout of laughter from the theater broke the spell as the theater doors were flung open and students spilled forth from rehearsal, talking, shouting, pounding down the pavement. As the sea of college students surged around him, David felt himself buoyed forward, walking to catch up with Eddie, his mind a whirl.

He tried asking Eddie more questions, but his youngest son shook his hand away impatiently. Eddie checked on his turtles, then flipped through the book Dr. Donahue had given to him as if he hadn't just dropped this supernatural bombshell on his father.

David turned the key in the ignition. He paused, staring into the back seat at his youngest child, the one who looked most like his beloved Cathy.

How does he know this? How?

12

David drove home so Eddie could return his turtles to their tank. At the house, David waited in the car while Eddie ran inside to deposit Teeny and Tiny into their terrarium. He drummed his fingertips on the steering wheel and stared at the pink dogwood in his own backyard. It was his last birthday present to Cathy.

He thought again about the tree at the college. What had Eddie meant? Did he actually see his mother, or think he saw his mother, or was it just the overactive imagination of a grieving boy?

Eddie bounded from the house, slamming the backdoor. He climbed into the rear passenger seat of the Yukon and snapped his seat belt tight. David had promised to drive him immediately to the pet store by the Rose Diner to purchase the supplies on Dr. Donahue's list. It was impossible to continue their conversation in the car with David's hands on the wheel. Instead, he stole glances of his son in the rearview mirror. Eddie's attention stayed fixed on his new book.

David parked the car outside the store. As he shifted into park Eddie leaped from the vehicle and marched into the store.

By the time David walked through the door, he spotted Eddie clutching a plastic basket to his chest waiting impatiently for his father in the reptile aisle. He bit his lower lip in consternation and raised his eyes to his father. David nodded and pulled the list from Dr. Donahue from his pocket. Eddie scanned the bottles of vitamins, supplements, and products, choosing them with the same care Cathy had used to choose baby food at the supermarket.

They paid for the pet supplies, stowed them in the back of the Yukon, and drove to the supermarket a half mile away. David pushed the shopping cart while Eddie loaded it with choice turtle treats. He dropped three heads of Romaine lettuce into the cart, and David had to pause to put them back, his hands raised in the stop gesture to indicate it was too much. Eddie frowned, lower lip pushed out, but David took him by the arm and steered him over to a display of cherries. Eddie brightened immediately and chose the biggest bag.

David's mind wasn't really on the shopping. He mulled over the campus visit while they worked their way through the bright supermarket aisle. The shadow, reaching out as if to cover Eddie, and the throaty notes of Chopin floating from the music building at the same moment...what were the odds that out of the entire classic repertoire someone would be practicing that exact piece at that precise moment?

But neither the shadow nor the music occupied his thoughts the most. It was Eddie's remarks. "Mom is watching us." David often felt as if Cathy's presence still lingered in the house, especially near the piano, but that was understandable – it was the last place she'd been inside the Majek's home, and the place she'd spent happy hours.

David reached for cans of soup, boxes of pasta, several thick steaks for their supper tonight as he puzzled over what Eddie had said. Why would Eddie feel so much blame for his mother's death? Why did Eddie think that whoever had killed Cathy had someone zeroed in on him?

Eddie piled two half-gallons of ice cream onto their overflowing shopping cart and helped David place the items on the conveyer belt at the register. David thought about the missing papers, Cathy's sudden flight from the house, Eddie's insistence that his mother was still watching them. Was she there with them in the supermarket? Did she watch him while he slept?

The cashier cleared her throat impatiently. David snapped out of his reverie. Both Eddie and the cashier stared at him. The bag boy placed the last plastic bag into the shopping cart while the cashier tapped a ballpoint pen at the total glaring from the register's screen.

"No, no coupons today." David swiped his credit card and signed the filmy keypad screen. Mission accomplished. Two bags of groceries, one per turtle, David thought ruefully as he hefted the bags into the back of the Yukon. Twenty bags for four men. How the heck did Cathy manage all of this with a smile, day in and day out, every day for the past twenty-three years?

At home, David put away the groceries while Eddie ran upstairs to coax Teeny into eating some Romaine. Once all the perishables were stowed and the cans and boxes stacked, David climbed the stairs to the second floor. He flicked the lights politely to alert Eddie he was at the door. Eddie leaned over the turtle tank but beckoned him to enter.

David pointed to the turtles and signed, *How is he?*

Okay, Eddie shrugged. He waved a slender piece of dark green lettuce under the turtle's snout. The reptile blinked and turned his head away.

Not hungry, David signed. Eddie agreed. He placed the lettuce shred like an offering on the basking rock, adjusted the heat lamp, and poked the cuttlebone that was floating in a shallow dish of water. Satisfied, Eddie fastened the cover of his tank and raised his eyebrows at his father. *What?*

David sat on the edge of Ed's bed. He patted the quilt. *Sit.* Eddie slid onto the bed impatiently. He tapped his wrist as if taking a pulse, his sign for his older brother

Yes, David nodded, pointing at his watch and then at the cell phone clipped to his belt. They had plenty of time. Alex still had to call from the train station to let them know he was nearing the Locust Valley station, the closest one to Brookville. It was around 1 o'clock, and they still had to eat lunch. But before they did, David had a few questions for Eddie.

He signed carefully, making sure he had Eddie's full attention.

You said Mom was with us.

She is.

How?

Eddie shrugged. He spread his arms wide, embracing the room. *Here, there, everywhere.*

Is this just make believe? Imagination? He struggled to sign the right word.

Eddie shook his head vehemently.

Eddie, why do you think Mom thinks you know who killed her?

Eddie turned away. He leaned forward, studying his turtles, biting his lower lip.

David's cell phone shrilled. Cursing, he glanced at the display. It was Alex. Eddie leaped from the bed and ran to the door. David fumbled with his cell phone. "Alex?"

"Dad – are you okay? You sound funny."

"I'm fine. Just trying to sort something out."

"I just changed trains to the Oyster Bay branch. I should be at Locust Valley in about forty minutes, I think."

"Okay, Eddie and I will be there to pick you up. Can't wait to see you, Son."

"And you, Dad. Are you sure you're okay?"

David watched as Teeny extended his leathery head from his shell and lipped the lettuce. He gulped the green shed into his gaping maw, then nosed about the rock for more. "I'm fine," David said firmly. "Fine. Just getting to the bottom of things. See you in a bit."

Eddie followed his father downstairs, happily running ahead of David at the prospect of lunch, all questions forgotten. David paused at the top of the stairs, then shook his head and continued. Eddie would tell him what was on his mind sooner or later. He knew from long experience that Eddie couldn't be pushed. His son had inherited his grandfather's stubbornness, and if he pushed Eddie on his answer, Eddie would just shut down. If he bided his time, Eddie would choose when to tell his father more, if there was anything more to say.

In the kitchen, Eddie rummaged around the cold cut bin while Josh grabbed the loaf of white bread from the counter. "You want a sandwich, Dad?" Josh asked.

"Sure," David said. He scanned Eddie's face to see what his youngest son was thinking, but Eddie was fixing a sandwich. Forcing himself to push aside any urge he had to demand more information, he merely said, "We have just enough time to eat, and then we've got to go pick your brother up at the train station. Did you get his room set up and the bathroom ready like I asked?"

"Um, sort of."

"Sort of isn't the right answer, Josh."

"I'll do it now, okay?"

"Please."

Josh dropped the bread onto the counter and grumbled out the door. David heard the tail end of his middle son's monologue. "...do everything around here...not fair..."

David took a plate from the cabinet and dropped two slices of white bread onto it. He was just reaching for the cold cuts when Josh stomped back into the kitchen. "I can't find the towels."

"What do you mean, you can't find the towels? Your aunt just did a huge load of laundry for us this week. We've got to have some clean towels."

"Can't find them."

"I don't think you looked hard enough."

Josh grabbed a clean plate from the cabinet, picked up the bread, and placed two slices on the plate. He dripped a blob of mayonnaise onto both slices and slapped four slices of bologna on the bread, slammed the top of the sandwich onto the bologna and pressed down, mayo oozing from the sizes. David shook his head as Josh grabbed his plate and slid into his seat at the kitchen table.

"You guys into a heavy conversation or what?" Josh studied his father over the edge of his sandwich. He wiped mayo from his fingers onto his jeans.

"Just finished a discussion we were having upstairs," David said. He reached into the fridge for the mustard and the pickles for his own sandwich. His cell phone rang as he was assembling his lunch.

"Yes?"

"Mr. Majek? This is Jennifer, from Excelsior Housekeeping Service."

"Yes, Jennifer," David nodded. "Thanks for calling back so quickly."

"My pleasure. We've found a candidate we think will be a great fit for your family, and I'd like to have her over to interview with you this evening. Would that be convenient?"

David glanced at the boys. Other than picking Alex up at the train station, they had no plans for the day. "Very well. What time?"

"Would seven tonight be convenient?"

"Yes, that's fine." He gave her directions. "What is her name? And her credentials?"

"Her name is Turquoise Daniels. She's thirty-seven years old and has twin girls of her own. She's been a housekeeper for some of the North Shore families, but the last family she worked for wants her to travel to Europe for the summer and she can't bring her daughters along, so she needs another position. She ran her own catering company before her marriage, and the family she works for now says she's a fantastic cook. I think you'll like her."

"Does she speak American Sign Language?"

"No, but she said she's willing to learn," Jen chirped. "I'll have her bring a resume with her tonight, all right?"

"That's fine. Thank you."

"Certainly. If your plans change for any reason and you won't be available at that time, please call and leave a message on our answering service. We check messages 24/7."

"Thanks." He disconnected the call and slipped the cell phone back into his leather belt holster.

"What was that all about?" Josh asked with his mouthful.

"Don't talk with your mouth full," David rebuked.

Josh swiped the back of his hand over his mouth and Eddie burped.

David sighed. Raising sons was like civilizing savages. He signed quickly to Eddie, no burping, manners!

Eddie signed, *pardon me*, and David turned back to Josh.

"I called the housekeeping service Aunt Eva recommended," David said. "They're sending a woman over tonight to be interviewed. Please be on your best behavior when you meet her."

"Wow, Dad, you've really changed your mind about not having strangers over, huh?"

"No, I'm just desperate to have my home in order again," David admitted. "I can't ask Aunt Eva for favors all the time, and I'd pay for her cleaning service, but we need more than just someone to dust and vacuum for us. I don't know how your mother did it all. I can't keep up with everything. I loathe shopping, I can never remember to do the laundry, and if we rely on my cooking skills, we'll starve."

"Your bacon and eggs aren't bad."

"It's the only thing I can cook except for heating a can of soup. My repertoire is limited to bacon and eggs, sandwiches and soup, and spaghetti."

"Well, you haven't burned the spaghetti yet," Josh mumbled into his bologna.

"How much spaghetti can we eat?" David asked. He sat at the kitchen table and took a bite of his sandwich. "And how often am I going to ask you to babysit your little brother after school? What do we do during the summer months when you're both home all the time? I can't leave you here alone."

"Eddie is away at camp for most of July," Josh pointed out. Eddie attended the Lions Club Summer Deaf Camp in Connecticut each year. It was a sleep away camp with plenty of wilderness activities, and Eddie loved being surrounded by deaf kids his own age for the two and a half weeks.

"True," David said, trying to remember if he'd mailed in the application and deposit form to enroll Eddie this year and relieved to recall that he had. "But what about August? And beyond? It's time I made this decision. No, Josh, we do need a housekeeper. We'll see if this woman works out but if not, the agency will likely have other people."

After they finished lunch, David nagged Josh into going upstairs to look for the lost towels again. Josh stomped upstairs, muttering under his breath about how unfair it was to be the middle child. Eddie nodded when David asked if he wanted to drive to the train station with him, so the two set out again in the SUV, threading through the back roads of Brookville, turning onto Chicken Valley Road and then to Piping Rock Road. They passed some fine mansions, the estates of many of David's clients at Majek Investments, and even some horse barns where beautiful bays and chestnuts grazed in fields bordered by old-fashioned post and rail fences. Eddie especially loved seeing the horses, and gazed longingly at the animals as they passed.

David felt a pang of guilt; he and Cathy had talked about taking Eddie over to HorseAbility, the therapeutic riding school at Old Westbury College, for riding lessons this year, but of course those plans had also been pushed aside in the wake of Cathy's death. There just aren't enough hours in the day, David thought. I never wanted to be a single parent. How do other people do this?

The Locust Valley train station parking lot was almost completely empty, with a handful of vehicles parked near the station building. The Spanish-red tiles gleamed in the bright May sunlight. A few cars idled in a line near the station as people awaited the train. David pulled into a slot and beckoned Eddie out of the car. It was too nice a day to sit in the car.

They walked around the station for a bit, Eddie picking up pebbles and tossing them at the pillars of the station building until David stopped him. Soon David heard the horn as the LIRR train wheezed into the station. Eddie raced to the platform, dancing from foot to foot as David ascended slowly behind him, scanning the cars as the train pulled in. The brakes squealed, and the doors dinged open. From the front of the train Alex emerged, wheeling a black suitcase and toting a backpack.

"Hey, Squirt!" he called, dropping to his knees on the concrete platform and enfolded Eddie in a giant bear hug. Eddie clung to his elder brother and David smiled, stepping forward.

"Do I get a hug, too?"

"Hey, Dad." Alex untangled himself from Eddie's embrace and reached out to hug his father. Alex came up to David's chin, and his hair was the lightest among the three boys, carrying hints of Cathy's red-gold among the plain brown strands.

He hugged his oldest son close then examined him at arm's length. "Alex, it's so good to see you." Alex had dark circles under his eyes and stubble on his chin. "Are you all right? You look tired."

"I've been up since four." Alex yawned, stepping back from his father's embrace. "I had to get take the six-something out of Boston."

Eddie pointed to the suitcase and Alex handed it over to his little brother, who wheeled it across the concrete to the handicapped ramp so he could tug it down to the parking lot from the raised platform. David and Alex followed slowly, watching with amusement as Eddie lost control of the suitcase, sending it careening down the ramp.

"I hope you didn't have anything breakable in there," David said. Eddie righted the suitcase and pulled it towards the Yukon.

"Nah, just laundry. Where's Josh?"

"Hopefully fixing up your room for you and not playing War Worlds on the computer with his friends," David said.

"I can fix my own room. Knowing Josh, he's already on the computer. How are you doing, Dad?"

"Me? I'm fine."

"Yeah, right. What's this about a test you have to take?"

"I'll tell you all about it when we get home."

Almost as soon as Alex marched into the family room, he was exchanging insults with Josh, wrestling with Eddie, and making his father laugh. It is so good to have Alex home again, David thought as Alex finally untangled himself from the wrestling match with both Josh and Eddie piled on top of him. How Cathy would have loved to see the boys getting along so well!

The younger boys let their brother retreat to the mudroom where he'd left his luggage. Alex pulled his case straight into the laundry room. David wandered in to see what Alex was doing, only to find his oldest son dumping the entire contents of the rolling suitcase into the washing machine.

"Don't tell me you brought home only dirty socks!" David exclaimed as another dirty sock tumbled to the floor. Alex picked it up and stuffed it into the machine, slamming the lid down. "Don't you want to separate any of that out?"

"Nah, I never do." Alex poured what looked like half a bottle of detergent into the dispenser tray. "You want me to wash anything for you? I can do the wash while I'm home."

David eyed the red sweatshirt in among the white socks and shook his head. "No thanks. Pink doesn't look good on me."

"Pink? What do you mean?" Alex pushed the tray into the machine, poked the beeping buttons, and set the machine for a normal cycle. Water gurgled in the taps.

"Nothing. Aunt Eva did the laundry this week, so I think we're set for a few days at least. It's good to have you home, Alex. I've missed you."

Alex smiled at his father. "I've missed you too, Dad."

Alex settled back into his own bedroom while David inspected Josh's handiwork in the bathroom. Josh had done a fair job of straightening up, even scrubbing the whiskers, dirt and shaving cream from the sink. David found the clean towels stacked neatly in the linen closet where Eva's staff had left them, and he handed them to Josh, who slung them haphazardly over the bars.

"You've got to fold them. Like this." David showed his son how to arrange the towels neatly.

"Why bother when he's just going to take a shower and use it anyway?"

"Honestly, Josh? I don't know. But it's what your mother would have done, and what she used to do all the time, so I just got into the habit of doing it too."

"Women are neater than men, aren't they, Dad?" Josh tried his best to even out the towels under his father's scrutiny.

"I wouldn't say that, necessarily," David said. "I'm neater than your Uncle Con, for instance. I'd fold my clothes and put them away even when I was a teenager; Uncle Con would just throw everything in a jumble on the floor. It used to drive your grandmother to distraction."

"Uncle Con is so different from you," Josh mused as they stepped out of the bathroom and headed together downstairs. "You and Aunt Eva are a lot alike, but Uncle Con is different."

"How so?"

Josh shrugged. "Well, it's like your laundry story," he said as he thudded down the stairs. "You'd hang up your shirts, right? Because, I don't know, you wanted to look nice for a girl, or to go to work or something."

"And I hate to iron."

"Yeah, that too. Okay, but Uncle Con? He'd dump his shirts in a big pile, pull out something wrinkly, then complain because it was wrinkled, like someone should just do it for him. He's always like that, like he wants what everyone else has but he's never willing to, I don't know, do something to get it. You know what I mean?"

David thought of math problems and homework at the kitchen table, of comic books tucked between textbooks and Con's assurances that he always got away with it. "Yeah, I know what you mean. And it's true, Josh. Very true. But your Uncle Con is a good man. He's got a kind heart, deep down, and he's really smart."

"I know that, Dad. I'm just saying he's not like you and Aunt Eva … and Grandpa. Not at all."

Dinner was actually edible, and while it would never pass as haute cuisine, Cathy would have approved. David managed to cook the steak without burning it and to bake the frozen French fries properly. The peas came out of a can, so he didn't ruin those, and the boys said it was the best meal they'd had in weeks. Alex, Josh and Eddie decided to go into the yard to play ball, so David scrubbed the broiler pan and cleaned the kitchen himself. He sprinkled scouring powder on the bottom of the charred pan just as the doorbell chimed.

He rinsed his hands quickly, wiped them with a dish towel, and hurried to the front door. He peered through the windows flanking the arched doorway to see who was calling on them on a Saturday evening. There standing on the front steps was a woman wearing a white sundress splashed with orange and pink daisies. She was so thin the bones of her shoulder blades stuck out from under the dress as if she wore a coat hanger tucked under her clothes. Matching pink sandals and tote bag completed the outfit. Her eyes were shaded by white rimmed sunglasses with huge lenses, and her flame-red hair was piled into a messy top knot. Chunky turquoise bracelets and tiered turquoise earrings completed her outfit.

Ah, David thought as he opened the front door, *this must be the reliable, responsible housekeeper they sent to care for my boys. I'm going to kill Eva for sending me to this agency. If they think I'm going to leave my kid with this nut job. She looks like a cross between Cindy Lauper and Lady Gaga.*

"Mr. Majek?" Turquoise Daniels removed her sunglasses and smiled. Deep sapphire blue eyes met his. Her smile crinkled the corners of her eyes, as if she smiled frequently. She held out her right hand and shook his firmly before he could respond. "I'm Turquoise Daniels."

"Please, call me David." He stepped back. "Come in."

"And I'm Turque." She pronounced it "turkey." He laughed.

"Yeah, I know," she grinned, stepping into the foyer and hefting her hot pink tote bag back on her shoulder. "My parents got creative with my name. You have to admit, though, it's memorable."

"That it is. Let's sit in the living room, Miss Daniels – I mean, Turque."

He led the way into the formal living room. Turque admired the soaring ceilings, the windows topped with colorful stained glass. Sunlight streamed through the red, gold and sapphire panes, touching Cathy's piano with streaks of watery color. The seating area in front of the fireplace was bathed in early evening light. Turque immediately gravitated towards the table nearest the family room door. She studied the group of family photos.

"If you'll excuse me, I was just finishing the dishes," David waved the striped dish towel in her general direction. "I'll just put this away, and then we can talk. Please make yourself at home."

"Would you like some help?" Turque asked as she picked up a photo in a silver frame. It was the last group photo of the entire family, taken at Easter a few months before Cathy was killed. David and Cathy stood on the top step in front of the house, while Eddie, Alex and Josh stood in front of them. Con had taken the picture, and he'd done a wonderful job capturing the moment.

"No, thank you," David said. He hurried into the kitchen to hang up the towel. When he returned, Turque had replaced the photo and seated herself on the burgundy sofa facing the piano. He sank onto the sofa opposite her, the coffee table between them.

"You have a lovely home," she said, nodding towards the dining room and soaring stairs ascending to the second floor. "It's warm and inviting. Not what I expected for a Brookville businessman and his family. Most of your type go for sleek chrome and technology everywhere, but this...this isn't a house. It's a home."

"My wife would have been pleased by your analysis. She grew up not far from here, and her home was like this, too. But I know what you mean about the chrome and gadget types. That's not who we are." He plucked a thread from the dishtowel off of his slacks, dropping it to the carpet.

Turquoise cleared her throat. "Jen at the agency said you're a widower. I'm sorry."

"Thank you." He crossed his arms over his chest and studied her for a moment. "You're not what I expected."

She threw back her head and laughed, the turquoise chandelier earrings flashing in the light. "I'm never what anyone expects, Mr. Majek."

"David, please."

"David, then." She fumbled in her oversized tote bag, pulling out a hot pink plastic folder from which she extracted a sheaf of ivory colored paper. Handing it to David, she said, "This is my resume, but I assume the agency gave you at least the highlights?"

"I think so, but why don't you tell me a little about yourself?" He let the resume sit on the table between them. Whenever he interviewed job candidates at Majek Investments, he preferred to listen first and review resumes later. Resumes could be fudged to reflect only the best about a person, but people rarely had the energy to hide their true personalities for long during an interview.

"Well, my name is Turquoise Daniels, and I'm divorced," she said. "I have twin girls, Elizabeth and Emily. They're eleven, the same age as your youngest child, I believe?" He nodded.

"I'm originally from New Jersey, but I moved to New York City to attend the Culinary Institute of America. That's where I went to college. I worked as a chef at Gray, the big restaurant at Columbus

Circle in Manhattan, but then I met and fell in love with Barry
Richter. Do you know Barry?"

"The name is familiar," David said with some surprise. "He's
a hedge fund manager, isn't he? I think I've crossed paths with him at
some function or another."

"Probably. He used to attend all the swanky gatherings, the
charity balls and such. Personally, and no offense if that's your thing,
but I couldn't be bothered with them. I'd rather be catering them than
dancing at them."

"They're not my thing, either," David said. "But when you're
in the business, you have to go to a certain number of them. It's
expected. It's where your clients are, and when you buy tickets to
support their favorite charity, they remember you when it comes time
to invest."

"I know. That's what Barry said all the time. Anyway, I gave
up my chef career and became the dutiful society wife. It wasn't until
I was pregnant with the twins and on bed rest that I learned that Barry
was cheating on me. So I gave him the boot, and started catering all
those swanky parties..." She hesitated. "You're probably wondering
why I'm telling you that part."

"A little, yes."

"Well, I know from researching you online that you're CEO
of Majek Investments. Your father, if I may say so, is a legend."

David smiled. "Indeed. He's quite a character."

"I thought you might need some help entertaining, too,"
Turque said. "I wanted to point out that I'm equally as comfortable
caring for your home and family as I am catering a party for 200 of
your top investors. I can do it all."

"What happened after you opened the catering business,
Turque?" It was starting to become easier to call her Turque even
though he kept picturing a Thanksgiving turkey on the table.

"It did well until the market crash," Turque said. "My clientele were all Barry's colleagues and friends. Most of them started losing their fortunes, however, when the housing bubble burst. I saw the writing on the wall and sold my company quickly to a rival catering firm. I did well on the sale, but I need to work. So I started working with Excelsior Housekeeping."

"Tell me about your last housekeeping job."

"I was working for Brian and Donna DeMartino," Turque said. "The printing company guy?"

"Never heard of him, but continue."

"He owns a chain of quick copy shops around the tristate area. Very wealthy but showy, new money, if you know what I mean? I mean, not to offend you or anything," she rushed in, correcting her mistake. "I know that you're sort of new money too, right?"

"My father was an immigrant with $2 to his name when he came into the United States," David said. "So yes, compared to some of the North Shore families, we're new money."

"But you're not flashy new money."

"No. I know what you mean. My wife was from old money, as they say, and she liked the good life but not the flash. I was raised with frugal parents; even though they became wealthy, my father still lives in the same house we grew up in, a modest little house in Queens, New York. We don't like fancy cars or boats or whatever."

"Right. That's what I mean. They did. They liked to entertain....and so I acted as their housekeeper for the past five years."

"What were your duties?"

"Managing their entire household," Turque said, crossing her legs and primly tugging the hem of her skirt over her knees. "Donna – Mrs. DeMartino – hated anything to do with housekeeping. So I did all the meal planning, the shopping, the cooking, cleaning, laundry. I scheduled maintenance men to do things like paint the house, and I supervised the gardeners. This was for two houses, mind you – they have a house in Oyster Bay and a house in the Hamptons."

"I see. Well, your duties here would be similar. Daily meal preparation, cleaning, laundry, errands, and watching my children until I get home. Making appointments for them and driving my youngest boy to the doctor, dentist, haircut appointments and what not. You have a car?"

"Yes, and I did the same for the DeMartino family. I like that kind of work."

"Did they have children?"

"Two sons, yes, but grown."

"So your child care experience is limited to your own children?"

"Please," Turque rolled her eyes heavenward. "I have twins. Double trouble. I have twice the experience most mothers get."

David chuckled. "Yes, I see." Well, perhaps she wasn't so bad, David thought as he studied her across the coffee table. Her odd outfit aside, she seemed to be genuine. If she was hard working and diligent, she might just do.

"You have a fine family," Turque said, gesturing towards the table of photographs. "Your wife was beautiful. When did she pass?"

"Last November, just before Thanksgiving."

"If I may ask...?"

"Hit and run accident," David said.

Turque nodded.

"She was walking across the parking lot by the Rose Diner and struck by a black SUV. That's all we know. She was killed instantly."

"I'm so sorry. Right before the holidays...that's hard."

"It is what it is," David said quietly. "But the fact remains that I need a housekeeper. My hours can be irregular, and your days may be long as a result. I'd like you to begin at eight and end around six.

Can you stay later if you have to? I'll pay you well for your time, but I need someone reliable with my son after school this fall."

"I can do those hours, but with one request."

"Yes?"

"My daughters," Turquoise said. "My neighbor watches them for me from three, when the school bus drops them off, until five when she has to leave for work. If you want me here until six, I'd have to pick my daughters up from school and keep them here with me until I leave. They're good kids, David, and we'll respect your privacy and your home."

"I see...I think it will work," he said. He couldn't believe what he was saying. What was wrong with him? He blushed, glancing away from Turque towards Cathy's piano. *I've gone from not wanting a stranger in my house to welcoming this woman and two little girls I've never met.* "Maybe they could play with Eddie."

"Maybe," Turque said. "Kids tend to get along better than adults. Eddie...he's your deaf kid, right?" She said it so bluntly and easily that it didn't feel like an insult.

"Yes, he's deaf. He was born that way – birth defect. His entire inner ear is missing on both sides. The normal organs that you and I have to hear never developed in him when Cathy was carrying him. No one knows why. He gets along quite well among both hearing and deaf people, though, and he says he likes being deaf."

"Wow," Turque said, her eyes brightening. "He sounds like an interesting kid."

"He is. He loves animals, and anything in nature...he's really a budding scientist. He wants to be a veterinarian."

"Can a deaf kid become a veterinarian?"

"There are a handful of deaf veterinarians in the country, so it's possible," David said. "Anything is possible. The deaf are just like you and me; he just communicates with his hands and his eyes instead of his mouth. Some days, when my middle boy starts mouthing off at me like teenagers do, I appreciate Eddie's quiet!"

Turque laughed that throaty, deep and free laugh again. Pink suffused her cheeks and she gestured again towards the photos. "Tell me about your other children."

"Alexander is the oldest, and he's home for a visit now. I'll have you meet everyone before you leave. The boys are in the yard playing baseball."

"How old is Alex?"

"He's twenty-three," David said. "He's in medical school. He's training to be a psychiatrist."

"A shrink? Wow! And the other boy?"

"Joshua, age sixteen for another couple of weeks. He's finishing his junior year in high school. He's smart, but unfocused. Popular, but doesn't have much direction. Art and baseball are his only passions, and I'm not sure how he's going to parlay any of that into a college major, but we'll see."

"And the woman in the photos...not your wife, I can clearly see the resemblance between Eddie and your wife...the woman with the crazy curly hair? She looks familiar."

"My sister, Eva," David smiled. "She's the owner of White Glove Maid Service."

"Oh right! I've met her a few times. I've used her cleaning company before when I worked for the DiMartinos. And the other two men? I see your father, I think – that has to be your father. He has the look of the lion about him."

"My father, yes. Tibor Majek. The other man standing next to Eva is my brother, Constantine."

"He looks a little...lost."

"He wasn't looking at the camera."

"No, I don't mean that. I mean...he doesn't have the look of lions that you have, that your father and sister have. All three of you are, I don't know. Visionaries? Leaders?" He found himself blushing and looked away. Turque rose from her seat and walked slowly over to the table with the photos, plucking the one with the Majek siblings and their father from the rear of the table and scrutinizing the composition. "You've all got a look like you're going somewhere and damn the torpedoes. Even smiling, even relaxed here, you've got the hungry look. I know that look. Barry had that look and his friends have that look. It's the look of people who succeed. Your brother looks like a nice guy, don't get me wrong, but he's got a softer look about him. A little lost. A little too kind. I don't know.... I'm sorry if I ramble on. I shouldn't say anything." Abruptly, she plunked the picture back onto the table, making a hollow clang as the frame hit the wooden top.

"No, no, it's all right. It's fascinating, actually. I've never thought of it that way before. Con resembles my mother more than either Eva or myself. My mom was short, and Eva inherited her height – or lack of height – from my mother. Eva and I have our dad's dark hair, and I got the waves and she got the curls. But Con gets that soft, misty look from my mom." David cleared his throat. He had made up his mind about Turque, but it was time to get on with the formalities. He picked up the resume and read through it; as he suspected, it was all top level stuff, and he nodded, mentally ticking off her credentials. "Right. Let's meet the kids, and then we can discuss when you start."

"You mean I'm hired?"

"You're hired," David nodded. "I'll work out the salary arrangements with the agency, add on a bonus for working longer hours, and yes, your twins can come here. They can play in the family room or in the yard, and they're welcome anywhere on the first floor. If they get along with Eddie, they can play with him."

"That sounds wonderful. David..." Turque hesitated. "One more request. Please."

"Yes?"

"The piano." Turquoise gestured to Cathy's instrument. "My youngest daughter, Emily, hopes to be a professional musician someday. It would be helpful if she could practice here when I'm working."

David started to say no, but something held him back. He took a deep breath, his gaze resting on the mahogany baby grand. He remembered traveling into Manhattan to purchase the piano. Rachmaninoff had practiced on it when he traveled into New York City. He and Cathy had just brought the Brookville home, and he had just been promoted to senior vice president of Majek Investments. Josh had been born that summer, and life seemed complete with his growing family and career. It was time for celebration, and he surprised Cathy with the fine instrument. It had been her pride and joy. He'd sworn on the day she died that he would never let anyone play it as long as he lived. Now, however, as he looked back at Turquoise waiting expectantly, and as he thought about shadows and Chopin, watchers and waiting, he swallowed hard. Perhaps he had been too hasty. Life was, after all, meant for the living.

"Yes, I suppose so," he finally said. "But it's a very expensive instrument. And rare. And it was my wife's. I don't want her to, you know, bang on it. Ruin it. If she's gentle with it..."

"She'll treat it with the respect a fine instrument deserves. I promise."

"Very well. It's probably out of tune."

"I can take care of that when you're ready."

"All right, then. It's a deal." David rose from the couch. "Follow me. I'll show you through the first floor and if I can round up the boys, I'll introduce you."

"Thank you," Turque said. She followed him past the stairs, to the dining room and the kitchen beyond.

13

"You spent what on a *what*?" Constantine's horrified exclamation made Eva laugh so hard she choked on her cigarette smoke.

"A turtle," David said mildly. "A red-eared slider, to be exact."

"Not just any turtle," Eva coughed. "It's Teeny."

"Oh, sure," Con smirked. "That makes all the difference."

The three Majek siblings stood on the back stoop of David's home on Sunday afternoon, leaning on the wrought iron railing and watching the boys play ball with their grandfather in the backyard. Of course, it was a rather slow game with the ninety-year old Tibor pitching, but the boys laughed and catcalled as if they were playing for high stakes, and Tibor loved it. He pitched underhanded to Eddie, who sent the softball sailing over the garage with a crack of the bat.

"Watch it!" David called as Eddie ran the bases and Josh ran around Con's Escalade parked nearest the garage. "You're going to break a window on your uncle's car!"

"Don't worry, Dad!" Alex called. "I'll tell Ed to aim to the right."

Eva blew smoke from her Marlboro away from her brothers. Con coughed and waved a hand delicately in front of his face. "Oh come on, Con. Those clubs you go to must get pretty smoky. Don't tell me you don't get more second hand smoke from a weekend of bar hopping than you do from me."

"Will you two stop squabbling?" David intervened. He turned to Con. "Yes, I spent that much on turtle supplies. I'll thank you not to judge. If you had kids, you'd do the same."

"You could just buy him a new one if that one croaked."

"You said that before. I'll say it again: Eva's goldfish."

"Goldy!" Eva cried, tapping her cigarette ash over the railing on the back stoop.

"Oh Eva, get over it," Con snapped.

"She's only teasing you," David said. "Come on, Con, relax. You're a little uptight today."

"Yeah, Con." Eva eyed her brother over the haze of smoke. "Why are you being even more of a jerk today than usual?"

"Shut up."

"Will you two stop it?" David sighed. "It's Sunday. Dad brought homemade blackberry wine. Let's have some before dinner."

"Dinner should be almost done." Eva ground out her cigarette butt under the heel of her boot before ducking into the kitchen.

The front doorbell pealed over the crack of the bat and Josh's yells. David frowned.

"Who could that be?" Con asked

"Maybe one of the boys' friends," David said. "Eva? Can you get that?"

"I'm on it!"

David leaned over the railing and smiled as his father pretended to throw the softball to Alex, then threw to Josh instead.

Eddie slid into home base, a garbage can lid on the grass. His brothers raised their arms in triumph for him, giving him the thumbs' up sign.

David smiled. But Con frowned. His eyes narrowed as he watched the boys. "Con, lighten up. Eva just jerks your chain. She's always liked to tease you. You want some wine?"

"Dad's homemade hooch? Sure."

David and Con stepped into the kitchen where the mouth-watering smell of roasting beef wafted through the house. David pulled the jug of homemade wine from the refrigerator as Con reached into the upper cabinet shelves for wine glasses.

"Con, are you sure you're okay?"

"I'm fine."

A man's voice rumbled from the entrance hallway. "I'm sorry to bother David on a Sunday like this..."

"It's no bother, really. I'm sure he won't mind. Mr...?"

"Scalia. Victor Scalia."

David fumbled with the wine jug, almost dropping it onto the granite countertop.

"Are you okay?" Con asked him.

"Yeah, the bottle is just slippery from condensation," David said. "Excuse me a moment while I see who it is."

David reached the dining room. Eva led Victor through the foyer and into the dining room. Victor nodded to David before turning back to Eva.

"And you're David's sister? I've heard so much about you."

"Yes, I'm Eva. It's nice to meet you." She smiled and held out her right hand to the investigator.

Con suddenly appeared in the dining room right behind David. "Hello!" He pushed past his brother, strode forward and held out his hand. "I'm Constantine Majek. Don't I know you from somewhere?"

"Hi, Constantine. I'm Victor Scalia. Yes, we met at the office on Friday."

"Right!" Con studied Victor. "Why are you here on a Sunday?"

"Con!" Eva admonished. She turned back to Victor. "I'm sorry for my brother's manners. Con, let's leave them alone." She grabbed Con by the upper arm as if escorting him to a cotillion, and steered him back to the kitchen. "Come on, Con. You can pour me a glass of Papa's wine while David and Victor talk."

"No, that's all right, Eva," Victor smiled easily at Con. "I'm here to see your brother."

"On a Sunday? About work matters? Can't it wait until tomorrow?"

"If it could wait, I would have waited."

"Thank you for stopping by," David said to Victor. "Will you excuse me for a moment?"

"Certainly, David."

"Please wait for me in the living room. It's to the right of the foyer."

"I can find my way." Victor sauntered from the dining room past the foyer and into the living room.

David strode into the kitchen and stood in front of his brother. Eva shook her head at Con and turned to check the roast.

"Okay, Con, why are you acting like a jackass?" David demanded. "You were a little rude to Victor just now."

"Why do you put up with employees like this who just drop by, unannounced, on a Sunday? If I were head of the firm, I wouldn't let him get away with this."

"But you're not head of the firm," David said. "And it's my house, and I don't mind, so why are you behaving like this?"

Con frowned and folded his arms across his chest. Eva closed the oven door with a bang.

"Eva, will you decant the wine, please?" David asked.

Eva straightened and put her hands on her hips. "I will, if Con tells me why he's acting like a paranoid nut job."

"Why are you so chummy with this guy, Victor? You've known Neil a lot longer, and he doesn't stop by on a Sunday."

"Why is this any of your business?"

"Guys..." Eva held up her hand like a traffic cop, stepping forward as if to get between them. David and Con glared at her, and she stepped back. "Okay, okay. But while you two fight about this, your guest is waiting in the living room, and I've got a roast that's almost done. Can you get on with it?"

"Victor lives in Oyster Bay," David lied. Con nodded. "I asked him to drop by to finish a discussion we were having on Friday. No, Con, I won't tell you what it's about. Yes, you are my senior vice president, and a Majek, but no, you don't need to know every detail of my business dealings. Dad didn't tell me everything when I was senior vice president, and I don't feel the need to tell you everything, either."

"Papa never kept anything from you, and you know it."

"Papa did as he saw fit, and now I do as I see fit. Back off, Constantine."

"Do I hear my name?" The screen door opened, and Tibor stepped through, wiping a yellowed handkerchief over his perspiring brow. Con dropped his gaze from David's unflinching stare. David watched as Con turned to fuss over their father.

"Dad, are you okay? You didn't over exert yourself, did you?" Con reached out to touch his father on the shoulder.

Tibor waved him away like a pesky fly. "I am fine," he huffed. "Just tired, that is all. It is warm out there. I came in for a glass of tea."

"It's in the refrigerator, Papa," Eva said. "I'll get you some tea."

Tibor's eyes sparkled when he saw the jug of wine sweating on the counter. "Perhaps something stronger would be like medicine."

"Perhaps tea first, then medicine," Eva chided, bustling to the cupboard for a glass.

The boys pounded through the back door behind their grandfather, Eddie in the lead, followed by Alex and Josh. Eddie's cheeks were flushed with victory. Eddie dumped his baseball bat and ball in the mudroom. Josh tossed his catcher's mitt with expert ease into the corner, where it landed in its accustomed spot and called, "Grandpa, are you okay?"

"I am fine. I just need to sit for a while and drink some tea. Or wine. Yes, wine would be good. Constantine, would you pour, please?"

"Tea first," Eva said sternly.

"Victor is here, Papa," David said pointedly. Con glared at his brother, then turned his gaze to his father.

"Victor?" Tibor asked in surprise. He pulled out a kitchen chair and sat down heavily, wiping his forehead again. "Look at me, like an old man. I cannot even toss a ball to my grandson without feeling ancient."

Ice rattled as Eva poured a glass of sweet tea. She handed it to her father. He wiped his brow again and gulped the beverage.

"You're ninety," Con chided as he wrestled with the screw cap on the wine jug. "You shouldn't be running around in this heat."

"It is only May. Not so hot. My papa lived to be one-hundred and one years old, and he only grew feeble at age ninety-nine," Tibor said. "I have nine more years of health, by my calculations. More if I drink that wine." The hint given, Eva accepted the empty tea glass and held it out to Con for a refill with wine.

"Need any help with that, Con?" She cocked and eyebrow at her brother and pointed to the jug.

Con snapped, "No, I do not need your help opening a screw top." The cap suddenly gave way and flipped high into the air, where Eva reached out and caught it. David laughed, and even Con smiled.

"Excuse me, then, everyone," David said. "Let me speak with Victor before Eva's roast is ruined."

"How did you find this guy, Papa?" Con asked. "David said you were the one who found him for the firm."

"I did," Tibor said, nodding. He stuffed his handkerchief in his pocket while Con poured a glass of wine for his father. "He came recommended from my former senior vice president. Do you remember him, Constantine?"

"Peter Krug? Yes, I remember him, Dad."

David hurried to the living room. Victor stood by the table of family photographs, studying the array of candid portraits.

"Seems as if my arrival caused a problem for you. I'm sorry."

David shrugged. "It's fine. Papa will hold Constantine's curiosity at bay. He's always been able to handle Con better than any of us. But this must be important if you're here on a Sunday, Victor."

"It is," Victor nodded. "Is there somewhere we can go to speak in private where we won't be disturbed?"

"The family room." David pointed through the arched doorway. "Follow me."

David drew the rarely used pocket doors that closed the family room from the living room. He gestured towards the couch, and Victor sat down. David pulled the chair from in front of his desk into the center of the room and swiveled it around so that they could sit face to face.

Victor said, "I believe I found Cathy's missing cell phone. At least I believe it's her phone. It matches the description that you gave to the police of the make and model."

David sat very still. "Where?"

"In the parking lot by the Rose Diner. It must have skidded out from her purse and slid into an open storm drain. The storm drain leads into a shallow ditch behind the diner, a sort of open dry well. It was wedged into the drain. It's dirty and didn't work, but I turned it over to the police. They will probably call you any minute now, but I wanted you to hear the news from me first."

"I'm grateful for your help. Do you think they can get anything from it?"

"My contact in the police department said that their forensic unit would look at it, but it's doubtful they can do anything with it. They'll probably have to send it to the state crime lab, or the FBI, to have experts examine it."

"Would money help move things along?"

Victor paused. He dropped his gaze to the floor and drummed his fingers on his knee. "You're paying me quite enough, David. I can't work any faster."

"No, no, not you. I mean for your contacts at the FBI lab. If I offer a bonus or something – either openly or under the table – would that speed things along? Is there a private laboratory that can handle it more quickly? If so, I will pay for them to outsource it to the private laboratory. I'm just saying that if money will solve this quickly, it is at your disposal. You just need to say how much is needed and where it should be sent."

Victor nodded. "I see. Yes, there may be ways we can get this done faster. I'm curious, though. Why the sudden urgency?"

David bit his lower lip and looked out the window to the dogwood tree in the garden. "I'm not sure," he said finally. "Just a hunch that things are coming to a head. It's been six months since Cathy died, and I keep feeling like it's urgent that we find the truth. Whatever I can do to help this along, I'll do."

"I'll get back to you." Victor stood and held out his hand to David.

They shook. David asked, "Will you stay for dinner?"

"Dinner?" Victor blinked.

"Yes. We're having Sunday dinner, and we have plenty of food. Eva, my sister, is a wonderful cook. She made extra just in case Constantine's girlfriend could come to dinner today, but Lisa couldn't make it, so we have plenty. I just thought it would give you time to get to know us all, so to speak, and maybe ask a few questions.... surreptitiously, of course."

"But if it's a family dinner...I don't want to impose."

"It is, but we used to...that is, before my wife was killed...well, Cathy would often invite people to stop by for Sunday dinner. Her brother would come, or neighbors like Mrs. Jenkins, or friends of hers from the neighborhood. We would sometimes start with just family and end up with quite a crowd gathered around the piano by the time dessert was served. The only one who will wonder why you're here is Con, but he's been acting strangely all day, and I don't particularly care what he thinks. Please stay."

Victor hesitated. "Con is on my list of people to investigate more thoroughly, David. This will give me a chance to watch him more carefully."

"Then stay. A home-cooked meal, some company, and some detective work."

"I haven't had a home-cooked family dinner in ages. I'd really appreciate it."

"Good." David nodded. "Join us in the dining room, then. Eva said that dinner is almost done."

The standing rib roast was indeed done, and it waited on a large wooden cutting board on the counter for David to carve. Eva placed baked potatoes into a shallow bowl and passed them to Eddie, who carried them to the table. He stopped in surprise at the sight of his father and Victor, but nodded politely before putting the bowl onto the dining room table.

"Victor, this is my youngest son, Edward, called Eddie. Eddie is deaf, and speaks American Sign Language. He reads lips a little, but not much yet."

David signed to Eddie to introduce them, and Eddie held out his hand to shake Victor's. Victor smiled and said "Hello," as if greeting a colleague, which pleased David. Many people were immediately uncomfortable around his son's disability, and Eddie sensed it. Like most deaf children, he hated being treated differently, as if he were stupid just because he couldn't hear. Some grownups unconsciously raised their voices or even shouted at him when they learned he was deaf, and while he couldn't hear them, of course, he could see by the straining cords in their necks that they were shouting, and it annoyed him to no end. Victor handled the introduction with just the right touch.

Josh entered next, carrying the salt and pepper and the butter dish. "Oh, hey. Company."

"Victor, this is my middle son, Joshua. Josh, this is Mr. Scalia from my office. He's alone tonight so I invited him to join us for dinner."

"Cool! Just like we used to do!" Josh said. He pointed to the seat at the end of the table closet to the kitchen on the long side. "My mom used to love to have friends join us for dinner. This will be fun. We have an extra place already set, Mr. Scalia. Please make yourself at home. Can I get you a glass of wine? Iced tea?"

"Iced tea will be fine, thank you." Josh hurried off to the kitchen.

Victor looked at David. "Your children have wonderful manners, David."

"Thank Cathy for that. She insisted on civilizing the savages."

Alex and Tibor entered next, Tibor leaning a little on Alex's arm while his grandson fussed over him. "Really, Grandpa, you should let us know when you feel tired. We could have come inside if you weren't feeling well."

"No, no. It is fine. Ah, Victor. Good to see you." The men shook hands, and David introduced Alex.

Con and Eva entered last, Con carrying the roast, Eva carrying a basket of rolls and a bowl of carrots. "All set," she called. "Everyone here? Good. Did you boys wash your hands?"

Alex rolled his eyes, and Eva amended her question. "Joshua, did you and Eddie wash your hands? The future doctor over there insists I am asking him stupid questions."

"It's just that I'm twenty-three years old, Aunt Eva, not three."

"You may be twenty-three, Doctor Majek, but I used to babysit you, so I will forever remind you to wash your hands, scrub behind your ears, and eat your peas. Sit down." Alex gave his aunt a quick hug before sliding into his seat between his father and uncle.

David carved the roast, then brought it to the table. He stepped behind the row of chairs to the head of the table and glanced with pleasure over the full dining room. It felt less lonely with Cathy's place at the table filled by Victor.

Eva left the dining room and returned with the iced tea and Tibor's homemade blackberry wine, now poured into an acceptably elegant Waterford crystal decanter. She slid into the end chair nearest the kitchen so she could easily get up for a forgotten item. Conversation rose into a babble of happy, excited voices. "Did you see Eddie's home run hit? He's going to be great on the school team if he tries out."

"Still no idea which college you want to apply to, Josh? You know, you need to decide soon. You can always start with an undeclared major and then figure out what you want to do."

"Aw, Uncle Con, I know, but it's so hard to decide. I really don't want to stay home, but I don't want a party school, either."

"Where are your friends going?"

Voices rose from David's right. Tibor waved his knife in the air for emphasis at some remark Alex made from across the table. David took a slice of beef, then called, "Papa!" to get his father's attention. Tibor dropped his knife and took the platter.

"I still say I am right."

"Of course you are, Grandpa."

"You are humoring me."

"Of course I am, Grandpa."

"Bah!" But Tibor smiled good naturedly at his eldest grandson. He forked a hefty slice of rare beef onto his plate before passing the platter to Eddie. Eddie took a small slice, then handed the platter off to Josh, seated to his right.

"I haven't had a home-cooked meal in months," Victor confessed to Eva as he passed the rolls to her. "This smells delicious. You must be a marvelous cook."

"I try," she smiled.

"She is!" Josh interjected.

"That's a long time to go without home cooking," Eva said to Victor. "What do you eat?"

Victor shrugged. Con studied Victor carefully as he cut his roast beef into small pieces on his plate. "Mostly frozen dinners. Sometimes I eat out. It's hard to cook when you're single."

"Bachelor?"

"Yup. Never married. And you?"

"Always a bridesmaid, never a bride," Eva replied lightly.

David glanced around the table. Everyone had filled their plates. He cleared his throat. "Victor, we pray before meals...please join us if you wish, but if you don't want to...no worries..."

"I'm good with that."

David grasped hands with Alex and his father, and soon an unbroken chain around the table linked family and guest alike. He bowed his head. "Let us pray."

Sparrows chattered in the rhododendron outside the open dining room window. David paused, cleared his throat, and said "Lord, we thank you for the food we are about to eat. Thank you for our health, and thank you for our family and friends. We ask your blessing on our day and on the coming week, that we may be helpful to our fellow men and women, kind to all we meet, and a witness to your love to the world. We ask this through Christ our Lord. Amen."

"Amen!" came the hearty response from everyone but Victor and Constantine. Victor glanced at his dinner companion as Con slipped his hand from Victor's. Victor realized he was holding Eva's hand a little longer than necessary and slid his hand from hers quickly, but not before Eva blushed. David noted Con's angry glare towards Victor. He frowned, chewed his meat, and waited.

"So what brings you to us on a Sunday, Victor?" Con asked.

"David asked me to drop by," Victor said easily. "We started discussing the prospectus for the Triad Fund on Friday, but didn't come to consensus on the opening materials. I mentioned to David that I would be passing by Brookville this weekend, and he suggested that if I had time, I should stop by to continue our talk from Friday."

Con raised his eyebrow. "Oh? I didn't see any papers. Or did you just remember everything you wanted to discuss?"

"I have an excellent memory." Victor held Con's gaze until Con looked away.

"My but you're a busybody today, Con," Eva teased. She took a sip of iced tea, watching her middle brother carefully over the rim of the glass. "Why the sudden interest in David's business?"

"Well," Con said, "His business is my business, you know. As senior vice president of the firm, I need to know what's going on."

"If you need to know, David will tell you," Tibor said. "As I did with him. It is how it is done."

"Only because that's how you both want it done."

David shrugged. "Honestly, Con, it's no big deal. You know most everything that I do."

"Well..." Mollified, Con reached for a dinner roll. "I suppose so."

"How's Eddie's turtle doing?" Eva asked. She didn't sign the question to Eddie, who was looking down at his plate while he ate; he would not be able to see her signing.

Josh answered. "Okay, I guess. Dad helped him set up the fancy heat lamp yesterday, and the thing was eating some of the new lettuce they bought, so I guess it's a success. How long does it take for a turtle to get better?"

"Dr. Donahue said it could take a while," David admitted. "It's too soon to tell. Soft shell disease is really hard to cure."

"Does Eddie know that?" Con asked. "I mean, after all this fuss, won't he be devastated if the turtle does die?"

"The opposite, I should think," David said after finishing his baked potato. "At least this way, he knows we did all we could to save the creature."

They continued eating, talking, and laughing as the Sunday afternoon lingered in a golden springtime glow. Tibor's home-brewed wine packed quite a punch, and after one glass, David felt mellow and sleepy, while Con grew more talkative. He listened to snatches of the conversation from the far end of the table. Con spoke softly with Alex about his studies and about a new girl Alex was seeing, a fellow medical student named Martha Tanner. David realized by Alex's sparkling eyes that his son was in love. He waxed poetic about Martha's compassion with the cardiac patients she cared for her, her intelligence...

"And is she beautiful?" David knew what the answer would be, of course.

David's cell phone rang. "Excuse me." He turned away slightly from the dinner table. "Hello?"

"David Majek?"

"Yes?"

"This is Lt. Halloran from the 5th Precinct," the man on the other end identified himself. "Am I calling at a bad time?"

Conversation around the dinner table stopped abruptly as David said, "No, Lieutenant, this is fine. What can I do for you?"

"I'm one of the homicide detectives at the 5th Precinct, and I wanted to call to inform you that your wife's cell phone has been found."

David met Victor's gaze across the table. The gesture wasn't lost on Con, who glanced suspiciously between the two men.

"What is it?" Tibor demanded. "David? What is wrong?"

David held up his hand for silence until he was finished. "I see, Lieutenant. Where was it found?"

"Oddly enough, it was still in the parking lot of the Rose Diner," Halloran said. "The private investigator that you hired found it there. It was inside a storm drain behind the diner. We surmise that it must have fallen from your wife's purse when she was struck by the vehicle. Then it either bounced or slid across the lot and into the drain under the curb. There's no grill over the drain. Storm water must have washed it back through the pipes and into the dry well at the rear of the store."

"You're lucky that drain doesn't empty into a sewer system," David said."

"Yeah, or into Oyster Bay," Halloran said.

"Have you found anything helpful on it? Is it even still working after all this time?"

"No, and I wouldn't expect it to," Halloran said. David heard the rustle of papers on the other end of the phone. "The display was cracked, the battery corroded from rainwater. We're sending it to the state forensics lab first to see what they can get off of it."

"What are you hoping to get from her cell phone that you can't get off of the record of calls, Lieutenant?"

Was it his imagination or did Con stiffen, ever so slightly? David glanced at his brother, but Con pushed around a carrot on his plate as if fascinated by the glistening trail the butter sauce made on the china.

"We've always worked under the suspicion that Cathy was meeting someone at the Rose Diner that day," Halloran said. "We checked your home phone records again when we found the cell phone, and there were no calls home that day except a call from St. Mary's School for the Deaf. I followed up with the school nurse, who confirmed from her log book that she had called your wife that day to discuss something, but couldn't remember what it was. She's checking her records, but in the meantime, we are hoping to find a text message that may indicate why your wife was in the parking lot that day."

"She texted with the boys all the time. I'm afraid there's going to be a lot of 'I need a ride home from baseball practice' kind of texts."

"That's fine. We'll sort through them, but that's if we can get to them. For now, keep your fingers crossed that the state lab boys will have better luck than our department here."

"Thank you, Lieutenant. Am I to assume that you're handling Cathy's case now?"

"I am. And I'm treating her death as suspicious. Going over the case records from last fall, I'm not satisfied that the original team looked into every lead. They treated it like a simple hit and run, but there are a lot of questions in my mind about it."

"Mine too. I'm glad you're on the case now."

"I'll let you know when we get an answer from the state lab."

"Very good. Thank you."

David slowly punched the end call button on his phone and lowered it to the snowy tablecloth. He raised his gaze to see seven silent people staring at him.

"The police found Cathy's cell phone," he said and signed. Eva bit her lip and looked away, while Alex started at his plate and Josh mumbled something. Eddie nodded.

"Where, Dad?" Alex asked.

"In the storm drain behind the diner."

"Does it work? How did it get there?" Alex demanded

"It probably fell out of her purse when she was struck by the Escalade," Con muttered, and look away.

"Yes," David nodded. "They think it fell out of her purse when she was struck. Anyway, the phone is in bad shape, and it doesn't work, so they're sending it to the state forensic laboratory to see if they can get it working again."

"Why?" Josh asked.

"To see if they can figure out why she was there that day," David replied. "If someone contacted her to meet here there, the phone might hold a record of who that person is. I've always thought that someone knows more than they're saying."

An enormous crash erupted from the living room, so loud that the vibrations shuddered through the table and stemware in the china cabinet rattled. David leaped to his feet, thrusting his napkin onto the table, while Victor, Con, Eva, Alex and Josh also tumbled to their feet. Eddie glanced about to see why the adults were running from the room.

What? Eddie signed.

Alex replied, *Big noise from the living room.*

Eddie just shrugged and turned back to his dinner.

"What was that?" Tibor demanded.

"It sounded like a picture fell off the wall!" Josh cried. He ran into the living room, glancing wildly at the walls.

"No, it was more from the front of the house!" Eva shouted.

"I know that sound," David replied. "I think it came from the piano."

He strode to the elegant instrument dappled by late afternoon sunlight streaming through the windows. David fumbled with the latch on the right side of the lid, then raised the hinged lid open as far as it could go, pulling the stem up from the base to hold the lid in place. A fat steel and copper string lay curled on the sound board as if ready to lash at them.

"Holy crow," Alex muttered as Eva, Josh, Victor and Con crowded around the piano.

David lifted the keyboard covered and spidered his long fingers over the keys, running an unpracticed scale from the deepest bass notes up. When he reached the F# just below middle C, he depressed the key, and the felt-covered hammer inside the soundboard struck air.

"How much tension is on those strings?" Eva asked. "It sounded like a gunshot."

"How did you know it was a string, Dad?" Josh asked.

"Because I've heard this before." He blinked, his mind racing.

"What makes strings break like that?" Victor asked.

"Tension, usually." David recalled what Cathy had taught him over the years about her instrument. "It's unusual, but not unheard of. Cathy had a string break in the middle of a performance when she was in graduate school. I was at that performance...that's how I knew what the sound was." He slid the keyboard cover down and moved to the side of the instrument to replace the soundboard lid.

"Mom had a string break in the middle of a performance?" Josh asked. "What do they do when that happens?"

"They waited until a break in the piece she was playing, then paused the concert while they rolled out a new piano from one of the practice rooms," David said. "It was upsetting for your mom; she said it broke her concentration. But she was the consummate professional, so she just smiled, bowed and went right back to playing."

David remembered that concert as if it was yesterday. He'd brought her favorite flowers, a dozen pink American Beauty roses. They'd dated six months, and he'd fallen madly in love with the red-haired musician. He couldn't believe his good fortune that the gorgeous girl he'd spilled coffee on six months before, this shimmering creature wearing a sapphire blue ball gown and playing Debussy and Ravel on a grand piano in the Tisch School of the Arts, was actually laughing at his jokes, slipping her hand into his, falling into his arms at night. Warmth suffused his chest, and he blinked back a tear at the memory as he closed the piano lid gently.

"Come on, let's finish dinner."

Alex had already returned to the dining room and signed to Eddie what had caused the vibration and noise. Eddie nodded and continued to eat, while Tibor waited expectantly.

"Everything all right?"

"Mom's piano acted up, that's all," Josh said. "Boy oh boy, that was loud."

Constantine slid back into his place. His gaze darted back into the living room and he paled. Everyone else began eating again, talking about the horrible noise the broken string made. David watched them silently as he mentally replayed the conversation just before the string broke.

It was when I said someone had been there, and wasn't talking, he thought uneasily. Glancing down at his now lukewarm dinner, he realized the string that broke was the F# – *Just like the Chopin piece at the college campus. It all points back to the afternoon she died. It's as if someone is trying to tell me something.*

"What do we do about it?" Alex asked his father. David blinked and looked up.

"Do?"

"About the piano. Can it be fixed?"

"Yes, it can. I'll take care of it eventually."

Constantine's cell phone shrilled. "Excuse me." Con pushed his chair back while reaching for the phone in his front pocket. "Hello?" He paused, standing by his chair. "I'm sorry. Yes, I can be there. Where? Okay, I know where that is." He clicked off and turned apologetically to everyone at the table.

"I'm sorry, but I've got to go. My girlfriend just called. Her car broke down on the Northern State Parkway."

"Is she okay?" Eva asked.

"She was able to coast to the shoulder, and she's waiting for a tow truck, but she needs to get to work on time. I'm going to have to leave now."

"But you'll miss dessert!" Josh said. His uncle had brought a chocolate seven-layer cake from the bakery. Missing that was like missing Christmas to Joshua.

"I know, Josh, but I've got to go. It can't be helped."

David stood and walked his brother to the back door, while the rest of the family and Victor spoke quietly about the phone call from the police. "Call me if you need someone to go out there, too," David said. "And be careful – the parkway is crazy on a Sunday afternoon."

"I'll be fine."

"Thanks for coming, Con. See you tomorrow at work."

"Bye, David. Tell Eva dinner was excellent."

As Con backed his SUV out of the driveway, David stood and watched from the back stoop. Something nagged at him, tugged at his memory, a sharp tug when he glanced at his brother's car. Then the tug ceased, and David shrugged and turned back to finish his meal with his family. *If it's important, it will come to me,* David thought as the screen door closed behind him.

14

"No, you can't have any, Dad." Alex folded his arms across his chest, planted his feet a shoulder's width apart, and waited.

"Don't stand between me and the coffee maker first thing in the morning, Alex. It's dangerous."

"Dad, it's going to screw up your test results. I'm a doctor. I know these things."

"This is truly cruel and unusual punishment."

"It's necessary for your health."

"Damn these tests," David snapped. "I have half a mind to cancel right now."

"They'll charge you a cancellation fee."

David stared at his son.

"Sorry. Forgot I'm talking to Mr. Money Bags. Well, if getting hit with a cancellation fee doesn't mean anything to you, then think about this: you'll leave us all orphans."

"You'll manage."

"We'll live with Aunt Eva and develop lung cancer from secondary smoke."

"Alex...."

"Better still, we'll all move in with Uncle Con and become rich playboys, with an endless parade of women..."

"Okay, okay!"

"...and we'll gamble away our inheritance at those nightclubs he likes to go to..."

"You win! I'll go!" David gave the coffee pot one last, longing look.

"It's only for a few hours, Dad." Alex reached out and touched his father's shoulder. "And I'll be there."

"What?"

"I'm coming with you." Alex poured himself a cup of coffee. David eyed the brimming cup hungrily. "You're terrible with medical things, Dad. Half the time you tune the doctors out, and the other half you're shouting at them like Grandpa."

"I do not shout like Grandpa." David scowled.

"On occasion, better than Grandpa." Alex took a sip and nodded. "Yes, better than Grandpa. So I'm going to go with you, help you fill out your forms, and listen while the doctors explain the results so that later on, when you have a million questions, someone is around to answer them."

David sighed heavily, shaking his head. "How did I end up with you boys? How?"

"Mom." Alex smiled.

"You're all tough as nails, too."

"Oh, that we get from Grandpa."

David laughed.

Someone rapped swiftly on the back door. "Hello!" Turquoise called from the back stoop. David unlocked the back door for her. "I hope I'm not too early." She bustled past him, wearing a smile and white-rimmed plastic sunglasses pushed back on her head. Today she'd chosen a wide turquoise silk bandana which she tied around her hair, blue Keds and a denim sundress adorned with embroidered cherries. Alex gaped openly at her as she sailed into the kitchen, plunking her bulging pink leather tote bag on the countertop, with her silver bracelets jingling. She held out her hand to Alex. "Hi Alex. We met briefly the other day. I'm Turquoise, the new housekeeper. You can call me Turque."

"Hi." Alex shook her hand. "Yup, I'm Alex."

"The oldest, if I remember correctly?"

"Yes, ma'am."

David reached for his suit coat, which he had tossed over the back of a kitchen chair. He shrugged it on and tugged the hem down to smooth out the wrinkles. "How late can you stay today, Turquoise?"

Turquoise leaned over and brushed lint from the charcoal worsted wool jacket with her palm. "If you don't mind my girls waiting here with me, as I mentioned to you about how they might need to do after school, I can stay until seven. But I have to leave around two-thirty to pick them up from school. When does Eddie's bus drop him off?"

"Usually around three-thirty. He gets dropped off in front of the house. The driver waits until he sees an adult greet the him, then drives off, so someone has to be here. Josh has been here for the most part, or my sister, but it will be a relief to have you here."

"That's fine, then. I can be back in time to meet him at the bus. Don't worry about a thing, David."

Eddie pounded around the corner and skidded to a stop when he saw the stranger in the kitchen. He looked questioningly at his father, and David signed, This is Mrs. Daniels. She will be our new housekeeper. You met her the other day, remember?

Eddie nodded, eyeing Turquoise warily. She held out her hand to him. "Hi, Eddie. Remember me? I'm Turquoise."

He looked at his father, who signed her name. *She wants you to call her Turquoise.*

Why?

That's her first name.

Eddie just shook his head. David glanced at the clock. "Damn, we're already late. Alex, did Eddie eat breakfast yet?"

"No, not yet." Alex dumped the remainder of his coffee into the sink and rinsed his cup.

"I'll fix him breakfast," Turquoise said smoothly. "What does he like to eat?"

"Anything. Captain Crunch is his favorite cereal. Bowls are over there, cereal – "

"I'll figure it out," Turquoise smiled. "I've got it under control, Mr. Majek. Go and finish what you need to do to before work."

"Make sure he takes his vitamin," David called over his shoulder as Alex hurried him through the kitchen towards the mudroom. "They're in the cabinet."

"I'll find them. Good luck with your test, David."

David paused in the mudroom and watched as Turquoise swiftly brought a cereal bowl to the table, holding it up to Eddie and communicating easily without ASL.

"You ready to go, Dad?" Alex asked.

"Ready as I'll ever be."

Eddie waved from the kitchen table and signed, *Hope you get an A or whatever.*

David smiled at his youngest. *Me too,* he replied.

David leaned over the sink in the patient restroom at the cardiologist's office, splashing his face and chest with water. He grabbed a fistful of paper towels from the wall dispenser and wiped at the gooey gel on his chest where the electrodes for the EKG had been attached. As he raised his arm, he noticed red lines etched into his bicep from the blood pressure cuff. "Told the damn nurse it was too tight," he muttered as he shrugged into his t-shirt and reached for his Oxford button-down.

"Dad? Are you okay?"

"I'm fine, Alex. I'll be out in a minute."

"Joan is on the phone. She says it's urgent."

The nurses had insisted he leave his cell phone in the reception area with Alex while he underwent the treadmill stress test. Parting from it had been like walking out of the house in his underwear; he felt naked and vulnerable. David tugged open the door and motioned his son in. "Okay, come in."

Alex entered and handed him the phone, shut the door behind him. "Joan?"

"David, we have a situation."

"What's the problem?

"I'm so sorry to bother you, and I hope I didn't disrupt the test, but I've got six angry Saudis in the reception area and I don't know what to do."

"Hang on for a second, will you, Joan?" He slipped on his trousers, buckled his belt, and tied his shoes. Throwing open the bathroom door, he pressed the cell phone between his left ear and shoulder as he strode back into the exam room where the cardiologist and nurse were conversing quietly with Alex.

"Whoa, slow down. Six angry Saudis? As in Saudi Arabians?" Alex met his father's eyes across the room. "Can you wait a minute? The doctor needs to speak with me."

Dr. D'Angelo pressed his lips together in a thin line. "Mr. Majek, I must insist that you put that cell phone away. There are patients other than yourself, you know...your selfishness might ruin their tests."

"Dr. D'Angelo, please," Alex interjected. "My father doesn't use his cell phone for fun, I assure you. This is urgent."

"So are the other patients' stress tests."

David rolled his eyes at the trio facing him across the exam room. "Joan, I'll call you back as soon as I leave this infernal place. I promise."

"Please, David." He had never heard her sound so panicked. With growing alarm, he clicked off the phone and snapped it back into his belt holster.

"What, Dr. D'Angelo? I have a situation brewing here. Are we done yet?"

"Mr. Majek, your doctor will review your complete test results with you and discuss your next steps, but I wanted to give you preliminary results immediately."

"Go ahead. I'm listening."

"I'm not sure I have your full attention. You keep glancing at your cell phone."

"I have an emergency situation at work, Doctor."

"You have an emergency here, Mr. Majek." Alex stiffened. "I don't mean to scare you, but you must take this seriously."

"I thought everything was fine." David folded his arms across his chest and waited.

"No, it's not. We stopped the test early not because your heart was fine but because it's not. Your test results indicate a potentially life-threatening condition, Mr. Majek," the doctor said.

"So what are you telling me?"

"I'm telling you, Mr. Majek, that you're a heart attack waiting to happen. You need further tests, but I believe your condition is urgent."

"What tests?"

"Tests to measure the precise amount of blockage in your arteries."

"How do you know I have blocked arteries?"

"By your test results," Dr. D'Angelo said. "My best guess is at least two, if not three, are completely blocked. You'll need to have this taken care of immediately, Mr. Majek."

"I can't," David said. He pulled out his cell phone. "I've got a situation brewing at work; I've got three children without a mother, and two hundred employees on both coasts depending on me for their paychecks. Will you take care of all of this while I'm getting tested, doctor?"

"Mr. Majek, I don't think you understand the seriousness of the situation."

"I'm well aware of it, Dr. D'Angelo. My mother dropped dead of a massive coronary around this age. Trust me, I'm aware of it." David turned away and walked towards the door.

Dr. D'Angelo seemed taken aback by David's abruptness, but Alex said quietly, "I'm a physician, doctor. I can go over them with my father and make sure he does what he needs to do."

"Any signs of a heart attack, he must go the emergency room immediately," Dr. D'Angelo said. "Chest pain, shortness of breath, pain in the arms, pain in the jaw, nausea. Take any symptom seriously, Mr. Majek. If you don't, none of what you just said will matter, because you'll be dead."

"Enough!" David snapped. "I'll handle this in my own way. Alex, can you schedule any of my follow up appointments or what not while I take this call?"

"Yes, Dad. I'll meet you in the parking lot by the car."

David stalked from the exam room and slammed the door behind him. He strode through the corridors in the testing facility towards the reception area, barely pausing to hold the door for a nurse heading into the reception area to call on the next patient. Once in the hallway of the medical building, he yanked his cell phone from his belt and punched Joan's number into the device. She answered before the first ring finished.

"Thank God," she said. "I hated to call you but I didn't know what else to do."

"What the hell is going on?" David barked as he took the stairs down to the parking lot two at a time. He didn't stop until he reached the exit door. Outside, he leaned against the brick wall in the shadow of a hedge, and listened to his pounding heart.

"Constantine had an eight o'clock breakfast meeting scheduled at the Garden City Hotel this morning with six Saudi Arabian investors," Joan said. "But he never showed up. The group waited until ten, and when he didn't arrive or call, they showed up here. They're furious.

"I can't find Constantine anywhere! He's not answering his cell phone, your father hasn't seen him and neither has Eva. I waited to call you, but I don't know what to do. The Saudis are threatening to pull all their money out of Majek Investments if someone doesn't meet with them today before they head back to the Middle East. And by someone, they want the boss, David. They have a 3 o'clock flight out of Kennedy."

"Which means they have to leave our offices at one, the latest."

"Right."

"I can be there in half an hour," David promised. "Order refreshments for them – tea, juices, whatever they want. Set up in my office. Make them feel comfortable. Get Neil down to sit with them until I get there. Tell them Neil is third in the company after myself and Constantine. Can you look at Con's appointment calendar and see why he was meeting with them?"

"There's nothing in his calendar about the contents of the meeting, David, just the date and time. The men say they were meeting with him to review their investments. David, I looked their files up on the computer. They have over two hundred million invested with us!" David glanced back at the door as Alex exited the building holding a sheaf of papers. Alex clicked the car doors open, and David slid into the passenger seat of the Yukon, allowing his son to drive him to the office.

"Pull their investment files," David said. "Print them and have them at the front reception desk. I'll take a minute in the elevator to look at them. Keep them in my office until I can get there."

"Dad, you really should go and get this next test done now." Alex bit his lower lip and waited for his father's response.

"I can't, Alex. I have to get to the office as soon as possible."

"Dad, this is really serious. You may need to get stents put in – today."

"Alex, I'm not going to the hospital and I'm not going for the next test. I lived with this yesterday and I will live with it today. Call the hospital, tell them I will come in next week. All right?"

"Dad..."

"No buts, Alex. Do it."

"Not while I'm driving."

"Fine. After we get to the office." David turned his attention back to Joan while pointing to the road and waggling his finger for Alex to go faster. Alex just shook his head as he turned the Yukon out of the medical office lot and headed towards the parkway.

"Nothing at all in his appointment calendar?" David demanded as Alex threaded through the parkway traffic.

"Nothing!" Joan said. "What shall I do?"

"Stall them." David glanced at the traffic and made an educated guess. "I'll be there in twenty minutes."

He clicked off the cell phone and leaned against the car window, sighing heavily. David slammed his palm against his knee. "Damn that brother of mine."

"What's going on?"

"Uncle Con didn't show up for an important meeting this morning, and now I have to handle it."

"Can't Joan find him?"

"He's not answering his cell phone, and Grandpa and Aunt Eva haven't heard from him since he left our house yesterday."

Alex threaded between the traffic. "That's weird. Has Uncle Con ever done something like this before?"

"No." David tapped his foot and stared at the traffic. Where could Con be? "What did he say yesterday – his girlfriend had car trouble?"

"Yeah, the call during dinner. The girlfriend said her car broke down or something and asked him to pick her up. He sure ran out in a hurry."

"He did." David picked up his cell phone again and hit his brother's number on speed dial. The phone rang six times, then dropped into standard voice mail. Frustrated, he disconnected Con's number, and rang his sister.

Eva answered her cell on the second ring. "White Glove Maid Service, Eva speaking."

"Eva? It's David."

"Hey! What's up? How did your test go this morning?"

"I've gotten better news, but that's not why I'm calling. It's Con, Eva. Have you spoken to him since last night?"

"Con?" Eva sounded puzzled. "No, I haven't seen or spoken to him since he rushed out from dinner to pick up his latest bed warmer. Why, what's going on?"

"He seems to be missing." David fumed. "He didn't show up for an important meeting with several foreign investors this morning, and neither Joan nor I can reach him. I don't even know where to start. Do you have the number for that girlfriend of his?"

"Phone number? Are you kidding me? Con hasn't even introduced me yet. Did you try Papa?"

"He's my next call."

"Okay, then. I'm not sure where to call next. Hospitals? The police?"

"If he was in an accident or something, wouldn't they call one of us?"

"They should...Majek isn't that common a name. But it can take them a couple of hours to call family. The son of one of the women who works for me was in a car accident and it took the Emergency Room four hours to call her. By the time she got to the hospital, her kid was already out of surgery."

David nodded. "All right. Can you call the local hospitals while I try Papa?"

"Sure. David, take a deep breath. You sound like Papa when he's about to explode. I'm sure there has to be a logical explanation for this."

"I hope so." David was about to say goodbye when something else occurred to him. "Eva? One more thing. Do you have a key to Con's house?"

"A key? No, I don't clean for him anymore."

"I was hoping I could just let myself in to check on him."

"Sorry, I don't have a key anymore. Can you ask his landlord?"

"I can try." David took a deep breath. "I may sound pissed, but I'm worried, Eva. This isn't like him."

"No, it's not. He can be a jerk, but he's usually a responsible jerk, and he wouldn't neglect a business meeting. Was there a lot of money riding on it?"

"I think so."

"He definitely wouldn't forget it, then. We'll find him, David."

"Okay. I'll call Papa, you call the hospitals. Talk to you later."

He dialed his father just as Alex exited the parkway and drove on the back roads to the Mitchell Field Office Park. David pictured his father's ancient rotary phone ringing. It rang six times before Tibor picked up.

"Yes?"

"Papa? It's David."

"David! What is wrong?"

"Papa, it's important," David urged. "Have you seen Constantine since last night?"

"Constantine? No, not since he left the dinner."

"If he calls you, will you have him call me, please?"

"Certainly. But what is it, my son? What troubles you?"

"He didn't show up for a meeting with investors today."

He heard his father's muffled curse. "Do you need my help?"

"Papa..."

"I come."

"No, Papa. I need your help finding Constantine. Can you call him in an hour? I'll be tied up with these investors. Maybe he'll speak with you if he's checking his phone. I'm just worried about him. This isn't like him at all." Whatever Constantine's faults, David thought as Alex turned into the parking lot by the Majek Investment building, he takes his work quite seriously. He would never simply not show up for a meeting. Especially not with this much riding on it.

"David, can you call the police? What if he is hurt?"

"I don't know if the police will do anything yet, Papa. I'm not sure what to do. Eva is calling the hospitals."

"Victor will know what to do. He was police, yes?"

"Victor! I'd forgotten about him! Yes, I will ask for his help." David unbuckled his seat belt and fumbled in the rear passenger seat for his briefcase and laptop. "Do you have a key to Constantine's apartment?"

"No. I thought Eva did?"

"No, she said she doesn't have a key anymore. I was hoping I could just get into his apartment to check on him. What if he's ill? What if he's hurt?"

"Drive there and see," Tibor urged. "If we cannot find him in a few hours, drive there and see."

"I will, or I'll send someone. Thanks, Papa."

"Let me know if you find him, David. I am worried now, too."

Alex turned to his father, "I can drive to Uncle Con's apartment and check on him."

"Alex, I won't ask you to do that."

"I've got to come back here anyway and pick you up later," Alex shrugged. "And I don't have much else planned today. Dad, you need to follow up on these medical appointments, too."

"I will. I promise. But for now, I've got to go entertain six very rich men who invested a small nation's income in our business and find my brother."

"Let me help," Alex urged. "I'll go. We can update one another by phone."

"All right, Alex. Thank you. Do you have Uncle Con's address?" David read it from his cell phone and Alex programmed it into the GPS.

"Okay, Dad. I've got the GPS to guide me and I've got the address. I'll call you no matter what I find, good or bad."

"Thanks, Alex."

"Dad? Take care of yourself."

"I will. When this is over!"

David strode through the doors of Majek Investments and grabbed the file folder that Gail, the front desk receptionist, waved at him as he hurried in. He stepped onto the elevator and flipped through the folder, scanning the documents. There wasn't much time. Breathe, he told himself, hoping he didn't look too disheveled. Between the stress test earlier, no coffee, Constantine missing and now this, he felt like he's run a marathon and climbed Mount Everest all in one morning.

He spied the six businessmen through the glass doors of the executive suite. Joan hovered nearby, holding a Queen Anne silver tea pot as if she were hosting an afternoon bridge party. David pushed open the glass doors and stepped forward. The first of the Saudis stood, lips pressed firmly, and held out a rigid hand to him. David shook it, mumbled apologies and moving to the next man, listening with half an ear to the introductions.

"Gentlemen? I'm sorry for being late. Please come into my office."

"We were just about to leave," the first man said. "We do not have much time."

"I understand. Please step into my office, and we can conduct business as quickly as possible."

David quickly tapped in his security code and showed the men into his office. Muttering among themselves, they took seats on the sofas while Joan tidied up the refreshments on the credenza. "Thank you," David said.

She nodded and offered more tea to the men, which they declined. Taking her cue, she exited the suite, closing the door firmly behind her. David thought he detected a little sigh of relief, but it was probably his imagination.

He placed his briefcase and laptop behind his desk and turned his full attention to the guests. Arrayed in the room before him were six of some of the wealthiest clients his brother dealt with. But he had no clue why Constantine had scheduled this meeting.

This is going to get interesting, David thought, pressing his palms together and calmly surveying his guests.

"Gentlemen." He stood before his guests and nodded. "How can Majek Investments help you today?"

The six Saudis left in a black stretch limousine Joan ordered for them. David watched from the windows of his office until the last trace of exhaust fumes blew away in the May afternoon. He slumped against the window frame, letting his cheek rest against the cool glass. Joan touched him on the shoulder.

"David? Are you all right?"

"Any word from Constantine?" His only thought was of his brother. Con had left a two hundred million deal on the table when he'd missed this meeting. The Saudis were eager to invest in several new funds offered by Majek Investments, and at the conclusion of their meeting, had asked David specifically to manage their investment in a new proprietary account he would establish for them. He planned to assign several of his senior fund managers to the daily tasks, but he would oversee it. Con had missed out on a considerable commission. His morning's rushed meeting had earned him several millions in fees, and the firm even more. Con never left money like that on the table.

"No. His planner and calendar all indicated he intended to be at this meeting today."

"Has Eva or my father called?"

"No, no one from your family has called."

"Where can he be?" David stared across the glittering asphalt towards the fountain in the office park as if he could peer into the distance and find his brother by sheer willpower.

"I don't know, David. We've tried everything. What shall I do?"

"Cancel the rest of his meetings for today, I suppose, and take messages until we figure out what to do. Any emergencies, direct them to Jack Noble until Con turns up or I can figure out who will take his accounts temporarily."

"All right."

"Can you send Victor in here, please? The new man working on the Triad Fund communications materials?"

"Yes, certainly." Joan hesitated. "Have you eaten anything yet today?"

David realized part of his exhaustion was hunger–and the headache seething behind his temples from lack of caffeine. "Oh Good Lord, no. Alex played caffeine cop with me this morning before my medical test. Coffee, coffee, stat."

"Yes, sir." Joan finally smiled. "How did your test go this morning?"

He turned away from the window, walking towards his desk. Without looking at her, he slid his laptop from his bag and clicked it into the first port on his desk. "Oh, you know these doctors. They always find something," he said without taking his eyes off his computer,

"Is it serious?"

"Nothing I can't handle."

"David..."

"Joan, just get Victor, please."

"Your health is important, David."

"Joan, just get Victor."

The phone in the reception area shrilled, and Joan hurried out to answer it. David logged into his computer, and while his emails downloaded, he collected his voice mail messages. Alex had called several times, asking him to call back. David quickly punched in his son's number on the speed dial.

Alex answered on the first ring. "Dad?"

"Have you found Uncle Con?"

"No," Alex said. "I spoke with his landlord, who said his car has been gone since yesterday. The landlord wouldn't let me into his apartment, but I looked through the window. There was a gap in the curtains and although the room was dark, it looked empty. Doesn't look like he's in there. What should I do now?"

"Do you have any plans?"

"No, not really. I was going to pick you up later when you need a ride home."

"Can you swing by the house first and check on the new housekeeper? Mrs. Daniels?"

"Turquoise, right? Love that name. Yeah, sure."

"I just don't feel comfortable leaving her alone the whole day, and it's her first time with Eddie. She doesn't speak ASL."

"Oh Dad, you worry too much. Aunt Eva knows her, right?"

"Yes but not well. I mean, they're not friends or anything, just business acquaintances. Can you just keep an eye on things at home so I don't have to worry about them?"

"Sure." Alex cleared his throat. "Speaking about worry, Uncle Jim called me."

Two messages on his voice mail had been from Jim Bjork, but he'd ignored those. "Surprise, surprise."

"Dad, he's worried about you. Those test results weren't good. You really need to keep that hospital appointment."

"What else did Uncle Jim say?"

Alex hesitated. "He said you probably need either a stent or bypass surgery. He's really, really worried about you, Dad. I am too. Please don't put this off. You really can't."

"Alex, I won't, I promise, but today I've got to find Uncle Con. In order for me to take time off from the firm, I need Con here at the helm. Until I find him, I can't so much as blink. I don't have time." His emails were still downloading. When the counter reached over seven hundred, he turned off the monitor so he wouldn't punch it.

"Dad, promise me."

"I promise," David said, and he meant it. "I'll finish up these stupid appointments and call Uncle Jim when I find Constantine. Okay?"

"Okay. Call me when you need a ride home, okay?"

"Thanks, son."

"Love you Dad. And we'll talk later about the stress test results and what they might mean, okay? It's important that you understand everything before you talk to Uncle Jim, and you already sound like you're just going to yell at him."

David grunted. "Yeah, sure."

"Dad...."

Joan knocked on the door, a sheaf of takeout menus in her hand. She waved them at David and placed them on the edge of his desk. "We can discuss it later, Alex. In the meantime, if you hear anything at all from your uncle, let me know, please."

"Right away, Dad. I promise."

It was past one, and David's stomach rumbled angrily as he scanned the menus. Joan waited. "My stomach says cheeseburger and fries; my conscience says salad."

"Go with your conscience."

"Okay. Diet coke, I guess, and a chicken Cesar salad. And coffee. Where is my coffee?"

"Coming up."

"Get that damned tea pot out of here. What did you serve them, cat piss?"

"Chamomile tea. They don't drink caffeine."

"Dear God, how do they live?" He flicked on the computer monitor. "Shit. Can you take any of these emails for me?"

"Yes, I'll go through them first and leave only the urgent ones for you."

"Thanks, Joan."

Joan rushed out as Victor hurried in. "Shut the door behind you."

Victor shut the door and hurried to the visitor's chair in front of David's desk. "Word in the cubicles is that your brother is AWOL today. The whole company is buzzing about it."

"News travels fast."

Victor nodded.

David leaned back in his chair and asked the investigator point blank, "Victor, what did you think of my brother? Give me an honest answer. Forget he's my brother. He's just an employee as part of this conversation now. What did you think?"

Victor didn't hesitate. "I think he's hiding something. And I think he's on something –drugs, booze, not sure. I didn't smell anything on him, but his hands were shaking during dinner last night, especially right after the piano made that God awful crash."

David nodded. "I think so, too. Do you think he's in trouble?"

"Some people in the office think he's skipped town." Victor paused. "But I'd say it's just gossip. Do you think it's possible?"

"He didn't show up for a meeting that would have netted him personally several million dollars in commissions, and he didn't even call me. That's not like him at all. I'm worried. Alex drove to his condo, and he never came home last night, or at least that's what we think. I'm rather at a loss right now as to what to do. Neither Eva nor my father has heard from him. Eva is calling the local hospitals. She hasn't called me, so I assume she didn't find him. He's not answering his cell phone. Is there anything we can do, Victor?"

Victor frowned. "Call the police."

"I thought you had to wait twenty-four hours or something to file a missing person's report?"

"That's a myth. If you have cause to worry, file a report. Worse thing that will happen is that Con will show up and you have to call the police back and tell them it was a misunderstanding."

"All right. I'll call the police." He reached for the phone, but Victor's next question stopped him.

"What does your gut say about this, David? You asked for my opinion and I gave it. Now I want yours. I watched you and Con interact yesterday. There's tension there, mostly on his side. What's your gut say about his disappearing act?

David closed his eyes. For an instant, he saw Con as they were as children. Con, furtively hiding comic books inside his textbooks. Con, swiping extra candy from their mother's hidden stash of chocolates, then fluffing out the remainders in the bag to make it look like none were missing. "We can buy Eva another goldfish. She'll never know." He sighed, opened his eyes, and met Victor's gaze.

"I think he's in some kind of trouble." Victor waited. "A few days ago, he asked me for a raise. I said no, then changed my mind and offered him a personal loan...but he said no again. He seems to be having some kind of money trouble, and I can't figure out why."

"Word among the staff is that his behavior has been erratic lately. Some days he's on the ball, other days he's furtive and secretive. Spends a lot of time with that fellow, Jack Noble."

David thought of Con's decision to put Jack on camera representing the firm. "He seems to favor Jack quite a bit."

"Shall I look into him, too?"

"Yes, but make Con a priority." David reached for the phone. "Just call the police? 911 or the precinct?"

"Call the precinct. Fifth precinct, Nassau County. Tell them you want someone to check on your brother because he didn't show up for work this morning."

"Thanks, Victor."

"David?" Victor pushed back the visitor's chair and rose to his feet. "Your brother is hiding something. I'll get to the bottom of it, but it may be difficult for you."

"I know, Victor." David took a deep breath. "Sometimes, the truth hurts."

"Hurts?" Victor snorted. "Sometimes it's a bitch. But you've got to know the truth. You've got too much at stake."

David thought of his children, his father, and the two hundred or so people depending on a paycheck from Majek Investments. He thought of Cathy, and memories crowded his mind.

He nodded. "I know," he said softly, dialing Joan's number so she could connect him to the police station. "Believe me, Victor, I know."

15

Alex knocked at his office door at six and peered through the doorway. David glanced bleary-eyed at his son. "Oh. Is it five already?"

"It's a little after six. I just passed Joan on the way out. Are you ready to go?"

"Yes, I'll take this with me." David saved the report he was reading and shut down his computer. He gathered his briefcase and tucked the laptop in a separate bag. After locking his office door, he followed Alex down to the parking lot.

"I wish Constantine would call," David muttered.

"Maybe he can't." Alex threaded the SUV through the traffic on Northern Boulevard.

"That's what I'm worried about."

"Did you call Uncle Jim back?"

"No. I've had a little too much on my mind today. I'll call Jim tomorrow."

"Please, Dad. It's important."

"Alex..."

"All right, I won't nag."

"You already have."

Alex gripped the steering wheel but said nothing further until they reached the Majek home in Brookville. David did a double-take at the white Honda parked in the driveway until he recalled that Turquoise was working today.

"You checked on the new housekeeper this afternoon, didn't you?" he demanded as they reached the back steps.

"Yes, I did. And I didn't mention it to you because everything was fine."

David paused on the threshold. "She's really working out okay?"

"See for yourself." Alex held the door for him.

The house felt different as soon as he walked into the mudroom. David couldn't put his finger on why until he realized Turquoise had tackled the boys' mess and straightened out the tangle of winter coats and boots. Hockey and soccer gear sat in their respective corners, and the snarl of shovels behind the bag of ice melt now marched in an orderly row across the wall. A note on top of a pile of winter coats read: Take to dry cleaners.

"Oh boy," Alex marveled. "She's already got us organized."

"Hello?" David called as they walked into the kitchen. "Turquoise?"

The granite countertops gleamed. The sink sparkled. An empty drain board awaited freshly washed dishes. Pleasant scents of garlic, tomato sauce and chicken wafted from the oven. A large pot of water boiled on the back burner, and a box of spaghetti waited next to the stove. The oven timer ticked on the counter. A new daffodil-yellow tablecloth spread across the kitchen table, with places for four already set out. Turquoise had even found Cathy's stash of colorful napkin rings and placed rolled cloth napkins at each setting.

David simply stood and stared.

Turquoise appeared from the dining room. She wore a professional chef's apron over her clothing and rubbed her hands on a dish towel. "Welcome home, Mr. Majek – I mean, David."

"I can't believe how good the house looks, and I've only seen the mudroom and the kitchen," David said. "And dinner smells delicious. Thank you. You don't know how grateful I am for this after the day that I've had."

"I've got some chicken Parmesan in the oven. All I need to do is make the spaghetti. There's a salad. I forgot to ask, do you drink wine with dinner?"

"Yes," David said as Alex said, "No." David glared at his son.

"I'm not nagging you."

"Yeah, right. Only on Sundays, Turquoise." Alex nodded and walked ahead of his father out of the kitchen, heading upstairs. Turquoise winked at him and reached for the corkscrew.

"How did everything go today?" David asked.

"Fine," Turquoise replied. "Eddie and Josh went upstairs to do their homework. At least that's what they said they were doing. You know kids – they're probably texting their friends. But I didn't know how strict you are about homework being done after school, so I gave them a pass today. Let me know how you want me to handle it from now on."

David walked past the freshly waxed and gleaming dining room table. Turquoise's work would give Eva nothing to complain about, he thought with satisfaction. Even the rooms smelled good, a spicy mixture of roses, cinnamon and cloves. It was a familiar scent which had faded along with Cathy's presence in the home since last November.

"I changed the potpourri," Turquoise hurried after him. "There were unopened bags in the linen closet and the bowls in the living room were a bit dusty. I hope that was okay."

"I didn't even know we had potpourri," David admitted as he carried his briefcase to the family room. He dumped it on his office chair, loosened his tie and nodded with satisfaction at the list Turquoise had left on his desk.

"I meant to show that to you after you've eaten." Turquoise tapped the paper on his desk. "I didn't want to hit you with a lot of things as soon as you walked in the door. I figured you'd want to change, have a glass of wine, then we could go over anything from the day that needed to be reviewed before I left."

"No, I can look at it now. I expect you'll want to pick up your daughters soon."

"Thanks for remembering," she smiled. "This is the week's menu and shopping list. I noticed someone had gone grocery shopping recently, and of course Eva's cleaning is noticeable throughout the house. Her crews do a very thorough job. But I'd like to take those winter coats to the dry cleaners, and I thought you might have some suits or other things that needed cleaning. We should discuss setting up charge accounts or another payment method so I can run your errands for you."

David gave silent thanks for Eva's help finding this woman. "You're a treasure."

"I'm Turquoise," she said impishly, and he laughed.

"What system did you use with your previous employers?"

"They added me to their credit card accounts," Turquoise said. "Some set up cards just for me so they could keep a closer eye on my spending. Depends on how you feel about it."

"I trust you." He found to his own surprise that he did. "I'll arrange for a charge card just for you with bills sent directly to me. Until the card arrives, I'll write a check out to cash. Spend it as you need and leave the receipts in an envelope for me to review at the end of the week."

"That would be fine."

The timer chimed in the kitchen. David handed her the menu and the grocery list. "This looks fine, except that neither Eddie nor I will touch a Brussels sprout. Sorry."

"You'd be surprised at the magic I perform with Brussels sprouts."

"There's nothing that can convince me to try them again."

"Everything tastes better wrapped in bacon."

"Bacon...?" His stomach rumbled. "Well, perhaps."

She smiled with satisfaction. "Trust me. Even Eddie will eat at least one."

Sweeping the papers into her competent hands, she strode back to the kitchen, humming Queen's "Bohemian Rhapsody" under her breath. David shook his head and hurried upstairs to change.

Turquoise had opened the windows in the master suite, airing out the rooms while she cleaned. The curtains billowed in the soft evening breeze. David changed quickly. He pulled several bills from his wallet and slipped them into a plain envelope, leaving it propped on Cathy's dresser for Turquoise to pick up in the morning.

Downstairs in the family room, Turquoise regaled the boys with a story. Josh and Alex sprawled on the couch, with Alex translating for Eddie, who leaned against the couch, smiling as Turquoise finished her tale.

"...and then Trump ATE the garnish. I didn't have the heart to tell him I'd sprayed all that parsley with laundry starch to keep it fresh for the photo shoot. He said he liked the crunchy taste. He called it, and I quote, 'unique'." The boys burst out laughing.

"Did you cook for a lot of celebrities, Turquoise?" Josh asked.

"A few," she said. "But he took the cake. Literally. I think he ate the whole thing!" She spied David leaning against the doorway. "Oh, your father is here. Dinner's ready. If you'll please be seated, I can serve."

"There's no need," David protested as the boys scampered happily towards the kitchen. Chairs scraped on the tile floor as everyone slid into their places. David had barely slipped the ring from his napkin when Turquoise, with the practiced ease of a chef, drained the pasta and slid the pan of chicken onto a trivet. Sliced garlic bread cradled in a linen napkin and a basket followed in the blink of an eye, along with a bright yellow ceramic bowl filled with luscious greens and baby tomatoes.

"It's no trouble at all." Turquoise fished in the refrigerator door for the bottles of salad dressing and the iced tea pitcher. She slid a glass of red wine towards David.

"He shouldn't have that!" Alex protested.

David sipped the burgundy, recognizing it as a bottle from his own collection. "Wine is good for the heart, doctor," he said mildly.

"Hush now and eat," Turquoise admonished them. "I'll be in the family room. You can call me or ring for me when you're done and I'll clear and clean up." A tiny servant's bell appeared from her voluminous white purse on the counter. She tried to leave it on the table, but David pushed it back to her.

"Turquoise, you've done plenty today. The boys will clear and clean up."

"It's no trouble..." Turquoise left the bell on the kitchen counter next to the toaster.

"I want the boys to continue doing their assigned chores, and you need to go home to your own girls, Turquoise. I'll pay you for another full hour," David added as he realized it was close to seven p.m. "I'll call the agency tomorrow and make sure they bill me for a 12-hour day today. Really, you've done quite enough for one day. I don't know how I managed without you."

The boys ate the succulent chicken smothered in mozzarella and the al dente pasta as if they hadn't eaten in weeks. "Look at them," David said, pointing to the boys. "I haven't seen them eat like this since their mother last cooked for them. You really are a treasure, Turquoise."

"Did I pass the audition?" she teased.

"With flying colors," he said around a mouthful of the most succulent chicken he had ever tasted.

Turquoise lingered by the stove. She untied her apron and folded it into a square which she slid into her white tote bag. "Are you sure, David? It really isn't a bother for me to stay."

"Good night, and thank you, Turquoise."

She nodded, bade everyone good night, ruffled Eddie's hair on her way out, and left as they dug into second helpings.

"Can we keep her? Please?" Josh begged, and Eddie signed two thumbs up: *Yes!*

David sipped his wine and felt a small measure of contentment. "Are you kidding me? If she's this wonderful every day, I'm going to pay her double. She's worth every penny of it."

As they ate and the boys polished off every crumb of garlic bread, pasta and chicken, David's cell phone chimed. He glanced at the display and leaped to his feet, napkin tumbling to the floor and fork clinking to the table. "Dad?" Alex asked.

"It's Uncle Con. Excuse me, boys." He clicked on the phone as he jogged to the family room and slid behind his desk.

"Con?"

"Yeah, it's me." Con's voice sounded muffled. Background noise, like the roar of a crowd, made it difficult for David to hear him.

"Are you okay? What happened to you today?"

"Today? What about today?"

"Con, I can barely hear you. Can you move somewhere quieter?"

A minute later, Con's voice came clearly through the phone. "Sorry about that. Now what were you asking me?"

"Con, where were you today?"

"Today?" Con paused. "Oh, today? Sorry, did I miss something?"

"Sorry? Con, do you know how worried we were? I called the damned police on you!"

"I know. They just showed up at my condo, pounding on the door, doing something called a "welfare check." Sounds like I'm on government assistance or something." Con laughed.   "Are   you sure you're okay? You don't sound like yourself. What happened to you today? Why weren't you at work?"

"I was sick. Home with the flu."

"Why didn't you call?"

"Couldn't get out of the bathroom. You know, stomach flu."

"Bullshit. Alex went to your apartment and you weren't there. Papa called, Eva called, I called you, no answer. Where the hell were you?"

"Out....I just lost track of time, that's all."

"That's all? You had a meeting with six members of the Saudi royal family today. And you lost track of time?"

"Shit." Con exhaled loudly into the phone. "Shit and double shit. What happened?"

"What happened is that I rushed from the stupid cardiac stress back to the office to cover your meeting and felt like a complete ass while Alex, Eva, Joan and Dad all tried to track you down, that's what happened," David fumed. He slammed his open hand on top of the desk. Blood pounded in his temples. "Con, Eva was calling hospitals. We thought you'd been in a car accident or something. How can you be so calm about this?"

"If I had known..."

"If you had known? How can you not know your own schedule?"

"I just didn't, that's all."

Your brother is hiding something, David heard Victor say again. Damn right, David thought.

"Let's start at the beginning." David forced himself to take a deep breath. "You left here around three yesterday to pick up your girlfriend. She had car trouble. Con, I want to know the truth. Was that what really happened?"

"Yes, it was the truth. Lisa called and the timing belt on her car broke. She's driving this beat up old shebang and it's falling apart. I met her on the Northern State Parkway. We had the car towed. Then..."

"Then what?" David's voice hardened. He drummed his fingertips on the desktop.

"I was going to drive her home but she wanted to go out. One thing led to another and we ended up driving down to the Jersey Shore."

"You ended up...where?"

"Jersey. You know. New Jersey?"

"You drove all the way down to the Jersey Shore." David repeated his brother's statement, hardly believing what he heard. "On the spur of the moment. You left a family dinner, you picked up your girlfriend, and instead of driving east, you, what? Headed west?"

"Something like that."

"Why the hell did you go to New Jersey? Nobody goes to New Jersey on the spur of the moment. On a whim. It's...it's New Jersey, for God's sake. You go there for a reason. The beaches aren't even open yet."

"We just felt like going...to the Boardwalk, you know?"

"You live on Long Island. There's miles of boardwalk at Jones Beach."

"Well, we just felt like going to the Jersey Shore. You know?"

"No, I don't know. I don't just run out to the beach on the spur of the moment. I honor my responsibilities and commitments. So where the hell were you, really?"

"David, always the hard ass. Can't you let this slide, just once?"

"No, I can't let it slide! Not only did you not show up for work, you didn't call, and on a day when I really needed you there. I was counting on you, Con. You're supposed to be my senior vice president. That doesn't give you a right to just come and go as you please. The opposite, actually. When you have a position of authority, you have even more responsibility."

David rose to his feet and paced in front of his desk. He could no longer modulate his voice and speak reasonably. He shouted, "Con, you lie worse than the boys did when they were little. I can't believe the bullshit you're shoveling at me. You realize that if you were anyone but my brother I would have fired you on the spot for today's shenanigans?"

"I know, I know, David. Just give me another chance..." Con's voice drifted off.

"This is your last chance." The veins at his temples throbbed. His stomach churned. His hands shook as he strode around the room.

"So you're giving me an ultimatum?"

"Yeah, I'm giving you an ultimatum," David snarled. "If you don't get your act together and act like a responsible employee of Majek Investments, you're going to be fired. This is your one and only warning. You left me in the lurch and embarrassed the firm in front of six of our wealthiest investors on a day when I was supposed to be taking care of my health."

"Oh yeah, how'd that go?"

"Oh shut up! Not well!" David shouted. He slammed his chair into place. "I've got other things to worry about than your nonsense." He forced himself to take a deep breath and stop pacing. "Constantine, get your act together before it's too late. I need you at my side. I need you watching my back. I can't do this alone."

His brother laughed bitterly. "What, the great David Majek can't handle everything? He's not God?"

"What's that supposed to mean?"

Alex, Josh and Eddie appeared in the doorway. Eddie's face was pinched and drawn, while Josh bit his lip and shuffled nervously. David held up a warning hand to them not to enter.

Alex backed out of the room, saying. "C'mon, guys. Wait for Dad in the kitchen."

David slid the pocket doors shut behind them.

"It means that I've spent my whole life in your shadow," Con snorted. "The elder brother. The tall, handsome athlete. The apple of Papa's eye. The eldest son who would inherit everything. Then not only do you show a talent for business, Papa entrusts you with everything he's built. Is that enough for you?

"No, not for David the Great. You walk into a coffee shop and spill hot coffee over a beautiful woman waiting in line behind you. She doesn't throw her own cup of coffee back in your face, oh no, not for David the Great. You end up getting her phone number and marrying her less than a year later. And you tell me you're not God, David? Only God works miracles. I'm 44 years old and I still haven't met Miss Right, and yet your clumsiness gets you the girl of your dreams. Tell me again how you don't have all the luck, David?"

"Con...."

"You know what, David? I was happy when Eddie was born deaf."

"Con, just stop now...."

"You want to know why I was happy? I was happy because your perfect little life just got a little less perfect. Happy because for once, you screwed something up. You created something imperfect. An imperfect little kid. Then what?" Con laughed bitterly. "The deaf kid turns out to be brilliant, happy and so fun to be around! Even your screwed up little kid turns out golden!"

"Con. Stop. You're going to regret this."

"Oh, go screw yourself, David. I'm done with you, done with Majek Investments, done with everything and everyone in the whole fucking family."

"Con." David exhaled and wished he hadn't gotten so angry with his brother. "I don't want you to quit."

"Then fire me," Con dared. "You said you would if I screwed up one more time. Well, here's your chance. Fire me."

"I'm going to have to. Please believe me when I say this gives me no pleasure."

"You're just scared of what Papa's going to say!"

"Con, you aren't being reasonable. What's going on? Are you drunk?"

Con laughed until he coughed. "Drunk? No. I wish I was. By God, I wish I was. There's not enough booze in the world to get me drunk these days."

"Con, you need help."

"I don't need your kind of help!"

"Take a few days off, Con. Cool down. We can work this out."

"Fuck off, David."

David stared at the cell phone in hands. The click of his brother disconnecting the call seemed overly loud. Outside the open windows, the Miller's Rottweiler barked. A plane droned overhead as it descended to LaGuardia Airport. His heart thudded wildly in his chest, and he pictured its anguish squeezing as sluggish blood spurted through closed arteries

Where had Con gone? To the Jersey shore? Why didn't that ring true? Con hated the beach. He rarely went into the water at the family summer home in Cutchogue. He complained about sand and sun. Why the Shore?

What was at the Shore? What would explain his brother's random outbursts, his loss of time? What would explain the sudden need for money, the rumpled clothing at the office, the furtiveness and mood swings?

David sat back on the couch. He dropped the cell phone. It took him a few minutes to piece together the puzzle, but soon an unpleasant picture emerged.

"Oh my God," he murmured. "Gambling. That's what's at the Jersey Shore – Atlantic City. He went to Atlantic City."

16

David sat for several minutes in the office chair with his cell phone on his lap. The perfect brother? The perfect life? Did it really seem like he had it so easy to Con?

And Con's strange dismissal of his own crazy behavior...going to Atlantic City on the spur of the moment.... Was this the only reason Con was acting so strangely or was there something else going on? Another tug at his memory made him pause. Something Con had said yesterday during dinner. It was gone again. This had been happening all day. It was like a light flashed on in his mind, then blinked off. David shook his head. If it was important, it would come back to him.

After several more minutes thinking through the troubling call, he rose and pushed his cell phone back into his belt holster. In the kitchen, he found the boys seated around the table. They had piled their dirty dishes on the counter near the sink and made half-hearted attempts on the pots and pans. All three looked expectantly towards the doorway as he entered.

"Is Uncle Con okay, Dad?" Alex asked.

David nodded and signed so that Eddie could follow the conversation easily. "He's home again. I think. He called me, at any rate." He slid back into his chair at the table where his cold dinner waited.

"What happened?" Josh demanded. "You practically called out the army to find him today. Was he sick or something?"

"Yes, boys," David sighed. "Yes, he's sick. We had a big fight. He quit the firm."

"Whoa," Josh whistled. "Shot heard around the world."

Eddie cupped his hands around his mouth and threw his head back as if roaring. Josh nodded. "Yeah, that. What's Grandpa going to say about Uncle Con quitting the firm?"

"I haven't told Grandpa yet, and I'd appreciate it if you wouldn't, either. There's a chance this could all blow over."

"Really?" Josh asked.

"Probably not," David admitted. "But honestly, guys, I don't want to call Grandpa tonight. I can't handle Con and Grandpa in the same day."

"Is there anything we can do to help, Dad?" Alex asked quietly.

"No," David replied. "But thanks all the same."

He couldn't finish the delicious dinner Turquoise had prepared. Shoving his chair back, he threw his napkin on the table and strode out the back door, letting the screen slam behind him. David leaned against the wrought iron railing. The dogwood shed its blossoms, shivering in the light offshore breeze.

Just yesterday we stood here and laughed, he thought. *What am I going to do about this?*

Behind him came the sounds of silverware plunking into the sink, a little good-natured bickering between Alex and Josh. The dishwasher door banged open, and one of the boys turned on the television. CNBC's announcer gave way to the blast of raucous heavy metal. For once, David was glad for the blare of guitars and the steady throb of drums.

Atlantic City...David shivered. What if Con wasn't just asking him for a personal loan the other day? What if he'd already...helped himself to something?

David clicked on his cell phone and dialed Victor. The private investigator answered on the second ring.

"Victor," David said without preamble. "I need your help."

"What happened?"

"It's Con. He called me this evening. Victor, I think he was in Atlantic City, gambling. I think he might have a gambling problem and, I don't know, maybe he's doing drugs on the side. His behavior is all over the place and he's acting erratically. We had a terrible fight on the phone and he quit the firm. I'm not sure what I should do."

"Change the locks and order an audit," Victor said crisply. "You've got no time to lose."

David swallowed. "Are you sure?"

"If he's got a gambling addiction, and maybe a drug addiction on top of that, you've got to act fast. Depending on where he is in his addiction, he may be desperate enough to do anything. Change the locks, get your books audited or whatever you need to do to account for every penny your investors have entrusted to you, and ask for your brother's forgiveness later. If he doesn't have an addiction, then he's just going to be angry, but he will understand. If he does have an addiction, then you've got bigger things to worry about with him than hurt feelings."

David nodded. He raised his voice a little over the blare of shouting and what passed for music among the boys emanating from the kitchen. "All right. I have one more task for you. Can you put surveillance on Constantine? I need to know where he's going, what he's doing. I need to know...if I'm right."

"It's your dime. You said he's home? Where's home?"

"I think he's at home. He lives in the Huntington Village Townhouses, the new condos on Woodbury Road. Gated community, the townhouses with the tennis courts and big fountain out front. He's in unit 3-C."

"I know the place. I'll get my team on it right away."

"Victor...do you think I'm overreacting? He's my brother. I can't believe he'd go so far as to steal from the firm, but then again, if you had told me yesterday some of the things he said to me on the phone just now, I wouldn't have believed it, either."

"I say go with your gut. I had a bad feeling about your brother the minute I met him. No offense."

"None taken. Why did you get a bad impression of him?"

Victor chose his words carefully. "He seemed...weak. Jumpy. A man with a guilty conscience, as if he was hiding something. I watched him at the office. He was alternatively charming and rude, schmoozing with some employees, barking at others. Then he'd disappear into his office for a while or go out for a walk or whatever, and emerge smiling. I suspected drugs, frankly. I think you need to search his office."

"I wouldn't know what to look for."

"I have a suggestion."

"What?"

"We could search his office tonight and put your mind at ease."

"Search for what?"

"Drugs? Paperwork? Anything to give you more insight into what he's doing."

David glanced at his watch. It was almost seven. Alex could stay with Eddie and Josh. He nodded. "All right. I'm not going to sleep easily tonight after that call, anyway. Yes, meet me there. I'll phone ahead to building security to let them know we're coming."

"Right. I'll see you there."

"Twenty minutes," David promised and clicked off.

He returned to find the kitchen clean, if not as sparkling as when Turquoise had left for the day. The boys had left his half-eaten plate of chicken and pasta on the table. David spread plastic wrap on it and slid the plate into the refrigerator.

"Alex?" he called. The boys were in the family room arguing over what to watch on the television. Close captioning scrolled across the bottom of the screen, and Eddie's hands flashed as he protested Josh's sliding by his favorite cartoons.

"*Zombie Havoc* is on tonight. I want to watch that."

"Josh, you always want to watch zombies. Let Eddie watch Sponge Bob for a while before he goes upstairs to finish his homework."

"I can't stand that show!"

"It's just a half hour. You won't die," Alex said.

"I might!" Josh laughed.

"I'm a doctor. I know these things."

The boys spied their father in the doorway of the family room. "Dad?" Alex leaped to his feet. "Everything okay?"

"Relax. I'm fine. Alex, would you mind staying home tonight and watching Ed?"

"Sure. I had no plans for tonight, anyway."

"All right. Make sure to do your homework." David signed the last bit to Eddie, who pretended not to notice until Josh punched him in the shoulder. Wincing, Eddie turned and slugged his older brother back in the chest. David wagged a finger at them. *No fighting. Get your homework done, Eddie.*

It's done, Eddie signed. *Turquoise is going to help me tomorrow with my blog project.* His sign for the new housekeeper was jangling imaginary bangle bracelets on his arm, and David smiled at the new sign despite his anxiety. *Just need to pick a recipe. Can I call Grandpa?*

"Joshua, can you make the call to Grandpa for Eddie?"

"Aw geez, Dad, do I have to?"

"No, but I'd like you to."

"I can do it, Dad," Alex said.

"Alex, you're already doing enough. Joshua?"

"Fine." Josh crossed his arms across his chest. "I'll call for the Squirt. Can't he use that stupid deaf relay? Isn't that why Mom got the service, anyway?"

"Grandpa hangs up on the relay operator," Alex reminded his brother. "Eddie's tried to use it to call Grandpa, but he always thinks it's a telemarketer. He won't keep talking unless he hears one of us."

"He could text Grandpa if Grandpa would ever learn to use his computer."

"Don't hold your breath," David warned. "Grandpa won't even install an answering machine on his telephone. He still thinks computers are a passing fad."

The boys laughed. "Where are you going, Dad?" Josh asked.

"Back to the office. If your uncle really isn't returning to work this week as he said, then I've got to take care of his work and I'm not sure what he had on his schedule next week." David let the little white lie slip from his lips easily.

"Can't you give it to someone else or something?" Josh asked.

"Yes, I can delegate some of it," David promised. "But I've got to go over it first. Boys, thank you for helping out. You take a big weight off of my mind when you act responsibly."

"Lay down the guilt, why don't you," Josh muttered.

Alex glared at him.

"It's called parenting," David smiled. "If I thank you for being responsible now, you're less likely to do something stupid later. No friends over while I'm gone, please, and if you need me, call my cell phone, or call Aunt Eva or Uncle Blake in a pinch, okay?"

"Okay," Alex said. "But we should be fine. Um, Dad?"

"Yes, Alex?"

"I meant to ask you before, but...while I'm staying here, can I drive Mom's car?"

David hesitated just a few seconds, then nodded. "Should work. I've started it a few times to keep the battery fresh, but it needs gas. Keys are in Mom's top dresser drawer."

"Thanks, Dad." Alex swallowed. "I didn't think you'd say yes."

David shrugged as he turned away. "It makes sense. You need a car to drive while you're here, and it will be helpful if your brothers need a lift anywhere. Can that be part of the deal?"

"Sure!"

"All right then. Boys, lock the doors behind me. No guests. Don't stay up too late if I'm not home by your bedtime, and I want homework done. Please don't leave a mess in the kitchen. Even though Turquoise will be here in the morning, I don't want her to think we're a bunch of pigs."

"She knows that already," Josh replied. "She cleaned our bathroom."

"That probably scarred her for life," Alex said.

"Shut up, Shrink" Josh retorted.

David raised a hand in farewell. "Later."

Traffic was light, and he made it to the office in just under 20 minutes. The setting sun turned the mirrored windows of the Majek building into sheets of molten gold. A few cars remained in the parking lot, and the security guard nodded from the front desk when David slipped his key card into the reader to unlock the door.

"Good evening, Mr. Majek."

"Hello, Brian. Is Jason still here?"

"Yes, Mr. Majek."

"Can you page him to my office, please?"

"Certainly." Brian reached for his walkie-talkie. "Oh, Mr. Majek? Mr. Scalia is here. I let him in a few minutes ago. He said he had a meeting with you and to let you know he'll wait by your office."

"Thanks, Brian."

David hurried through the reception area. He passed the darkened Human Resources cubicles and turned towards the elevator. A few employees from the IT department sat in their cubicles across from the elevator still hard at work, and a fresh pot of coffee gurgled invitingly from the hot plate in the corner.

"You folks sure burn the midnight oil," David said to a woman hurrying past him. She clutched a hard drive to her chest with cords trailing like tentacles.

"We're usually here until midnight, Mr. Majek. It's easier to work on the computers when the rest of the staff have left."

"That makes sense. Have a good night."

"You too."

Victor waited for him in front of the elevator on the second floor. The private detective wore a black t-shirt, jeans and sneakers. As he greeted Victor, a burly man in black security windbreaker rounded the corner. The newcomer raised an eyebrow towards Victor and nodded at David.

"Jason, hello," David said. "Thanks for getting up here so quickly."

"Brian said you wanted me?"

"Jason, I'm going to tell you something in confidence. I need you to give me your complete assurance you won't say anything."

The security chief folded his arms and tucked his chin to his chest. "Say it."

"My brother won't be returning to the firm this week and he still has his keys. I can't explain everything but I'd like the locks changed."

"Just his office?"

"Front doors, executive suite, records room, and Con's office."

"I'll need all day tomorrow to do it. Need to collect keys, reissue new ones."

"Fine. Just do it. I'll approve the expense."

"Yes, sir."

"Thank you."

Jason moved off, and Victor nodded. "Glad to see you're acting on your hunch. I think it's the right thing to do."

"I hope so." David slid his card into the locks outside the darkened executive suite. He flipped on the overhead light and held the door open for Victor. It seemed odd to arrive without Joan's crisp greeting, but even she had to go home sometimes. Her desk was precisely arranged with the stapler and tape dispenser parked next to the telephone and papers neatly stacked in her in- and out-trays. Even her pencils were sharpened to approximately the same height and placed precisely in the metal cup on her desk next to a highlighter and two pens. David wondered if dust ever dared settle on the glossy surface of her desk.

Victor nodded towards Constantine's office door. "Ready?"

"Ready as I'll ever be. What's the plan?"

"We go in together. I search. You're my witness and permission to be here."

"All right."

David made only one mistake using the override function programmed into the door lock. It had been so long since the security service company had demonstrated the feature to him that he'd forgotten how to activate it. He had to fumble around in the drawers of his own desk to find the little laminated card they'd left for him. Once inside Constantine's office, he flicked on the overhead lights. The office was dark and stuffy, as if it hadn't been opened for weeks instead of days. A red light blinked frantically on Con's phone, indicating voice mail messages, and a Styrofoam cup with an inch of congealing cream-laden coffee stood on the desk. David tossed it into the trash can before they set to work.

"What do you want me to do?" David asked.

"Stand by the door and watch. Don't touch anything. Let me search."

"Is that all?"

"It's more than enough," Victor grunted as he bent to test the desk drawers, which were locked. "Are these keys universal?"

"I'm not sure."

"Mind if I pick the locks?"

"Do what you need to do."

Victor slid a black case from his jeans pocket. Inside was what looked like tiny flat-head screwdrivers, the kind jewelers used to open the backs of watches and peer into the gears. He slid one out of the case and within seconds, the lock clicked open on the top desk drawer. Soon the other locks followed and Victor slid the tool back into his case.

"You're here," Victor said as he bent to riffle through the top desk drawer, revealing nothing more interesting than a half-eaten pack of breath mints, a pile of rubber bands, and a stack of chewed pencils, "As a witness. First of all, to make sure I'm not accused of taking anything out of the office that I shouldn't. Second, to make sure I'm not accused of planting anything. You are here to verify that what I am doing is with your permission as the owner and head of this company, and that you are observing what I am doing. If this comes to a court of law, you will be called upon as my witness. Got it?"

"Got it." David folded his arms across his chest and leaned against the open doorway. Victor slid the top drawer shut, but something rustled, and the drawer wouldn't close all the way. Nodding, he pulled the drawer all the way out on its track, seesawing it up and down until it came away from the desk with a metallic clunk.

"What is it?" David moved closer to see.

"Something taped to the bottom of the drawer that's coming off," Victor replied. He dumped the contents of the drawer onto the desktop, scattering paperclips, pencils, scissors, breath mints and rubber bands and flipped the drawer over. A crisp business-sized envelope was taped to the bottom. Grabbing a pair of scissors from the top of the desk, he slid the blade under the tape securing the envelope. Victor looked at David, who nodded permission. Slowly, Victor pulled out a sheet of paper from the envelope.

"What is it?" David stepped closer.

Victor scrutinized the page. He handed it to David. "See for yourself."

It was a simple 8 1/2 x 11 sheet of paper, the kind they printed every day on the office printers. Printed in black ink was a list of 30 names, with numbers in parentheses after them. David glanced down the list, puzzled.

"Do you know what it is?" Victor asked.

"No," he said finally. "Although some of these names look awfully familiar. This one – Gertrude Van der Peyser. That's not a name I'd be likely to forget. Shall I look them up?"

"When I finish my search."

David watched in fascination as Victor checked the entire office from desk to floor. When he moved a chair into the corner, David asked curiously, "What are you doing?"

Victor pointed to a worn spot on the carpet near the corner. "Someone has been moving this chair over here a lot," he said, stepping up onto the sturdy visitor's chair. "And that usually means one thing."

"What?"

Victor stood on tip toes and pushed his palms against the white acoustic tile panel in the ceiling. He reached into the space, feeling with his fingertips. Finally, he drew back his hand and wiped the grime from his fingertips on his jeans.

"Anything?" David asked, peering into the yawning blackness above.

"Nothing now," Victor said, sliding the panel back into place. "But I can feel a sticky spot where something was taped there. He probably removed it. I'm guessing he had a bag of something stashed up here by the size of the tape marks. I've seen it before. Cocaine, probably, or pills of some kind. Given his behavior and sudden need for more money, I'd say he's on coke. It's expensive, habit forming, and would account for his bursts of energy and crazy mood swings."

"Shit." David leaned against the doorway. "I wish we knew for sure."

"Act as if you do, ask forgiveness later if you're wrong. Does anyone check Con's work here?"

"Check for what?"

"Accuracies, inaccuracies. You guys get audits done regularly, right?"

"Of course. We have independent auditors review the accounts quarterly."

"Who hired them?"

David hesitated. "Constantine."

"Get new ones immediately."

"I'll see to it."

Victor gestured towards the envelope they'd found taped to the bottom of the drawer. "Is there any way we can dig into this list tonight?"

"Let's take it to Joan's computer. She's got a desktop unit. I took my laptop home, and Con's is missing, so I assume it's with him."

David picked up the list and walked across the reception area to Joan's computer. Sliding into her chair, he logged into the company's intranet with his own user name and password, and accessed the client files. He began typing the names into the list.

Victor emerged from Con's office and pulled the door shut behind him. He hoisted a visitor's chair over to the desk to sit next to David and watched as David clicked methodically through the names on the list. "What's the list?"

"So far, all investors in Con's Triad fund," David said, He studied the screen and frowned as he scrolled through each name. "Everything seems to be in order. Just the usual account stuff."

"What do the numbers correlate to?"

"Social security numbers." David pointed to the upper left hand corner of the screen. Each client's name, address, telephone number and social security number were prominently displayed. "Here's Gertrude Van der Peyser."

"He shouldn't have those on the printout."

"No, he shouldn't. We have strict rules about data security for a reason. Not everyone on staff can access this information, and Con shouldn't have copied it over. But unfortunately he wouldn't be the only one to make mistakes with security. I confess, I've taken home some paperwork I shouldn't have, which did have people's social security numbers on them."

"You guys are a data breech waiting to happen," Victor muttered.

"My dad ran a rather loose ship in that regard."

"So I can see. But you're the captain now. Steer the ship off the reef."

"I'm trying, but it's not easy when you don't know what you're steering away from."

David clicked through the list until he reached the 18th name. "Any mid-level or above employee in our firm could access the names of people invested in this fund. Wait. This one is odd."

On the screen flashed "Name not found." David tried alternative spellings, but no "Andrew Rothschild" was in the database. He grabbed a highlighter and marked the name. Victor nodded as he continued. It wasn't until he hit record number twenty-eight, a Stephen Baylor, that the same thing happened. Two of the names on the list weren't in the database.

"I wonder if these are the same two records that were missing from the records room," David mused as he logged off and shut down Joan's computer.

"I'd bet the farm on it," Victor said.

David shuddered. "Don't say the word bet. Please."

"David..." Victor paused. "I've been thinking a lot about Constantine's behavior and the problems you described. From what your father originally hired me to do and from what you're saying, you know we might uncover something even worse than gambling losses or some nose candy here."

"I know what you're thinking." David rubbed his eyes and leaned back in Joan's chair. The chair protested with a loud squeak. "Something Con said at dinner yesterday is bugging me. I can't put my finger on it."

"What?"

"If I knew, I'd tell you."

"Walk me through it, then," Victor urged. "It may be important. When did this happen?"

"During dinner." David replayed the conversation in his mind. "We were talking and then the tremendous crash from the living room happened just as I was struck by something Con said. And then it fled from my mind, and now I can't put my finger on it. It was important." He shook his head and looked wearily at Victor. "I'll call the auditors in the morning. Meanwhile, did your men find my brother?"

"Yes, they did. He was at his condo. I've got a two-person team, husband and wife, who I trust completely, following him tonight. I've got him on around the clock surveillance."

"Good. I want to know what he's been up to and who he is with. I'm glad it's not that idiot in the fedora. If I thought it was going to be the man who watched my place, I'd look for another private investigator."

"I do apologize for that."

"You've apologized already," David said. "My father would say, never apologize twice or it takes it back."

"That sounds like a folk saying."

"It probably is." David rose from Joan's chair and glanced at his watch. It was half-past eight. It had taken less time than he thought. "Are we done?"

"For now. You'll call an auditor tomorrow?"

"I will. I want to get some recommendations first."

"Very good."

Just as they walked to the glass double doors, someone exited the elevator. David stopped abruptly, motioning for Victor to be silent. At first, he thought the newcomer was Constantine. His heart leaped with both hope and anger. But within seconds, he realized his mistake. The newcomer was shorter and as he emerged into the overhead light near the executive suite, David saw the glint of silver hair.

"Jack." David held open the door to greet Jack Noble. Jack stopped abruptly. Fear flashed across his face, replaced by a smooth professional mask.

"David! I'm surprised to see you."

"So it would seem. You're here late. What can I do for you?"

Jack cleared his throat. He clutched an envelope in his right hand, and tried to slide it unobtrusively into his suit pocket. "I, uh...I was actually looking for your brother. Is he working late, too?"

"No, not this evening," David replied. He nodded towards the envelope. "What's that, Jack? A message for Con?"

"Yes, yes, a message for him," Jack said too quickly. "Follow up to a meeting we had last week."

"Oh?"

"Papers," Jack babbled on, oblivious to the impression he was making. "Reports on the Triad Fund he was waiting for."

"I see. Well, why don't you give them to me?" David leaned towards the shorter man. Jack shrank back with his back to the wall. Victor smiled and nodded to David.

"I don't want to bother you..." Jack licked his lips. His eyes darted back to the darkened office suite. "I can give it to your brother tomorrow. If he's over his flu, that is."

"It's no bother for me to make sure he gets it." David held out his hand for the envelope. "I'll put this right on his desk. I promise."

Jack hesitated. Then he slapped the envelope into David's open palm. "Thank you. Good night."

"Good night."

After the elevator doors slid shut, David turned on his heel and marched back into the executive suite, sliding his key card back into the lock. "Let's see what that was all about."

"I thought you'd never ask."

They stepped into Constantine's office and Victor shut the door. Jack had sealed the envelope, but David use the scissor blade again to slide open the gummed flap. A single piece of paper floated out. Victor scooped it up from the carpet. It was a check for $5,000, made out to LePonto Enterprises, LLC.

Victor whistled. "Well, now," he said. "This is interesting."

"LePonto Enterprises? LePonto is the last name of Con's girlfriend."

"Interesting. I think I'll run a check on LePonto Enterprises tomorrow. It's certainly not a Triad Fund report."

"No, that's for sure. What do you think it is?"

Victor handed David the check and envelope. David slid the check back into the envelope. "Could your brother be selling as well as using?"

David shook his head. "Jack doesn't strike me as the type to take drugs."

"Does your brother strike you as the type?"

"Perhaps. I'm not sure. I just don't think that's it." David paused. Then he said, "Air time. That's what this is about."

"What?"

"Jack. He filled in for Con on CNBC without my permission a while ago. We're strict about who represents us on camera, as you can imagine. You say one wrong thing on television and you could start an investor panic. It's usually one of the family who goes on camera when we're asked to comment on something. I'm usually the face of the firm, but when I'm busy, Con fills in. That morning, Con was supposed to be on camera, but I turned on the T.V. and there was Jack. I hadn't approved the change. I raked Con over the coals over that one. Shit. I'm betting he's selling his slots on camera to that slimy bastard."

"I take it you don't like Jack."

"He's a jackass, but a good fund manager. My father liked him. I keep him as long as he does his job. Shit and double shit. Con's selling his air time!"

"Now that's the most unusual fundraiser I've ever heard."

"Sure beats a bake sale." David slapped the envelope onto the desk. "There. Did as I promised the man."

"That you did. I'm a witness."

"Let's get out of here. I need to go home and clear my head of this mess, and figure out how I'm going to tell my father about everything tomorrow."

"That," Victor said with a knowing nod, "is not something I envy you."

17

David returned home just in time to tuck Eddie into bed and wish Josh goodnight. He sat up in the family room, listlessly flipping through reruns. He couldn't call his father this late and dreaded the conversation he'd be forced to have with him in the morning. Around midnight he staggered up to bed, finally falling into a dazed, exhausted sleep around three.

The next morning, the boys were as subdued as he was. Josh barely grumbled about rising early, and Eddie stuffed his laptop and books into his backpack without a fight. David poured his third cup of black coffee in the kitchen when Turquoise rapped softly at the back door.

"I'm glad you're here a little early today," he said as she breezed past him into the kitchen. "I may be late this evening; I know you mentioned that you could stay later, if your daughters can come over to stay here. Does that offer still stand?"

"It does," she said. "On one condition...."

"Yes?"

"The piano." He stiffened and set his jaw, folding his arms across his chest. She rested a hand on his forearm. "I know it's special to you. I promise that Emily will treat it gently. She may only be 11 years old, but she's a genuine musician. Your wife would approve of her playing the Steinway, I think."

David exhaled. "Yes, I suppose she would. She loved children."

"Did she teach piano to children?" Turquoise asked the question casually as she dumped her enormous pink purse on the counter and tossed her white-rimmed sunglasses next to it.

"Just when we were first married," David said. "Cathy stayed home with the boys when they were small, and it was easy for her to teach piano lessons around their schedule. When Eddie entered preschool, she began teaching at C.W. Post."

Turquoise rummaged within her voluminous purse until she extracted a hot pink coffee mug with a handle shaped like a flamingo. David stared at the mug as she strolled to the coffee pot and poured herself a cup of coffee.

"You didn't have to bring your own mug."

"The boys said the enormous one in your hand is yours."

"We have others."

"Still, a man needs his own coffee mug. I'm territorial about mine. I figured you were the same." She raised her cup to his and tapped the rim. "I need quite a bit of fuel to get me going in the morning. None of the others would do." She cleared her throat. "Wouldn't your wife have approved of a young musician playing her piano, David?" Turquoise spooned two teaspoons of sugar into her coffee and liberally doused it with milk. When it turned the color of a paper bag, she stirred it and tapped the spoon on the rim three times, then dropped the spoon into the sink.

"Yes, she would." A thought occurred to him. "Oh, but it's broken."

"What happened?"

"Darndest thing...we were eating dinner on Sunday, and a string broke."

"Just like that? They don't usually do that."

"Yes, just like that."

Turquoise took a sip of her coffee. "How about I call a technician in to work on it today?"

"Well, don't bother..."

"It's no bother." She drew a small pink leather covered notebook and matching pink pen from her pocket and scribbled a note to herself. "I'll call Vincent Itorio. He's a genius with pianos."

"That's who Cathy used to call! She'd only call in Mr. Itorio to work on her pianos here and at the university."

"See? I knew she'd approve of me." Somehow, he found himself gently ushered to the back door. She handed him his laptop, which he shrugged over his shoulder, then exchanged his briefcase for the coffee mug. Turquoise held the screen door for him. "Have a wonderful day, David, and don't worry about a thing. I'll handle everything here."

"You should have been named Diamond," David said. "Thank you." She smiled and closed the door behind him.

A locksmith's red van was parked directly in front of the main entrance of Majek Investments. Jason from security growled a good morning. He nodded over his barrel chest towards David. The locksmith grunted and stepped aside from his work. He had popped out the front door lock and held a replacement in his hands. Good, the locks would be changed. One hurdle down, David thought as he greeted his employees and stepped onto the elevator.

Joan waited for him next to her desk. She scowled at her computer. "Someone," she said, "Has been sitting in my chair. Someone around six foot four, I should think."

"And has that someone been eating your porridge too, Goldilocks?" He flipped through the stack of mail and messages she thrust into his hands.

"Very funny. You know that I make few requests of you, David, but one request I am firm about is not using my desk. I am very particular about the height of my chair."

"I didn't change the height."

"When you sat upon it, it dipped in slightly, here." She pointed to a miniscule mark on the back of the chair.

"You actually note where the seat is positioned – with a pencil mark?"

"Indeed I do. That temp we had last year was horrible. She actually exchanged my chair for your brother's!"

A sudden thought struck David. "Joan," he said, "Do you remember the name of the temp who filled in for you while you had that awful flu last Thanksgiving? The week Cathy died?"

"I don't think I ever knew her name, actually," Joan answered. She took the junk mail from David and fed the hungry shredder. It hummed and spat ribbons into the bin underneath her desk.

"Where did we get the temp from?"

"I assume AccuTemps. That's who Human Resources uses."

David nodded. "Would you please call Connie and ask her which temp agency we used last year? I have a question for them, or more specifically, for the woman who filled in for you."

"Certainly." Joan fussed with her chair, then straightened. "David, what about Con? Did you hear from him?"

"I did." David hesitated. "He won't be in today."

"Oh....is everything all right?" Joan hesitated, but he knew she cared for both his brother and himself as if they were her own siblings. Joan had been with Majek Investments for almost twenty years, first as his father's assistant, then as his. She had grown very fond of the entire clan during her tenure as their executive assistant, gatekeeper and den mother.

"No, Joan, it's not okay." He glanced at the closed door to his brother's office. "Con called last night and we had an argument. We agreed it's best if he takes a leave of absence from the firm." David swallowed. No sense in letting it be known he had pretty much fired Con. There might still be a chance to salvage the relationship. "I am having the locks changed."

"Oh no. Not that."

"Yes, that. Certain information came to light that makes me wonder if Con's behavior these past few months wasn't, well, due to something other than stress or whatever. Let's leave it at that."

He expected Joan to ask questions, but she merely let her hands rest lightly on the back of her office chair, watching David's face intently.

"So you have noticed."

"Noticed what?"

"Con."

Joan hesitated. "I didn't want to bother you, but he has been acting strangely lately."

"Yes. Well, it all came to a head last night, I'm afraid. I'm having the locks changed, and his passwords changed, and he is not to have access to this building without my permission. Is that clear?"

"Yes, David."

"I came in late last evening and went through his desk to see what loose ends might need to be tied up today, and that's why your desk chair was moved. I apologize, but Con took his laptop with him and my own was at home, and I needed to look up a few accounts on the intranet. So I borrowed your desk. I'm sorry."

"I'm such an ass about my space." Joan's voice trembled. "I'm so sorry that you and Con had a disagreement. Does....does your father know?"

"No, and I'd appreciate it if you didn't tell him," David responded. "I'll get to Papa later today." He picked up his briefcase in his right hand and his laptop in his left. "Joan, I need you to keep the information about Con highly confidential. Please don't tell anyone, not even my father, that we quarreled, or that he won't be in to work. Until he returns, please review his calendar and find people to cover his meetings. Any of his work goes to me or to Neil. If we need some extra help, I'll think of something or call my father in. But not until I say so."

"What about your medical tests, David?" Joan whispered.

"I can't even think about that now. I've got to get things straightened here, and with Con, before anything else." "I   suppose so."

He hesitated as the door lock light flashed red, then green, and the security system clicked his door lock open. "One more thing."

"Yes?"

"Jack Noble. Have you ever noticed him being...friendly with Constantine?"

"Certainly. Jack drops by Con's office frequently during the day. I'm surprised you never noticed."

"My door is often shut when I take calls or participate in meetings."

"That's true."

"And have you ever heard of LePonto Enterprises?"

Joan frowned. "No, the name isn't familiar."

"Thanks, Joan."

He made several phone calls to friends and colleagues from graduate school that morning, using his business network to secure several references for forensic accounting firms. That task complete, his next call was to his Human Resources Director. David briefed her quickly, merely stating that Con would be taking an extended leave of absence. Until David rescinded the order, Con was not to have any decision-making capacity in the company. Neil was to suspend his brother's access to the accounting system and his signatory powers. IT was to change his brother's passwords. David had already taken care of changing the locks. Connie asked no questions, but he could tell she understood that something was deeply wrong. David appreciated her brisk professionalism and thanked her.

By ten o'clock he'd secured a new forensic accounting firm. One of his MBA school buddies was now CEO of an accounting firm and promised swift, confidential action. David decided to walk up to Neil's office to speak with him personally. He took the stairs two at a time, noting with relief that he wasn't out of breath as he ascended the steep stairwell to the third floor.

Majek Investment's CFO had a corner office above David's. Margaret, Neil's assistant, looked up in surprise from her computer as David approached the open reception area near the accounting offices.

"Mr. Majek!"

"Hi Margaret, how are you?" David smiled at the assistant. "Is Neil in?"

"Yes, he's in. He's just meeting with Donna and Carl."

"I can wait."

"It's not a formal meeting. They just had some questions for him. Go on in."

David found Neil behind his desk, leaning back with his hands cupped behind his head. Coffee and Aqua Velva mingled in a nauseating cloud punctuated with the scent of government ink from the many IRS documents strewn about the office. Donna and Carl, two of the firm's accountants, sat across the laminate wood desk from their boss, balancing folders and Styrofoam coffee cups on their knees. They glanced up in surprise as David knocked on the open door. "Hi all. Sorry to interrupt. Neil, can I see you privately for a minute?"

"Sure thing, David." Neil dropped his hands and sat upright. Carl and Donna scrambled to gather their papers and coffee cups.

"Don't rush, guys. It's fine."

"No, that's okay, Mr. Majek." The pair hurried out, Donna easing the door shut behind her.

Neil's office was brightly lit by overhead fluorescent lighting and cluttered with putty colored filing cabinets. Stacks of official reports, IRS publications, and other reference books towered in the corners. Coffee rings dotted his desk. His purple tie was askew as if he'd knotted it in the dark, and the edge of his left hand was stained with ink.

"David, what can I do for you?"

David sat heavily onto a still-warm guest chair. "Neil, we've got trouble."

"I saw the locksmith outside. I didn't think Con had the flu." Neil's lips thinned and his eyes narrowed. "Did you fire him?"

David started in surprise. "Fire him?"

"I was wondering when you'd get around to that."

"Why would you think that?"

Neil rose and paced to the windows overlooking the parking lot. Like David's office, his windows faced west, towards the Roosevelt Field Mall. Acres of concrete parking lots, roadways, and green swathes circled the fountain in the courtyard. Neil searched the distance before he turned back to David.

"I've suspected Con was up to something for months now. I tried to look into his dealings quietly, because I would never want to approach you with an accusation like that without any proof."

David's mouth went dry. "Neil, you should have told me."

"He's your brother, David. And I know how protective you are with him."

"That shouldn't matter!" David swallowed, but his mouth was dry. "What did you suspect?"

Neil dipped around the side of his desk, navigating the sea of file cabinets and reference publications. Leaning over one of the taller stacks, he fumbled with a locked combination drawer on his file cabinet; clicking the three-digit code into place and sliding open the drawer. He tugged out a stuffed manila file folder marked "Triad Fund II."

Spreading the papers on the desk, Neil pointed to several Excel spreadsheets and line graphs among the first pages in the file. "This. Con's fund invests in up and coming IPOs, these internet companies are preparing for an IPO or have just launched one."

"Correct..." David peered at the papers.

"Notice anything?"

David studied the lines. Something was off, but he couldn't put his finger on it. He met Neil's eyes. "What?"

"The trend. It's just up and up, up and steady. No IPO does that. Ever. They should be jagged, all over the place. IPOs are risky. Con has, somehow, magically taken out all the risk of investing in what should be a very risky investment."

"Damn," David swore. "How did I miss that?"

"Because these just came out last Friday," Neil said, slamming the folder closed. "You haven't seen them yet. I only got around to looking at them this morning. I had suspicions all along that something was off, but this graph was the last straw. I'd meant to visit you later this week to discuss it."

"You think he fudges his numbers?"

"Easy enough to prove, I think. But why?"

"To fool the investors."

"So they stay in the fund?"

"And he continues to collect a fat commission without doing the work." David stood, pushing the visitor's chair back and thinking about comic books hidden inside textbooks. "Neil, I came to tell you that I've hired a forensic accounting firm to investigate the Triad Fund and our accounting in general. I was afraid you'd be upset, but I see that with this knowledge you aren't surprised."

Neil snorted. "I'm not surprised. I'm just surprised he let you catch on. He's good at getting his act together when you're around, David. He should have been an actor instead of a businessman."

"How long have you noticed this?"

"What, his behavior? Let me see...he started acting funny last summer. Then, right around Thanksgiving, he was really off. Snapping at everyone. Right before you left for Los Angeles, he was like a maniac, roaring at everyone."

"Worse than my father?"

"Your father?" Neil laughed. "Tibor roars, but he's also an old softie, and everyone knows it. No, this was different." Neil grew serious. "David, there's a cruel edge to Con that people sense...it's hard to explain. He has a sense of entitlement that gets on people's nerves."

"You mean as the founder's son? But I'm the founder's son..."

"Who worked his way up through the ranks, and earned his way into the CEO's chair," Neil finished. "This is different. I'm sorry, it's hard to explain."

"When did Con's behavior really strike you as odd, Neil?"

"Right after Cathy died. Oh, it was awful. We knew how hard hit you were, and Con, being your brother, we just thought he was upset for you. After that, he seemed to rally and rise to the occasion while you were out, and he did a good job as interim CEO although he could be a dickhead at times. No offense intended."

"None taken. And then?"

"Then you came back after your leave of absence at the start of the year, and things were going smoothly. Until April. Then his behavior changed again."

"What did you notice?"

"Moodiness. Some days he's on fire, got a million ideas and can't contain himself. Other days, he's grouchy and simmering, angry one minute and silent the next. It's gotten so bad the European Markets crew doesn't want anything to do with him."

"How...how could I not have noticed this?" David bit his tongue to keep from adding, "My father would have noticed it."

Neil nodded, though, as if reading his mind. "David, we all know you've been through the wringer this year. Hell of a thing, losing Cathy like that, and raising three boys on your own. Nobody blames you. In fact, the opposite. Betty, Connie in HR and I have been trying to handle things on our own as much as possible so we didn't have to bother you with any of this about Con. But with him not showing up for that big meeting with the Saudis, and now his sudden attack of the 'flu'" – Neil drew air quotes around the word – "and the locks changed on the front door, I had a feeling you'd noticed on your own, and decided to take action."

"Something like that, at any rate. I hired a forensic accounting firm. I would like them to go over everything, every account, every transaction. Every nook and cranny, so to speak. If there's a problem, I want it rooted out and dealt with. Is that clear?"

"It will be my pleasure." Neil leaned back in his chair. He nodded.

"Good."

"I'll set them up in the third floor conference room and get IT to give them temporary network access."

"Perfect. Thanks, Neil. I appreciate your cooperation and... enthusiasm."

"David, you may not understand this, but many of us feel like family here," Neil said quietly. "Tibor can be difficult, but he's a beloved pain in the ass around here. He's the reason a lot of us have the careers we have. I've worked here for over a decade, and Betty too. Neither of us want to see anything happen to this firm. We believe in the work we do here and the wealth we create for our clients. Tibor ran an ethical ship and you do, too. We know you won't stand for anything unless it's completely above-board. That's why we stay, and why I agree with your actions. Whatever you need us to do, whatever support we can offer you, we will give it."

David swallowed as he rose and shook hands with Neil. "Thank you. I appreciate it more than you know."

Back on the second floor, Joan waved a sheet of paper at him as he entered the executive suite. "This is the name of the temporary agency Connie called during Thanksgiving week last year," Joan said. "Here's the strange thing, though. After I asked her for the information, Connie called them today to ask about the gal who covered for me last year, and they said the order had been cancelled."

"What? You mean she called to request a temporary executive assistant, and someone called back to cancel it?"

"Exactly."

"But then who was at the desk that week? Someone was here. I know it, because I called a few times to gather messages and spoke with someone. I can't remember her name, and I never met her in person, but I know there was someone covering the desk."

"There was indeed." Joan hesitated. "Does the name Lisa LePonto ring a bell?"

"Lisa..." David couldn't believe what he had just heard. "Lisa LePonto? Isn't that Con's girlfriend?"

"Bingo," Joan said.

"Oh my God. He never said."

"No, he didn't. Connie said that he called her, told her he had someone in mind to cover the desk for the week, someone he wanted to try out for a permanent position. It was an unusual arrangement, but not so unusual that she wouldn't go for it. She thought you knew about it. Con told her you'd approved it, and you didn't complain that week to Connie, so she thought it was okay."

"I didn't complain because I had no clue the woman I spoke with was Constantine's girlfriend. I would never have approved that!"

"Connie thought it strange, but chalked it up to something you two agreed on privately."

"So Lisa LePonto covered your job that week. And she is the one who spoke with Cathy on the day that Cathy died." David felt the blood rise to his cheeks. "Why didn't Con mention any of this? Why?" He banged his fist on Joan's desk and whispered. "LePonto. LePonto Enterprises?"

"It's the same name," Joan said. "There's got to be a connection."

"Is there a number where I can reach this Lisa person? I need to ask her a lot of questions."

"Connie said they mailed her a W2 form in February but it was returned as undeliverable. Moved, left no forwarding address sort of thing. Her cell phone is disconnected, too. They tried to call her when the W2 came back."

"Oh dear God."

"Your brother told Connie in HR to mail it to his condo and he would give it to her. She was between apartments, he told Connie, and temporarily living with him."

"He never.... he never said anything about this!"

David paced the reception area, fists balled in his pockets. Joan's telephone rang. "Majek Investment, Mr. Majek's office, Joan speaking. How may I help you?"

Fuming, David walked the perimeter of the office like a caged lion. "Why didn't he tell me any of this? What is he doing? What is he hiding?" he raged while Joan held up a hand begging for silence.

"He's right here." Joan handed the phone to her boss, her eyes pleading with him for patience. "David, it's the 5th Precinct."

David snatched the phone from her and barked, "Lieutenant. Any news?"

"Yes, Mr. Majek. I'm afraid there is." The Lieutenant paused. "The state police forensic laboratory was able to access your wife's cell phone. There's a text message on her phone that's led me to request a search warrant to pull all her messages."

"I don't understand."

"We ruled her death suspicious, a vehicular homicide, Mr. Majek. We thought it was a random hit and run so we didn't bother to pull her cell phone records at the time of her death. Your insistence on doing so now via your private investigator, Mr. Scalia, has led us to some new information. Mr. Majek, the last person to call Cathy's cell phone was your brother, Constantine Majek."

"I don't understand." David felt the blood drain from his face. He grew cold. Joan rose silently and walked to his side, sliding a hand under his arm as if supporting him. It dawned on him that he probably did look faint.

"At two-thirty, she received a call on her cell phone from your brother, Constantine Majek. They spoke for roughly 10 minutes, and then the call terminated. From there we know only that she was killed by someone driving a black SUV at three-ten or so in the parking lot a short distance from your home."

"Wait." David leaned against the office wall, gathering his thoughts. Something pulled at his memory, something from the weekend. It was all happening too fast. He felt his thoughts swirl, then from the ball of voices and memories, he tugged the thread he was seeking. "Did you say a black SUV or a black Escalade?"

"Just a black SUV. We had a tentative identification of the vehicle as an Escalade, but we didn't release that information to you or to the public. We had nothing to confirm it."

David licked his lips. "Con," he said miserably.

"Sorry?"

"My brother, Constantine, Con... he drives a black Escalade. A Cadillac Escalade, an SUV."

"I see."

"No, you don't. Over the weekend, he..." David took a deep breath. "You see, he was at my home on Sunday. We had a family dinner. He said that Cathy was hit by a black Escalade. Not a black SUV. He specifically said Escalade."

"Are you sure?"

"I'm positive."

"Well now. That's interesting. Very interesting."

"Can you...is there any way to tell?"

"We'll follow up on this lead, Mr. Majek. Thank you."

"But – "

"We will call you as soon as we know anything," the Lieutenant promised.

David closed his eyes. "I see. Thank you." After the detective hung up, he remembered he'd asked Victor to have Con tailed. He grabbed the phone to contact the detective, but decided instead to wait. Let the police find Con, David thought. I need time to think about what I'm going to say to him when I finally see him.

He's got a lot of explaining to do. A lot.

Joan rubbed his arm and murmured his name. Blood roared in his ears, blotting out any sounds of comfort. He pressed his lips together and squeezed his eyes closed, as if to shut out what he had just heard and said. Finally, he opened his eyes and turned back to Joan.

"It's all crashing down, Joan. It was him. I know it was him."

"Oh David." She had heard his end of the conversation and had drawn her own conclusions. "I'm so sorry. What will you do?"

He blinked back tears. The phone in his office shrilled, and Joan's computer chimed as emails arrived. David took a deep, steadying breath.

"We have work to do," he said quietly. "I've got to pull myself together. The accountants will be here soon. Joan, say nothing."

"I won't, David," she said quickly. "You have my word."

"I know I do. This is only just beginning, and I'm going to need all the friends I have."

"You have many. You just don't know it."

He thought of Neil, of his father. He thought of Turquoise and Victor. Mostly, he thought of Eva. And Con. Con. Why, Con? he wondered as he walked slowly, miserably back to his office. The phone shrilled again. Coffee wafted from the freshly perking urn on the credenza. Oh why, Con?

18

David pushed open the screen door into the mudroom. Discordant sounds crashed through his headache as he dropped his briefcase and laptop onto the kitchen table and rummaged in the refrigerator for something to eat. *Mr. Itorio must be here*, he though as he hunted for something quick to take the edge off his hunger. A flash of white caught his peripheral vision. A little girl in a white sundress patterned with strawberries watched him from the doorway. She peered at him from around the corner of the kitchen entranceway.

"Hello," he said to her, straightening up.

"You've got a house like a castle," the girl said flatly. "It's too big."

"Um...." He loosened his tie. "Is your mother around?"

"She's in the living room with my sister and Mr. Itorio. He had to replace a string on the piano. It was the one that makes F-sharp and G-flat."

"Okay, thanks."

He closed the refrigerator, picked up his bags and strode past her through the dining room and into the living room. The sounds grew from a frenzied pounding to chords crashing together, a ripple of scale, then the crunch of a ratchet as the technician worked his magic tightening and adjusting the tension on the strings. The cover of the piano was raised to its full height, and Mr. Itorio leaned into the sound board while Turquoise and the twin of his new friend hovered nearby.

Itorio wielded his magic wand, only in this case it was a chrome socket wrench and tuning forks he struck while turning the wrench. His large, competent hands spanned the keyboard striking chords as he whirled back to the keyboard to test his magic.

"Hello," David said simply, walking past them into the family room, where he dropped his bags by the computer. He returned to the living room, where Turquoise hurried from the platform near the piano to meet him. Her twin daughters stood by the piano, watching him curiously.

"David, I was hoping we'd be done by the time you came home. Girls, this is Mr. Majek. Please say hello to him and thank him for letting you play here today."

"Hello," the girl with the red sneakers said. Her sister whispered, "Hello," clearly, the shy one of the two.

"Hello," he said, trying to be friendly. It wasn't that he disliked children; he loved his boys fiercely. But he was always uncomfortable around other people's children, ill at ease, afraid of stumbling out of his conversational depths and keenly aware of how disinterested he was in a child's world. "Who do I have the pleasure of addressing?"

The girls glanced furtively at their mother, who translated his grown up speak for them. "This is Elizabeth, known as Lizzy." She pointed to his new friend in the strawberry-patterned sundress, "and this is Emily, the musician." Emily wore a similar sundress to her sister's, but her outfit was yellow, with yellow sneakers to match.

"Emily, I hope you enjoy playing this piano," David smiled tiredly. He raised his fingertips to his temples and winced. "It's a very special piano."

"Indeed it is," Turque said. "Mr. Itorio was telling us about it. I had no idea it was such a fine instrument."

"There's only ten in the world like it, Mom," Emily said urgently, tugging her mother's wrist. Emily pointed to the scrolled music stand. "Rachmaninoff touched that, Mom. Rachmaninoff played on this piano!"

"Indeed he did," David said, surprised. "This piano stood in the Empire Hotel in New York City near Carnegie Hall. When the musicians came to perform and stayed at the Empire, they used this piano to rehearse. Rachmaninoff loved it so much he wanted to buy it, but the Empire refused to sell it. I managed to snag it at an auction right after my own little boy, Joshua, was born. It was a gift for my wife. Do you know Rachmaninoff's music, Emily?"

"Know it?" Emily's eyes glowed. "I want to play it someday. I can, but not quite. My hands aren't big enough yet."

Mr. Itorio laughed from the depths of the piano, and raised his head, resting his hands on the fame. The piano strings hummed with vibrations, dwindling to blessed silence. "You're a fine musician, Emily. Hello, Mr. Majek. It's good to be here working on this instrument again."

"Hello, Mr. Itorio. Yes, I'm glad you're here. Cathy would be, too."

Mr. Itorio bowed his head at the compliment. "I was telling the girls what a fine musician your wife was. I wish there were recordings of her playing."

"Unfortunately, other than some home videos her brother Blake has, I don't think there are any. Cathy never pursued a recording career. She loved to teach."

"Dinner is waiting for you," Turquoise said quietly. "I'll just heat it up when you're ready."

"Thanks," David said. "Did the boys eat?"

"Yes. Alex went out – said he was meeting up with some friends from high school. Josh is out too, playing baseball tonight, he said. Eddie is upstairs at his computer."

"If you'll excuse me, I'll see you later."

"Do you want me to stay a while longer?"

"Please, if you don't mind. I have a terrible headache."

"Probably just hunger."

"And stress." David winced again as the pain in his temples intensified.

"I'm almost finished," Mr. Itorio confirmed. "It took me a little while longer than I thought it would since I had to replace the string, and the piano was very out of tune. It's odd."

"Why is it odd?"

"Shouldn't be that badly out of tune after only nine months," Itorio said. He shrugged and returned to pounding keys and creaking his ratchet. "Probably because it hasn't been played. But still, odd."

"Well, it should be fine for now, yes?"

"Yes, if it is played. Pianos must be played."

David nodded. "Miss Emily here will play it, won't you?"

"Oh, I will! Now, Mama?"

"No, not now," Turquoise said firmly, running a hand over Emily's flame-red hair and smiling at her daughter. "Tomorrow or the next time you're here."

"I'd love to come back. Tomorrow, I mean."

"I don't," Lizzy scowled. "Eddie's boring."

"Elizabeth Anne Daniels!"

David laughed. "That's fine. I'm sure Eddie thinks girls are boring, too."

"He just wants to play War and talk about his stupid turtles."

"Well, what do you like to do?"

"Play other games. Make crafts. Read."

"Eddie likes to read, too. Maybe you'll find books in common."

Lizzy shrugged. "Whatever."

With a sigh, Turque started to apologize again, but David waved her off and turned to the stairs. "Never mind. Don't worry. They're just kids."

"Honestly...they're eleven going on thirty some days."

"Don't worry about it Turque, I've raised three of my own. I know the drill."

Mr. Itorio shooed Emily away from the piano bench. "Move aside, Miss Emily. I must test this fine instrument."

Emily slid off the bench and stood with rapt attention at his right. David smiled at the little girl's obvious obsession with the instrument; she would have been a child right after Cathy's own heart, he reflected sadly. She had tried to introduce both Alex and Joshua to the piano, but neither boy showed any interest in the instrument. Now he watched as Vincent Itorio raised his hands, paused and listened as if to an unseen voice.

"What will you play, Mr. Itorio?"

David expected the opening strains of "The Blue Danube" waltz by Strauss to fill the house. Every time Mr. Itorio had tuned the piano in the past, he had played the Blue Danube to test the action of the instrument. Today, however, Itorio merely shook his head. He dropped his gaze to the ivory-colored keys and frowned.

"Mr. Itorio?" Turquoise asked quietly. "Is everything all right?"

Slowly, his hands rippled over the keys, gaining speed. David felt the hairs on the back of his neck rise as the familiar opening strains of the Chopin Polonaise in F-Sharp Minor gurgled from the depths of the bass. The deep-throated sounds rose, fell, crested until the dance-like trills and rising momentum of the Polonaise filled the house.

Why Chopin? he wanted to ask, but his throat seemed dry. And why this piece?

"Wow," Turquoise said as she watched Mr. Itorio's hands develop the bass, the trills in the right hand, the cascades of notes back down to the bass as the Polonaise continued. "I've never heard you play that one before. What is it?"

"Chopin," David whispered.

"That's right," Mr. Itorio nodded, gliding back to the treble notes as the Polonaise continued. "I haven't played this in years."

"You usually play The Blue Danube after you tune a piano," David said. Turquoise glanced sharply at him.

Itorio nodded. "I know. I don't know...I don't know why I started playing this. It was as if the piece just suddenly came to mind."

David turned abruptly. Turquoise asked, "Is everything all right?"

"Fine," he managed to say. "I'll be downstairs in a minute. I need an aspirin."

Mr. Itorio left around seven-thirty, handing David a hefty bill and a promise to return in two weeks to check the instrument. David was used to the bills; Itorio was a master craftsman, and Cathy only used the best craftsman to care for her instrument. He knew Itorio's talents were worth every penny.

The master craftsman shook his hand solemnly at the front door. "As always, David, it is an honor to work on such a fine instrument. I'm glad you are going to let the little girl play it while she is here. Cathy would have wanted that."

"Yes, I think so, too. Mr. Itorio..."

"Yes?"

"When you sat down to test the piano...the Chopin...you said it just came to mind."

Mr. Itorio waved him aside and switched his tool kit from his left to his right hand, shrugged as he turned to walk out the front door. "Oh, it was nothing. Just a fanciful mind. All artists are alike, you know. We hear whispers of inspiration everywhere."

"Yes, but...whispers. You said whispers of inspiration. Did you actually think you heard something?"

Itorio just laughed and continued down the walkway. "Ah, who knows? I thought I heard someone whisper to play it. In my mind, you know. I was all set to play The Blue Danube, and it suddenly felt wrong. Then I thought I heard a whisper. But I am sure it was my imagination."

"Imagination. Yes, probably."

"Goodnight, David."

"Good night, Mr. Itorio."

Turquoise stood in the hallway, hefting her large pink tote bag over her shoulder. Emily and Elizabeth stood next to her, staring curiously at David. Elizabeth held her tablet, while Emily held a bright pink Hello Kitty book bag.

"What was that all about?" Turquoise asked.

"What?"

"The Chopin. It seemed to upset you."

"Ah, it's nothing," David said. He forced himself to smile. "Thanks again for staying and overseeing everything. It's been a rough week for me and likely to get rougher."

"I'm sorry to hear that. Work problems?"

"Work, family...when it rains, it pours, I suppose." David squatted down so that he was eye level with Emily. Her eyes grew big and she stepped back, suddenly shy as the tall Mr. Majek spoke directly to her.

"Emily, I want you to know that I am very happy you'll be using Mrs. Majek's instrument," David said solemnly. "She would very much have liked to have met you, I think. And you too, Elizabeth."

"I'll take good care of it, Mr. Majek. I promise."

"I know you will." He straightened and smiled at the group. "Good night. And thank you again."

"Good night. David..." Turquoise hesitated by the doorway as the girls bolted through, eager to go home. "If there is anything I can do for you, just let me know. I know what a rough day at work can be like for finance guys. Married to one all those years. Ah, you know."

"Thanks Turquoise. But this is something I'm just going to have to weather through. Just knowing you're here, taking care of things, is enough."

"Well," she smiled, suddenly embarrassed. "Good night."

"Good night."

David heated the plate Turquoise had left for him in the refrigerator in the microwave and ate hastily, feeling guilty about gobbling the delicious supper of lamb chops, minted peas and rosemary balsamic potatoes. But he had many things to do, and his mind whirled with all of the problems of the day. He rinsed his plate and slid it into the dishwasher. When he was done, he reluctantly walked to the family room to make the phone call he was dreading all day. At least his headache had faded thanks to the aspirin and meal.

Tibor picked up on the second ring. "Yes?" his father barked.

"Papa? It's David."

"Ah, I was hoping it was that brother of yours. I have called him three times today. No answer. I even left a message on that, what do you call it? Answering machine? No reply. None!"

"That's why I was calling you, Papa." David slid the pocked doors shut so that he was alone in the family room. Eddie was still upstairs, and Alex and Josh were out. The house was quiet. "There's a problem. A big problem. I need you to be calm."

"I am calm!"

"Papa...."

"Well." Tibor took a breath. "Has something happened to Constantine?"

"He's not injured," David said hastily, offsetting some of the fear in his father's voice. "But yes, Papa, something has happened to him, and it is bad. Very bad. I had to suspend him from the firm today and lock him out of the building."

The seconds ticked by. David waited for Tibor to say something. Finally, his father sighed heavily, muttered something unintelligible in Czech, and said, "It must be bad indeed for you to take that step, my son. In all the years of Majek Investments, we have only suspended traders twice. My own son now makes the third. I had a feeling...yes, I had a feeling it would come to this. What has he done, this troubled son of mine?"

"Why did you call him your troubled son, Papa? You aren't surprised by this?"

Tibor sighed heavily. "You asked me once why I didn't vote him into the senior vice president seat the first time around," his father said after a long pause. "You asked me why it is that the Board did not want him the first or second vote. Well, he is not trusted, David."

"Not trusted? By who?"

"By me," Tibor said simply. David was so surprised he was actually speechless for a minute.

"Papa, why?"

"I cannot say why...it is not something easily spoken. It is a feeling. Do you understand?"

David thought of Con's wrinkled suits, his erratic behavior, on top of the world one day, grumbling and sullen the next. He thought of the coffee stains on the desks and the aggressive laughter, the sly suggestions of overnight romps spoken at inappropriate times. "Yes, I do. I understand. Your feelings were not without cause, Papa"

"What has happened? Tell me the whole truth. Do not hold anything back. I may be old, but I am not stupid. I have seen signs that all is not well with that boy but I could not find out what was wrong. He would not tell me. He hid from me. I know something is wrong. Now this...tell me. There is more in your voice than suspending him from the firm. That alone is bad, but there is more. Much more."

David took a deep breath. "Papa...Constantine may be stealing money from the firm. We are looking into it, but he may have been falsifying records as well. He and I had a big argument over the telephone after he didn't show up for that meeting with the Saudi investors. I suspended him indefinitely for these reasons.

"And... this is hard to say, Papa, it is very hard. The police found Cathy's cell phone and were able to trace the last call made to it. Constantine was the last person to call her.

"So? He called her. What of it, David?"

"Why has he never mentioned this, Papa?" Tibor remained silent. David continued. "Yesterday at dinner he said the make and model of the car that struck her. No one, not even the police, knew that information." David drew in a deep, shuddering breath. "I think.... I think he killed Cathy, or he knows who did."

"No!" Tibor shouted so loudly that David cringed and pulled the cell phone from his ear. "No! I cannot believe he would do such a thing."

"It could have been an accident...I'm sure it was. I can't believe he would do anything like that on purpose, either."

"Then why did he not say anything all these months? Why?"

David shook his head wearily. "I don't know, Papa. I just don't know. It's like he's a stranger to me. I was angry at him for missing that meeting with the Saudis. I had other things on my mind. I admit it, I was harsh with him, but it was with cause. We had words. He refused to come to work. I found evidence he may be up to something illegal that could harm the firm. So I suspended him immediately and closed off his access to the company accounts. I also had the locks on the building changed."

Tibor muttered angrily under his breath. "We need to talk to him. To hear his side of the story about the day Cathy died."

He swallowed the lump in his throat. His father's first concern wasn't the firm. It was with Cathy. The weight seemed to lift from David's shoulders as he continued.

"Papa, Con had nearly six months to tell me his side of the story. Six months to come forward and tell the truth. He came to her wake, to the funeral. He came to my home for dinner. He sat next to me at Easter Sunday Mass. He said nothing, nothing at all about this. He never once mentioned the phone call. If he wanted to come clean, to tell the truth, he had ample time to tell me his side of the story."

"David, my son. Listen to me. Constantine loved Cathy like he loves Eva, like he loved his mother. Cathy was his sister as Eva is his sister. He would never harm her. Never!"

"Don't you think that I've thought that? I've thought about nothing else all day." David paced in front of the couch, barking his shin momentarily on the coffee table and letting out a strangled exclamation. The clatter of baseball bat, mitt and ball dropped in the mudroom, Josh's "I'm home!" shouts and the thud of his footfalls as he careened upstairs told David that his middle child was home.

"We need to speak with him. All of us. The family."

"This is between him and me."

"If he is dragging his troubles into the firm, it affects us all," Tibor said. "The firm bears my name. It carries our fortunes with it. My money, your money, his, Eva's...it is all tied into the firm."

"Papa, I think Constantine has another problem." David hesitated. "I think he may have a gambling problem."

Tibor inhaled sharply. "So. I thought it was the drugs. And women. Now you say gambling?"

"Wait, drugs?" David thought of the ceiling tile in Con's office that bore tape marks, Victor's assumption that Con had hidden something there, his brother's disheveled appearance and strange mood swings.

"Something Eva said," Tibor replied vaguely. "I think she found something in his apartment when her company did his cleaning. This was why he stopped using her firm...she came to me to talk to me, to tell me, but Constantine refused to talk to me about it, so we dropped it, Eva and I. I should have told you."

"You're damn right you should have told me. What did she find?"

"Drugs of some kind, I think. She was very upset, more so by his attitude than by what she found."

"That explains where all his money is going, then."

"Yes..." Tibor paused. "If this is his problem, and the gambling too, he must not return to the firm. Not now and not ever."

"Never?"

"Never," Tibor snapped. "Too much temptation to steal money and go back to the gambling. All that money at Majek Investments, all that access to ready cash. It is like a drinking man working in a saloon. Can he do it? Yes, if he has willpower of steel, a willpower like a Tibor or a David or even like Eva. Your brother is too much like your mother. Ah, your mother was a wonderful woman, David, but not strong. Weak."

David thought of what he'd said when showing Turquoise the family photos. "Con takes after my mother..." It was true, in more ways than one.

"What are you doing to protect the firm, David? You must stay one step ahead of your brother and the media on this."

David ran down the list of steps he'd taken, starting with searching Con's office to hiring the forensic accountants. "I've asked

Victor to have his men follow Con. They should have a report for me soon."

"Are you telling the police this?"

"The police are the ones who told me about the phone call to Cathy," David said. "At this point, they just want to talk to him."

"Be careful, son."

"I know. Police reports are a matter of public record. The media, our investors..."

"Yes. This could cause great damage to the firm, David." Tibor paused. "But you must do what you think is right for Cathy."

"I will, Papa." Nausea rose in his throat. He swallowed.

"David? Are you all right?"

"Just stress, Papa."

"Did you go back to the doctor yet?"

"No. I've had a little too much on my mind with this nonsense."

"*Můj syn*, you must take care of yourself! You are all those children have now."

"All right, Papa. Soon." David glanced at his watch. It was getting late. "Con may call you, Papa. He may try to get his job back. Until we know exactly what trouble he is in and the extent of his involvement, if any, with Cathy's death, I don't think we should say much to him."

"I agree. Ah, my son. What has become of us?"

David wondered the same thing. He glanced at his watch and realized he had only a little while to talk to Eddie before his youngest son fell asleep.

"I don't know, Papa," he said finally after a long pause. "But we'll work it out. We always do. You survived worse; we must stay together."

"Yes. We are a family."

David climbed the stairs heavily, pausing at the top, listening. Josh's bedroom door was open, the overhead light spilling onto the steel gray hall carpet, casting dark shadows from the wooden banister and newel posts. Alex's door remained closed, and Eddie's door was closed too, but he saw a crack of light underneath. Water hissed and fizzled from the closed bathroom door. The clunk of dropped soap hit the tiles. Josh must be in the shower. He walked to his left, past Alex's closed bedroom door and to Eddie's room. He hesitated on the threshold, then simply opened the door, not flicking the lights to warn his son he was entering.

Eddie was at his desk, face inches from the computer screen, watching the scroll of words from an instant chat. David moved behind the chair and read over his son's shoulder.

Lucky7:	Just do the same thing again and I'll go away
Turtleman:	No. I told you. Passwords don't work anymore
Lucky7:	Can't u guess them
Turtleman:	NO
Lucky7:	If u don't do what I say I'll tell
Turtleman:	I can't do what u want it doesn't work

At that point, David tapped Eddie on the shoulder. Eddie jumped, hands flashing to his face, eyes wide. He twisted in his chair to see his father looming behind him.

David pointed to the screen, his face white with rage. He could barely sign; his hands were shaking so hard. *Is Lucky7 your uncle?*

Eddie tried to slip out of his seat and leave, but David grabbed him by the upper arm. He jabbed an index finger at the screen, forcing Eddie to watch him. David signed, *Did you take money from my bank account for your uncle, Ed?*

At first Eddie shook his head no, adamantly. But then on the screen flashed Lucky7's next message: I need you to get me money again.

David leaned over and started typing. Eddie frantically grabbed at his father's hand, but David pushed him away.

Turtleman2:   LEAVE MY SON ALONE

                YOU NEED HELP, CON

Eddie was furious with his father. His eyes begged, pleaded, all the while flashing with anger. He grabbed at his father's hands, trying to make him stop, but it was too late

The screen flashed, indicating a new message. David leaned forward.

Lucky7:   YOUR SON KILLED HIS MOTHER.

                DID YOU KNOW THAT?

Lucky7 exited the chat room. David whirled around to Eddie, but his son was gone.

19

David pounded after Eddie down the stairs. His feet slipped from under him on the third step from the bottom. He gasped as he hung onto the banister to avoid tumbling down the remaining steps.

From the kitchen, he heard a thud and a scuffle. "Whoa, there, little man, what's up?"

"Alex!" David shouted. "Grab Eddie. Don't let him leave."

"Hey now," he heard Alex's voice soothing Eddie as he ran to the kitchen. "What's wrong? Why are you crying? Dad won't kill you. No, stop saying that. Trust me. He can get mad, but he won't kill you."

David burst into the kitchen. Alex held a struggling Eddie by the refrigerator. A take-out bag from Poppy's Place, the local Italian restaurant, stood on the counter. "Dad, what's going on? He's freaking out."

"Alex, let me talk to him."

"Yeah, okay. But I don't think I can let him go just yet. Everything okay?"

"We just need to have a chat. A long chat."

Alex glanced from his father to his little brother and shook his head ruefully. "Hope you're not in too much trouble, little man." He released Eddie to his dad.

David dropped to his knees in front of his youngest son. Eddie sobbed, his eyes streaming with tears, snot hanging from his nose. David fished into his pocket for a handkerchief, holding it out to his youngest son while Alex, whistling, stuffed his take out bag into the fridge and headed into the family room. David was left alone with Eddie.

Ed, he signed carefully when his son regained some composure, *whatever he says, I don't believe it. Your uncle is...sick.* David made a sort of vague sickness sign to his head and stomach, then more adamantly pointed to his head. *Lucky7 is Uncle Con, yes?*

Slowly, Eddie nodded.

Okay, start from the beginning. Why are you on a chat with him?

He asks me for money! Eddie gestured violently.

He has plenty of money, David signed back. *Why?*

He told me you would hate me and put me in jail because I killed Mommy.

Eddie started to shake. David reached out to draw his son to him, but Eddie shrank from his touch. He paused, then signed very carefully.

What happened, Ed?

Eddie fumbled through the signs, gaining confidence as he spoke.

I told the school nurse I was sick. David nodded encouragement. *She called Mommy. Only I wasn't really sick. I didn't want to take my math test. I didn't study for it. I was on the computer the night before when Mom said I should study. Only I lied and told her that I studied. So now I couldn't take the test because I would fail and Mom would know I lied.*

It was convoluted logic, but it was 11-year old logic, and David felt his heart breaking with every flutter and gesture of Eddie's hands. All he wanted to do was gather his son into his arms and make it all go away, but he couldn't. He had to wait. The truth was there in front of him, waiting in Eddie's tale.

Eddie continued. *Mom picked me up at school.*

When, Eddie? he interrupted, pointing to his Rolex.

Eddie signed back, *Around two-fifteen.*

Then what?

We drove home. Mom was at the piano. I went to my room. Mom came and got me a while later. Said we had to go out.

What exactly did she say?

Eddie scrunched up his face, trying to remember. Then he nodded. *She said she had to give Uncle Con papers you left home.*

The hairs on David's arms stood up. *She said Uncle Con?*

Yes.

Not someone else? You're sure?

Yes. Sure.

She had to meet him?

Yes. We drove to the Rose Diner.

So many unanswered questions. David could barely breathe. *What happened?*

Mom parked the car. She saw Uncle Con drive in. She gave me money for a milkshake so she could talk to him. I ran to the diner to buy it.

Then what?

Mom and Uncle Con were in the parking lot. I could see them from inside the diner. Mom was mad. I never saw her so mad. So was Uncle Con. He was yelling at her. He pushed her. Eddie held both palms up and shoved at the air.

He pushed her? David repeated the gesture.

Eddie shoved David in the shoulders.

David nodded and signed. *Then what?*

Uncle Con got into his car.

Was there anyone else around?

Nobody out there.

Okay. What next? David's heart thudded in his chest.

Mom walked to her car.

I thought she was by her car.

No, she walked away from it to talk to Uncle Con. She walked back to her car.

Okay.

I don't know what happened next. I got my milkshake. I hate those milkshakes. I never want another one again after that day.

Sweetie, what happened next?

I was walking outside. I walked...

Eddie's eyes filled with tears again. He wiped them away with the back of his hand. David nodded gently to encourage him to continue. Slowly, Eddie raised his hands to speak.

I didn't look before I crossed, Dad.

I know, honey, it's okay. This time he did gather Eddie into his arms. *I know, it's okay, I know.*

Eddie wiped his nose on his arm. He looked up at his father with watery eyes and signed, *Uncle Con was mad. He drove like a crazy person. He was going so fast. He didn't see.*

Didn't see what, Eddie?

ME!

David could picture it. Eddie, happy to have his milkshake, glad to be free from his hated math test. Cathy, distracted by her meeting with Con and upset by whatever she had uncovered in those papers, not caring that her supposedly sick son craved a milkshake.

Eddie, stepping off the curb while Con barreled by, driving a two-ton death machine....

He hit her with his car, didn't he, Ed?

Mom ran in front of his car to grab me. I didn't look both ways and didn't see him. I was just drinking my stupid milkshake and happy I wasn't in math class – and I wasn't looking where I was going. I walked right in front of his car.

Eddie nodded miserably. His hands shook as he signed. *It was my fault, Dad. All my fault. It's because I'm deaf. I couldn't hear her shouting, so she had to run and grab me...and then he hit her, not me.*

"Oh my God...my baby," David whispered. He blinked back tears and signed, *What did you do next?*

I fell on the curb. Mom hit her head. She didn't get up. I grabbed her. I shook her. She didn't move. There was blood on her head. Her purse was open, stuff everywhere. She just lay there. Uncle Con pulled around the parking lot again. He was coming after me. I got scared. I ran.

I ran and ran until I couldn't run anymore. I ran down to the corner. Uncle Con pulled up. He grabbed me and told me to get in the car. I was so scared. I didn't know what to do.

I know. I understand. What then?

He drove me home. When we got home, he told me if I ever told, no one would believe me. I was a liar. I had lied about the math test, lied about being sick, lied about studying, and nobody believed liars even when they told the truth.

David closed his eyes. He felt numb with shock, and grief. Frozen with rage. Slowly, he opened his eyes. Eddie started at him, terrified. His hands shook as he signed.

He said you wouldn't love me anymore, Daddy.

Oh my baby.... David couldn't even sign his love. He had clenched his fists so tightly he had lost all feeling in them. If only he could clench his heart shut so tightly he couldn't feel anymore.

Something in his eyes must have told Eddie the truth, some fire behind the darkness. Eddie crumpled into his arms. David held him and rocked as if he was an infant instead of an eleven-year-old going on twelve. Eddie felt frail, slight, as if a strong wind would blow him away. He sobbed on David's shoulder and David stroked his hair, their reflection in the polished steel surface of the refrigerator making them look like one tangled ball.

When Eddie calmed down enough to step back from his father's embrace, David stood, feeling the crunch and pop of his joints as he righted himself. He held out his hand to Eddie and led him to the kitchen table. He poured his son a glass of water from the spigot on the refrigerator, and quietly poured himself a glass of orange juice. Eddie watched from watery, bloodshot eyes.

David sat opposite his son. He waited until Eddie sipped his water. Nodding to his son, he tapped the table to get his attention. He began signing.

I believe you. I believe every word you said.

Eddie nodded. He rolled his hands over the condensation on the sides of his glass.

It wasn't your fault. I will never blame you for this.

Ed looked away for a second, then looked back at his father. David continued.

I will love you no matter what. Always. Do you understand that?

Slowly, Eddie nodded.

Eddie, this is important. Did Mom have those papers with her when she met Uncle Con?

Eddie shook his head no, and David felt his hopes sink.

Do you know where she put them? The papers she said she had to talk to Uncle Con about?

Again, Eddie shook his head, no. David nodded.

Okay. Now... did you go into my bank account a few weeks ago and transfer money to Uncle Con?

Eddie hesitated, but again, David signed, *Tell the truth. This is on your uncle. Not you.*

Frowning, Eddie finally nodded.

Why did you do it?

He told me he would tell you that I killed Mom if I didn't get him the money.

How did you access my account?

It was easy. I guessed.

You guessed my password?

Sure.

And my user name?

User name, David Lion. Password is always Cathy and your wedding date.

David blinked. Eddie, of course. Why hadn't he thought of Eddie?

You knew I knew your password, Ed said. *From school. Remember?*

He flashed back to the evening a few weeks ago when he had confronted Eddie about the note from Eddie's school, and Eddie had shown him details about his project online. Of course, Eddie had easily accessed the parent notification bulletin board. If his account was so easy to hack, Eddie must have had full access to everything. For once, he was glad that the Majek Investments IT staff insisted they change their passwords each month and that his office passwords were random combinations of letters and numbers. They were horrifically difficult to memorize, but at least no one else could guess them.

I couldn't get him the money this time, Ed signed. *I couldn't get into your account.*

No, I changed it when the money was stolen.

Eddie bit his lower lip. *Am I going to jail?*

Jail? For what?

Murder. Bank robbery.

Not you. Uncle Con is in a lot of trouble.

I didn't mean to get him in trouble, Daddy.

He got himself into trouble.

David stood up and gulped the sweet orange juice. Eddie also stood. Go to bed, David told his son. He patted him on the shoulder, then leaned down and gave him a hug. Eddie hugged him back. *No jail, so don't worry about it. I will call the bank tomorrow and tell them it was a mistake. Uncle Con won't hurt you anymore.*

Are you sure, Dad?

Yes.

Okay.

Don't chat with him anymore. Please. Leave him to me.

Okay.

Eddie scampered upstairs. David heard his feet pounding the stairs, his bedroom door slam shut. Alex was in the family room watching television. David strode up the stairs to his bedroom, closing the door behind him. He leaned against the closed door and shut his eyes.

Cathy, what am I going to do?

He knew what he had to do. Shaking, he walked to Cathy's dresser. His face was white in the mirror, his dark eyes huge and glassy with unshed tears. He touched the perfume bottles remaining on the dresser top, her hairbrush, the ornate hand mirror she'd bought in an antique store in Cutchogue one summer. Although he'd offered Eva anything of Cathy's that she'd wanted, she'd declined, and he didn't want strangers holding these objects, using her perfume, touching her hairbrush. He had left everything just as it was on the day she died, giving away only her clothes to charity. Now he touched her objects like talismans, hoping some of her spirit lingered among the fragrance of L'Air du Temps and Chanel No. 5.

Cathy, he's like a worm at the heart of an apple. You can't cut it out without destroying the fruit, but if you don't rid it of the worm, the apple isn't any good. If I don't destroy the worm, the whole tree is ruined. What will become of us? What is Con hiding in those papers?

Slowly, he drew his cell phone from his pocket. He dialed the Fifth Precinct and left a message for the homicide detective working Cathy's case. Numbly, he supposed the man might call back tonight, but he thought it more likely he'd have to deal with it in the morning.

"Detective, this is David Majek. You are investigating my wife's death, Catherine Majek. New evidence has come to light. My youngest son, Edward, was with his mother that day. He was afraid to come forward...tonight he told me more facts about the case so that I believe we can say with certainty who it was who killed her. My brother, Constantine Majek, was driving the SUV that struck and killed Cathy, according to my son. Please call me on my cell phone number as soon as possible."

Message completed, David switched off his cell phone and slid it into the charger on his dresser. He leaned against the mahogany highboy, grief and anger mingling.

Then, straightening his shoulders, blinking away the tears, he vowed to himself, *I will find those papers. Cathy, no matter what happens, I will find them and the truth will be known.*

20

David received his call back from the detective promptly at seven the next morning, and they arranged to meet, with an official American Sign Language interpreter present to take Eddie's statement. Although he would remain with his son during the interview, the police, like hospitals, preferred to have a non-family member translating.

Eddie was hollow-eyed the next morning, dark circles rimming his eyes. He picked at his Captain Crunch. When all the boys were at the table, David told them what was going on.

"There's been a break in the investigation around your mother's death. I think the police will announce the name of the man who killed her very soon."

Joshua and Alex nodded, exchanging glances with Eddie. "Dad, does Ed have something to do with this?"

"Yes, guys," David said heavily, sipping his second cup of black coffee. He had no stomach for breakfast this morning. "Eddie finally told me last night what happened. He was with your mom the day she died."

"Ed was there?" Josh's voice rose. "I knew he didn't go to his last class that day, Dad, but I had no idea."

"This is why I don't want you pretending to be me, even in fun," David said. He raised his eyes to Josh's. "If I had known he wasn't in school that afternoon, we may have cleared this up a lot sooner."

"I'm sorry, Dad," Josh mumbled, dropping his gaze back to the little O's floating in his cereal bowl.

A key turned in the back door, and everyone jumped as Turquoise bounced in. "Hello!" she called cheerfully, dropping her enormous bag onto the counter. She took in their tired, drawn faces. "My, my. You look like something bad has happened."

"Dad says there's a break in Mom's case," Alex said quietly.

Turquoise's smile vanished. "I'm sorry," she said. "Do you want me here today?"

"Today? Yes, of course. You're the one bright spot of sunshine in this rather bleak week." David stood and walked to the sink, dumping the remains of his coffee and rinsing out the cup.

"Here, I'll do that," Turquoise fussed, taking the cup from his hands. For an instant, her hands enfolded his, and she squeezed them gently, meeting his eyes. He averted his gaze and reached for the dish towel to dab his wet hands.

"Turquoise, I may be late this evening. Can you stay again with Eddie again?"

"Certainly. I promised Eddie we'd work on his cooking video for his school project. Right, Eddie?" She gave him a warm smile and patted her bulging tote bag. Eddie merely looked at her, not understanding what she said. Reaching into the tote bag, she drew forth a video camera, and Eddie brightened a bit. With flat palms, his left hand facing up and his right facing down, he air-clapped the heel of his palms together a couple times.

"What's he saying?" Turquoise asked.

"It's the sign for school," Josh said, gathering up his cereal bowl and walking towards the sink as his friends honked the Jeep's horn outside to let him know they were there. "He understood that the video camera is for his school project."

"Turquoise, I don't know how to thank you," David said to her. "I'd forgotten all about his blog."

"He mentioned it to me the first day. He shoved a note under my nose while I was dusting. I think he's a little desperate to finish it."

"He thinks he's going to flunk sixth grade," Josh said, gathering up his books.

"Josh, don't say anything to anyone about your mom's case. Not even Grandpa or your aunt and uncle, okay? The police don't want us to say anything until they've arrested the suspect." David didn't meet Turquoise's questioning gaze.

"Can you tell us who you think it is, Dad? Does Eddie know the guy?"

David didn't answer. He only repeated, "Please keep this between us until tonight. Then I'll tell you everything."

"Okay, Dad. I won't say anything. Good luck, Dad."

"Yeah, Dad," Alex said. "Good luck." Alex scraped his chair back and grabbed his dirty dishes, walking them to the sink. Turquoise took them from him before he could rinse them. He smiled his thanks.

"Are you angry with me, Alex? I honestly can't tell you boys anything until after Eddie meets with the police in a little while. It's...it's a lot more complicated than we could ever guess."

"I'm not angry about that, Dad. I'm concerned about you," Alex said quietly. "I know how serious those medical test results are, and I don't want to lose my dad the same year I lost my mother. Talking about Mom's death this morning made me think about losing you too. I'm really worried about you."

"I promise to take care of it, but right now I have more pressing matters to tend to."

"What is more pressing than making sure you don't have a heart attack?"

"Alex, I swear this really is more important. I wouldn't put off the medical stuff if I didn't think so."

"Okay, Dad."

"What are your plans today, son?"

"I was going to head out to Caumsett State Park for a while, but now I'm not sure if I should leave the house." Alex studied his father from across the kitchen. "You might need me."

"Go," David urged. "The walk around the loop to the beach there will take your mind off your troubles."

Eddie's school bus honked outside. David said, "Wait a minute while I tell them I'm driving him to school today."

"Don't run!" Alex called but his father jogged instead, letting the back door slam behind him.

The police station both fascinated and frightened Eddie. He peeked out from behind his father's legs as they stood at the reception desk while the officer on duty buzzed the homicide division. Eddie brightened, however, when the K-9 unit dogs arrived for the day shift. If it wasn't for the cops pulling back on the big German harness, Eddie would have hugged both dogs before David could stop him.

"What an adorable little boy," the woman at the front desk smiled at Eddie. "He's a quiet little thing."

"He's deaf," David said.

"I'm sorry."

"I'm not." David smiled at her to show no hard feelings. He reached down for Eddie's hand. "Come on, Ed, let's get this over with."

They were shown to a small interrogation room furnished with a table and four chairs. Eddie pointed to the rings built into the table and raised his hands with palms open, shrugging in the what? gesture.

To hold prisoners, David signed carefully. He didn't know the sign for jail or prisoner, but he mimicked handcuffs, and a key turning into the lock, and Eddie got it. Fascinated, Eddie ran his fingers over the loops.

Lieutenant Halloran stepped through the open door into the small room. David had only met him a few times, but the tall, 40-something detective had a steady, calming air about him. Behind him came a short black woman with swinging beaded braids. She wore a lanyard with the name "Sheila" and "ASL Interpreter - Nassau County Police" on it.

She signed briskly to Eddie before David could even shake her hand. *Good morning, Eddie. My name is Sheila. I will interpret for you.*

Eddie, like most 11-year-old boys, loved to be treated like an adult, and he nodded to the interpreter and held out his hand like a grown up. Pleased, she smiled and shook it, then gestured to the chairs.

"Now, Mr. Majek," Detective Halloran said, nodding to Eddie and David sitting side by side across the table. "Let's begin. Eddie told you a story last night and says he can identify who struck and killed your wife. You mentioned a name on my voice mail last night. For the record, I am recording and videotaping this interview so that we can see Eddie's sign language responses, but would you state the name he gave you?"

David felt his throat tighten. "Constantine Majek. Eddie's Uncle Con." His voice came out just a few notes above a whisper.

"I'm going to ask Sheila to repeat the question to your son, and translate."

Eddie responded with the same name. The interview began. Eddie told his tale.

Statements taken, Sheila offered to show Eddie the rest of the police station while David finished speaking with Lieutenant Halloran. David gratefully agreed. He sat back in his chair, utterly drained at hearing the story again from the beginning. Halloran got him a bottle of cold water and he drank the entire bottle in one gulp.

"Are you sure your son is telling the truth, Mr. Majek?" the detective asked bluntly as the door clicked shut behind Eddie and the ASL interpreter.

"Lieutenant, what are you implying?"

"It's just that it's taken him quite a long time to come forward with this information."

David glared at the detective. "Do you have children, detective?"

"No, I don't."

"He's telling the truth!"

"Okay, okay!" Halloran held up a hand as David's shouted response.

"Do you honestly think I'd bring him in here, accusing my brother of killing my own wife, if I wasn't 100 percent certain Eddie was telling the truth? I've had to choose my son's word over my brother's, and if you've never faced that choice, Detective, you have no idea of what that means. None." David shoved back his chair angrily and rose to his feet.

"I know, Mr. Majek," Halloran said, dropping his voice. He gestured towards the chair David had just pushed aside. "Please, sit."

Reluctantly, David sank back into the uncomfortable metal chair. He folded his arms across his chest. "What happens now?"

"I'm going to ask your brother to come in for questioning. We never even looked at him as a suspect, given that he was supposed to be at work the entire day. No one thought he might be in the parking lot by the Rose Diner, miles away from your office, on the day Cathy was killed."

"And what if he refuses to come in?"

"Then I get an arrest warrant for him and hold him for 24 hours on suspicion of manslaughter."

David nodded slowly. "I must tell you, Lieutenant, that he also coerced my son into stealing from my bank account last month. I think he may be up to something at work. I hired forensic accountants yesterday, and they are working with a private detective to look into all of Con's work. He's in trouble, Detective, of that I have no doubt."

"Any idea what could be behind this?"

"Money problems." David looked away.

Halloran raised an eyebrow at David. "Are you saying that he's having financial difficulties, Mr. Majek?"

"Yes."

"When last I checked, Senior Vice Presidents of large financial firms don't usually have financial difficulties unless there's something else going on. What's he into, Mr. Majek? Drugs, booze, gambling, bad investments?"

"A little of everything, I think," David said. He leaned his elbows on the table, cupping his chin in his hand and studying the scarred and battered tabletop. Someone had carved a list of crude words into the table on his side, and he dropped his right hand and traced the letters with his index finger while he spoke.

"Con has always been...impulsive. A dreamer, living on wishful thinking and imagination, yet wanting to be a man of action and accomplishment. It's a fatal combination, I think."

"What do you mean?"

David looked up. "He dreams big dreams of making millions, but he gets easily frustrated when things don't happen right away. Then he takes shortcuts to make them happen. Sometimes, his shortcuts work. That's the dangerous part, because it makes him think they will always work."

"Give me an example."

"When we were boys," David began. "He would fudge his school work. I'd be slogging ahead with my algebra, or biology, or whatever I had to study, and he'd be reading comics or doodling or just fooling around. Then we'd have a test, and he's cram for it, or cheat, or pay a kid for the homework answers.... you know how those kind of kids do it. He wanted to get into Harvard or Yale, and he did, but he couldn't keep up with the work. Partying too hard. Sometimes he'd be on top of the world, then a few months later, down in the dumps. Staying up all night or crashed out in his dorm room and sleeping for days at a time.

"He always envied me, but he never understood that what I have, I earned. He thought that somehow God gave out rewards, and I was always just ahead of him in that line, getting the best of everything and keeping him from having it, too."

Halloran said, "Those papers keep coming up, the ones Cathy called you about on the day she died. Your son was adamant that she wasn't carrying any papers with her when they drove to the diner to meet your brother. We didn't find anything in her purse. You said you've gone over the house from top to bottom looking for them?"

"The house and the office. I checked the records room at work, Con's office, everything. They aren't in the family room, and they aren't in Cathy's dresser. I don't know where else she might have stashed them, Detective. My sister cleans the house for me, and now we have a housekeeper, and they're both very thorough. If Cathy had hidden anything in the couch cushions or in a drawer somewhere, we would have found it."

Halloran shook his head. "We need those papers. If there's something there that points to a motive for the meeting that day, and for your brother's rage, it would make the case against him even tighter."

David winced. Halloran immediately put out an apologetic hand. "Look, David, I know this is hard on you. I'm sorry."

"Everyone is apologizing to me today," David said wearily. "And it's not their fault. What my brother may or may not have done, it's done. We just move on."

Sheila returned with Eddie, who carried a sheaf of police crime dog stickers and a coloring book. "Well," David smiled at his son, who ran to show him his bounty. "Did you two have fun?"

"We did," Sheila beamed. "He's a bright boy, Mr. Majek."

"I know it," David said. He signed to Eddie, *Time for school.*

Eddie scrunched up his face in disgust. "Come on, Ed," David chided, rising and holding out his hand. To Halloran, he said, "Thank you, Detective. What happens now?"

"We need to bring your brother in for questioning. You said you have private detectives following him?"

"Yes – Scorpion Investigations."

"A good firm. I know Victor well. I worked with him many years ago when he was a cop. We'll call them. I'll also try calling your brother now. It would better for him if he comes in voluntarily to tell his side of the story."

"Agreed. There's so much we just don't know...I still can't wrap my head around this. Con loved Cathy like a sister, Detective. They were friends. The thought of him killing her and not saying anything...if it was an accident, wouldn't that count in his favor?"

"Yes. If he had come forward. Since he hasn't, however, it gets more serious." Halloran walked them to the front doors. "You mentioned during the interview that you'd had an argument with him and that he was on suspension from work. Is there any chance he might make contact with you or the office today?"

"A slight chance, I suppose, if he's had a change of heart, but I don't think so. You'd have a better chance of finding him through the private investigator," David replied.

"If he does contact you, have him call me, please."

"I will."

David dropped Eddie off at school. They stood together by the Yukon, Eddie shrugging off his navy nylon backpack. David leaned down and gave his son a hug and a kiss, which Eddie squirmed out of, pointing to the school windows. Yeah, I know, your old man is embarrassing you, David thought, kissing Ed on the top of his toffee-colored hair anyway. Too bad.

See you tonight, David signed.

Later, Ed replied, and raced to the front doors of the school, bearing the hastily scrawled note David had written for the principal and his teachers. David waited until his son was safely through the front doors, then he turned around in the horseshoe-shaped driveway and headed to the office.

Majek Investments buzzed with an odd energy as soon as he entered the front doors, nodding to the first floor receptionist on his way to the elevator. Conversation stopped as he walked past desks, web browsers hastily covered or closed. *Oh no,* David thought wearily, *They're all looking at CNBC's website. What now?*

He punched the second floor button on the elevator and stepped through the double glass doors into the executive suite to find two grim-faced men waiting for him.

Joan rose from her desk, her face pale. "David, this is Mr. Ogden, from the SEC." The elder of the duo rose to his feet, nodding impassively. The Securities and Exchange Commission. David quietly placed his laptop bag and briefcase next to Joan's desk. "And I believe you met Mr. Worsham yesterday from Worsham, Scott and Daily, the forensic accounting firm."

"Mr. Ogden, Mr. Worsham. Won't you come in?"

"Thank you," Ogden said, and Worsham nodded. Joan slipped back behind her desk, waiting.

David picked up his briefcase and laptop. "Joan," he said. "Hold all my calls and meetings. Unless you hear from Con or a Lieutenant Halloran at the Fifth Precinct."

She jotted a note, her hands shaking. "Yes, of course."

"Fifth Precinct?" Ogden studied him. "What is this in reference to, Mr. Majek?"

"It is in reference to my wife's death last year, Mr. Ogden," David said quietly. "Please, come into my office where we can speak privately."

He unlocked the door, ushered them in, and closed the door firmly behind him. After dropping his bags behind his desk, he walked to the seating area. "May I offer you coffee? Joan will bring it for you if you wish."

"No, thank you," Ogden said swiftly, perching on the edge of the sofa like a gray-suited stork. "Mr. Majek, I'll get straight to the point. We received a complaint about Majek Investments. Several investors contacted the local SEC office to state they believe some improprieties have occurred. Mr. Worsham and I met this morning quite by accident in the elevator, where I overheard him speak to one of his staff about the Triad Fund. Apparently you have also suspected some sort of financial impropriety and have hired an independent investigation team, for which you are to be commended."

David relaxed slightly as he sat down opposite the two men. "Yes. This has all happened within the past few days, Mr. Ogden. I can assure you, we will do everything in our power to correct any potential mistakes."

"Indeed. Did you receive a complaint?"

"No," David said. "I have not heard of any investor complaints regarding the Triad Fund or even our firm. Your news comes as a surprise to me."

"The investors tried to work directly with your brother to address their complaints. It was only when they were unable to speak with him personally this week that they became alarmed and contacted our office. After the most recent banking and investment scandals, we cannot take a chance that investors will be hurt again."

"I see. Well, we are looking into it, Mr. Ogden. I can assure you that Majek Investments will cooperate fully with the SEC in all matters."

"Thank you, Mr. Majek. We appreciate your cooperation. Tibor Majek was well known for his ethical business dealings, as are you, David," Ogden nodded. "However, we must investigate the complaints from Triad Fund investors in the past month. Each invested through your brother, Constantine."

David winced. If Ogden noticed, he gave no sign of it, but continued.

"These investors were told that their initial ten million investments had been deposited into the Triad II Fund. Upon inspection, however, only eight million of each deposit went into the Majek Investments account at the clearing house. The rest is missing."

A knock on the door startled them all. Joan peeked in. "David? I thought Len should join you." Len was Leonard Cohen, the firm's corporate counsel. David smiled. Thank God for Joan.

"Why yes, Joan, please show Len in."

Leonard Cohen strode into the room, a bear of a man who rumbled greetings and pumped hands with the two men. He dropped onto the sofa next to David. David summed the conversation for his attorney. Cohen nodded and gave David a look which said, don't say anything. David nodded. "It appears we have a situation brewing here, Len."

"Indeed, Mr. Cohen," Ogden cleared his throat. "Approximately eight million is missing from the Triad Fund. Somehow eight million dollars of a fund went astray."

"We will, of course, ensure that the investors receive every penny of their money." David waved his attorney aside. "No, Len, this is something my father would agree to immediately. It's by no means an admission of guilt, gentlemen, but a statement of good faith. Majek Investments has always stood for integrity, and I mean to run this firm with integrity if I need to refund that money from my own pocket. Please assure those investors that their money will be refunded to the penny in the unlikely event that we discover something other than a clerical error."

Worsham looked pained. "It's not a simple clerical error, David," he said.

"We need to investigate, Mr. Majek," Ogden said. "This could be just the tip of the iceberg."

"Majek Investments will cooperate fully with the investigation, Mr. Ogden," David said quietly.

After the men had left, David walked slowly to his desk. Len stood.

"I've been talking to Neil and that Worsham fellow. David, your brother is a worthless piece of shit." The attorney stuffed his hands into his pockets. "No offense."

"None taken, Len," David said. "He's in more trouble than you can imagine."

"More trouble than embezzling $8 million and almost getting you arrested by the SEC? They could have arrested you, you know, and had you held while they investigated. The fact that you started looking into this before they arrived on the scene is the only thing that saved your ass, David." Len paced the length of the room. "If they can find a paper trail on your brother's illegal doings, he's screwed. The only thing saving him is that we still can't prove he took the money. If we had a paper trail..."

"I started my day at the police station with my son, who told the detectives investigating my wife's death that he saw his uncle run his mother over with the car. Then I find that my lovely brother has been threatening my son and getting him to embezzle money from my personal accounts. Next, I walk into investigators from the SEC, who tell me that $8 million is missing, probably stolen by my brother. So how was your day, Len?"

Len hissed an expletive through his teeth. "I told your father not to make Constantine Senior Vice President. This one's going to be tough to get us out of, David."

"You think, Len?" David raised an eyebrow at his corporate counsel. "Just protect the firm, all right? I've got 200 people depending on this company for paychecks, not to mention our investors who depend on their dividend checks. Con's already ruined enough lives. I don't want him ruining more."

"Agreed." Len reached out and touched David on the shoulder. His hard-angled face softened. "David, I'm sorry. Really. I know how close you are with your family. And Cathy..."

"Cathy." David bowed his head and bit his lip. "You know, Len, much as everything else matters, it kind of pales in comparison to that."

"Yeah. I know."

Len hurried out to alert his team of the impending storm and to find Ogden. David had just finished clicking his laptop into the docking bay when Joan came in, bearing a cup of coffee and a donut for him.

"Thanks, Joan, but I don't think I can eat." His stomach rolled.

"Is it bad, David?"

"It's bad," he replied. His shoulders slumped, and he ran a hand over his tired eyes as his computer booted up.

"How...how was your meeting with the police this morning?"

David blinked at her. "It's done," was all he would say.

After she left, he took one bite of the cinnamon sugar donut, and pushed it away. Even the scent of coffee was unappealing to him this morning. He was so nauseous that even the smell of coffee made bile rise in the back of his throat. David had never felt so alone as he did, tapping his password into the computer, staring out into the sun-streaked parking lot beyond the Majek building. Is Con being arrested now? Will I be arrested, too?

After a few minutes of deleting emails, he turned aside. He picked up the telephone, and dialed Eva's cell phone number. She answered on the third ring.

"White Glove Maid Service, Eva speaking."

"Eva."

"David, is that you? It doesn't sound like you. Are you all right?"

"No, Eva, I'm not okay."

"My God, what's going on? You haven't sounded like this since the day Cathy died. Is everything okay? Is Dad okay and the kids? Did Con get in touch with you?"

"Eva, it's complicated..." He took a deep breath and gave her a summary of what had transpired. She didn't say one word. The silence stretched between them.

"Eva? Are you still there?"

"If I get my hands on him first, I'll kill him," she said quietly.

"Wait your turn," David replied.

"David..."

"Eva, I have to go. I just have one more question. And this question is going to seem out of the blue to you, and you may need some time to think about it, but it's important. I can't say why it's important now. It just is."

"Okay, David. What?"

"Eva, I need to appoint a guardian for the kids – for Josh and Ed. Alex is old enough to take care of them if anything happens to me, but I don't want to saddle him with that responsibility. Eva...things are happening. I need to know someone will look after them, especially Ed, if anything happens to me. Anything. Do you understand me?"

"David...you aren't thinking of doing anything stupid? You know I was just joking when I said I was going to kill Con. You're not...?"

"I need peace of mind. Will you be their guardian, Eva?"

"You know I will. Yes."

"Okay, then. I'll call Cathy's brother next and tell him I'm appointing you and that you accepted. He might need you to sign something, I don't know how this stuff works."

"Okay. David...please...do you need me to come over? I can. I'm just in the office today doing the books and stuff. I can drive over."

"And what? Clean my office?"

"David...."

"Eva, I'm sorry. There's nothing you can do now, okay? Just call the police if you hear from Con, okay? And tell them what you found in his apartment."

"What I found? Oh. Papa told you?"

"Just that you stopped cleaning for him because you found something there that disturbed you. Drugs?"

"Yes," she said shortly. "Heroin or cocaine, I think. I'm not sure. I don't know anything about that stuff. It was a white powder, that's all, and some other stuff in a little pouch in his bedroom. I had a bad fight with Con over it. He told me to get out. That was it. We didn't talk for weeks."

"I didn't know."

"I didn't tell anyone. Papa figured it out. He always knows when we're fighting."

"So you told him?"

"A little. He guessed most of it. He's sharper than we give him credit for. He's talked to Con a few times about his behavior when you were Senior Vice President and Papa was still CEO."

David nodded. "How long has this been going on?"

"On and off since college, I think," Eva said. "Papa's always worried about Con's odd mood swings. You know Con. He goes through phases. First, the mood swings, then I think he dabbles in this crap, then stops. I think this time, he couldn't stop."

David put his head in his hands. "Look, I've got to go. I've got messes to clean up here. I'm sorry for that crack about your cleaning."

"I've already forgotten it. David?"

"Yes?"

"Please take care of yourself. Call Blake about your will. But call the doctor too, okay? You've got to take care of your heart. Alex is really worried about you, and I am, too."

JEANNE GRUNERT

"When this is over," David said wearily. "When this is over."

21

The rest of the day passed in one nauseous blur for David. He huddled over spreadsheets with the SEC, the accountants, and Victor, going over every file, every bit of paper, every account. Len hovered nearby, hissing under his breath anytime David opened his mouth to say something that might vaguely sound apologetic. David finally sent the corporate counsel back to his lair; he couldn't handle the constant interruptions.

Joan kept calls at bay, but by the end of the day, word had leaked out from the office to the press that something was amiss at Majek Investment. Reporters camped out in the parking lot until Jason and his security team encouraged them to leave. They pushed back and set up an easy cordon around the parking area, remaining on the grass edges between the Majek building lot and Sun Bank next door.

David spoke briefly to his father to let him know about the SEC investigation. It was perhaps the most painful call he'd ever had to make to his father. Surprisingly, Tibor did not shout; he was so quiet that David was afraid his father had hung up.

"Do what is necessary, and do what is right," Tibor sighed. He didn't even say goodbye. David sat for a minute, thinking about what his father must be feeling, knowing his own son may have been responsible for the death of his daughter-in-law and the collapse of his firm. He wanted to drop everything and race to his father's side to offer comfort, but what could he say? What, if anything, could anyone say?

Victor's team called around four to let them know that Con's car had disappeared from sight during heavy rush hour traffic. He'd either realized he was being followed or luck was on his side. They alerted the police that he'd last been seen in Queens, and the police promised to look for the Escalade.

David left the office around six, his head still ringing with numbers and calculations of all that had been stolen from his investors. His cell phone shrilled as the Yukon idled in bumper-to-bumper traffic on the Northern State Parkway.

"What news, Lieutenant? Did you speak with my brother?"

"No," Lieutenant Halloran said. "No one has seen him since Scalia's men lost him around four o'clock. We can't get hold of him on his cell phone. We've got a notice out to find him and bring him in for questioning."

"Did you check on that girlfriend? Lisa LePonto?"

"There doesn't seem to be anyone with that name. It's probably an alias."

"Surprise, surprise."

"Yeah, shocker."

"Thanks for the update, Lieutenant."

"My pleasure."

By the time David pulled into the driveway, it was nearly 7:30. He hurried from his car into the kitchen. As soon as he opened the door, he smelled onions, cabbage, and the scent of fried grease. Turquoise had left his meal of sausage and cabbage neatly wrapped in plastic on the table. From the living room, he heard the doleful sounds of Ravel's 'Pavanne for a Dead Princess' issuing from Cathy's piano.

"Turquoise?"

He hurried into the living room. Emily, Turquoise's youngest daughter, sat at the keyboard, playing with the maturity and confidence of one several years older. Her sister Elizabeth sat curled up with her legs underneath her on the sofa, scowling at her cell phone, texting a friend, probably. Turquoise stood by the barrister bookcase, the top glass rolled up. She flipped through piano scores while Emily played.

"David! I'm glad you're home."

"Wow, Emily, you sound good. I thought for a second it was Cathy playing." David stepped into the living room and gave the Daniels family a tired smile. "It's been a long day. It's nice to come home to some peace and quiet like this. How is everything here?"

"Peaceful and quiet," Turquoise promised with a smile. She shifted the stack of music scores from her left hand to her right, leaning forward and pushing aside the remainder in the bookcase to return the books. "Eddie is upstairs on his computer. His homework is done. We worked on a video for his project so he's got one more done. We cooked dinner together and filmed it. I don't speak sign language, so Eddie wrote out a script for me."

"Excellent! Thank you!"

"I hope you like sausage and cabbage. That's what we made."

"I'm famished. I'm sure I'll enjoy it." His stomach was still roiling, but he managed a wan smile.

"Which is a nice way of saying you hate it."

"I didn't say that! I'm sure I'll enjoy it, that's all. Where's Josh? And Alex?"

"Josh and Alex are in the family room."

The boys, hearing their father's voice, stepped out of the family room. "Dad? Did everything go okay today?"

"I suppose so. Could one of you get Eddie? Let's go into the family room. We need to talk."

"Okay." Josh ran upstairs without being asked to fetch his brother.

"Come on, Em, Lizzie, it's time for us to go."

"Aw, Mom. I'm not done practicing."

"You can practice at home." Turquoise reached over the piano for the score, but Emily protested.

"Can I borrow it? Please?"

"I don't see why not," David shrugged. "None of us are using it. You play wonderfully, Emily."

"Thanks."

Turquoise gestured towards a small stack of music scores she'd set aside on the bench next to Emily. "Em browsed through your wife's music. Is it okay if she borrows some?"

"Help yourself. Emily, you can borrow whatever you like, as long as you return it. All right?"

"Yes! Mom, can we stay a few more minutes while I look through Mrs. Majek's music?"

"Yes, yes, I suppose so."

"Mom!" Liz rolled her eyes impatiently. She twisted around on the sofa. "Do we have to?"

"Yes, I just said so. One more minute won't kill you, Liz."

Eddie and Josh bounded down the stairs. "Okay, boys, into the family room. It's time I told you everything that's going on."

Turquoise nodded. "If I don't see you before I leave, good night, David."

"Good night, ladies, and thank you again for staying late."

David drew the pocket doors shut. The older boys sat together on the couch, while Eddie sat cross-legged on the floor at their feet, pulling at the threads on the carpet. David drew his desk chair around to sit down and face them.

"You know that this morning, I told you there was a break in the case of your mother's hit and run accident. What we didn't know last year was that Edward was there. Ed, why don't you tell them what you saw?" He signed and spoke.

Eddie shrugged. *Do I have to?*

Don't you want to?

I've told this story twice already – once to you, and once to that nice lady at the police station.

Please. It's your story. You should tell it.

Eddie related his story while Josh and Alex watched quietly. "Oh geez," Josh said, slapping a fist on his thigh when Ed had finished. "I can't believe it. Uncle Con? Why, Dad?"

"It's those damned papers," Alex said. He surged to his feet and paced to the windows, folding his arms across his chest and staring out at the backyard. His face was like stone. "I wish we could find them."

"I've been all over the house," David said. "Aunt Eva and I went through Mom's things right after she died and we didn't see any papers. We've been through all the drawers in the kitchen, the laundry room, the dining room...where else could they be?"

"Mom's office at work?" Josh asked. Eddie followed the conversation; his brothers signed as they spoke out of habit.

"I don't think so. I'm sure they cleared out her office by now. No, she must have had them here at home," David said. "The attic?"

"We would have found them at Christmas, wouldn't we?" Josh asked. "We did put up a tree even though we were sad." Eddie nodded.

"We don't have much junk up there, anyway," Alex said.

In our rooms? Eddie signed.

"Nah," Josh replied, "We would have found it by now, wouldn't we?"

Not in your room. It's a mess!

"Shut up, Squirt." Josh snapped.

Mom's car?

"I've been driving her car this week, and there's nothing in it," Alex said. "I didn't check the trunk or anything, but there can't be anything hidden inside. It's empty except for the spare."

"I doubt she would have hidden anything there. Where else?" David asked.

"The piano?" Josh asked.

David thought for a moment. "That's a good idea, but Mr. Itorio was here to tune it, and he went over it inside and out. If she had taped anything inside the lid or hidden something under the soundboard, he would have found it. I've already checked inside the bench."

They sat quietly, thinking. David interrupted them by saying, "No matter. Boys, there's more trouble going on. I can't go into details yet, but suffice to say that Uncle Con has also been doing something peculiar at work."

"More?" Josh asked. "He's done something else?"

"Oh no," Alex said. "Embezzling?" He didn't sign the word.

Eddie looked questioning at his father. David signed, *Stealing money.* Eddie nodded. He knew all about his uncle and stealing money. He'd had a long talk with his father in the car after their visit to the police station about stealing.

"So he made Ed steal money, and then he's stealing from work? He's got some nerve!" Josh fumed.

"He's got big problems," Alex said quietly. He looked up at his father. "What's wrong with him, Dad? Why is he doing this? If he asked you for help, you'd give him money, wouldn't you?"

"If he'd told me the truth or asked me for help, I would," David said. "And I tried to give him a loan but he pretended like it wasn't a big deal. I think he's in trouble, deep trouble. How deep, I don't know yet."

"I wish we could find those papers," Alex said. "I bet that somehow, they prove that Uncle Con is behind your problems at work, Dad."

"Yeah, isn't that what you need?" Josh asked. "Proof that Uncle Con took the money from the Triad Fund?"

"Why can't they figure it out from the computer?" Alex asked.

"They're trying," David said. "But it takes time. If the papers your mom had were some sort of proof that Uncle Con was up to no good, it would be a lot easier to protect the firm."

"And easier to get him arrested," Josh said grimly.

"What should we do if he calls us, Dad?" Alex asked.

"Get me on the phone, quick. And if you can't get me on the phone, just find out how we can reach him. Okay? The police are looking for him and the men at work investigating him want to talk to him, too."

"Is he going to jail, Dad?" Josh asked.

"I don't know," David said honestly. "I...I just don't know. I don't know how these things work. The embezzlement at work is bad enough, even if your grandpa and I repay the investors. But your mom...I don't know what the rules are, boys. I don't know if the police charge stuff like this as an accident or...or as murder." There. He said it aloud. He dropped his hands after signing the word as if they were burning. Eddie lowered his eyes to the carpet and traced an aimless pattern in the rug, thinking. Josh glared angrily at his father, while Alex just nodded sadly.

"I'm going to be honest with you," David continued, gazing at each of his boys. "Part of me wants him to pay if he was the driver of the car that killed your mother. For weeks, months, I lay awake at night and prayed...I prayed that God would make the driver have a change of heart and come forward. I prayed that the truth would come to light. I had no idea that what I prayed for would turn out to be this.

"So I don't know. I do know that whatever we find with the Triad Fund, he's fired from Majek Investments, and I doubt any other investment company will hire him after this. Big or small, the second you mess around with company money, trust is shattered forever. As for me, if he would return the money to me and apologize, I won't press charges about the work problems or the money he stole from me. I've already called the bank and let them know the money has been found, and it was a misunderstanding.

"But your mother...leaving the scene of an accident where there's a fatality? His own sister-in-law? Lying to me all these months? I don't know how I can forgive him, and I'm not sure what the law says."

"Uncle Blake would know," Josh said.

"I called your uncle Blake this afternoon about another matter and asked told him briefly what's going on. He's not just a lawyer, he's also your mom's brother, so I thought he had a right to know. He said that leaving the scene of an accident where there is a fatality is a Class D felony. That means that at best, Uncle Con is going to be hit with a big fine and maybe jail time."

"How much jail time, Dad?" Josh asked.

"Up to seven years, according to Uncle Blake, but a lot has to do with the circumstances, the particular judge assigned to the case, and the family's wishes. He said that judges often take into consideration what the family wants, especially in a case like this. So I think it's up to us, and what we want, to some extent. We can ask for the maximum punishment or for leniency. The judge may think differently, but we can ask all the same. That's a long way off, though, boys."

"Just so I know.... What do you want, Dad?" Alex asked and signed. All three boys watched him expectantly.

"I don't know," David admitted. He looked from one child to another, his boys, Cathy's sons. "How do you all feel about this?

Cathy was my wife, but she was your mother. And Eddie, you have more of a say in this than anyone, I think...given the circumstances."

The boys were quiet for a moment. "I can't feel anything right now," Josh said abruptly. He stood and joined his brother by the windows, leaning his forehead against the glass. "I can't even begin to figure this out. My uncle, my mom, my grandpa and dad's business...I mean it's like everything is going to pieces at once, you know?"

"I know," David said heavily. "Believe me, Josh, I know."

"Well, we don't have to figure this out right this second, do we?" Alex asked. He turned resolutely from the windows and walked back to the couch, flopped down onto the left side and settled his sneakered feet on the coffee table the way his mother hated him to do. "We can figure it out once Uncle Con talks to the police, right."

"Right."

"Okay, then. Let's think about it."

"Always Mr. Peacemaker," Josh muttered, glaring at his brother.

"What, you want the death penalty for Uncle Con?"

"Yes!" Josh shouted, spinning around. "I do, okay? He left her like a dog, lying on the curb like that. All he cared about was his own ass. He didn't care about Mom, and he sure as hell didn't care about Eddie or Dad. He's been lying his face off for the past six months. He sat at our dinner table, for God's sake, Alex! He looked you and me in the eye at the funeral parlor and said how sorry he was, patted me on the fucking back..." Josh was crying now, big ugly sobs. David rose and started walking to him, but Josh raced by, shouting, "Leave me alone! I can't take this anymore. I just want it to be over."

Alex moved as if to go after his brother, but David held up his hand. "Let him go, Alex. He needs to get this out of his system."

"But he's crying. Josh doesn't cry. Ever."

"All the more reason he needs to do this now, while he can."

Eddie's face scrunched with worry as he watched Josh run from the room. He looked up at Alex, at his father. *What about Grandpa?* Slowly, he drew his head back and cupped his hands around his face, like a lion roaring.

"What about Grandpa, Eddie?" David asked.

Ask Grandpa, Eddie signed. *Ask Grandpa what he wants.*

"That's an interesting thought," Alex said.

"Yes," David said slowly. "You're right, Eddie. The four of us have a say...but so does Grandpa. What if we go to him tomorrow night and ask him?"

Eddie nodded. He tapped his wrist, like tapping a watch. "Tomorrow after dinner," David promised.

"You want us to all go?"

Eddie shook his head before David could respond. He pointed to his father and to himself. "Ed says just us, and I think he's right. Poor Eddie...he's been caught in the middle of this from the start."

"You're right." Alex looked fondly at his little brother and signed, You're one tough kid, you know that? Eddie gave him two thumbs up.

"Alex, let me know what you would like me to do about Uncle Con. I'll ask Josh, too. It doesn't have to be tonight. You can take your time with this decision."

"What are our choices, Dad?"

"I think Uncle Con needs help," David said wearily. "Psychological help, maybe a rehab. Do they have rehab for gambling problems?"

"I'm sure they do," Alex said.

"Well, then. Let's say our choices are asking the judge for prison time or leniency, whatever that may be."

"Okay. I'll tell Josh." Eddie nodded.

David looked down at Eddie, who was now scrambling to his knees to get up from the carpet. "How did Eddie get to be such a strong, smart kid? He's really incredible."

"It's all from mom," Alex said with a ghost of smile and a wink at his father.

"Amen to that," David replied with a wan smile of his own.

The next day, David left for work early to face the SEC, the forensic accountants, the media, his investors, and of course, the employees, who had probably been reading internet reports about their boss' problems all night long. David had briefly clicked on CNBC at breakfast, heard his name mentioned derisively by the commentator comparing him to the last CEO sentenced for embezzling, and he clicked the television off. Better not to hear the news than to deal with that kind of stuff.

He was also still feeling dreadful, like had the start of a bad stomach flu coming on. He shivered, took one sip of his coffee, and dumped it into the sink. Not even coffee could stay in his stomach this morning.

Alex promised to make sure his brothers left for school on time. "I'll be home most of the day," Alex said to his father. "Along with Turquoise. If Uncle Con shows up or calls, I'll be here to handle it. I want to go over this house one more time, from top to bottom, to make sure we didn't miss anything. Those papers have got to be here. They just have to be."

"I was thinking about that last night," David said. "What if Uncle Con found them already and destroyed them?"

"It's possible, I suppose. But somehow, I don't think so. Do you?"

"No, not really. But it is possible."

David arrived at the office by seven. Joan was just turning on her computer. "Good morning. Did you get any sleep?"

"Barely. Welcome to shit storm, day two." David keyed in the code to his office and dumped his briefcase and laptop by his desk. The red voice mail light blinked frantically on his desk.

"I've got an extra umbrella to weather the storm," Joan said lightly as she bustled to the credenza to start the coffee.

"There's no umbrella big enough for this, Joan," David said as he slid into his desk chair.

The morning passed in a blur of phone calls, meetings, and David taking phone calls from both the media and frantic investors. The entire company was in an uproar, with clients phoning once gossip reached them at their clubs and golf courses about the state of the Triad Fund. David spent most of the day speaking soothing words to the well-heeled investors spooked by scandals in the news and imagining the worst at Majek Investments.

The news wasn't all grim. By four, Neil, the forensic accountants and Victor were waiting for him in the conference room to review their findings.

They gathered in the same glass-walled conference room where David had seen Constantine rallying the Asian and European markets not a week before. As David took his seat at the head of the conference table, he glanced down and saw a sticky coffee ring on the surface. Con. His chest tightened. A sharp pain ran down his arm. He winced and rubbed his forearm. *Too much damn computer work,* he thought as the pain subsided. He leaned back and made a steeple of his fingers.

"Well, ladies and gentlemen, what is the verdict?" he asked, scanning the assembled team.

"Better than we had hoped, David," Worsham from the forensic accounting firm said. "Although not great. There's about eight million, total, missing from the Triad Fund. We're still not sure how he managed to get the money out without raising red flags. There's some pretty complicated computer work behind this that doesn't seem like Con's handiwork, so we suspect there's someone else he's working with on this. Someone, most likely your brother, also fraudulently reported the fund's earnings."

"How so?"

One of the two female accountants seated at the far end of the table next to Victor spoke up. She tapped her pencil on the yellow note pad in front of her, reading off her findings.

"Quarter one appears to be an accurate reporting of the fund's earnings," she said. "In Quarter Two, he fudged the numbers a bit, but nothing more than could be chalked up to a simple mistake. It was enough, however, to encourage more investors to join the fund, and thus might be construed by our colleagues in the SEC investigation unit as outright fraud.

"Quarter Three is where he really got creative. You'll note from the graph I'm passing around" – a line graph showing a blue line that leaped acrobatically into the upper levels in Q3 made its way to David, who scanned it with mounting disgust – "shows how much he overstated the fund's earnings. I won't go into details now about how he accomplished this feat of computer programming, but suffice to say that your computer systems aren't as sophisticated as you believe them to be. He was able to conduct a sophisticated fraud, using a loophole in the software you have to compute and publish earnings, to make earnings on Triad II appear greater than they actually were."

"What about in November?" David asked. "And at the end of the fiscal year?"

"Same pattern. Your report for Q4 is garbage."

"Damn," David swore. He threw the graph onto the conference table. "Can any of this be directly attributable to Con?"

"Not yet," Worsham admitted.

"The SEC is still working on his computer files," Victor said. "It's going to take a while. So far, no, they can't lay this at his feet."

"We know it," Neil said quietly. "Or at least we guess it. But proving it? Not yet. If we had a paper trail...some tangible evidence...something to tie him directly to it, we could get closure on this quickly."

David folded his arms across his chest. "Now what? How do we clean up this mess?"

"That's where the SEC gets involved," Worsham said. "I spoke with Ogden, and the SEC is willing to talk about fines and penalties instead of jail time if we can rectify this quickly. Certainly it appears that neither you nor your father had any knowledge of the fraud, and you were actively taking steps to investigate it before they got wind of it, which all counts in your favor. Between us? You're off the hook, David. The publicity damage isn't something we can easily fix, I think, but we may be able to weather this storm yet."

"Let's bet on that," David said. His stomach twisted, that odd, nauseous feeling he'd been fighting on and off for the past week. He suddenly felt hot, but he ignored it, and pressed on. "What's our next step?"

The meeting continued. He pressed a hand to his side. *Not now*, he thought as the assembled team continued to craft a plan to save his company. *I can't be sick now. Not now.*

David arrived home a little after six. "Hello," he called into the house where piano music once again issued from the living room. "Anyone home?" A warm, buttery smell filled the kitchen with sweet overtones of apricot. It was a familiar smell, but one he hadn't encountered in many years. He started to peek into the cupboards when Emily called from the living room, "Hi, Mr. Majek. Mom is in the family room helping Eddie with his homework."

David gave up on his search for the entrancing odor and strode into the living room, where Emily sat, poised and confident, on the edge of the piano bench. Her fingers deftly sought the melody and counterpoint of the little Bach prelude she was playing. Her right foot barely touched the sustain pedal. David thought, Cathy would have adored this little girl as her student.

"Hello Emily. Hi Lizzie." Lizzie just grunted from her place on the couch, eyes glued to her iPhone screen.

Turquoise came out of family room holding a video camera. Eddie followed her carrying one of his mother's cookbooks, a notebook and a pen. "Hi David," Turquoise said.

"Hi," David said, nodding towards the camera. "Another video done?"

"Yup. Two down now. Eddie won't fail sixth grade on my watch."

Eddie smiled up at Turquoise. David could tell his son liked her. He motioned as if moving a spoon to his mouth, then pointed at Eddie. *Did you eat yet?*

Eddie nodded yes. He cupped his hands to his mouth and pointed to the door. *Let's go to Grandpa's now.*

"What are you saying?" Turquoise asked. The piano music stopped. Emily hopped from the bench and wandered to the barrister bookcase, sliding open the glass door covering the second shelf. She pulled out a music score, pushed it back into place, then continued scanning the spines for what she wanted.

"Ed and I have to take a run over to his grandfather's place," David said. "I was just asking him if he ate."

"Yes, he did," Turquoise said. "We made kolacky."

"I thought I smelled it when I came into the house!" He loved the buttery apricot jam-filled pastries. "I haven't had one in ages. My mom used to make them for Christmas and Easter."

"I knew they were a Polish treat, but I didn't realize they were also Czech. There's a plate of them in the dining room. You walked right by it."

"That tells you how distracted I am. Where did you get the recipe?"

"We found a hand-written recipe tucked inside one of your cookbooks," Turquoise said. "Eddie thought it was his grandmother's *recipe.*"

David watched Emily riffle through Cathy's music books as memory stirred in him. "Yes," he murmured. "Cathy had a bad habit of tucking loose papers into books..."

As soon as the words were out of his mouth, he realized what he had said. He stood very still.

Books, he thought. *We never checked her music scores for the papers. We looked everywhere else but in her books.*

What music had been coming up lately, over and over again?

"Chopin," David whispered. "Emily, wait!"

Emily froze with the canary-yellow covered book in her hands. David hurried over to the little girl's side. She shrank away from him, glancing worriedly at her mother.

Of course it was that book, David thought, glancing at the cover. *Of course. What else? I've been so blind. And deaf. Mostly deaf. Cathy, I'm sorry.*

"What you got, sugar plum?" Turquoise called to her.

"It's just a book of music, Mr. Majek," Emily said. "It's Chopin's nocturnes and polonaises. You said I could borrow a book, right, Mr. Majek?"

"Yes, but may I look inside that one first?"

"Oh. Okay."

She handed him the Schirmer score. He let the book fall open to a creased spot where the spine broke on the score for the Chopin Polonaise in F# minor. David pulled two sheets of white paper tucked between the pages. The Majek Investment lion roared in the upper right corner, and the Triad Fund triangle was in the upper left. At the top of each page were the names Andrew Rothschild and Stephen Baylor.

It was the missing papers.

"David? What is it? You look like you've seen a ghost." Turquoise took the score from his trembling hands as he walked away.

"I haven't seen one," David whispered. "I've heard one."

He carried the papers from the living room to the dining room table. He pulled out a chair and sat down. Turquoise, Eddie and Emily followed curiously, while Lizzie continued texting. Placing the missing papers on the table, he used the edge of his left hand to smooth them out. The handwriting on the signature was unmistakable: Con's. His brother had done little to protect his forgery.

Cathy, he prayed, reaching out to his wife, *if you can hear me, show me what I'm missing. I can't figure it out. I know Con faked these applications, but how did you know it?*

Eddie pointed to the papers and signed, *Is that what you were looking for?*

David nodded. He tapped his wrist three times, then pointed to the stairs. *Can you get Alex?*

Eddie pounded upstairs while Turquoise leaned over his right shoulder. "What is that? Something important?"

"Something that was missing," David said. "There's something wrong with these documents, but I can't figure out what. Your husband was in investments; can you see anything wrong with these?"

"I was a caterer and a business woman, not a financial advisor, but I'll do my best," Turquoise pulled the Andrew Rothschild application towards her. "Other than the signatures looking the exact same on each document, I don't see anything wrong."

Alex ran into the living room with Eddie and Josh in tow. "Ed says you found the papers?" Alex asked.

Josh grabbed the chair to the left of his father and flipped it around. He sank onto the seat and leaned against the back. "Hey," he said, pulling the Stephen Baylor page towards him. "What's my social security number doing on this guy's paperwork?"

"Your what?" David peered at the application. Josh pointed to the social security number.

"This guy's got my birth date, too. Same date and everything."

"Let me see the other one," Alex said. He grabbed "Andrew Rothschild" and pulled the page over to look at it more closely. "Dad, this one's got my birthday on it and my social security number. This explains it all, doesn't it? These are papers to open the funds, and papers showing money withdrawn from the fund, too, but it's Uncle Con's handwriting and our social security numbers. This why Mom was so upset that day, and why she drove off to confront Uncle Con in person. She probably saw these lying on your desk and noticed the birthdays and social security numbers."

What must Cathy have thought? David wondered. He remembered Cathy's tone of voice when she'd called him in California to ask about the papers she'd found. Confused, hurt, hesitant. As if she wanted to ask him more, but didn't dare. Did she think he had asked Con to forge these papers?

But of course, he did have access to his nephew's social security numbers, David realized. He'd set up college funds for his sons as well as investments as soon as they were born, and their social security numbers and dates of birth were on all the papers. Con had access to all of the records at Majek Investments, and he'd stolen his own nephew's personal information, perhaps hoping to beg forgiveness if David ever caught him.

But it had been Cathy who caught on to his scheme, and Cathy who paid the ultimate price for David's careless mistakes of bringing home the pile of papers. He'd been in such a rush he'd just scooped up the papers on the edge of Joan's desk. She'd gotten violently ill right after lunch − food poisoning, David remembered. She had left a stack of documents for him on the edge of her desk and he's simply stuffed them into his briefcase as he'd run for the door, hurrying home to pack for his trip.

Con must have used their social security numbers to create these two fraudulent accounts. Using the numbers, he could pretend that each investor had sent ten million to the Triad Fund, then he could withdraw the money at his leisure. No wonder the company was eight million short. Between these forgeries and the complaints from real investors, his brother had already begun tapping into his own special line of forged credit and stealing from the firm.

"Your mom knew," David said, studying the papers carefully. "Con must have been desperate to get these back."

"Why did she rush off to confront him like that, though?" Josh asked.

"I told her to call the office to have someone pick them up," David remembered. "I brought these home by accident and left them on my desk in the family room. You know how nervous I get when I travel. Joan went home sick that day and the office was a mess. It's always a mess when she's not there to organize things. I just rushed out of here without taking all my papers with me. I grabbed all of the ones I needed for my trip, but I left these and a few others on my desk. Mom called me in California to ask if they were important, and I told her to call the office and they would send someone over to pick them up."

"Mom must have called work, and Uncle Con knew he had to get them back quick," Alex said. "If he's the one who drew up these phony papers, Dad, then he knew he could get in big trouble if you saw them."

"So he insisted on picking them up himself," David said quietly. "And he asked to meet Cathy by the diner."

"And then..." Josh swallowed, finishing the story. "He didn't count on her having Eddie there. Dad, do you think he actually meant to hit Eddie or Mom?"

David looked over at his youngest son, who was leaning on the table staring intently at the pages. "God, I hope not. I still hope it was an accident."

"What now, Dad?" Alex asked.

"You're still going to ask Grandpa what he wants to do about Uncle Con?" Josh asked.

"It was Eddie's suggestion," David said, gathering his car keys from the kitchen counter where he'd left them. "We won't be long."

"What are you going to do?"

"Ed and I will go to Grandpa's," David said. He scooped up the papers, folded them into quarters, and slid them into his front pocket. "We'll show these to Grandpa, and if he's in agreement, then I'll bring them to the police tonight. But I want to talk to him first about what to do about it and what he thinks we should do about Con." He looked at his sons. "What do you want me to do, boys?"

Josh folded his arms across his chest. "He's a murderer."

David reached out and touched Josh on the shoulder. Josh shrugged him off. "Your uncle may be responsible for your mom's death, or he may not be. But he does have a problem, a big problem. If he's an addict, above all, he needs treatment. I need to talk to Grandpa and hear what he has to say. And we need to call our lawyers to help us through the legalities of this mess. This happened on my watch, kids, and I'm the CEO."

"That means you're in charge."

"Yes. And I made a mistake trusting Uncle Con, so I may need to pay for this mistake."

"Losing Mom was payment enough." Josh turned away.

"Yes, it was, Joshua," David said. "But you know I wasn't speaking of that, Joshua."

"It's always about money with you, isn't it?"

"Josh, that's not fair," Alex snapped. "That's not where Dad was going with this, and you know it."

Even Eddie frowned at Josh and tapped on the table. "What, Squirt?" Josh demanded. He signed, thumping his fist on the table angrily.

Dad takes care of us all, Eddie signed back to Josh. *Grandpa. Us. Work people. Stop being selfish.*

Josh's cheeks flushed crimson "Okay. I get it. It's not just about us. Uncle Con's screw up will affect...gee, how many people?"

"Over two hundred, if something happens to the firm," David said, jingling his car keys in his hand. "More, if you include the investors in the company. But it won't come to that. I'm not sure what will happen, but Majek Investments will stand. Grandpa and I will see to that. We will pay everyone back." He looked again at his sons. "What will it be, boys?"

"I'll go with whatever you and Grandpa decide," Josh said.

Alex nodded.

"All right." David looked at Turquoise.

"I'd better get going," Turquoise said quietly. "Emily? Lizzy? let's go."

"Dad, did you eat yet?" Alex asked.

"I'll grab something when I get home," David said. He walked over to the plastic-wrapped plate of cookies and slipped a few out from under the wrapper. Munching the cookies and handing one of the buttery jam-filled treats to Eddie, he said, "Or I'll just eat kolacky. This is my mom's recipe. Oh man, I haven't had this in years. Let's take a few to Grandpa, Ed."

"I'll fix a plate before I go," Turquoise said, hurrying into the kitchen.

David tucked the wrapped plate of cookies into the passenger seat of the Yukon while Eddie buckled himself into the rear seat. Turquoise, Emily and Lizzie said goodnight and waved as Turquoise drove the white Honda down Edgewater Drive.

David smiled at Ed and signed, *You like her?*

Eddie nodded vigorously and smiled. *Me too,* David said, nodding and pointing to himself.

They drove from Brookville to Bellerose in moderate traffic, passing C. W. Post University, the Miracle Mile, and the North Shore Towers. David turned off the exit onto Little Neck Parkway, thinking hard about what he wanted to say to his father. Deep within him, anger and grief dueled, each taking a turn having the upper hand. At one moment, he was so angry he found himself careening down the parkway faster and faster until a sigh or shuffle from Eddie jerked him out of the red haze that threatened to engulf him like a fire. Then, he would ease off the gas pedal, glancing at his son's profile reflected in the window glass, grateful for the reminder that he had a life worth living for. The next moment, he'd feel grief well like a tide, a sweep of loss so hard it made his eyes sting. Grief gave way to rage, and he swung full circle again.

Eddie, he thought as he turned onto his father's block and pulled into the driveway. *I'm thankful you're here, because without you I'd be chasing after Con myself to put him in a cage for the rest of his life for what he's done to me and to us all.*

David parked the car and Eddie leaped out of the passenger seat. The front storm door of his father's house stood wide open. He left the cookies in the car and hurried across the lawn as the sound of raised voices floated through the screen door. Eddie patted the stone lions flanking the steps and reached for the screen door before he could stop him from entering.

He recognized the voices and shouted, "Eddie, NO!"

Eddie threw open the front door ran straight into the living room, skidding to a halt, his sneakers making marks in the carpet. David bolted after him.

Con stood next to the fireplace. Tibor sat on a threadbare wingback chair, facing his middle child. Con held a gun to his father's head.

"Get in here," Con said harshly to David. He grabbed Eddie and shoved him onto the floor next to Tibor.

22

David hesitated. Con met his eyes. He clicked off the handgun's safety and leveled the weapon not at David, but at Eddie. "If either of you so much as blinks, I'll kill Eddie."

"Con..." David licked his lips. "What the hell are you doing?"

From the bedroom, he heard a crash. "Con, I can't find anything. If he's got money stashed here, he's got it well hidden." *I know that voice,* David thought. *Who is that?*

"I told you," Tibor said hoarsely. "I have no money here."

"Shut up." Con gestured for David and Eddie to sit on the couch next to Tibor. David grabbed Eddie by the arm and pulled him down next to him, keeping his son between himself and Tibor.

"Con, don't do this. Please. We can figure something out...." David watched his brother pace the familiar room.

Con laughed harshly. His white button-down shirt was stained under the arms from sweat, and he had several days' stubble on his cheeks. He stared at David from red-rimmed eyes, and his hands shook.

"Figure something out?" Con asked. "Like how many years I'll spend in prison? I know you're onto me. I heard all about the forensic accountant you brought in and the SEC investigation. But you don't have proof of anything. You need proof to put me in jail, and you don't have it."

David fingered the papers in his front pocket. *Con doesn't know,* he thought. *He really doesn't know that I found them. Steady, David.*

Footsteps tapped down the hallway leading from the master bedroom on the left into the living room. "He's got nothing in there except a diamond ring that might be worth something." Lin Liu stepped around the doorway. Her eyes opened wide when she saw David and Eddie.

"Oh Con. No."

Con's eyes glittered. "We have company."

"Lin Liu," David sighed. "Well, now this is a surprise. Lisa LePonto, I presume? Which is your real name, Lin or Lisa?"

"Lin." She licked her lips and glanced unhappily at Con. "Con, you said he wouldn't find out. You said..."

"Shut up and bring the ring to me. I can sell it."

"Papa was saving that for your bride-to-be." David nodded towards Lin. "I suppose that means it would be yours someday, Lin. Might as well have it now."

"Oh God, Con," Lin cried, raising her hands to her mouth as she saw the gun leveled at Eddie. "He's just a little boy! You've got to stop this now. This has gone too far."

"Constantine, my son, do not do this," Tibor said tiredly. He tried to rise, but Con shoved his father back into the chair. "David is right. Whatever you have done, it can be worked out. We will repay the money. Is it the drugs, son? If it is, we can get you to a doctor. No matter what, we stay together. *Jsme rodina.*" Tibor swallowed and repeated the phrase in English. "We are a family."

"Nothing can help me now, old man." Con's laugh was harsh and grating. "Lin, go check upstairs in our old rooms. The old man may have hidden money there."

"I have no money hidden in this house, Constantine. You know this is not my way."

"Con..." Lin protested.

"Just do it, Lin."

"I'm sorry," Lin whispered as she whirled around on her high heels and raced back up the stairs.

"So that's the wonderful Lisa," David said quietly. "I see why you wouldn't bring her to dinner. You're into this up to your neck, aren't you, Con?"

"Shut up. How much cash do you have on you?"

"About two hundred dollars. Why?"

"Give it to me. Stand up slowly and give me your wallet."

"My own brother is holding me up like a common criminal. Great." David stood and slowly reached into his back pocket, taking his black leather wallet out and handing it to Con. Con pawed through it, greedily grabbing at the bills. "Now why don't you have any money, Con? You made thousands, millions. Nothing left?"

"Shut up. I made some bad investments. My luck's going to turn."

"You mean you gambled it away. How much did you lose?"

Con licked his lips as he stuffed the bills into his back pocket. "None of your business."

"All of it," Tibor nodded. "He would not be here stealing from us if he did not lose all of it."

"Why do you keep fingering your front pocket, David?" Con sneered. "Going to cry? Need your handkerchief?"

In one snakelike move, he reached out and grabbed for David's pocket. David tried to smack his brother's hands away, but Con shoved the gun right into his chest above his heart. "One move, and your kid gets to watch you die," Con whispered as he stuck his fingers into David's front pocket. "Well, well, what is this?" He drew out the papers.

One glance told him exactly what they were. "Lin! Get down here!"

Lin clattered to the top of the stairs. "What is it? What's happening?"

"He had them. He had them all along, the jackass."

"Had what?"

"The papers. The papers I told you about. See?" Con waved them in the air. Lin returned to her search of the bedrooms. David heard her high heels clipping across the hardwood floors above as she moved from his parents' bedroom to Eva's old bedroom. "I've got them!"

"Those are the papers?" Tibor asked David. "The papers your Cathy died for?"

"Those are the papers," David confirmed. "And I bet Lin was searching the Records Room for them that day I found her there. Or did you send her up there to keep an eye on me, Con?" He was so tired, and that odd queasiness was back in his stomach. He sank back to the couch. Con whirled around, gun pointed on him again.

"I didn't tell you that you could sit!"

"I'm not asking." David rubbed his left arm. "Con, what do you want?"

"I'm getting out of town. Lin and I are heading to South America. For good."

"Go, and Godspeed." David casually slid his left hand into Eddie's right, using his fingers to spell on Eddie's open palm.

Run. Call 911.

Eddie squeezed his father's fingers in reply.

Con stared at the three of them as if they were strangers. "It's not that simple now."

"What are you going to do about us?" David asked.

"Tie you up, and take Eddie along as a hostage," Con said. "We'll leave him at the airport. That should give us enough time to get out of the country without a problem."

"Con, do you know why Eddie and I came here tonight?" David asked.

"Do you think I care?"

"Eddie told me what happened in the parking lot by the Rose Diner last November, Con," David began. He kept his voice low, never taking his eyes from his brother's face, all the while hoping he could distract him long enough to let Eddie make a run for the front door. "We came to talk to Papa about what to do, Con. You've made quite a mess, but there's time to fix things. Just don't do anything foolish. Don't take Eddie with you. There's hope we can get you out of this mess, Con."

Con laughed that ruthless laugh again. "No, there isn't. I'm broke, David. Broke."

"Is that it, Con?" David scanned his brother's watery eyes, his runny nose, his sweat stained shirt. "I think there's more."

"Yes, there's more. More than you can imagine."

"Lin. How did she get involved?"

"I met her a few months ago at Ocean Blue, just as I said," Con licked his lips. "We started dating, and when I needed cash to cover some debts, she told me about a scam she had worked at Hadley and Keene." Con named the rival investment firm. "Lin taught me how to set up the paperwork so I could easily cover my tracks. She's a whiz at computers, Lin. She was able to fix the reports and everything. If only I hadn't lost those papers! They were the only actual proof that I did anything. The rest of the stuff is all computer work, and it would take a long time to unravel that evidence. It would be hard to pin that on me. But the papers? Much easier to prove it was me.

"The day I lost the papers, I called Lin. I was frantic. I put some stuff into Joan's soda at lunch to get out of the way, then got Lin into the office as the temp. We still couldn't find the papers, though."

David felt his stomach turn. His left arm was going numb, and pains starting shooting from his wrist up to his armpit. He tried flexing his fingers, thinking he had just kept it too long in Eddie's hand, but it didn't work. Suddenly, he gasped as crippling pain ripped through his chest, a searing heat that made it hard to breathe. He pressed a hand to his chest and gasped. He couldn't breathe.

"Don't pull that fake heart attack shit on me, David."

"I don't think this is fake," David wheezed. Pain made his eyes swim. "Oh God, it hurts."

"Constantine, this is what your mother looked like on the day she died! Stop! Call an ambulance!" Tibor roared.

Eddie hopped down from the couch and leaned against his father's knees. He raised his eyes to David's, worriedly looking into his father's face He glanced up at Con, raising his hands to sign.

"You know I don't speak sign language well. What did he say, Dad?"

"Please. He said please, Constantine."

"Please what?"

"Constantine, can you not understand? Call an ambulance for your brother, now!"

David moaned as searing pain ripped through his arm, his neck, his jaw, his chest. A thousand-pound weight sat on his chest, and even though he gasped air into his lungs, it was as if he was drowning in fiery pain. Every cell screamed for air. He was glad Eddie couldn't hear him. Sweat poured down his face as the pain increased.

He gathered every ounce of strength he possessed. "Con," he gasped. "Just let Eddie go."

"I set up fake accounts using your kids' social security numbers," Con said. "Then the papers went missing. You picked them up from Joan's desk last November, David. I'd walked into the reception area and hid them fast under a stack of papers on her desk so you couldn't see what I was holding. You were so nervous about flying that you weren't thinking straight. You barked at Joan "Where are my papers?" and she pointed to her desk and you just scooped them all up, whoosh! Including the papers that could get me sent to prison or get me killed if my new friends found out. Way to go, David.

"I thought for sure you'd recognize your own kids' social security numbers and birthdates on the papers, but you didn't." Con laughed. "You didn't even look at them, and you were so preoccupied that when Cathy called you, you brushed her off. I thought my luck was holding when she called the office asking for someone to pick them up. I agreed to meet her by the diner. Said I was out on client appointments or some shit like that, and she bought it."

David's world narrowed to a pinprick of pain and fire in his chest. He could barely hear his brother ramble on.

"Constantine, your brother is in trouble! Call an ambulance, now!" Tibor shouted.

Con laughed. "Poor Joan. I meant to give her only a little bit of that stuff to mimic food poisoning, but she was out the whole week. Slipping Lin into the office as a temp was easy. A few weeks later, getting her the full time job? A little harder. But you'd never seen her, and nobody remembers a temp. It was easier than I thought."

"Con, for God's sake, I need a doctor!" David wheezed.

"Oh shut up and stop faking." Con paced back to the other side of the room, peering out from behind the fiberglass curtains to the roadway beyond. "I met Cathy in the parking lot by the diner. She wouldn't give me the papers. All she wanted to do was talk. She sounded just like you David – talking about forgiveness, restitution, making things right. It was too late for that, I said, too late. But she wouldn't listen and I got so angry I tried to shove her, but she got away.

"It was then that I saw Eddie. He was coming out of the diner, holding a milkshake, oblivious to the world. I was pissed, I admit. I wanted to get her back. I wanted to scare her a little, not hurt her. Frighten her enough and maybe she'd go home and get me the papers like I'd asked her to do. Believe me, I never wanted to hurt her or Eddie.

"Eddie was in the roadway, walking to her, smiling. She was shouting at him, but of course – he couldn't hear her. A mother's instinct to shout, I'd say."

"Constantine!" David heard his father shout as if from far away. "I think David is losing consciousness. You must call ambulance. Now!"

"She leaped right in front of the Escalade. I couldn't stop. I'll never forget that sound, as long as I live. Never."

The rose pattern on the carpet swam into murky shadows. From far away, he heard the front door bang open and his father shout, "Victor! Over here! Constantine has a gun!"

And then the worst words he'd ever heard his father shout. "Eddie, NO!"

The gunshot blast was the last thing he heard before he slipped away.

23

"Did you see her?" Turquoise asked.

David sat on the sun-warmed rock and dangled his bare feet into the shallow water of Peconic Bay. Gulls screamed and wheeled overhead against a shimmering blue sky. Off to his right, the children played on the shoreline. Eddie held up a hermit crab to show Emily. The little girl squealed and ran away in mock terror. Eddie grinned and raced after her. David smiled, remembering long-ago days of chasing Eva around the beach with his own hermit crabs. Then he remembered Constantine by his side, and his smile faded.

"So?" Turquoise leaned against the jumble of boulders on which David had perched to watch the children. "Was she there or wasn't she?"

From the gray-shingled house on the hill, a ripple of laughter rose to greet the shrieking children. Eva flipped hamburgers at the grill while Tibor, Alex and Josh sat at the picnic table playing Uno, laughing at something Tibor said.

If it wasn't for the ten-inch-long incision on his chest and the angry purple scars on his arm and leg where they'd taken veins for his heart bypass, David could almost forget that this wasn't a typical summer day. They'd kept the Majek family tradition of gathering at the beach house for the Fourth of July weekend. It was Friday, the start of the long holiday weekend, and they were just waiting for Blake and Victor to return from court before the festivities could start.

"David? Earth to David?"

"Oh Turquoise, I'm sorry. I was just thinking." He pushed his mirrored sunglasses up to the bridge of his nose. The breeze teased a tumble of dark hair over his forehead, and he shoved that back, too. He suddenly noticed that the skin on his hand was golden brown, glowing from the sun. How long had it been since he'd been outside in the sunlight long enough to tan?

He'd done nothing but lay on a deck chair and stare at the sky, thinking, since his release from the hospital a month ago. Eva and Turquoise had taken over his household, Neil and Betty had taken over the business, and he had the summer off.

He thought he'd go mad with boredom.

"No, I didn't see Cathy," David admitted. "No white light, no bright tunnel. Jesus wasn't there to greet me. I wish He was. I have quite a few questions I'd like to ask Him."

"At least it wasn't the other guy," Turquoise said lightly. "No pitchfork and cloven hooves, either."

"That's something, at least." David hopped down from the rocks. "Sorry to disappoint you, but the only thing I knew was pain and feeling like I was suffocating from the heaviness in my chest, and the last thing I remember seeing before I woke up again in the ambulance after they restarted my heart was the roses on my father's carpet. God, I never want to feel anything that bad again." He shuddered. "They don't tell you how much a heart attack hurts.

Apparently all that nausea I'd been experiencing was my body's way of warning me I had an impending heart attack on the horizon."

"That and the results of your stress test," Turquoise said ruefully. "Alex had a complete meltdown in the emergency room when they brought you in. He blamed himself for not making you go to the hospital right away after the stress test. Poor kid. It took us all quite a while to peel him off the ceiling and make sure he wasn't going into the operating room to assist. David, why didn't you take care of yourself?"

He watched Eddie pluck some seaweed from the water and throw it at the squealing girls. "I had more important things on my mind."

"Turquoise! David! Kids! Lunch is ready!" Eva shouted from the deck. Tantalizing clouds of charcoal smoke and the aroma of roasting meat wafted towards the beach. The group on the deck set their cards aside, and Josh and Alex carried bright ceramic bowls filled with salads from the kitchen just off the deck. The Majek's beach house was built on stilts to protect against floods, and the deck jutted out over the bay like the prow of a ship cutting through the blue-green Atlantic.

"Coming?" Turquoise asked him. "Blake and Victor should be here soon. I think Joan and her husband, Stephen, said they'd by coming by tonight for the town fireworks." She had gotten to know all the members of the clan in the weeks while David was recovering, including Joan, who Turquoise had laughingly called David's "other sister" when she'd seen them interact.

"Did Joan say how things are going at work? I know Neil is in charge but..."

"Will you shut up already? You're going back in August. Until then, you're on vacation. Doctor's orders. Joan's orders. Everyone's orders. Stop thinking about work. Neil, Betty, and Joan have it under control. Your father handled the media and the SEC guys brilliantly while you were in the hospital. I hope I'm that sharp when I'm ninety. There's nothing to worry about. The world went on turning without you, David."

"So you say..."

"Bah!" Turquoise punched him playfully in the arm. "You're just bored. You really do need a hobby."

"I don't need a hobby. I have work."

"Global financial domination isn't a hobby, David. Something like, oh, I don't know, painting or gardening or something."

"Can you honestly see me painting happy trees like the guy on television, Turquoise?"

She laughed. "You've got a point. World domination is more your style. Okay, fine. Maybe we'll find you a nice manly hobby, like golf."

"I'm not wearing plaid pants."

Turquoise paused. "Are you sure you don't want me waiting with you until Blake gets back from...you know?"

"From court. From Con's hearing. No, I'm fine. I just need a few minutes alone."

"Okay, then." Turquoise smiled and bent to pluck a stone from her sandal. She had painted her toenails blue to match her fingernails. *Turquoise blue*, David mused. "If you're not up there eating one of those delicious veggie burgers Eva fixed for you, then I'm coming down to get you."

"Damned things taste like cardboard."

"Doctor said to say goodbye to cheeseburgers for a while."

"Did he also tell me to say goodbye to fun forever?" David grumbled.

"Pile some extra onions on your burger. You won't notice the difference."

"It will just taste like cardboard and onions instead of plain cardboard. Mm, good."

She waved him off and started walking back to the house. David hopped off the rocks and ambled down the beach away from the house, stopping to pick up the round sandstone bits they'd called paint pots as kids.

The Indians, he heard his mother's voice in his mind telling Con and him when they were little, *used to put water inside the hollowed out stone. The warriors would make a paste and paint streaks on their faces. War paint, for bravery.*

David had told his own sons the same story many summers ago, spending a carefree morning hunting paint pots with them along the shore. He plucked up a round stone the size of a golf ball and turned it over in his palm. The depression in the center of the red stone was deep and smooth. A perfect paint pot. He slipped it into the pocket of his cargo shorts in case Eddie wanted it.

The only thing missing from this happy summer day was Con...and Cathy, of course. Always Cathy.

Eddie splashed out of the water after Lizzie and Emily, who pounded up the wooden stairs to the deck. The girls grabbed beach towels from the deck railing, bright pink and rainbow colored things, and flung them over their dripping shoulders. Instead of joining Emily and Liz on the deck, Eddie turned and ran to his father, shedding water like a seal from his sleek tanned skin.

Hi, David signed with a smile.

Hi, Ed waved back.

David slipped the paint pot from his pocket and placed it on his palm, holding it out to Eddie. With a delighted grin, Eddie picked up the stone, turning it and examining it. He nodded and gave his father two thumbs' up, sliding the rock into his own swimsuit pocket before reaching out and taking David's hand.

An engine purred from the driveway, and Blake's silver-gray Mercedes glided into sight. His brother-in-law parked his baby in the shade under the deck and unfolded himself from the driver's seat, a tall figure in a navy blue suit. Victor emerged from the passenger side, also wearing a suit and tie. Blake waved up to the deck where Josh and Alex clamored down the stairs to greet their uncle.

Eva waved a spatula towards him. Victor's answering wave as he ascended the stairs told David he'd be seeing a lot more of the private investigator in the future, probably by Eva's side. He smiled.

Eddie looked questioningly at his father. *Yes,* David signed. *Uncle Blake is back from court.*

Blake turned away from the house and walked towards Turquoise, who made her way along the beachside path. He kissed her on the cheek and asked a question, and she pointed to the beach. Blake nodded, raised his eyes, and saw David. He waved and David waved back.

Go, David signed to Eddie, *I need to talk to your uncle alone.*

Eddie nodded. He ran up the path and practically leaped into his uncle's arms, heedless of his wet trunks and his uncle's good suit, showing him the paint pot and scampering up to the house to show his grandfather and brothers his new treasure.

David turned and picked his way back to the sun-warmed rocks. He slid onto his favorite rock. There, seated on the ageless stone, with his bare feet dangling in the cool salt water of Peconic Bay, he could forget about Con. Just for one moment more.

Blake called, "Hello, David."

"Blake. Pull up a rock and sit."

Cathy's brother stepped among the seaweed encrusted stones to the water's edge. A wavelet lapped against his black wing tip shoes and he winced. David laughed. "Oh, just take the damned things off. And your socks, too. I hope you brought your bathing suit, or did you only pack business suits?"

"Glad to see you're in a good mood," Blake grinned. "I brought t-shirts, shorts and sandals. And yes, SPF 100 sunscreen for the pale look favored by Scotch-Irish descendants everywhere." His

grin faded. "Court adjourned early because of the holiday weekend."
Already the hot summer sun had brought out the freckles sprinkled on
his boyish face. His ginger hair, cropped short, was speckled with gray
at the temples.

Blake leaned against the rock at David's right and shaded his
eyes. "What's that boat out there?"

"Freighter, I think," David said. "They go by at about one
every five minutes on a nice day like this. A few sailboats out of
Montauk, too."

"Ah..." Blake cleared his throat. "You want to know about
your brother's hearing?"

"I suppose so." David paused. "How...how did it go?"

"It was a closed hearing," Blake said, "meaning it was just the
judge, your attorney, Con's attorney, and a few interested parties like
myself and Victor. No jury, of course. The judge rendered his verdict
and that's that. Your attorney is good, by the way."

"Did you know him?"

"I've seen him around the courthouse in Mineola, but I've
never faced off with him. Len was there, too, your guy from work,
representing the firm. So all in all...mostly attorneys and the judge."

"And..." David drew in a breath. "And Con? How...how is
he?"

Blake paused, watching the freighter chug along the horizon.
"Sober, probably for the first time in a very long time. On psychiatric
medication, according to his attorney. Con's being evaluated for
bipolar disorder, which is probably the most likely diagnosis I've
heard bandied about by the court experts. Con didn't say anything,"
Blake added. He kept his voice steady. "He just sat there and stared at
the table. His attorney entered a no contest plea, meaning he doesn't
contest anything the state entered in evidence against him, so it won't
go to trial. The judge already had the evidence from the SEC and the
forensic accountants. Your attorney presented your request and your

father's to the court, and Len presented his on behalf of Majek Investments. The judge had a few questions for Victor about the day you had your heart attack and Con tried to shoot him. The judge asked what he saw when he and his men burst into your father' house. After we gave our testimony and the lawyers said their piece, the judge went to his chambers to consider the evidence. He took a few minutes to think it all over, came back into the courtroom, and rendered his verdict."

"Which was...?"

"Mandatory psychiatric commitment," Blake said. "Ninety days in a drug and alcohol rehab center, followed by psychiatric commitment for at least one year. Time served as his sentence. Leniency, as you requested."

"I didn't request it." Anger flared between them. "Eddie begged me to be kind to him. If it were up to me..."

"I know," Blake took a deep breath. "Believe me, I know. She was your wife, but she was my sister."

"I know, Blake. I'm sorry." David glanced at his brother-in-law. "I'm not the only one hurting here."

"No, but you've been the most hurt, I think," Blake said. "You and Eddie. I'm just grateful that Victor and his team picked up Con's tail when they did. If they had been just a little slower, or hesitated to call the police..."

"I'd be dead from a heart attack, and my dad might be dead, too, if Eddie hadn't tackled Con when he fired the gun," David said. "Thank God Victor was there to hold Con down until the police and ambulance came. Yeah, and Eddie asks for leniency. Go figure." He plucked at a few barnacles clinging to the stone, wincing as the razor edge seared his thumb.

"Why did you agree to let Eddie make the final decision about whether or not to press full charges against Con?"

"Because," David said, "after all we've been through, the only thing I could think of was, what would Cathy want? And I kept looking at Eddie and thinking, she'd want him to make the decision for her. I don't know why, Blake, but it's what I felt. So I went with it. I couldn't find much compassion, but I trusted that Eddie would. I know it seems crazy. An eleven-year old boy, going on twelve, but there you have it."

The two men sat silently, watching the heavy freighter chug westward around the bay's bend.

Suddenly, Blake jumped. "Oh, I almost forgot. Con asked me to give you something." He reached into his pocket and drew out a plain white business sized envelope. David took it, but didn't open it.

"What about Lin Liu?"

"She wants to go to trial."

"Idiot," David muttered. He folded his arms. "She should have taken the deal we offered her."

"She should have, but she didn't. That's her right."

"Her right," David snorted. "What about Cathy's rights? My rights? Eddie's rights, or my father's?"

"As far as we know, she didn't have anything to do with Cathy's death," Blake said. "Con says he was alone in the car, and that he was driving it. Lin agrees. Con says he meant to scare Cathy, not to hurt anyone."

"Do you believe him, Blake? Because I don't believe anything he says these days. He's given me nothing but lies for years, I think."

"I don't know, David. I really don't. But Len said that you offered Lin Liu a plea deal, which her attorneys urged her to take. We'll see. There's still time for her to change her mind. Jail has a tendency to do that – help people change their minds."

The envelope in his hand seemed to weigh a thousand pounds. David wanted to chuck it into the sea and let the freighter's wake carry it far away.

"Anyway..." Blake turned. "I thought you'd want to know what happened."

"Where...where will Con be sent? For treatment?"

"I'm not sure yet. His attorney suggested a few private places. Your father said he would pay for whatever Con and his doctors decide, and the judge agreed, so that's that. He can get the best care money can buy. There's one private hospital in Vermont, if the court agrees, that's probably the best place for him right now. The psychiatrists who examined him think he's got something called dual diagnosis...addiction issues along with psychiatric disorders, most likely bipolar disorder. He's going to be in the hospital for a long time, David."

David nodded. Eva had already told him this from her last visit with Con and his attorney. "And this place in Vermont? It's a good place?"

"It's a good place. He'll be supervised. He'll get treatment."

"And then?"

"Then," Blake winced as the water licked his expensive dress shoes. "Then, the rest of his life. Whether or not you and the rest of the family are part of that is up to you."

"And you?"

"Me?" Blake shook saltwater from his shoes. "I hope I never see him ever again. No matter what happens, he killed my sister, plain and simple. I know, David, I know. It's not that easy for you, or your father and sister. But for me, the choice is simple. I never want to see him again. If it were up to me, I'd put him in a cage for the rest of his useless life. No offense."

"None taken."

"Right now, I'm heading up to the house to change into shorts and a t-shirt, crack open a beer, and eat one of your sister's amazing hamburgers before we go out to the fireworks. Aw hell, maybe I'll have two burgers. Maybe get some time in for a swim, and try to wash off the stink of this whole mess."

"Don't let my father convince you to play a game of Uno. He's a card shark."

"Hell no. I remember last summer. What did we play for, potato chips? The old man won like six bags worth of chips. If it wasn't for Eddie eating them, we would still be playing. I was getting ready to send Eva out on 7-Eleven run to buy more just so we would have a chance of winning one hand."

David laughed. "Thanks, Blake." He reached out and shook his brother-in-law's hand. "I mean it. Thanks for being there. I just couldn't."

"I know."

David watched until Blake reached the deck. Then he took the envelope in his hands and turned it over and over, fighting the urge to throw it into the sea.

Footsteps splashed in the shallows. He glanced up and saw that Eddie had returned. His son had towel-dried his hair, and thrown a t-shirt on over his bathing trunks. Alex had taken Eddie to the aquarium in Riverhead while David was in the hospital and bought him the t-shirt. Eddie wore it every day, like a talisman, until David came home. Now he just wore it on the beach. David smiled to see the sea turtles on the t-shirt. Eddie and his turtles.

Ed, he signed, *I need to be alone. Private time. Please.*

Eddie merely climbed up onto the rock by his side, and leaned his cheek against his father's chest. David hesitated, then drew his son close to him.

Suddenly, Eddie raised his head, looking out to their left away from the house. He tapped his father's arm urgently, then pointed, his gesture unmistakable. *Look!*

A misty figure walked along the shoreline. Rippling red-gold hair, a white sundress, bare feet. Turquoise? But she was up on the deck. He could see her from where he was sitting; the figure walked in the opposite direction. David blinked behind his mirrored sunglasses and swallowed.

No. It couldn't be. It was impossible.

Cathy?

Eddie's sign was unmistakable. He tapped his heart three times. *It's Mom!*

Ed, you see her too?

The figure raised a hand in farewell and slipped into the sea. For a moment, he caught a glimmer of red-gold hair, white dress and green sea. Then, she was gone.

She said goodbye, Eddie said sadly, leaning back against his father.

All of the anger inside of David flowed out with the tide that took the image of Cathy into the sea.

Have you always seen her, Ed? David signed carefully. *Has she been with us the whole time?*

Not always. But she's been near. Now she's leaving because we don't need her anymore. She said you'll be okay.

Turquoise's laughter trickled down from the deck, and Tibor's roar filled the air. Eva, Victor and Blake joined in the merriment. David couldn't make out the words, but he turned to stare at them. Turquoise stuck out her tongue at him and he couldn't help but laugh. He bent his head and smiled.

"*Jsme rodina*," David murmured. He watched his new friends, Turquoise and her family, and Victor, the man who had turned from foe into friend, mill about the deck, handing plates, soft drinks, napkins to his father and sons. "We are a family."

The envelope beckoned. Slowly, he slid his thumb into the flap and tore it open. A single, handwritten page slipped out of the envelope.

Together, the two began to read.

ABOUT THE AUTHOR

Jeanne Grunert is an award-winning freelance writer, blogger, and novelist. She is the author of a previous work of fiction, *An Ancient Gift and Other Stories*, as well as several non-fiction books including her Amazon best-seller, *Plan and Build a Raised Bed Vegetable Garden*. She lives and works on a seventeen-acre farm with her husband, John, and menagerie of rescued pets.

Follow the author through her Facebook Page:
https://www.facebook.com/jeannegrunertauthor

Author website: http://www.jeannegrunert.com

Bricks & Brambles Press

Bricks & Brambles Press publishes tales of imagination and suspense. Visit www.bricksandbrambles.com for more books by this author and information about our forthcoming releases.

Please leave a review.

Please leave a review for this book on Goodreads.com or Amazon.com. Tell a friend if you enjoyed it!